THE ALIEN ALGORITHM

Encoded Orbits Book 2

JEANNETTE BEDARD

Cover design by Rook Books Designs (rookbookdesigns.com)

Edited by Charlie Knight (cknightwrites.com)

Chapter One

Orin tried not to stare as a little yellow octopus slunk across the cockpit ceiling. With a complex arrangement of tentacles, the alien dropped onto the dashboard. Veena had warned him Click was on board; still, it was disconcerting to see a real-life alien— especially one that didn't appear anything like the aliens in the horror vids Mary used to make him watch back when his life was normal. Orin let out a long exhale and focused on his new companion.

With a body about the size of a loaf of bread, Click's skin glistened as it reflected the dashboard lights. Just as Veena said, it looked exactly like the little alien sidekick in the children's comic *Bubble and Click*, a coincidence that seemed unlikely.

"Um… Veena. Is that the alien you're travelling with?" Orin yelled over his shoulder as the alien moved towards him.

"Yep. That's Click," Veena replied from the small common room behind the cockpit.

"Great. It's like you said... fantastic." Orin stared at Click, and the little alien flashed orange, then pink. "Hello, Click. Nice to meet you."

A wave of magenta dots ran along Click's tentacles.

"I don't know what that means." Orin frowned. "Veena, can Click understand what I'm saying?"

"Maybe? Sure."

"Is that maybe or sure?"

The alien made a loud click and flashed green.

In a cascade of coloured pixels, Nigel appeared in the space between the pilot's and co-pilot's seats. The repurposed AI adjusted the buttons on his dinner jacket as if his holographic projection were somehow out of alignment. "Click wants me to tell you hello. And that they are capable of receiving and understanding your auditory information."

"Right. Veena set you up to translate."

"Yes, sir. However, my base code doesn't support this task. I fear...." Nigel's words trailed off as he futzed with his cravat.

Click emitted several slow clicks. Nigel nodded. "You're right; we need to make do." He turned to Orin. "Please excuse me while I perform some maintenance."

"Sure, do what you have to do." Orin blinked as the holographic Victorian gentleman vanished. He made eye contact with Click. "I guess it's just you and me now."

After waving three tentacles and flashing their tips pink, Click settled in, perched on the dashboard.

Orin let out another long exhale—his day kept getting weirder. If only there was a way to return to how his life had been before. He sighed and gazed through *Buttercup's* windshield at the ribbed interior of the battle cruiser *Defiant's* ship-sized airlock. When the air finished cycling, their escape would be complete.

He sighed again. Getting away from the battle cruiser was really only the first step in escaping, but he didn't dare think that far ahead.

"Stay positive," he whispered to no one but himself.

He didn't dare admit it to Veena, but his shoulder throbbed where the blaster beam had grazed him. Fortunately, the injury wasn't bad. He'd push through the pain—he had no choice.

2

"Now, let's get out of here." This time, he spoke with certainty.

Click let out a loud click, which Orin took as agreement. It rotated to face outwards, their skin now alternating from red swirls to orange dots. Orin did his best not to focus on the alien that shouldn't exist and studied the heads-up display instead.

As soon as the enormous doors ahead slid open, he accelerated out into space. Whatever Click had done bought them enough time to escape—but *Buttercup* was a survey ship, not a fighter, and the *Defiant* had squadrons of maneuverable short-range fighters. How would he escape them? His piloting skills were rusty, and even at his piloting peak, he'd never come close to being in a dogfight.

Keeping both hands on the controls, he swallowed as *Buttercup* emerged back into the debris field created by the destruction of the *Garden Princess*.

"Look at that mess. Now, what's the best path?" he asked aloud, more to himself than to the alien.

Click let out a long hmmm as their skin went pale blue.

"How about we take a better look at what's out there?" He reached forward and activated all of *Buttercup's* scanners, setting them to the widest electromagnetic band he could. Data started streaming in, adding to the heads-up display.

"We need to find a place to hide. Somewhere General Swa's people won't follow." He scratched the back of his neck as he started searching for a large enough piece of debris to hide behind.

Click pointed to a ragged piece of the *Garden Princess* hull one hundred metres ahead.

"Oh, shit." Orin jerked the controls hard left and slid the ship behind it.

The sharp motion tore at his injured shoulder, creating a raging pain that threatened to pull him into unconsciousness. The blaster's beam had only grazed him, yet now it was nearly incapacitating him. He wasn't in a state to fly.

"Stay focused. It's not like Veena can fly this thing if you pass out." Taking a deep breath, he pondered his next move.

The alien on the dashboard rotated until its enormous eyes faced him. Within the liquid-dark orbs, Orin thought he could see stars. Click flushed a deep purple and emitted a long click.

"*Buttercup*, we order you to return to the *Defiant* immediately," came a voice over the ship's external comms system.

"Damn it." Orin reached to turn it off. "I'm all out of ideas. What do you think our next move should be?"

The top of Click's head flashed green.

Orin pursed his lips. It seemed the little alien wanted to communicate, but their big eyes and bold colours added to a child's toy image more than anything else.

"Sorry, but I don't know what you mean. Can you bring back Nigel to translate?" As an excuse to break eye contact, he changed the scans to the infra-red spectrum. The new perspective added nothing, so he changed it back to visual.

Lifting themselves up onto their tentacles, Click's entire body flashed red, and they let out a loud click. They lifted one tentacle and pointed at the anchor world—a gesture Orin could decipher.

"Right, the anchor world. Yeah, that rocky planet is probably a better option than hiding out in this debris field."

Orin narrowed the scanner's focus to the planet. Every gate had an anchor world; the two were connected using physics no human understood. But the field of debris interfered with *Buttercup's* readings of the rocky world. Even though he couldn't get any definitive readings, it was still the best hiding place he could reach.

"We might find suitable shelter there. Good idea."

He plotted a weaving course to the anchor world, keeping as much debris between them and the *Defiant* as possible.

"Orin Akton." The external comms came to life a second time. Orin flinched as General Swa's face appeared in the middle of the front screen, completely blocking his view. Every part of him wanted to hide, put his head in the sand, and avoid his former supervisor's face.

He reached forward to activate his camera, but she didn't need to see him. She wasn't his boss anymore; he owed her nothing. He cleared his throat and activated audio only.

"We've decided not to accept your terms."

"If you don't return to the *Defiant* immediately, we will declare you a traitor." As she spoke, little wads of spit formed at the edges of her lips.

"I see.…" Orin's gut knotted. Everything he'd done since the war began had been to serve the Protectorate. All his sacrifices. He thought of Mary and how he'd put his work ahead of seeing her, and now the love of his life was gone. He swallowed as he stared into the projection of Swa's face. In that moment, he realized he didn't have to speak to her ever again.

"Click, can you turn her off?"

After emitting a series of choppy clicks, Click slithered over to the co-pilot's seat. With two tentacles, they worked the display, and a moment later, Swa's projection vanished.

Orin released a breath he hadn't realized he was holding, then relaxed back into his seat. Other than the throbbing shoulder, he suddenly felt much better—like a weight had been lifted from him. He stared Click in the eye and said, "Thanks. That woman is just too much. Let's focus on our escape."

Click flashed hot pink, then leapt back onto the dashboard.

Orin tuned the sensors as best he could before finishing plotting their course. "I suspect Swa is going to send out her short-range fighters to intercept us. I wonder how much time we have?" Trying to ignore his throbbing shoulder, he sped towards the anchor world.

"How's it going up here?" Veena asked as she stepped onto the bridge. Wisps of her black hair had escaped her ponytail; they stood straight up in the dry air. She ran a hand over her head, forcing many of them back down, as she sat and buckled herself in.

"Well, as expected, Swa threatened us." Orin tensed his muscles until he could feel the strain in his forearms as he dodged the ship past a piece of wreckage tumbling in their path. "So I assume they'll be out to shoot us down momentarily."

"Swa's predictable that way, but I don't think she'll kill us."

He glanced in Veena's direction. "I'm not sure they can just tow us back. Did you see a tow ship in the hangar?"

She studied a side display and fiddled with the settings. "Nope. But then, I didn't look for one. I'm sure Swa has a plan to haul our assess back."

"I appreciate your optimism, but...." Orin pursed his lips and focused on the debris field before him. He told himself he could manage the pain in his shoulder—he couldn't afford to let it distract him too much. As he swerved and dodged several more pieces of the former luxury liner, beads of sweat formed across his brow. The anchor world loomed ahead, yet it seemed so far away.

"She can't kill us. She needs us to decode the alien text."

Orin frowned. "Do you seriously think whatever that code says is worth the hassle of bringing us back in?"

"Yes, and they've launched their fighters." Veena's tone was flat as she brushed a lock of hair behind her ear.

"Damn." Gritting his teeth, Orin accelerated past the speed he was comfortable with. The throb in his shoulder morphed into a stabbing that threatened to take his breath away. "How long until they reach us?"

"We have minutes at most."

The debris was coming at him too fast now. It felt like a video game out of control—and he was playing with their lives. A wave of dread washed over him as a bead of sweat dripped down his forehead. He was teetering on the edge of control— one misstep, and he could kill them all.

Click waved two tentacles over their head, then started miming some sort of action with them.

"I have no idea what that means," Orin said.

Nigel materialized between the two seats. "Click would like a turn at the controls."

"That's insane. Are you mad?" Orin didn't dare take his eyes off his path. The pain from his shoulder was only getting worse, and maintaining control of *Buttercup* at this speed was getting harder and harder. A sour taste formed in his mouth as worst-case scenarios scrolled through his head.

Click emitted a series of loud, sharp clicks and flashed olive green, pulling Orin from his focus.

Buttercup shuttered as a piece of something bounced off the hull.

"I need to focus!" Orin roared. More debris hit the ship, sending reverberating gongs through the hull. Swa might not want to kill them, but the debris field might.

"You okay?" Veena asked.

"I'm fine." Orin gritted his teeth until his jaw cramped. With each movement, the fire of pain in his shoulder increased.

"No. You're not."

Click's skin faded to grey.

"Yes, yes, of course. I'll tell him." Nigel turned to Orin. "Click is concerned that your injury is impacting your control over this ship. They claim to know how to fly and would like to take over."

"Let Click take over." Even though Veena sat next to him, she sounded far away.

As Click made a series of undulating clicks, a wave of dizziness washed over Orin. He swallowed, trying to push the sensation away. "Fine. Click can take over."

Orin let his hands drop to his lap as Click slithered into Veena's. The little alien took the controls.

Orin clenched his jaw again as his fingers twitched. He itched to take over again. But Veena was right; he wasn't in the state to fly. He might damage the ship, or worse, kill them all. But could a cartoon alien do a better job? He squeezed his teeth even tighter together but said nothing.

Click sped up until *Buttercup's* accelerometer red lined. Somehow, they smoothly dodged everything in their way while maintaining a direct path to the anchor world. The planet's rocky surface came towards them so fast, it seemed impossible they wouldn't crash.

Orin grabbed hold of the armrests and squeezed his eyes shut. "Holy shit. Now it's all over!"

"Stop distracting them," Veena yelled back.

At what had to be the last second, Click pulled the nose of the ship up. The extra gs flattened Orin into his seat. For a moment, he couldn't breathe, and the throbbing of his shoulder expanded, threatening his consciousness once again. Then gravity returned to normal. He opened his eyes and wished he hadn't. They were flying so close to the ground he felt like he could reach out and touch the rock pillars surrounding them.

"You okay?" Veena asked, her voice shaky. Her dark eyes were wide as she stared at him.

Orin swallowed, then gave a nod. Nothing about their current situation felt okay.

Click flashed pink and yellow before making a pop.

"Click says the planet will shield us from their sensors," Nigel translated. "They are looking for a suitable place to land now."

Click angled the ship down into a deep ravine. The rock walls blocked the sunlight, creating an inky blackness ready to swallow them whole. The feeble lights on the ship ended only a few metres in front of them. Beyond, the heads-up display superimposed a mesh of yellow lines to show the walls.

"This place is impossible. There's nowhere remotely flat." Even though his shoulder throbbed more than ever, Orin itched to take back control. He swallowed and clasped his hand tighter together.

"We need to trust that Click knows a place," Veena said.

Orin glanced at the alien. They still sat on Veena's lap with three of their tentacles wound around the controls and another two on the throttle. They flushed green, then went transparent.

"Click says we are almost there." Nigel remained stationary in the narrow space between the chairs, his feet vanishing into the deck. "We will be safe there. We can wait until the *Defiant* gives up and leaves."

Veena glanced his way. "I don't think they're going to give up that easy."

"I have to agree with that." Relieved of piloting duties and unwilling to continue doing nothing, Orin fiddled with the sensor display and tried to find an electromagnetic band that would show if they were being pursued. He frowned. "All I'm getting is static. It's like the surrounding rocks are completely blocking the signals."

"If we can't see them, they probably can't see us," Veena said.

Click made a loud click followed by a softer one.

"Click says the walls should hide us," Nigel said.

"Let's hope that's true." Orin returned his attention to the scene on the other side of their windshield.

Click dove deeper into the ravine, which seemed more like a rift that split the planet. Orin turned on every light *Buttercup* had, which barely illuminated the grey walls.

Veena let out a low whistle. "I'm half expecting we'll come out on the other side of the planet."

Orin rubbed his injured shoulder. Now that he'd stopped straining, the pain had subsided back to a manageable level. Hopefully, *Buttercup* was well stocked with medical supplies.

"I—" Orin stopped when Click forced the ship on a nearly ninety-degree turn.

Around them, *Buttercup* groaned.

"What the…" Orin glanced at Click.

The little alien let out a series of dismissive sounding clicks while waving a free tentacle his way. Their huge eyes remained focused on the view outside the windshield.

"I think we've entered a side cavern," Veena said.

Click purred in reply as they slowed the ship down. Shades of grey and black marbled the sleek walls. Then the two-toned pattern became more regular until it resolved into a honeycomb.

Veena gasped. "This can't be natural."

Then Orin noticed the ground—the black and glossy surface extended completely level out to the perpendicular walls. "I agree. Someone made this cavern. Nigel, can you ask Click about this place?"

Click flashed grey, then made several frustrated-sounding clicks.

Nigel's face went blank for a moment, then re-animated. "Among other things, they say their kind lived here once before the Slip."

Orin raised an eyebrow. "Please explain what you mean by 'the Slip?'"

Click clicked and extended the landing gear, leaving Orin's question unanswered. At the back of the main cavern, Click set *Buttercup* down with barely a bump. The ship's bright lights lit up the wall, illuminating multiple hexagon-shaped passageways leading deeper into the rock.

"Now what?" Veena shifted in her seat.

Click moved off of her lap and back onto the dashboard. Their colour changed to greys and blacks that mimicked the marbled pattern they'd passed on the way in.

"I guess we just hang out here for a bit." Orin looked from the alien to the view outside, then back to Click. "Can we explore?"

Click lifted two tentacles, roughly reproducing a shrug. When Orin turned to the holographic steward, he shrugged as well.

Veena unbuckled and stood. "How long should we wait?"

"I'm hoping that Swa assumes we crashed." Orin ran a hand over his head, sure that he had earned more grey hair in the last few hours. "Let's say six hours, maybe longer."

Orin reduced *Buttercup's* systems to the bare minimum for life support. As he powered things down, he turned off the outside lights. For a moment, there was just blackness outside the windows, then faint lights emerged. A greenish glow came from the rocks themselves, as though lit from within.

"What's out there?" Veena's voice held more curiosity than anything else.

Click made a popping sound.

Orin turned off all the lights on the bridge. It took a moment for his eyes to adjust to the low light, then the surrounding details appeared. A honeycomb pattern stretched across the walls and glowed a vivid green, creating enough light to see.

"Wow." Orin leaned closer to the windshield as if that would give him a better view.

"They found the alien code on one of these anchor worlds," Veena said. "The reports described how the symbols, reminiscent of ancient Egyptian hieroglyphics, were etched into stone walls."

"Do we know which anchor world they found them on?"

"Nope. Someone redacted that information." Veena scratched her head, pulling a few strands loose from her already messy ponytail.

"Let the sensors test the environment out there. If it's safe, we have plenty of time to look around."

Veena turned to him, her eyes sparkling. "If we find more text, it might help us decode what we already have."

Chapter Two

"Did your scans pick up anything?" Veena took a seat at the table in the ship's common room. She cradled a steaming mug of mint tea between her hands, letting the warmth seep into her. She would've preferred a coffee, but *Buttercup* didn't have any—fucking tea was the only option.

She took a sip and sighed. Although it wasn't her favourite, Molly loved mint tea. Before the bombing of their home, before Hwicce was called to war, before her secondment to Rock 13-5A, before the army took Molly, the three of them used to sip mint tea together after dinner—but now was not the time to get lost in memories.

Their hideout was unexpected. A facility built by aliens ripe with possibility. What if she found more alien symbols written on the corridors out there? Maybe a clue to solve the puzzle? Swa still wanted her to decode the alien text she already had. Maybe the key was here, and she could use it to barter for her daughter's freedoms.

"I've picked up absolutely nothing on any of the scanner's frequencies." With a wince, Orin slid into the seat across from her. He gazed around as though he could see through *Buttercup's* hull. "It's like the walls are shielded."

Even after all the excitement of their escape from the *Defiant* had died down, Orin's balding forehead still glistened with sweat. With every movement, he held himself stiffly—then Veena remembered he'd been shot during their escape.

She set her mug down on the table. "You okay?"

Orin rubbed his shoulder. "It's not so bad. The blaster beam just grazed my shoulder. As long as I don't move too quickly, I'm fine."

"You could lay down for a bit. I can keep watch."

"Thanks, but no. Really, I'm fine. I need the distraction of exploring this place, and I think you do too." He took a sip of his tea. "Besides, I found painkillers in the ship's medkit—they should kick in any minute now."

Veena nodded, her thoughts returning to their impossible surroundings. She re-wrapped her hands around her mug, lifted it to her lips, and inhaled the mint-laced steam. After taking a sip, she turned to where Nigel, in his normal elegant suit, stood next to the un-used coffeepot. "Can you ask Click what this place is?"

Above, Click walked across the ceiling, mimicking the yellow of the ship's interior. At her words, they stopped and flushed grey.

"Click says it's a haunted place." Nigel glitched, and when his pixels reformed, his face assumed a solemn expression. "They say there isn't anything for their kind here anymore."

"What about this?" Orin raised one of Molly's *Bubble and Click* comics. "Can you ask how Click ended up in a child's book?"

Veena's gaze fixated on the brightly coloured pulp pages. She'd read that one to Molly at least a million times—it was Molly's favourite. She used to laugh every time Bubble and Click tricked the evil Dr. Ash and escaped his lab.

Without making a sound, Click dropped from the ceiling onto the table. They picked up the comic and flushed green. They flipped through the pages using a bizarre combination of tentacles. At times, their skin went white with orange polka dots, then indigo. At other times, Click went transparent, then blazed yellow.

"This," Nigel said as Click held up the comic and faced them. "What is this?"

"It's a comic my daughter loves." Veena sipped her tea, then continued in a quiet voice. "She regularly pretends to be Bubble."

"Are there more?"

"Yep. I have more with me." She cocked her head and set her mug down. She realized she hadn't questioned why an actual alien would look identical to the illustrated one. "But Orin has a point. How are you in the comic?"

Click let out a series of sharp clicks, and the holographic projection of the steward AI floated closer to the table.

"Not me." Nigel's expression went blank as Click talked directly through him. "Fun to read. I read more."

"You can read our language?" Orin asked.

"Yes. I learned after they took us."

Veena tucked an escaped lock of hair behind her ear as she leaned forward. "Was it Dr. Greer who took you?"

Click flushed grey. "No, other humans found me when I got lost. They weren't kind to me like you." Click's enormous eyes focused on Veena. "The ones that found me passed me off to Greer."

"I'm sorry you had to go through that." Veena stared into their mesmerizing eyes. It was as though they contained a whole starfield within. "I meant it when I said I'll help you get home."

Click flashed hot pink. "Click feels safe now."

"Good." Veena smiled and pulled out her datapad.

"And Click promises to help Veena too. I will help put your consortium back together."

Orin frowned. "Consortium?"

Nigel glitched, reappearing at the edge of the table. "Is that not what a group of related humans is called?"

"I think you mean family, and thank you, Click." Veena brought up the alien code on her datapad. "Can you read this?"

Nigel glitched, blinking out of existence, then blinking back. "I'm sorry my link to Click got severed." The hologram adjusted his cravat and glitched again. "Ah good, they're back. No."

Veena drew her eyebrows together and stared at Click. "No, you can't read it?"

Click went pale blue and slouched down. "It is old, from before the Slip."

"What's the Slip?" Veena kept her focus on Click, even though it was Nigel who did the talking.

"That's when we lost the worlds like this." Click made an expansive gesture with five of their tentacles as Nigel relayed their words. "It happened a long time ago, well before I hatched."

Veena glanced down at the symbols and pursed her lips. "So, this is no longer your language?"

"After the Slip, we changed." Click pulled themselves up off the table and balanced on three tentacles. "Can I read the comics now?"

Nodding, Veena retrieved the rest of Molly's comics from the backpack and put them on the table. Click picked up the top one and opened it, flushing bright colours as they flipped through the pages. Veena watched as she finished the rest of her tea.

A few minutes later, Orin glanced up from his datapad. "What I'm seeing doesn't make sense. The readings here are flat-out weird."

Cocking her head, Veena stared at him. "Good weird or bad weird?"

"Just weird. I ran a detailed analysis of the air outside and... well... there's air outside."

"Huh. I thought anchor worlds were just dead rocks." Veena scooted around the table to see Orin's screen. Click remained engrossed by the comics and ignored them.

"That's what I thought too." He slid the display over so she could see. "But here, the air's even breathable."

"Dare we breathe it?"

"The readings show the air in this cave is stable, with no organic readings at all. Oxygen levels are on the low end, but it's breathable."

"What about exotic elements?"

"Nothing that will harm us in the short term," Orin said. "*Buttercup* may be old, but its sensors are designed for this kind of analysis, and my friend Rosie kept them well maintained."

Veena tapped a finger on the tabletop. "So, you're saying you trust the readings?"

"Yes, I do."

For the first time in a long time, enthusiasm washed over Veena. Their hiding place was safe, they had time—and they had a puzzle right in front of them. She rubbed her hands together and smiled.

"Since we're waiting around anyway, let's go exploring."

Veena took a few minutes to rig a data-drive onto a harness for Click, so they could bring Nigel along to translate. Click flashed cyan and orange when she finished before skittering along the floor to the airlock.

"It seems your little friend is as curious as we are," Orin said as he entered the airlock after Click.

"I guess so." Veena followed.

With a clank, Orin sealed the inside door. "Let's go see what's out there."

Click flashed a neon orange, then yellow, which Veena took as more excitement.

"Let's do this." She opened the outside door. A waft of warm air hit them, followed by a tidal wave of fresh asphalt scent. She nearly gagged.

"That odour reminds me of last time I visited New Haven." Orin stepped past her and lowered the stairs.

The three steps extended down, revealing about five centimetres of viscous liquid covering the ground. Click clicked and climbed up Veena, settling onto her shoulder. They wrapped a tentacle around the back of her neck as an anchor, their grip gentle, before emitting a faint click. A surprising warmth radiated from their body.

"I don't blame you." Veena pointed to the liquid-covered ground. "I wouldn't want to get that on me either."

Click emitted another click.

"They had just paved outside our house. All the air inside smelled just like this." Orin stepped down and into the liquid; the toes of his boots nearly disappeared into the blackness. "We had to run the air filters on maximum to get the stench out— and that took several hours."

Veena descended to the bottom step, then paused. The dark liquid lapped at her boots as an iridescent sheen moved across the surface in a chaotic pattern. "What if there's a hole some-where? We wouldn't see it."

Nigel blinked into existence beside her. He hovered a good five centimetres above the liquid as though he was afraid to get some on himself as well. "Click tells me the floor should be flat."

"Nevertheless...." Veena fiddled with the thin rope she'd brought with her. "Orin, I think we should tie ourselves together."

"Right." Still gazing around at the cave, Orin stepped closer. "This place is...." His words trailed off as he lifted his arms.

Veena tied the rope around him, then tied the other end around herself. "This place is so deep in the rift I wouldn't be surprised if no other human has ever set foot in it."

Since the patterns on the walls glowed bright enough to see

by, Veena clipped her flashlight to her belt and trudged towards the closest wall.

Orin turned to his ship and frowned. "Oh, no… the mess. When we get out of here, we'll be cleaning *Buttercup* for weeks."

Veena glanced back. Black splatter covered the lower parts of the ship. The hull's jaunty yellow combined with the black reminded her of a wasp.

"This way." Nigel gestured towards the nearest hexagon tunnel.

A slight step up to get into the tunnel prevented the black liquid from extending in. Veena stooped as she walked inside. The rock ceiling was less than a hands-width above her head—barely enough room to stand. The walls glowed pale green, brighter than the main cavern.

Veena turned to Nigel. "Click, what was this place was for?"

Click flashed green, then leapt off Veena's shoulder, landing elegantly on three tentacles.

"They are as curious about the purpose of this place as you are," Nigel said.

Click glowed a pale purple as they began moving deeper inside the hexagonal passage. The alien took Nigel's projector past its transmission limit, and the holographic AI winked out.

"I guess we follow." Veena untied the line between herself and Orin.

Orin glanced back at his ship one more time, then to the corridor ahead. "I guess so."

Side-by-side, the two of them started walking. Further in, the corridor branched in multiple directions, including straight up and down. As though gravity was irrelevant, there were no handholds or ladders. Click could climb walls, but they certainly couldn't fly. Maybe water once filled the space.

A pace from the edge, Veena stopped. "Maybe Click's ancestors were aquatic."

"That would explain this." Orin pointed to the awkward junction of corridors. "Even with sticky tentacles, this would be hard to traverse. Hey, didn't the octopuses of old Earth have suckers on their tentacles?"

Veena smiled. "Molly had a thing for octopuses for a while, and we had to watch endless vids on them—first, an octopus' appendages were called arms, and yes, they were covered in suction cups."

"I wonder why Click doesn't… but I guess they don't need them as they seem perfectly able to stick onto ceilings and walls."

"Also, Click and old Earth octopus are from completely different evolutionary paths." As Veena glanced over the edge, her stomach churned. The corridor's glowing walls continued down as far as she could see. A ledge barely wide enough to scoot sideways along continued at her level around the junction. She swallowed as she watched Click skitter around like the drop was nothing—and maybe to them, it was.

Trying not to think about the smooth wall without a single handhold and how, if she lost her footing, there would be nothing to grab hold of, she stepped onto the ledge. By keeping her back to the wall and shuffling sideways, she reached the other side. The horizontal passage ahead continued straight for another fifty metres, then opened up into another cavern.

Orin let out a sigh as he stepped off the ledge beside her. "Let's hope we don't have to get out of here in a hurry."

From ten metres down the corridor, Click emitted a loud click as though to remind them to keep moving. Veena and Orin exchanged a glance and continued on. Once they crossed the threshold into the cavern, Click flushed orange and green.

"What is this place?" Veena followed, gaping at the walls.

Nigel flickered back to existence. He drew his eyebrows together and stared down at Click. He shook his head as though disagreeing with the alien. Then he turned towards Veena.

"I can't translate Click's description." Nigel pursed his lips together. "We just don't have the right words."

Veena walked forward. The carved-out room was a hexagon

on the horizontal. The walls extended up several stories coated in glowing hexagons the size of her hand. Inside each one was a symbol. Her chin dropped when she realized the symbols were from the alien text she'd been working on deciphering.

"Wow." She circled the room. "There's so much here."

Orin followed a few paces behind. "This is quite the place. Does every anchor world have a space like this?"

Click flushed indigo.

"We need to capture all of this." Veena pulled out her datapad to take pictures.

Chapter Three

Like the start of an epic flood, big drops of rain pummelled the planet's surface in an endless stream. Long since saturated by the tea-scented liquid, Baker continued her vigil, staring at the moss-covered cliff where Hwicce had fallen. Did he survive his fall? Was there some way she could help? But how could she even find him? The night was so dark, she could barely see her hand in front of her face.

"Come on. Let's find another mushroom for shelter until it gets light." Emiko moved close enough that Baker could feel the heat radiating from her body.

Baker slowly turned, scanning her surroundings one last time. The feeble beam of her flashlight revealed darkness that could be infinite, except she knew it wasn't. She shifted her weight back and forth, toes to heels, as she tried to focus on anything beyond the rain.

Hwicce's plan had been flat-out foolish—she should've stopped him. How could he have thought it was a good idea to climb on top of the giant mushroom to search for lights from the greenie village? The mushroom couldn't support his weight, and the top snapped off. In an instant, the falling fungi dumped him down the steep slope into the black. She'd heard him slide further down, but she didn't dare follow in the darkness.

"I'm a fucking clay-brained coward." She kicked the ground at her feet.

Hwicce needed her help, and she hadn't even taken two steps to find him.

Emiko rested a hand on her forearm. "Bullshit. Trying to find him right now would be a dumbass move on your part— even he'd admit that."

Baker swallowed and turned to her shorter companion. "Why in the hell did he climb up there?"

In the low light, Emiko's eyes glinted. "The sun will rise soon, then we'll be able to find him. He probably just slid to the bottom of the slope and is waiting out the night like we should."

"Even last night, when it was still light, it was impossible to tell how high up we are. The moss forest is just too fucking thick." Baker ran a hand over her normally shaved scalp—now stubble covered her head.

"I would've thought a veteran soldier like you would be used to waiting for the most opportune time." Emiko's words rang true.

Even though she'd only met the other woman a few days ago, Baker valued Emiko's company. She closed her eyes and tilted her face up towards the dark sky. Rain rolled off her skin. She wanted to wrap an arm around Emiko but couldn't work up the nerve to do it—besides, she needed to stay focused on finding Hwicce.

"Why the hell did the greenies stay on this awful planet?" Emiko stepped closer to Baker again. "A space station is way cozier than this place."

Baker snorted. "You say that because you grew up on a station."

"True. There's also no random rain on space stations—and they have restaurants and food kiosks."

Baker's stomach grumbled as if to remind her there was

nothing she could eat in the moss and fungi forest surrounding them. Emiko was right—this world wasn't meant for human habitation. She let out a long exhale as she realized Hwicce's pack sat with theirs beside the stump of mushroom. Wherever he'd ended up, he had no food or clean water with him. She groaned.

"This hell hole is the worst fucking place I've ever been!" Baker resumed staring out into the darkness.

"It does have death trap potential." Emiko's voice was soothing.

The sky at the horizon seemed a shade lighter now, or that could just be her wishful thinking.

"I think the rain is easing up." Emiko took Baker's hand in hers. "But I'm still wetter than a drowned rat."

Baker forced a smile and squeezed Emiko's hand. "Mythical creatures like that are smart enough to avoid getting stuck out in this kind of shit weather."

"I'll split a meal bar with you." Emiko pulled Baker away from the edge towards an intact mushroom a few metres away.

With a sigh, Baker let Emiko lead her. She hated having no idea what happened to Hwicce. Was he okay? She swallowed. Was he injured? He needed her help, but she was doing fuck all to find him. But then, she didn't know what she could do to help in the darkness.

"You're right," Baker said in a tiny voice.

"Huh?" Emiko shone her flashlight away from her pack and at Baker.

"It's only logical to wait until there's light." She sat down next to Emiko. Moisture saturated the spongy moss covering the ground—but it didn't make any difference, as she was already soaked. The mushroom cap above meant a respite from being pummelled by raindrops. With a sigh, Baker leaned her head back against the stalk.

"Damn right." Emiko opened a meal bar, broke it in two,

then handed Baker a piece—the larger piece. "We'll find him in the morning. It'll all work out; you'll see."

"I admire your bloody optimism." Baker shifted closer to Emiko. Even stranded on an alien world and her best friend lost, just having Emiko at her side warmed her heart. The feeling surprised her.

"Yep, I'm all sunshine and rainbows."

Baker took a big bite of her half of the ration bar. "Too bad you didn't pack food with flavour."

"What do you mean? Chalk is absolutely a flavour."

"Hmph, spicy cricket would've been better."

"Tell you what." Emiko slipped her hand back into Baker's. "If we're ever on Indigo Station, I'll take you to the best taco place—their spicy cricket tacos are to die for."

Baker smiled. "Sounds like a date."

As they each chewed their piece of the meal bar, the sky continued to brighten. Morphing from complete blackness to grey to a pea soup green.

"I swear this world is nearly monochromatic." Baker tried to ignore the metallic aftertaste of her snack. Her stomach grumbled, reminding her she needed a proper meal—and that she had no idea when she might get one. First, they needed to find Hwicce....

"Well, green's my favourite colour," Emiko said.

Baker turned to her. In the early morning light, Emiko's facial features were just visible. Her perfect nose, her full lips, and that pixie hair cut—she looked like a doll, yet she'd made it through fighting the Long Enterprise forces at Hamber Hole, abandoning the *Shimmer* and their harrowing crash landing on Smaragdos. She could have been a former soldier like Baker and Hwicce—but she wasn't. Baker wrapped an arm around Emiko and pulled her in close.

"You've never told me your favourite colour," Emiko said.

"Hmmm." Baker gazed out into the brightening sky. "That's a hard call... but I'm going to have to go with blue."

Emiko rested her head on Baker's shoulder. "I'm sure he's fine."

"I really hope so." A slight breeze picked up, and Baker shivered. "I don't want to face his wife and tell her all I did was sit under a mushroom after her husband fell."

"You'll find him," Emiko said. "I know it."

Chapter Four

Capturing images of the glowing walls as she moved, Veena circled the perimeter of the hexagonal room. Questions churned through her mind—she needed to understand what she was looking at. Were these new messages? Would they give her enough information to crack the alien code? The excitement of the possibilities masked her gnawing fear for Molly.

On the far side of the room, she stopped next to a waist-high, podium-shaped plinth—it was the only object in the room not glowing. Its darkness was an anomaly but not an interesting one.

"Hmm." Returning her focus to the walls, she set her datapad down on the plinth.

From across the room, Click emitted a high-pitched whine and flashed bright red. They rushed towards her and galloped up the plinth. Veena snatched her datapad back before Click reached the top.

She drew her eyebrows together. "What?"

All the lighting in the room went out, leaving a blackness so thick Veena felt like she could reach out and touch it.

"Well... shit." Veena grabbed her flashlight.

"This isn't good. What did you do?" Orin's voice came from somewhere in the darkness to her right.

Before she could turn on her light, the ceiling glowed, casting a green light over the space, brighter than before. In the centre of the room, a hexagon etched into the floor flickered, then shone with the same intensity.

Like a cascade of water, an incandescent wire mesh flowed from each side of the ceiling hexagon. The see-through honeycomb connected with the matching hexagon on the floor. At first, the far wall was visible. A shimmering wave passed through the honeycomb mesh and the scene inside changed to an inky darkness that felt different, as though it was no longer part of the same room.

"Interesting. Is this a hologram?" Orin took one pace towards the glowing mesh.

"No," Nigel said. The colour washed out from his projection, leaving the same green shades as the rest of the room. He cocked his head, then turned to Click.

Click clicked, and Nigel nodded.

"It's a portal."

"A portal?" Veena walked over and stopped beside Orin. The darkness inside made her think of a dark room or another cave. "Does it use the same physics as the gates?"

A deep groan sounded from somewhere deep beneath them, and Veena's heart skipped a beat. A moment later, the ground trembled.

A beep drew Orin's attention to his datapad. "Umm... this doesn't look good." As he glanced up at Veena, the green light in the room cast odd highlights across his dark skin. "*Buttercup's* sensors are picking up something strange."

Veena raised an eyebrow. What could be stranger than the discovery of portals? If this technology got out, it could change everything—and maybe in a good way.

"It turns out this world isn't as seismically stable as we thought."

"Is the portal creating the instability?" Veena scratched her chin and stared at the glowing mesh, then at the surrounding walls. Did the alien code contain instructions on how to make portals? "And I wonder what powers this thing."

Orin pursed his lips. "My readings suggest these caves might collapse. I don't think it's safe here anymore. We need to head back."

"I'm sure we've got a couple of minutes." Veena nodded, then returned her attention to the portal. "But where does the portal go?" She squinted as she tried to make out shapes inside.

"Wherever there's another transceiver. We lost the full map in the Slip."

Veena glanced at Click. "Can it get you home?"

Click flushed aqua with white dots and shook their head.

"No," Nigel translated. "There isn't a portal on Click's homeworld."

"This place isn't safe. We really need to go," Orin cut in, pointing to the readout on his datapad. "The instability is increasing."

"Give me a sec." Veena's words trailed off as she focused on the portal. She took out her flashlight and shone it through. The light illuminated a swath in the space on the other side. The light reflected off of ripples of water, creating flickering lights that danced across a low ceiling. There was definitely another world on the other side of the mesh. She cocked her head.

"Assuming this works like the gate system and based on our limited understanding of the physics in play, portals this small shouldn't be possible," she said. "This technology could rock our society."

Orin grabbed onto her arm and started pulling her towards the exit. "I don't want to get trapped in here if the ceiling collapses."

Ignoring him, she continued to sweep her beam of light around, resolving where the water gave way to a stone ledge. "Where is this place?"

Click shrugged.

Halfway between the water's edge and the wall, Veena's light landed on a familiar form, one she would recognize anywhere. Her jaw dropped, and the flashlight fell from her hand. It clattered to the ground as she tried to process what she'd seen.

"What was that?" Orin released her and turned his flashlight on. He shone it on the same spot.

She clamped her hands over her mouth as spots started spinning in Veena's vision. Her mind scrambled to understand.

Hwicce lay on the other side of the portal.

Keeping his light fixed on Hwicce, Orin approached the hexagonal mesh of light. "Click, where is this?"

Click emitted three long clicks.

"They don't know," Nigel translated.

"If light can go through, why not sound? Hwicce!" Veena yelled as loud as she could. He shifted slightly but didn't wake.

Something inside her wound up like a coil. Hwicce was right there! He could finally explain himself. Veena bit her lip. She needed him—and his help to get Molly back. She took a pace closer to him.

Nigel stepped in front of her, so close some of his pixels passed through her. "You can't go through unprotected!"

At her feet, Click flashed crimson and wrapped a tentacle around her leg.

Veena swallowed, staring at the still form of Hwicce. "But..."

"The portal will rip you apart," Nigel said.

"I could go back to the ship and get a suit." Veena turned and was about to break into a sprint when Orin grabbed her arm.

"There isn't enough time. We need to leave before the ceiling collapses and crushes us."

As if to punctuate his point, the ground beneath them shook, and several large rocks fell from the ceiling.

"But..."

Click let go and emitted a series of choppy clicks.

"The suits you have won't provide the right protection. We will go," Nigel pointed to Click, then himself. "Click can pass through the portal just fine, and I...." He looked down at himself and shrugged. "I'm not real."

Click pulled themself up on all their tentacles as though standing to attention. They flashed violet, then green.

"Click vows to save your companion." Nigel blinked out of existence.

Pulling their tentacles in and under their body, Click jiggled, and the band containing Nigel's code swayed with each movement. They launched themselves through the mesh of light, landing on the ground on the other side. Without hesitation, they skittered on top of Hwicce and smacked him on the cheek.

"What the hell?" Hwicce sat up and tried to grab onto Click. But Click darted out of reach, and Nigel reformed beside them, back in his normal colours.

"Hwicce!" Veena shouted. She desperately wanted to try the portal. What if Click was wrong, and she could pass through with no problem? In that moment, all she wanted was to have Hwicce wrap his arms around her. He could explain why he'd left his army post and why he didn't contact her. He had good reasons, and Veena knew it.

On the other side, Hwicce turned towards her, and his lips opened in an 'o.'

At the edge of the shimmering barrier of light, Veena fell to her knees. "Tell us where you are." Her hands trembled— Hwicce was so close, yet she couldn't reach him.

"Did I hit my head?" He ran his hands over this skull. "I'm seeing things that can't be. Like my love and..." He pointed to Click. "And Mol's stuffy?"

"Hwicce!" she said as the ground beneath her shook, stronger this time. Their time was running out. "Focus."

"Where are you?" Orin used the tone of a military commander. "You need to tell us where you are."

Hwicce scratched his head as he stared at Orin. "Why would I hallucinate Veena's boss?"

"You can really see us. We're really here." Veena's heart ached. She'd been so focused on getting Molly back, she hadn't realized how much she missed him.

"Veena, I love you so much." He ran his hands over his face. "I...I... was trying to get back to you. But things went sideways."

Veena bit her lip as a tear made its way down her cheek. "We can come get you. Just tell us where you are."

"After the *Garden Princess...* oh shit, what happened to that ship?" He perked up. "Did we avert a head-on collision?"

"Hwicce, we don't have much time. Where are you?" Veena shifted forward until less than a centimetre separated her nose from the glowing mesh. Her skin prickled this close to the barrier.

"We crashed on this damn planet, and now I've lost the others." He pushed himself up to his feet. He wavered a bit as he stood. "I fell a long way. I should be dead."

Veena bit her lip as she stood as well. "What planet?"

"Smaragdos."

"Click and Nigel are there to help you." Veena pointed to them.

"We need to go." Orin put a hand on her shoulder. "But Smaragdos is only one gate away on the main loop. We can get there in less than a day."

The ground shook, and a piece of the ceiling gave way. When it crashed down, the honeycomb mesh winked out.

"Hwicce?" Veena reached a hand out to where he'd been just a moment before.

Orin pulled her arm. "We really need to go."

Veena nodded. Hwicce was close, and he needed their help. "Let's get out of here."

Chapter Five

After jutting her chin out and clenching her fists at her side, Molly glared at Dr. Greer. She shifted her gaze to the examination table, then back to the man wearing a stupid white lab coat. Except for the lab coat, he looked nothing like Dr. Ash, the villain in her *Bubble and Click* comics—but Dr. Greer belonged in the same league of mad scientists.

Ever since she'd arrived, she'd been poked and prodded, and she was done with all that. She closed her eyes, picturing her hero Bubble. How she wouldn't put up with this. How she would refuse unless she got what she wanted.

Opening her eyes and fixing her gaze on her nemesis, Molly pulled her shoulders back. "I want my mom!"

Greer frowned. "How about you get up on the table and let me take a blood sample, and then I'll call your mom."

"You said that last time." Molly clenched her teeth together. "And you never did. You lied to me."

She squeezed her fists tighter. Jars, tools, and medical implements she didn't recognize rattled. Frowning, Greer glanced around. A bead of sweat dripped down his forehead.

"I need you to stop that," he said, blinking more than he

should. His voice was even, but she could tell she'd made him afraid of her.

"No." Molly stomped her foot, and things crashed off the counters and shelves.

Greer put up a hand. "Okay, okay.…" He backed away and retrieved something from his lab coat pocket. "How about I give you this package of Space Chew?" He opened his hand, exposing a silvery package of candy.

Everything stopped vibrating as Molly took a step closer. "What flavour?"

"Cosmic Crush."

"I want the latest *Bubble and Click* comic, too." She reached up and took the candy.

Greer frowned. "We don't have any comics here. This is a remote moon; I can't just run down to a shop and pick it up for you."

"Then call my mom. She'll bring them." Molly glanced at the mess of medical tools littering the floor—a mess she wouldn't have to clean up. "And I don't want to be poked today."

"Molly, I need you to cooperate." Greer bent down and started picking up the tools. "The anomaly in your genetics may help a lot of people."

"My mom and dad told me never to talk about that." Molly unwrapped a Space Chew candy and popped it in her mouth. The sweet orange candy stuck to her teeth as she chewed. "They said people would use it to hurt me."

Greer ran a hand over his face as he stood and faced her. "I have more Space Chew, including Galactic Grape."

Molly looked down at the roll of Cosmic Crush. "My favourite is Lemon Sun." She cocked her head and studied the doctor.

"I may have some of that flavour," he said as he straightened his tools. "If you cooperate and let me take a blood sample, I'll go look."

"No." Molly put the rest of the roll of candy into her pocket and crossed her arms over her chest. "You need to look first."

Greer sighed. "Fine. Come into my office."

Molly followed him through a side door into an exceptionally bland room filled with drab office furniture and not a toy in sight. Dr. Greer's office was as boring as the lab. The floor-to-ceiling windows running along one wall caught her attention; she walked over and put her hands on the glass as Greer hunted through his desk.

A gas giant hung just over the horizon. Green and yellow storms spun across its surface. She didn't recognize it, meaning it wasn't one of the planets she'd learned about in school—she'd aced the test on those. Her mom always said that astronomy was one of her strengths, just like Bubble.

How would her mom find her if she was stuck on a moon circling a planet no one knew about? She needed to gather some intelligence. "Where are we?"

"Ah-ha!" Greer stood and held up a yellow and silver roll of candy.

Molly turned and clapped her hands as her focus shifted to the candy. The shiny yellow and silver package glinted in the low light. "You found it."

Greer handed her the roll. "Let's go back to the lab."

"I want the Galactic Grape too."

Her captor frowned and turned back to his desk to look. Molly took the time to survey his office for a radio or some other communication equipment. That's what Bubble would do—and her hero wouldn't give up until she escaped.

Chapter Six

"Oh, shit." Veena paused at the threshold to the main cavern where *Buttercup* sat waiting. The tar-like liquid had risen. She took a step forward and sunk down into it halfway up her calves.

Orin stepped down beside her. "This isn't good. We've got to get out of here right away." He started wading towards the ship.

Veena followed. With each step, the viscous fluid slowed her down, but she forged on, not wanting to think about what would happen if it rose higher. Orin was right—they needed to get out of here. As if to punctuate her thought, a few rocks fell from the ceiling, hitting the liquid with loud plops. If a big one hit their ship...

She swallowed and forged ahead. At the airlock door, she stared at the splatter on the hull as the next problem surfaced in her mind. "How are we going to get past Swa and the battle-cruiser?"

"We're not fast enough—or maneuverable enough to evade her forces. We'll be sitting ducks as soon as we leave this cave." Orin frowned.

"True." She cocked her head as she continued to stare at the splatter patterns. For a moment, she started counting the marks, then a bubble of optimism rose in her chest. "What if we were invisible?"

Orin turned her way. "What do you mean?"

"Our sensors are blocked down here. What if—"

Orin cut her off. "The tar has the same properties as the surrounding rocks?" He pulled out his datapad and started analyzing a patch of the liquid on the hull.

"What are you getting?" Veena leaned in to see the readings.

"This just might work," he said, holding up the datapad. "My sensors don't see past it."

"If we coat the ship, at the very least, we'd be nearly invisible on the visible spectrums."

Another cascade of rocks fell across the corridor they'd just emerged from.

Orin rolled up his datapad and shoved it in his pocket. "We don't have much time."

Veena nodded. "Buckets. We need buckets. And we need to work fast."

Working together, the two of them coated most of the hull in less than twenty minutes. Their luck held, and no big chunks of ceiling fell while they worked. Ninety-seven bucket loads later, Veena stopped and took a deep breath.

With her shoulders and back throbbing from exertion, she backed up to examine *Buttercup*. Black tar now hid the entire yellow hull, leaving only the front windshield clear—it was the best they could do with the time they had.

"Let's get out of here."

"I'm on it," Orin said as he headed inside.

Veena followed, pulling in the stairs and sealing the airlock as she passed. Black imprints of their boot treads marred the floor—it probably wouldn't come off easily, but she didn't have the energy to worry about it.

In the cockpit, she found Orin racing through his pre-departure checklist, doing only what was necessary before lifting off. She buckled herself in the co-pilot's seat and gritted her teeth.

"It's time to get going. Are you ready?" Orin asked without looking her way.

Veena stared out at the fantastic alien place, still glowing as it crumbled. There was so much they hadn't seen—a tremendous opportunity lost. Her shoulders slumped. "No, but let's go."

Orin pulled back the controls. For a moment, the engines whined as the ship struggled to break the liquid's surface tension. With a slurping sound, they broke free.

"I can't fly like Click did." Orin didn't take his eyes off the view ahead.

"How's your shoulder?" Veena asked. Their frantic work coating the ship couldn't have helped.

"I took more painkillers. It's okay if I keep my movements smooth."

Without the drama of Click's flight path on the way in, Orin flew *Buttercup* back out into the rift and brought it up.

The matte surface of the rocky world absorbed most of the light coming from the nearby star. Complex rocky formations, some reaching up like spires, while others ending in flat table-tops, comprised the little they could see. But darkness was the dominant feature of the landscape, creating plenty of cover to fly through.

Keeping a low altitude, Orin continued until the right side of the gate appeared on the horizon, its glistening green surface like a beacon in the sky.

Veena bent over the displays from their survey ship's various scanners. There was no tactical display, as *Buttercup* was never intended for combat. But the *Defiant* wasn't trying to hide. She easily found the behemoth of a warship.

"It's as we expected." She turned to Orin. "Swa is guarding

the gate. I can't tell if any of their fighters are out on patrol, but my guess is they are."

"Let's see how well the tar keeps us invisible." Orin accelerated as he angled up on a course for the gate, quickly gaining altitude.

Veena strained her neck as she watched the battlecruiser get larger. How close could they get and not be seen? She glanced down at the display showing the range between *Buttercup* and *Defiant*. For a moment, the decreasing numbers pulled her in. With a shake of the head, she re-focused and started working on a backup plan.

An hour later, the gate dominated their view. Its shimmering surface beckoned them—Hwicce was on the other side, and he needed their help. Veena had to admit to herself that she needed him too. As she studied the displays, she did a quick calculation.

"We'll have to pass just under a hundred metres from the *Defiant*."

"Damn." Orin looked at her with wide eyes. "That's really close. The tar won't be enough to hide us at that range."

Veena scratched her head. "At our max speed, it'll take us about ten minutes from our closest approach to the *Defiant* to reach the gate."

"So they'll see us and be able to follow us through. Great." Orin didn't sound hopeful.

Running her hand over her ponytail, Veena let her mind churn. Being spotted was unavoidable, so they needed a trick up their sleeve. They'd be followed through the gate... unless Swa's people didn't think *Buttercup* made it.

"Do we have anything we can set to explode?"

Orin stared at her. "This is a survey ship, designed for looking at things, not blowing them up."

Veena raised an eyebrow.

He sighed. "The spare fuel core might work. Without it, we'd need to find somewhere to get fuel within the month."

"So getting to Smaragdos will be no problem."

"We can get there just fine."

"Can we just eject it and detonate it?" Veena stared at the looming battlecruiser. It was only a matter of time before they spotted *Buttercup*. The last thing she wanted was to end up back on board. Swa would make sure they didn't escape a second time.

"I'd need to set it to overload before ejecting." Orin unbuckled himself. "At that point, we'll have about thirty seconds before it goes."

"Okay." Veena swallowed. Her plan was risky—and Swa might not buy it—but it was all she had.

"You don't need to touch anything. The autopilot is on, and our current course will take us right through the gate." Orin stood.

Veena fixed her gaze on the battlecruiser. "I'll get them talking to us. Wait for my signal before ejecting the fuel cell."

"I best get to work then. It'll just take me a minute or so." He left her alone on the bridge.

Veena took a deep breath and slowly counted to sixty. She activated the comms. "This is Veena Oswiu, calling General Swa." She leaned back and waited.

An emotionless voice told her to stand by.

"This is going to work," she whispered before counting each breath she took.

Ten minutes later, the general's head appeared in the front windshield. "This is Swa. I demand you land on the *Defiant* immediately. A squadron of fighters is converging on your position as we speak."

Veena glanced down at the sensor display. None of the fighters were visible yet, meaning they wouldn't reach her for at least twenty minutes.

"We'll come in to land," she said. "I have new information on the alien code to share."

"You'd better have it translated. I will not ignore your recent foolish escape attempt—consider it a strike against you and Dr. Akton."

"I'll send you a taste of what we found." Veena transferred a single image from the portal cavern on the anchor world.

As Swa studied the image, she seemed to struggle to maintain her stern expression.

"You found more."

"Yes."

Swa cocked her head. "Is that why you ran off?"

"Yes," Veena lied.

"And there's more than just this one image?"

"Lots more."

Swa slowly nodded. "This will go a long way to redeeming you and your companion."

The *Defiant* loomed close now. Veena checked the sensors. They were one minute from their closest approach. The time was now.

She frowned at the display. "Stand by. I've just received an engine alert." She cut the external comms link and activated *Buttercup's* intercom. "Orin, do it now."

A clunk sounded from somewhere aft of her, and Veena was tempted to hold her breath. Instead, she crossed her fingers.

Thirty-seven seconds later, Orin returned to the bridge. "It's going to be bumpy." He bucked himself back in.

Veena opened her mouth to speak, but the fuel cell explosion cut her off. The ship shunted to the side, and gravity failed. Orin took over the controls and kept them on course for the gate.

"This better look like we exploded," she said as the flotsam of daily life on the ship began floating around.

"It should have caused them some damage too—at least to

their most sensitive sensors." Orin glanced at her. "So, it might have done the trick."

"We just need to buy some time before they come after us." She stared out the windshield. "Swa will probably figure out that the *Buttercup* didn't explode."

"So, the best we can hope for is a head start."

"Yeah. If we get really lucky, she might assume we've gone straight on to the Delta System."

The surface of the gate shimmered as they got closer.

"We're going through in 5... 4..."

Veena closed her eyes as Orin continued his count down. Hold on, Hwicce, I'm coming.

Chapter Seven

Hwicce stood staring at the spot he thought he'd seen Veena. She'd seemed so real. Oddly, she had Molly's favourite stuffy with her—except the stuffy seemed to move under its own power. No. that didn't make sense.

He scratched the back of his head. His imagination must have been playing tricks on him. There was no way she'd been real; the animated stuffy was proof. Maybe he'd hit his head harder than he'd thought when he'd fallen. A head injury-induced hallucination explained what he'd seen.

A dim light of an undetermined origin now shone—a new and exciting improvement. He could now make out some details of his surroundings. The cavern rose to twice his height, forming a rock-hewn room with the water that filled half the floor space. The liquid's surface was still and black; he couldn't see anything beneath.

He shivered and shifted his attention to the wall. A hexagon pattern covered the flat wall at the back of the cavern. Weird symbols filled each shape, and none of it made any sense.

"No, not symbols, just some sort of weird mineral formation."

The more he stared at the patterns, the more deliberate they seemed—like something Veena could decode and make sense of. He sighed and turned his back on them.

"Now, how in the hell am I going to get out of here?"

Something touched his leg.

Hwicce froze and reminded himself there were no native animals on Smaragdos. He held his breath and glanced down. Molly's stuffy sat at his feet. Moving… and glowing—it was the source of light. It rose on a tripod of tentacle-like limbs and reached out with another limb to tap his leg. With big, inky eyes, it stared up at him as though expecting something.

"Whoa!" Hwicce stepped back a pace without taking his eyes off of Molly's stuffy. "How can a hallucination produce light?" He ran his hands over his scalp on a hunt for a bump to confirm his head injury theory.

A flicker to his right drew his attention. A hologram of a man dressed in a dark formal suit formal with an emerald green cravat appeared. The man stood about a hand's width shorter than Hwicce, and his outfit combined with impeccable grooming suggested he was about to star in one of those historical vids about ancient Earth.

"Greetings," the man said. "I am Nigel 378, and my companion is Click." He pointed to the octopus-like animal at Hwicce's feet.

"Okay…." Hwicce let his voice trail off.

"We have come to help you find your way out of these caves."

Hwicce cocked his head, still unsure if he was hallucinating or not. "How can a hologram and my daughter's favourite comic character help me?"

Click let out a series of clicks and flashed green, then yellow. Nigel nodded.

"Click wants me to assure you they are real." Nigel's voice carried a prim and proper accent.

"What are they?" Hwicce bent down to study the animal. It

didn't seem dangerous, just unexpected. He reached out a hand towards Click, and Click extended a tentacle to make contact.

Ever since the generation ships arrived in this corner of the galaxy, rumours about aliens kept surfacing. But in the almost two-hundred and fifty years humans had been here, there had been no official proof of first contact, just ancient relics. Hwicce always assumed it was only a matter of time until aliens showed themselves—but appearing here in this cave was unsettling.

"They are part of the alien race who made the gate system. Their ancestors once lived in these caves."

"Huh." Hwicce stood. It couldn't be a coincidence the illustrated alien in his daughter's favourite comic matched the alien before him. He scratched the side of his head. "Maybe I'm hallucinating after all."

"I can assure you, sir, that you are not."

Hwicce turned to the hologram. "And how do you fit in?"

"I am a steward AI from the *Garden Princess*. Dr. Oswiu saved me when the ship went down."

"So Veena sent you?"

"Yes, she is on her way to this world with her ship as we speak."

Hwicce exhaled. Veena had seemed so real—maybe she actually was. Besides, what did it matter if he followed hallucinations? He didn't have any better ideas. "Okay then, let's get out of here."

Click flashed red before moving over to the walls. They climbed up and traced the hexagons with their tentacles. The lines glowed a pale green, and more symbols appeared in the spaces. Click jumped down and returned to the centre. They made a series of clicking sounds as they pointed at the symbols.

"Veena could make sense of this," Hwicce said as he slowly turned around.

"Yes." Nigel frowned. "Unfortunately, I do not have enough memory to save these images for her."

"Right, how are you here?" Hwicce turned to the shimmering image of a man.

"Veena downloaded my algorithms into that." Nigel pointed to the band around Click's neck. "So I could be mobile and able to translate."

Hwicce pursed his lips and nodded. It sounded like something Veena would do.

Click slapped a tentacle on the ground, drawing their attention. Nigel cocked his head, then glitched back to holding his head up straight.

"Click says you need to swim out, and you need to leave soon as water levels are rising."

Hwicce strode over to the water's edge and peered down. More glowing, symbol-filled hexagons extended beneath the surface. "How far do I need to go underwater?"

"Click thinks there will be more air in the next chamber."

"They *think*?" Hwicce turned to the toy-looking alien and raised an eyebrow.

Click flashed blue, then pink.

"They say that if you stay here, you'll drown." Nigel moved to stand next to Hwicce.

"Fine." Hwicce bent down and removed his boots. Tying the laces together, he wrapped them around his shoulders.

"Click will lead the way; you'll just need to swim after them." Nigel frowned. "My projection won't work underwater, so I'll see you on the other side." He winked out of existence.

Hwicce sighed and looked down at the little alien. "Well, Click, let's get going."

Click flashed cyan then slid into the water, glowing bright red.

"This is nuts," Hwicce said before jumping in.

Cold water engulfed him. Flavours of burnt tea combined with something metallic filled his mouth. Beneath the surface, a current caught Hwicce and Click, pulling them deeper and deeper. Kicking hard, Hwicce kept the glowing form of Click in view; the alien was pink now, their colour fading as they tried to navigate the current.

The flowing water shoved both of them up against another wall covered in hexagons. As Hwicce turned in the eddy there, he grabbed Click and shoved himself back into the main current.

As the water swept them further from the glowing hexagons and symbols, Hwicce's lungs began to burn. He needed to breathe. Kicking with all his might, he headed up, hoping he wasn't propelling himself into a rock lid.

Click wrapped their tentacles around his neck, holding their head against Hwicce's. The faint glow of the alien barely illuminated an arm's length in front of him.

Gritting his teeth, with his arms out like superman, Hwicce kicked again. His hands contacted rock—there was no surface to break through, no air to breathe.

This was it; he was about to suffocate with a probably hallucinated alien wrapped around his neck. His vision started to darken as he let the current pull him along.

Moments later, churning water pushed him up, and his head broke the surface. In a split second, he filled his lungs with fresh air, then the water pulled him down again. This time his feet contacted the bottom, and he pushed off back towards the surface.

The cavern was narrowing, and the water was speeding up. Every time he broke the surface, he tried to find something to grab on to, but there was nothing but water-worn rounded rock formations that his hands just slipped off.

The water pulled Hwicce and Click on without an end in sight. Although he was getting plenty of air, the water was draining the heat from his body. It was getting hard to think. Every time he tried to come up with a solution to his situation, his mind went blank.

The channel turned sharply, squeezing in diameter to the

point where he could keep his head out of the water. A growling roar of rushing water filled the cavern.

All the water dropped away, for a moment leaving him hanging mid-air. He filled his lungs, then gravity took hold, and he fell.

Chapter Eight

When the wind blew off the cloud cover, exposing an expanse of white sky above, Baker decided it was time to do something. Standing, she put her hands on her hips and surveyed their surroundings.

"I can't see shit," she said, turning to the other woman.

Emiko met Baker's gaze with her gorgeous obsidian eyes. "You're going to need to get a higher view."

"You mean climb up on a bloody mushroom?" Baker looked back at the field of mushrooms; their damp caps glistened in the morning light.

"Yep."

Baker exhaled with a forceful whoosh. "Hwicce used that bloody logic last night—and look what that got him." She swallowed, trying not to think about where his fall into the darkness might have taken him.

"Be smart." Emiko pointed to a mushroom away from the edge. A boulder stuck up out of the ground beside it.

Without a word, Baker approached Emiko's suggested mushroom. It was far enough back from the edge that even if it broke, Baker wouldn't tumble downhill. She climbed up onto the boulder. From there, it was just a step to get onto the mushroom top.

With the clear sky, she could see further than they'd been able to the day before. But as she gazed out, her heart sank.

The undulating terrain of oversized moss extended to the horizon in all directions, punctuated by occasional brightly coloured fungus structures rose like abstract art installations. No hint remained of where their escape pod had crashed the day before—it was like the foliage had swallowed it whole.

She turned towards the drop-off that had claimed Hwicce. Lush moss obscured any view of the slope. The only hint to where he had fallen was the stump of the mushroom stalk at the edge.

"Hwicce!" she shouted as loud as she could, then waited. No response came. She shouted two more times and got the same result.

"See anything useful?" Emiko asked from the ground.

"Hold on. I'm still looking." Baker did a second full turn, silently cursing the blanket of moss. Then she stopped—there was something. Squinting, she tried to make out what it was.

At first, she thought it was another fungal formation—but the shape was too regular. The structure had to be human-made. Her heart started beating faster. A tower extended above the moss about a kilometre away—it had to be the greenie village.

"Hey Em, come up. I spotted something."

Emiko scrambled up the boulder, and Baker extended a hand to her, pulling her over to the mushroom top.

"What should I see?" Emiko squinted as she gazed out.

"There." Baker pointed.

As the dawn provided more light, sunlight glinted off the metal structure.

"Well, shit. I'll bet that's the town."

"Bloody hell, we could've found it last night." Baker pursed her lips and returned her attention to where Hwicce had vanished. "We should go find Hwicce, then head to the village."

Emiko stared down at the moss-covered slope and bit her lip. "That direction looks steep, and we don't know what's under the moss. What if there're caves or sinkholes or a deep pit?" She turned and stared at Baker with her big eyes. "We could end up in the same predicament as he's in."

Baker scratched her head while studying the slope. "What are you suggesting?"

"We go to the town and ask for their help."

"Fucking hell." Baker frowned. "I can't just abandon Hwicce."

"We're not abandoning him." Emiko put a hand on Baker's forearm. "We're being smart and getting proper help."

Screeches of playing children greeted them as they made their way through the dense moss. Somewhere close, a gaggle of kids loudly engaged in some sort of chasing game. Baker gritted her teeth and continued forward; they had to be getting close to the hamlet.

A few metres past a mass of pale pink fungi reminiscent of an oversized termite mound, the moss forest ended. Beyond, lichen-covered ground extended fifty metres to a cluster of round homes—the greenie village. It had the kind of handmade feel that suggested a pre-industrial community, like the ones from Old Earth she'd been forced to study in grade school.

Emiko continued forward into the clearing.

Baker paused. "What if the greenies refuse to help us?"

"They won't," Emiko said, stopping a few paces ahead. "Come on, we're here."

"But—"

"We need their help." Emiko cut her off. "Dial-up your charm; we're going in."

Baker groaned but followed.

From all around them, children shouted a warning. Some of them raced towards the homes, while others stared from a distance. The kids were naked, the greenness of their skin blending into their environment. The ones they could see watched them with concern. No doubt more lurked out of sight.

Emiko turned and tilted her head to meet Baker's gaze. "Now what?"

"Step one—find the town elders." Baker continued towards the group of structures as she smiled and waved at the kids. "Hi there," she said, doing her best to appear non-threatening.

The bulbous homes had to be hollowed out mushrooms. Most rose two stories with small round windows randomly peppering the walls. Colourful flowers cascaded down from window boxes while neat flower gardens circled the homes.

A lingering scent of smoke suggested fires burned inside— but not to cook as the greenies photosynthesized to meet their energy needs. Maybe they still liked their coffee. At that thought, Baker pictured a big mug of the bitter liquid in her hand and craved both its caffeine and warmth. Her stomach rumbled when she realized they likely wouldn't have any breakfast to go with the coffee. The best she could hope for was more meal bars. She frowned.

As they passed the first house, a group of adults as naked as the kids approached them. Baker put on a smile and headed their way.

"Hello." She stopped a few paces away from the group of five, presumably all elders. Not one of them would come past her elbow—even Emiko seemed tall here.

"Greetings," the lead man said, continuing closer while the others held back. His silver hair and beard made an odd contrast to the green hue of his skin. He pursed his lips as his gaze passed over Baker, then Emiko. "Are you the crew of that ship that crashed?"

"Yes. We have a third companion who got lost."

The man snorted. "And you need our help to find him."

Baker glanced at Emiko, then back to the man. "Yes, we humbly ask for your help."

The man cocked his head and continued studying the two of them. Emiko hugged her arms around her chest and stepped slightly closer to Baker. Baker just stood still and accepted the man's inspection. Finally, he gave a curt nod.

"I am Han, elected leader of this village."

"Good morning, Han." Baker tried to sound as diplomatic as she could while wishing Hwicce was there to negotiate instead. Playing nice with strangers wasn't her strength. "I'm Baker, and this is Emiko. We didn't mean to disturb your peace. I can assure you our crash was an accident."

Han pursed his lips together. "Our scouts found your escape pod yesterday. You're lucky you landed where you did."

Emiko dropped her arms and took a step forward. "You found the pod yesterday? That must have been shortly after we crashed."

"Hmmm." Han's voice was deeper and richer than Baker would have expected from a man of his diminutive size. "We had hoped to find your party yesterday and get everyone to safety before the storm."

"Thank you." Baker wished they'd stayed with the ship instead of spending the day wandering and the night shivering. She swallowed. If they'd stayed put, Hwicce would be with them now.

"Now, come inside, and we will discuss your departure." Han gestured to a dome structure in the centre of the village. Clearly constructed of natural materials, it reminded Baker of the biodomes covering many of the human settlements. Constructed of thousands of triangles, this dome arched up several stories. The translucent covering on each triangle glowed warmly in the morning light.

Han led them through a rounded opening into the building. Both Baker and Emiko had to duck to make it through the door. Inside, raised beds filled with tomatoes, lettuce, peas, and other vegetables filled the gaps between three mushroom houses contained under the dome. At least there was some food, but Baker didn't dare ask the greenies to share.

"This way." Han led them into the first house. Inside, mismatched orange and blue cushions were scattered over a stone floor. He gestured for them to sit.

Baker settled herself onto the floor and leaned against the far wall, keeping a view out the door. Emiko sat close beside her. Han sank down onto a cushion across from them.

"Will you help us find our companion?" Baker stared Han in the eye. "He fell in the night, down a steep slope not far from here."

Han slowly nodded. "You spent the night under the clorot mushrooms on the hill?"

"If you mean mushrooms big enough to sit under, then yes." Baker took a deep breath and reminded herself to play the diplomat. Snide comments wouldn't help—and she should probably watch her language. It was clear these people didn't want her here, and angering them wouldn't help get Hwicce back. "Our companion climbed on top of one to look for the village lights."

"We don't emit any light at night," a younger woman said as she entered the room. She held a tray with three steaming mugs. She handed a mug to Han. Then she lowered the tray before Baker and Emiko, who each took a mug.

Baker sighed. Luck was finally turning her way—the mug contained coffee, no doubt an expensive import to a remote world like this.

"Moss." Han turned to the woman. "Please stay."

Moss nodded before setting down her tray and sitting beside Han.

"Your companion likely fell into the caves." Han maintained an expression as though he were talking about flowers as he took a sip of his coffee.

Moss' mouth formed an 'o', then she clamped a hand over it. "The cave network is vast, and most of it is flooded. With the rain last night..." She dropped her hand and bit her lip.

"True, this man's fate is in question," Han continued.

Baker did her best to not think about worst-case scenarios as she stared Han in the eye. "We need to start searching. Can you send someone with us as a guide? We need to find him."

"Moss can take you." Han put a hand on Moss' shoulder. "She has ventured the furthest into the caves. Once your search is complete, we will discuss how you plan on leaving Smaragdos."

"Thank you." Baker tried to sound positive.

Han gave his mug to Moss, then stood. "I will speak to the council and make arrangements." He left.

Baker turned to Moss. "When can we go?"

"First, finish your coffee." Moss put Han's mug down on her tray. "I need to prepare some supplies." She left too.

"We should have stayed with the pod," Emiko said as soon as they were alone.

"Hell yeah, we should've. At least the greenies seem willing to help us—even if they aren't happy about it." Baker sighed and took another sip. "In fact, they're being a lot friendlier than I expected."

"I wouldn't call them friendly exactly."

The sound of shouting children came from outside—the same excited calls they'd made when Baker and Emiko emerged from the forest.

Leaving the coffee mug on the floor, Baker leapt to her feet. "Maybe he found us." Without waiting for Emiko, she raced outside.

The children all pointed at the sky. Baker stopped and gazed up.

A black and yellow ship circled overhead. The round nose, high set engines, and belly sensor array suggested it was an old survey vessel—the kind that should have been decommissioned long ago. The ship swooped lower and extended its landing gear.

With a smooth motion, the ship landed in the centre of the open area, sending up a billow of debris.

Chapter Nine

As they passed through Smaragdos' atmosphere, Veena strained against her seatbelt to view the planet's surface beyond the windshield.

At their latitude, the deep green of the ground extended to the horizon in all directions like the fuzzy blanket she'd cherished as a child. But this blanket didn't soothe her one bit. Instead, the knot of worry in her chest kept tightening with every breath.

Her husband lay trapped in a cavern somewhere below the planet's surface. Even though Click and Nigel were now with him, she doubted the glitchy AI and octopus-like alien would be much help other than company.

She took a deep breath and exhaled slowly to a count of seven. Hwicce needed her. She needed to get on the ground and start searching.

"The ground looks so lush," Orin said from the pilot's seat. The bright sunlight highlighted the bald patch on the top of his head. "It's no wonder the first settlers here thought they could make a go of it."

"Hmmm." Even though she knew Orin was just trying to distract her, she wished he'd shut up. He'd been droning on with endless greenie facts since they'd passed through the gate several hours ago.

"I heard the first year the settlers were here, over three-quarters of them died of starvation, all that lush green and not a bit of it edible." He remained oblivious to Veena's desire for silence. "It's no wonder they resorted to genetic alterations."

"Yeah." Veena brought up the topographical maps out of *Buttercup's* database. Below the oversized moss forest, the cave networks extended out over most of this hemisphere. Where would they even start?

"Of course, that was before they imposed GenEn laws."

Veena ignored him and continued scanning the cave networks. She started counting the caverns—but there were too many. Fractal arms of cave networks extended out in all directions, and these were only the ones that had been mapped.

She let out an audible sigh as she leaned back and ran her hands over her ponytail. "I don't even know where to start looking."

"There's a settlement over there." Orin pointed to a spot near the horizon that was a paler shade of green. "Let's ask the locals for help."

They circled the village situated in an area mostly cleared of the oversized moss on the edge of a cliff with a river at its base. A dozen quaint mushroom-like homes formed an arc between the cliff and forest. In the centre sat three larger domed structures of an unknown purpose. Since *Buttercup's* sensor array remained coated in the tar-like substance they'd picked up on the anchor world, they wouldn't know more until they landed.

"Looks like they have a landing pad." Orin angled *Buttercup* towards an open area beside the largest dome. As he extended the landing gear, a loud thunk reverberated through the small survey ship.

"What was that?" Veena twisted to look back into the ship. Debris from their recent gravity loss littered the floor, but that wouldn't have caused the noise.

"Sounds like I need to do some maintenance."

Veena turned to Orin. Even though he sounded calm, a glistening sheen of perspiration coated his head. She bit her lip and focused on the world outside. The ground came up fast, then Orin flared the thrusters. Debris from the field billowed all around them as they touched down.

A red light flashed on the dashboard. After he'd powered down the engines, Orin turned his attention to it. "Hmph."

"What?"

"We have an electrical problem." Orin wiped his hand over his head. "Maybe the goo we picked up is causing us some problems. Who knows, maybe it's conductive or corrosive...."

"The goo is why we made it this far." Veena unbuckled and leaned forward. A group of naked greenies approached the ship, but not in a threatening way. "The welcoming committee is here."

A tall woman in the back drew Veena's attention. The woman was defiantly not a greenie—both the black hue of her skin and Amazonian height disqualified her. Her closely cropped hair suggested military, yet she wasn't in uniform. She moved with the physicality of a predator. The woman seemed vaguely familiar, but Veena couldn't place her.

Veena stood and headed aft. Three steps on, it hit her. She'd seen the woman's image in a group photo Hwicce had sent her a few months ago—the woman had to be the soldier that Hwicce had run off with. Baker was her name—presumably her last name since Hwicce had never mentioned her first.

She put a hand on the kitchen counter and took a deep breath. Once she found him, Hwicce had a lot of explaining to do. Even though General Swa had implied an illicit arrangement with the subordinate Hwicce had disappeared with, Veena still refused to believe he would ever abandon her. But she didn't look forward to facing that woman now.

Closing her eyes, she pictured Hwicce's last visit to their home on New Haven. How he and Molly ran around the yard with that orange kite until Molly was so exhausted, she fell asleep on their picnic blanket. Later, Hwicce carried his little girl into the house and put her to bed, then returned with a bottle of wine.

Veena shook her head. Hwicce would explain himself, and his answer would satisfy her. She took another deep breath to calm herself, counting on the exhale as always.

Pulling herself up tall, she strode to the airlock. She opened the outside door and extended the steps. After pausing for one more deep breath, she stepped outside to greet the crowd and face Hwicce's subordinate.

The crowd stayed a few metres back from *Buttercup*, just staring at her—not quite hostile, but certainly not friendly. In the bright morning light, the green shades of their skin ranged from dull lichen to the rich hues of grass and new leaves. The colours were actually quite pretty and fit their environment.

After an awkward moment, a lone elder approached.

"Welcome to Smaragdos." His voice reverberated at a lower tone than she would've expected from such a small man. "Why have you come?"

"We're here on a rescue mission. My husband is trapped in a cave nearby."

Baker wove her way through the crowd with her jaw set as though she expected a fight. She stopped next to the elder and met Veena's gaze.

"You're Hwicce's wife?" Her question sounded like a demand.

"Yes." Veena forced herself to stare into Baker's dark eyes for a count of ten. "I'm here to rescue him."

Baker gave a curt nod, then walked away.

The elder watched Baker go, then turned back to Veena. "It seems this man warrants quite the rescue party."

"Will you help us find him?" she asked.

"My name is Han. Come with me. A rescue attempt has already been negotiated."

A few minutes later, Veena and Orin sat side-by-side in a mushroom room under the dome. The other two non-greenie women sat across from them. Han sat to the side, his face relaxed as he studied each of the outsiders.

As she sipped her coffee, Veena did her best not to scowl at Baker; instead, she studied Hwicce's army companion. Baker sat cross-legged with her back military-straight. The planes of her face were angular, with sharp cheekbones and a straight nose. Her dark skin was perfect, with her only flaw being the scarring on her right hand. Veena had to admit Baker was a stunning woman.

"So you're Hwicce's wife?" the petite woman sitting beside Baker asked.

Veena racked her brain to dredge up the other woman's name. Then it came to her: Emiko. "Yes. We've been married for ten years." Veena shifted her gaze back to Baker, who maintained her chiseled stone expression.

"He told us about your little girl, Mary," Emiko said.

"Molly." Veena pursed her lips. "Her name is Molly."

Emiko shifted on her orange cushion. "Hwicce couldn't stop talking about her; he's beside himself with worry."

Veena turned to Han. "We need to get out there and go find him."

"Agreed." Baker's voice held a rich, husky tone Veena couldn't help but be jealous of.

"You all need to culture patience." Han took his time to sip his coffee. "We will help you hunt for your missing companion.

However, we aren't used to this many visitors, especially ones demanding things from us."

Veena said nothing as heat crept into her cheeks. She was so close—Hwicce was stuck in a nearby cave. Taking a deep breath, she reminded herself to be patient. She needed these people's help to find him.

"My ship requires repairs," Orin said. "While the others go on the rescue, I'll stay here and get to work on that. Hopefully, we can be ready to leave when everyone returns from the caves. I don't want to impose on your kindness any longer than necessary." He nodded to Han. "I'm happy to take everyone with me when I go."

"I can help," Emiko said, looking at Orin. "I have enough engineering skill to be useful."

While Emiko and Orin began a discussion of ship repairs, Veena continued staring at Baker. Her mind wouldn't stop racing about why Baker would leave the army with Hwicce. She began counting each breath she took.

Veena just worked up the nerve to ask Baker when a greenie woman wearing a moss-toned jumpsuit walked into the room. Han smiled at her.

"I'm ready to take the visitors to the caves." The woman spoke as though Veena and the others weren't right in front of her. "We'll use the cliff entrance."

Han nodded. "Thank you, Moss. The others have already been informed."

"Well, I'm ready." Baker nodded and pushed herself up to her feet.

Emiko tipped her chin up and gazed at Baker. "Hey, dumbass, don't slip into any holes."

Baker grinned. "Fucking hell I won't."

Veena stood and faced Moss. "Are the caves close?"

"The cliff entrance is not far. The caves themselves extend out for kilometres beneath us." Moss turned and walked out of the room. "Follow me."

She stopped at a table outside to pick up three water canteens with shoulder straps. "The water in the caves is saturated with tannins," she said as she passed them out. She then distributed headlamps, barely waiting until the other two women had put them on their heads before continuing on.

Without a word, Veena and Baker followed. One hundred and three steps from the dome, the three of them reached the edge of the village. Twenty-five metres ahead, the lichen-covered rock just ended. Veena swallowed as she continued towards the precipice edge. When Moss had said 'cliff entrance,' it turned out she meant that literally.

"Hwicce needs you," Veena said under her breath as she forced herself to keep putting one foot in front of the other. The precipice was only metres away now; beyond it, only air.

Moss continued right up to the edge with Baker on her tail. The threshold between rock and empty air made Veena's breath catch in her throat, but she forced herself to keep up with the others.

A stunning and terrifying vista extended before her. Farther down than she expected, a great river flowed. Its tea-hued water blended into the forest on the visible bank. Wisps of mist further obscured the view and added to the sensation of great height. A wave of nausea swept over her, and her footing felt unsteady. One wrong step and she could fall to her death—who would find Hwicce and Molly then? Her heart hammered.

At the cusp, Moss stopped and sat on the bare rock. She rolled onto her stomach and pushed herself over the edge, vanishing from sight.

"Holy shit." Veena couldn't look away from the spot where Moss had vanished.

"You're next," Baker spoke in a calm tone. She took a step closer to the edge and looked over. "There's a ledge. It's not far down." She turned and stared at Veena, scrutinizing her.

"Right." Veena closed her eyes and counted to ten, then vowed not to show Baker any weakness. When she opened them again, she fixed her gaze on the spot where Moss had disappeared over the cliff. Veena's feet felt encased in lead as she shuffled closer.

"Lay down on your stomach with your feet pointing to the edge and push yourself over," Baker said, as though that was an easy thing to do.

Ignoring the tremor in her hands, Veena lay on the rough rock and did as she was told. Little pieces of lichen came off on her hands and clothing as she let her feet dangle over the edge. Inching slowly back, she kept herself tight against the rock face.

Once her hips crossed the edge, she slid and almost let out a scream. Then her feet contacted solid ground again. Pressing every square centimetre of herself against the rock, she slowly looked around.

The ledge was less than half a metre wide—a single wrong step would send her tumbling. What was she thinking? Why weren't they using safety lines? If she fell here, Molly would never see her mom again. She swallowed and let her eyes follow the ledge. It sloped gently down until it passed under an overhanging formation of rock. With a frown on her face, Moss stood not far off, waiting.

"You need to move," Baker called down from above. "So I can climb down."

Veena nodded, knowing Baker wouldn't see the gesture from above. Staying as close to the wall as she could, she took a step forward, then another. A few metres on, a loud thump came from behind her. She spun around to look and nearly lost her footing. As she shuffled to regain her footing, a cascade of tiny rocks tumbled over the edge, bouncing down the rock face.

"Easy there," Baker said from right behind her. It had been her who'd made the sound when she jumped down. Baker put a hand on Veena's back and pushed her into the wall. "Hwicce would never forgive me if I let you fall."

"Right." Veena turned her back to Baker, vowing not to give

the woman any more reason to treat her like an inept child. She gritted her teeth and continued towards Moss.

The ledge widened out the further they went. Once it passed under the overhang, a cavern opened up to the side. Moss turned on her headlamp and went inside. Feeling more comfortable moving away from the precipice and its promise of falling doom, Veena followed.

"This antechamber leads into a series of other caves," Moss said as she kept walking. "Running water carved out a substantial network."

"Where would the closest caverns to where we camped last night be?" Baker asked as she strode past Veena.

Fighting to keep her composure, Veena swept her light over the walls. Tiny crystals embedded into the rock reflected the light back to her. The surrounding air alternated between blowing into the caves and out as though she stood at the threshold of a great set of lungs.

"We can start in the hex caves," Moss said.

"Hex? Like some goddamn witchcraft?" Baker's stoic features took on an expression of concern.

"Nah, just some weird geological formation that created massive hexagonal rocks."

Veena turned to Moss, thinking of the hexagons on the anchor world—the ones created by aliens like Click. They'd activated something there that opened a portal to Hwicce that Click and Nigel had passed through to help him. Moss was taking them in the right direction, yet Veena still had questions.

"But this isn't this system's anchor world." Veena ran a hand down her ponytail.

"No, the anchor world here is the next planet out from our suns." Moss turned and followed the cavern as it sloped down.

"What does being an anchor world have to do with anything?" Baker asked.

"It just...." Veena glanced at the retreating cone of light from Moss's headlamp. "I'll explain later." She turned and strode after their guide while debating how much she should tell Baker.

Baker didn't inquire again, just followed a pace behind.

———

It felt like they'd been walking deeper into the cave network for hours, yet the air didn't smell stale. Instead, occasional whiffs of rotting foliage and wet soil blew through. Each cavern flowed into the next with smoothly curved walls—the kind only water could excavate. The glittering crystals added a festive air while drips of tea-coloured water cascaded down from lower points in the ceiling.

As they crossed into a junction of caverns, a hint of tar wafted through the air—a scent just like the anchor world with the alien caverns.

"Are we close?" Moving her whole body, Veena swung her cone of light around. Above, stalactites reached down like tentacles reaching for their partner stalagmites. But the stalagmites weren't there, suggesting this cavern experienced regular gushing water flows.

Moss gestured to a cavern that looked the same as the rest. "Just a bit further down here."

"Why didn't Hwicce call me?" Veena asked, falling into step beside Baker as they followed Moss.

Baker didn't answer. Instead, she stretched out her pace and caught up with Moss. Veena frowned. Baker was gruff and rude. With a sigh, Veena followed the other two.

The cavern narrowed, and the sound of rushing water echoed along the walls. Standing water now covered the floor as though recently water levels had been higher.

"Hey, I see something." Baker rushed forward and picked up an object from the ground. She held it up to the light. It was a ripped piece of brown cloth. "This is the colour of the pants Hwicce was wearing."

Veena's heart sank. It was a hand-sized chunk of fabric—meaning he'd suffered some kind of impact that ripped it free.

"Hwicce!" she shouted, and the sound of her voice echoed. "Where are you?"

No response came.

Chapter Ten

"So you're an engineer?" Orin asked Emiko as they stood staring at *Buttercup*.

"Not exactly." She tipped her head back to study the sky. "Looks like it's going to rain."

Orin stared up at the sky. Thick, green-tinged clouds had rolled in, blanketing the sky. The change in weather had been quick. Working on the ship would suck in the rain. He sighed. "Maybe the greenies will let us move *Buttercup* into one of their shelters."

A large set of double doors on the nearest dome faced them, suggesting it could be a hanger of some sort. Han stood with a crowd of other greenies a short way off, watching, so Orin went over to him.

"Can we move my ship into there?" Orin pointed to the dome with the big doors. "I'll be able to fix it faster if I don't have to work in the rain."

Han gazed at the sky. "Rain is a given."

Orin nodded, uncertain if Han's answer was a yes or no. As he opened his mouth to ask again, two youths sprinted towards the dome. A moment later, the doors slid open. He made eye contact with Han. "Thank you."

"Be quick with your work," Han said. "Our code says we must welcome you, but your presence may cause unexpected effects."

"Of course." Orin turned and headed towards *Buttercup*, and Emiko followed in his wake. He hoped the young woman had decent mechanical skills as he wanted off this world as soon as possible. Even though Han seemed friendly enough, it was clear they weren't welcome.

Emiko went inside as Orin pulled up the stairs. Just as he closed the outside door, he noticed Han and his group of villagers deep in a discussion. Several of them pointed at *Buttercup* and scowled.

"The sooner we're out of here, the better," he said.

"Are the locals turning savage?" Emiko stood just inside the airlock doors. "I've heard stories."

"I'm sure they're an urban myth." He headed up to the cockpit, hoping that was true. He shifted his focus to the tar-like liquid he and Veena had tracked in from the anchor world—their black footprints marred the flooring.

"Did you hear about the greenie colony on Prathas-5?" Emiko stayed with him as they entered the cockpit.

"Only a rumour." He sat and powered up the ship.

"By the way, where'd you score this antique?" She slid into the co-pilot's seat.

Orin went through his pre-flight checklist, ignoring the warning lights. "A friend," he said as he lifted *Buttercup* about a metre off of the ground and slowly approached the hangar.

"Your friend must be a gifted mechanic to have restored this beast." A touch of awe laced Emiko's words.

"She's a genius."

The ship fit through the door with plenty of room to spare. Inside was a single open space with a perfectly level floor cleared of the lichen that coated the rocks outside. No clues betrayed the dome's purpose—but it would work just fine as a hangar. He set the ship down and turned off the engines.

Orin turned to Emiko. "Does your experience include diagnosing electrical faults?"

"That I can do."

Orin and Emiko spent the morning working through the various faults in the ship's electronics. Once *Buttercup* reported green on the diagnostics, they cleaned the now-hardened tar-like goo off all the external sensors. The damage hadn't been nearly as bad as Orin expected.

Pleased with his morning work, he walked to the open hangar doors to watch the rain fall outside. The hum of the relentless but light precipitation soothed him, and his mind wandered to his late wife. Mary would be proud of his newfound sense of purpose. Instead of drinking away his days, like he had since her death in the bombing of New Haven, he was part of a team with a goal to rescue a little girl—a noble cause. Once Veena found Hwicce, they'd be on their way. He felt confident Molly would be back with her parents in no time.

He inhaled the moist air, relishing its earthy scent.

"A ship, a ship," a young boy shouted as he ran through the town, splashing through puddles as if on purpose. The dark mud splatter was the only covering on his vivid green skin. At his warning, villagers began shutting up their buildings and ushering their children inside.

With his brows pulled together, Orin looked up at the sky. A black speck just beneath the cloud cover approached. As it got close, he recognized the shape of a military shuttle. The timing couldn't be a coincidence—General Swa must have sent it. Their ruse hadn't fooled the general.

"Emiko, get the other door." Orin began pulling the door beside him closed. "Swa's soldiers are here."

"Oh, shit." Emiko sprinted for the other door. They got them closed just as the shuttle came into land.

Orin turned and looked back at *Buttercup*. Swa's people would search this dome, and his ship was distinctive. He ran a hand over his head as he tried to come up with a plan.

"The elder asks if your ship will run," asked the young male greenie, who was scowling at him from a smaller door.

"Yes, but...." Orin pointed to the shuttle landing outside.

"We recognize the Protectorate ship," he said. "They have searched us before. They do not respect our ways or our autonomy."

"Please help me hide our ship." Orin wracked his brain to come up with a good reason for the greenies to help them instead of just handing them over to Swa's people. He couldn't come up with anything. His heart sank as he realized capture was inevitable.

The man nodded. "So they are after you."

"Most likely, yes."

"As you are our guest, our code dictates we must help." The man pursed his lips together as though the idea of offering help was distasteful. He turned and went towards a part of the wall that looked like every other space. Bending down, he lifted a panel of lichen and exposed a control box with a level of sophistication Orin had not yet seen in the village.

Orin followed. "What do you propose we do?"

"You need to get into your ship and lift off." He turned and stared at Orin. "I'll open the doors."

Orin turned back to the main doors of the hangar and pointed. "*Buttercup* can't outrun a military shuttle."

"In the cavern, you won't be detected."

Orin glanced down at his feet, then around at the space under the dome. "This is a secret entrance to a cavern?" It had seemed odd that they had left such a large space completely empty. But the fact they were standing on massive doors seemed impossible—how could the greenies have constructed such a thing?

"The Protectorate forces have never found the cavern. But they'll find you here if you wait too long."

"Mysterious cavern it is." Orin turned and jogged back to the ship. They'd said the cave network beneath the village was extensive—maybe they had a hideout down below. Emiko followed him inside and took her place in the co-pilot's seat.

"We've been working on doors all this time?" She bucked in.

"Seems so, my dear."

Using the least amount of thrust he could get away with, he hovered *Buttercup* a metre or so off the ground and kept his eye on the greenie man at the controls. He pressed a button, and the entire floor sunk down about two meters. Then it separated into two halves and retracted out of the way, leaving a dark hole extending into inky blackness.

"Activate the survey sensors and take a sweep of what's below us," Orin said as he slowly descended.

"Looks like the bottom is about one hundred metres down." Emiko turned and looked at him. "And we'll fit no problem."

"Great." Orin turned on the ship's lights, highlighting the shaft through the rock. It was too regular to be natural, but he didn't have time to worry about that now. He continued their descent. Twenty metres down, the cavern opened up, and their lights no longer touched the walls.

Emiko let out a low whistle. "Holy shit, this place is enormous. The radar says we're in a rift extending more than a kilometre."

Orin couldn't help but think of the rift they'd entered back on the anchor world. If the alien portal came here, did that mean this was all an ancient alien construct? For a moment, he wished Click was still with them so he could ask.

Far above, the doors closed, sealing out the outside light. As they approached the ground, their lights highlighted several other shuttles. Most were older models, but all of them appeared to be in good order.

"I guess they're not as primitive as we thought," Emiko said.

"Hmmm." He'd never figured the greenies were primitive; it turned out he was right. He set the ship down and powered it off. "Let's go see what this place offers."

A different greenie greeted them as soon as they left the ship —the only difference was this one wore clothes, a pale green jumpsuit. She held a lantern on a stick, creating a cone of light. Now that *Buttercup* was powered down, her light was the only beacon in the cavern's darkness.

"They won't find you here." She didn't offer her name.

"Thank you." Orin bowed his head to her. "We will leave as soon as we can."

"Our hospitality can only go so far."

While Orin tried to figure out if she'd just threatened them or not, she turned and started walking away. Emiko raced after her. With a sigh, Orin followed.

The greenie woman led them into a side cavern, then opened a large metal door. A dim light glowed from within. As soon as they went through, the greenie closed the door behind them.

"Our elders demand you swear to keep our secrets when you leave." Her tone was solemn.

"We swear," Orin said, wondering what would happen to them if they didn't. The greenies had maintained their freedom despite being in the Protectorate's territory—a difficult feat.

"I'm authorized to take you into the city, where you can wait until the Protectorate scum leaves." She turned and continued along the corridor. "Our security chief wants to see you."

They passed several side rooms and narrow passageways, disappearing into the darkness. All the while, the ambient lighting became brighter and brighter. Around a corner, the corridor opened out into a larger, well-lit space.

"Wow." Emiko tilted her head back and gazed up.

"Another rift?" Orin glanced around.

The space was about fifty metres tall by about twenty metres wide. The entire ceiling emitted light, making it as bright as the surface, even though they were still clearly underground. They stood in what appeared to be a market complete with small stalls and milling people—hundreds of people all wearing pale-hued jumpsuits. The only thing missing was the scent of cooking. A few shops opened into the rock face, and above, a series of balconies suggested apartments lined the second level.

Their guide continued through the crowd, still holding her lantern. The egg-shaped light was the only way Orin managed to follow her. As they moved through the crowd, most of the greenies just stared at them. A few backed away while others turned to their companions and whispered. Orin swallowed. The awkwardness in the air could swiftly turn against them. He hoped they wouldn't have to stay long.

Past the market, she turned into a corridor leading off the main rift. Just inside, it opened into a rounded room bisected with a waist-high counter. Behind the counter were three greenies in jumpsuits. The heaviest one stood when they entered.

"I've brought them," their guide said before turning and leaving.

"You're the outsiders," the standing greenie said, more as a statement than a question. "I'm chief Pan." Grey streaks ran through her short-cropped hair.

"Thank you for your help," Orin said. Beside him, Emiko remained silent, her eyes wide as she looked around.

"Come. We'll watch the surface cameras." Pan gestured for them to come through a gap in the counter, then into a smaller room.

Camera feeds were projected across the polished walls in the smaller room. Each one showed the village above at a different angle.

"Huh, there's no sneaking up on you," Emiko said.

"No." Pan settled down on the padded bench in the middle of the room. She gestured for the others to sit as well. "We've been forced to take steps to protect ourselves."

"Seems wise." Orin had seen the military reports of greenie settlements being wiped out for dubious reasons. The Protectorate had never been a fan of their kind.

Walking slowly around the room, he studied each image. The Protectorate shuttle sat on the landing pad, its raptor-like shape of sharp lines out of place amongst the organic lines of the structures.

"They're searching the main dome." Emiko pointed to another image depicting the inside of the dome they'd first visited.

"Another group is searching the houses." Pan gestured to where a family huddled outside their home. The parents clutched their two young children tight as they moved further away. A moment later, two soldiers emerged.

"I'm sorry." Orin watched groups of soldiers go from house to house. He sunk down onto the bench next to Pan. "We didn't mean to bring them here."

"They come a few times a year." Pan shrugged. "You just provided them a reason."

"What do they expect to find?" Emiko asked, sitting on the other side of Orin.

"We're the only engineered groups that originate from within the Protectorate. Even though we've followed the GenEn protocols since they were adopted, we still pass down the results of genetic tinkering with each generation."

Orin nodded. "They suspect you're still tampering with your genes."

"And so what if you are?" Emiko crossed her arms over her chest.

"There's been reports of genetically altered super-soldiers." Orin had read the reports back on the Rock. "The Nader Alliance uses them, but no one knows where they are being made. Now the Protectorate wants help to make their own."

Pan snorted. "Well, they won't find that here."

For over an hour, they watched as the Protectorate soldiers went through every home and building on the surface. Finally, the soldiers all piled back into their shuttle. It took off and quickly rose out of the camera view.

Pan checked a handheld computer, then nodded. "They've left orbit."

"Any word from Veena and Baker?" Orin asked.

"No." Pan swiped her screen, and all the camera views changed to infrared displays of various caverns. "I don't see them."

Orin stood. One image caught his attention, and he wasn't sure why. He cocked his head as he studied it. "Is that camera underwater?"

Pan jumped to her feet beside him. She grunted, then checked her handheld. "Looks like water levels are rising. They might have to call off their search."

"Oh crap," Emiko said. "B's going to hate that."

Chapter Eleven

Veena followed Baker and Moss deeper into the cave. The sound of falling water grew with each step she took until it became a roar threatening to drown out her thoughts. She cast her light around, hoping for another sign of Hwicce while holding the scrap of fabric tight to her chest. The others remained silent, which let Veena stew.

They entered another massive cavern where Moss set off a flare. The spot of red light arced upwards until it exposed a waterfall at least three stories high. The water cascaded down into a large basin before flowing into a wider river. Well-rounded gravel made up the riverbank on their side.

"Hey, I found something," Baker shouted, crouched at the water's edge.

Veena ran to look just as Baker stood. The other woman held up a pair of boots with their laces tied together.

"They're Protectorate army issue." Baker shone her light down on her own boots. "The same as mine."

Veena's gut twisted. "They have to be Hwicce's."

"But he took them off on purpose." Baker pointed to the

knot tying them together. Her expression was less optimistic than her words.

"Right." Veena swallowed; the spray in the air tasted foul and left her mouth dryer than before.

She surveyed the bank of the underground river while Baker stared at her as though expecting an order. Veena took a deep breath, then slowly exhaled. They would find Hwicce soon—he had to be close.

"I'll go downstream. You look near the waterfall."

Baker gave a curt nod and walked away, still carrying Hwicce's boots.

"We can't stay here long," Moss said as she came in close. "The water's rising. We could get trapped."

Veena nodded. "Just a few more minutes. He has to be close." Not waiting for Moss' answer, she headed downstream at a jog.

She continued as fast as she could in the shifting light. The flare created blood-red shadows while the large space swallowed the feeble white light on her head.

"Hwicce," she shouted, knowing the falling water would overpower her words but unwilling to remain silent. "Hwicce!"

She stopped when the gravel beach gave way to a field of stalagmites. The maze created a million places that could hide him, and the rising water now lapped at her ankles. Her breath caught in her chest as she admitted Moss was right. It was time to turn back—Molly needed a parent to find her.

Veena turned her back on the field of stalagmites and focused on the cavern they'd entered through.

"Excuse me, madam."

Veena spun as her jaw dropped. Nigel stood a few paces away, looking like the day she'd first met him on the *Garden Princess*, his tweed suit and poofy cravat as perfect as before. She rushed forward to hug him and passed right through.

"Um, I must remind you I'm only a projection." Nigel

winced and rubbed the back of his neck. Veena swore she watched his ears go red.

"Did you find Hwicce? Where's Click?"

Making a series of high-pitched clicks, Click skittered out between the nearest rock formation and grabbed onto her calf with all of their tentacles. Veena interpreted the gesture as a hug.

"This way." Nigel gestured into the field of person-sized stalagmites. "We've been here for some time. Your gentleman awaits."

With Click still attached to her leg, Veena followed Nigel deeper into the rock formation. Ten meters in, a sandy alcove rose barely a hand's width up out of the water. Within, Hwicce lay on his side with his feet still in the water.

Veena clapped her hands to her mouth as he slowly pushed himself up to his knees. She rushed forward and wrapped her arms around him. "My bear." He felt so solid, as he always did. "I was so worried…."

Putting a hand on the back of her head, he squeezed her in tight. "You're really here." He buried his face in her hair. "And you found me. Like I knew you would."

Even though water still dripped off him, Hwicce's warmth radiated into her. Veena swallowed back tears. He was here, and he was okay. Together, they would get Molly back. She squeezed him tighter.

"I missed you," she whispered into his ear.

Hwicce released her and pulled back enough to gaze her in the eyes. "I love you."

Veena squeezed him in again until her cheek rested against the bristles of his beard. "I love you too."

"Umm." Nigel walked close to them. "I don't mean to interrupt, but..."

"You're going to need to explain these two." Hwicce released her and pointed to Nigel and Click.

"Dr. Osiwu, it would be wise to evacuate these caves." As

Nigel wrung his hands together, his fingers glitched and passed through each other. "However, I'm afraid I do not know the best path to the exit."

Veena shivered, already missing Hwicce's warmth as she backed up a pace and looked him up and down. "Are you injured?"

"I'm somewhat surprised I didn't die going over the water-fall. But I'm sure as hell going to walk out of here." He stood up taller. "I just hope you know the way out."

Veena smiled as she noticed his left big toe stuck out through a hole in his sock. "I even know where your boots are."

In a flash of red, the flare flickered out, leaving Click's pale pink glow and Veena's light as their only illumination. The little alien now perched on her shoulder as she made her way around the massive fingers of rock. The water was coming up fast now —the ripples that had only licked at her ankles before now reached her knees.

When they reached where the gravel beach had been moments before, Veena realized it was now submerged. Slog-ging through the water, she led Hwicce to the narrow rock ledge running along the wall.

From near the waterfall, Moss fired off another flair, re-illu-minating the cavern in sinister glowing red.

"Holy crap." Hwicce stopped, and he put a hand on Veena's shoulder. "That waterfall has to be thirty metres high. I can't believe I'm walking away from going over that."

Veena smiled. A layer of tension within her released. Taking Hwicce's hand and not letting go, she led him to the others waiting by the mouth of the cavern that would lead them out of there.

"You're turning into a kit bomb, sir." Baker grinned as she held out Hwicce's boots. "Plus, you made me walk for hours just to find your sorry ass."

Hwicce sat on a ledge to put on his boots. "Well, I appre-ciate your efforts."

Baker gasped as Click leapt off Veena's shoulder and onto the wall. She shuffled backwards until her back was up against the wall. "What the fuck is that?"

Moss frowned as she stared at the alien, putting as much space between herself and Click while continuing ahead. She didn't say anything.

Click flashed yellow.

"That's Click. They're an alien I found on the *Garden Princess*." Veena forced herself not to show any amusement at the other women's responses.

"An alien?" Baker stayed put, eyes fixed on Click as though they presented a threat. "But there aren't any aliens." She shifted her gaze to Hwicce. "Right, sir?"

Hwicce smiled. "There's at least one. As for why they look exactly like my daughter's favourite comic book character...." He raised an eyebrow.

Veena shrugged. That remained a mystery to her, too.

Moss put her hands on her hips. "We need to get out of here." Without waiting, she turned and headed back into the cave they'd followed to get here.

Veena glanced to the water's edge. The water would soon flood their escape route. Even though the air was humid, her mouth went dry. As soon as Hwicce tied up his boots, he took her hand and let her lead him away. Only after their path had wound around several bends did it become quiet enough to hold a proper conversation.

"How did Click end up on a cruise ship?" Hwicce gestured to where the alien slithered along the wall, flashing with alternating stripes of green and yellow. "They look just like Molly's comics."

"The man who took Molly also took Click." Veena frowned, her positive mood crushed. She sighed. "I couldn't stop him from taking Mol."

Hwicce pulled her close and cupped her chin in his hands. He stared into her eyes. "I should never have left the two of you alone. I see that now. With Mol's… talents, she needed both of our protection."

"Come on," Moss said from a few paces ahead. "If we delay, we may not be able to get back to the cliff entrance."

Veena squeezed Hwicce's hands. "We'll have time to talk above."

Moss led them back through the maze of caverns, taking so many turns, Veena suspected they were lost. Keeping her grip on Hwicce, she said nothing as the familiar sound of rushing water came from up ahead.

"Fucking hell! We've gone in a bloody circle," Baker said loud enough for all to hear.

"No… no… no." Moss rushed ahead and fired a flare.

The red light highlighted a dip in the passageway ahead. Light reflected off a watery surface which blocked the path out. As the flare descended into the inky liquid, it cast crimson highlights across the faces of everyone present—except Nigel, whose hologram maintained its usual colouring.

"Dirt and rock," cursed Moss. "That was the exit."

"I'm not up for another swim." Hwicce licked his lips and stared at the water.

From their perch on the wall, Click let out a series of clicks that reminded Veena of fingernails raking down a chalkboard. A shiver ran up her spine.

"Click says they don't want to swim out either," translated Nigel.

"There's another way." Moss charged past, back the way they'd come. "But the elders will not like this."

Hwicce raised his eyebrow, and both Veena and Baker shrugged. They followed their guide as she backtracked down the tunnel. Click kept pace on the wall, now glowing pink.

Hwicce scratched his head. "How does she even know where to go?"

Baker snorted. "Hell if I know. Glad to have you back, sir."

"Did you leave Emiko surface side?" he asked.

"She's helping Orin fix the ship," Veena said.

"Your boss is here?"

"Yep, and somehow he got an old survey ship."

Moss stopped at a junction and turned to face them. Her face took on a serious expression. "I need you to turn that off." She pointed at Nigel.

"What? Me?" Nigel flinched, and his eyes went wide.

"I'm going to take you somewhere we don't let outsiders see." She swallowed. "I don't want any recordings."

"But I don't have the memory—"

Click flashed red, and Nigel vanished.

"If there was another path... but the water's rising too fast." Moss bit her lip. "I have no choice, even though the elders may exile me." She turned and headed down the other tunnel.

The tunnel rose at a steady pace, becoming dryer as they went. A faint whiff of lavender and rose filled the tunnel—unexpected on a world that couldn't grow the plants of Old Earth.

"Where are you taking us?" Veena asked, stepping faster to catch up with Moss.

"Into the city," she said.

They turned a corner, and a set of metal doors blocked their way. A biometric scanner sat off to the side. Moss put her thumb on it, and the doors slid open. Bright light filled the tunnel. Veena raised her hand to shield her eyes as Click climbed up her leg and grabbed onto her shoulder, sitting like a parrot on a pirate.

Veena took a step forward and into a different world—as modern as any place she'd lived.

Chapter Twelve

As they climbed the stairs to a second story, Veena still couldn't believe that a secret greenie city existed. Contrary to how they were portrayed on the vids, the greenies lived sophisticated lives with the same comforts that she expected. On the walk through the streets, questions had bubbled through her, yet Moss had refused to answer. She just reiterated over and over how the city must be kept secret while every greenie they had passed adverted their gazes and moved away.

From the landing at the top of the stairs, Moss directed them to a door on the right. Baker and Veena handed Moss their lights and canteens before opening the door to a living room, complete with several couches and a bar in the corner. The basic decor created a comfortable environment—like any regular home on New Haven. This time, it wasn't the decor that surprised her; it was the fact that Orin and Emiko were already inside.

"B!" said an excited voice from within. "You made it!"

Baker grinned as she strode inside. Veena followed with Hwicce close behind her. Click leapt off her shoulder, landing on the wall before scurrying further in. Veena still found it hard to believe that someone carved the entire space—no, the entire city—from rock. Everything about it was fabulous.

"Did they leave anything to eat?" Baker headed right over to the bar.

"Ration bars is all they have," Emiko said from her seat on the couch. She grinned, keeping her eyes fixed on Baker. "The chocolate cherry isn't bad—not even a hint of caulk."

Veena sank down on the couch perpendicular to where Emiko sat, grateful for a moment to rest. The emotional roller coaster of the last few days had left her exhausted. Above, Click crossed the ceiling and hung on one tentacle to peer out the window. Hwicce went to the bar and returned with two ration bars. He handed one to Veena before sitting beside her.

"We saw you coming in on the cameras." Orin went to the bar and poured himself a drink. "With the reports of increased flooding, we were getting worried."

"We got lucky, and Moss seemed willing to bend some rules," Veena said. "But how did you two end up down here?"

"A search party—" Orin's words were cut off as Baker pushed past him.

She slumped down next to Emiko, holding several ration bars, which she dumped in a pile on the couch beside herself. With her teeth, she ripped open one in a green package and started eating.

"This place is something." She spoke with her mouth full. "I had no bloody idea greenies built a place like this, and it's so well hidden. There's no fucking way the Protectorate will find it."

"On that note, Swa's people appear to have departed." Orin took a seat, a tumbler of greenie liquor in hand.

From over by the window, Click let out a series of three clicks and flashed pink and yellow.

Veena frowned. "The Protectorate followed us to this planet?"

Orin nodded. "While you were in the caves, Swa's search

party arrived. They went through all the buildings on the surface before leaving." Hwicce let out a low whistle as he leaned forward. "You've got General Swa looking for you? She won't give up easily."

"Her soldiers have already packed up and left." Orin swirled his glass, then took a sip. "I told Han we'll leave as soon as the coast is clear."

"Good. We need to get back on track to find Molly. She must be so afraid out there alone." Veena swallowed. A fear that Swa would guard the gate welled up, but she ignored it.

"I'm sorry I wasn't there when they took her." Hwicce met her gaze.

"How about I grab you some of this?" Orin raised his tumbler. "Han left us a bottle of the good stuff." Without waiting for their answer, he got up and headed back to the bar.

Veena shifted towards Hwicce. "I…" Words failed her, and she bit her lip.

Hwicce wrapped his arm around her. "We'll get her back. Those fools don't stand a chance against us."

With a sigh, Veena let herself sink into him. There were so many obstacles in their way, but at least now they were together.

When Orin set two tumblers of the greenie liquor on the table. Veena pulled away from Hwicce and took a glass. On the other couch, Baker and Emiko seemed engrossed in each other. She couldn't see Click but assumed they were around somewhere. She let out a long exhale before looking from Orin to Hwicce. "We're going to need a plan."

"I can ping my sister; she might be able to get us a location on the Defiant," Hwicce suggested.

Veena nodded. "That would be a start." She doubted Selene would help, but it was worth a try. She swirled the opaque greenie liquor before taking a sip. It had a faint anise taste followed by an alcoholic burn.

"Is there somewhere I can send a message?" Hwicce asked Orin.

"Yes, there's an open terminal over there." Orin pointed to a console embedded into the wall.

Hwicce went to the terminal, and Veena slid down lower on the couch. It was such a relief to have Hwicce back. If only the two of them could slip off somewhere alone....

She sighed and sipped her drink. Across from her, Baker and Emiko both held drinks of their own and sat so close, their sides pressed together. Baker whispered something into Emiko's ear, and they both laughed. Neither of them seemed aware of the others in the room.

Veena smiled. She'd never been one for public displays of affection like that, but maybe she should be... her eyes drifted to Hwicce. In damp clothing with mud caked in his hair, he looked more like a bear than ever—but he was her bear. She sighed. He was here in person. Together they'd find Molly.

From above the bar, Click let out a click as they reached down and grabbed an emergency ration bar with two tentacles. They flashed green and yellow before ripping open the packaging.

Letting out a long exhale, Veena closed her eyes and tipped her head back against the couch. Things were going to be okay.

"That was weird." Hwicce sat down, causing Veena to nearly dump her drink.

She took the last sip from her glass. "Did your sister get back to you right away?" Selene had a habit of ignoring her little brother's messages.

"No, I didn't get to even send that message." Hwicce frowned. "Remember my Aunt Darla?"

She sat upright and ran a hand down her ponytail. "She came to our wedding, right?"

"Yeah, that was her."

"And she sent you a message out of the blue?" Veena set her glass down on the table.

"No. It turns out she died in a shuttle fire last week."

"Oh, no!" Veena tried to picture the woman but couldn't.

She'd only met her that one day, and she'd met so many others. They all blurred together. "Was the message from Selene?"

Hwicce scratched his head. "No, it was from Darla's lawyer. She left me her ship."

"A ship?" Orin leaned forward and cocked his head.

"It's an ancient water tanker currently docked at Indigo Station."

Veena blinked a few times. They were one gate past the link to Indigo Station. To get there, they would have to go around the entire loop. "We don't have time to deal with that right now. We've got to focus on getting Molly back."

"Yeah," Hwicce said.

"A water tanker could be a good disguise." Orin cut in. "Swa's forces know what *Buttercup* looks like and will be on the lookout for it. But a water tanker... That kind of ship can go anywhere, and the Water Guild likes to ensure its member's privacy. No one would question us."

"But Indigo Station is a long way past where we need to go." Veena frowned. "We've already delayed too much. Molly needs us."

"*Buttercup's* capacity is four people, and there are now five of us, not counting Click," Orin continued as Click flashed yellow from their current perch above the bar.

Veena set her drink down and frowned as she stared at the two men. "They took Molly on an off-loop link from the Delta System. We need to look for her trail there."

Emiko leaned forward. "Don't forget Boris. That scum bag should be put behind bars."

"Who's Boris?" Veena stood, fixing her eyes on Hwicce. "Never mind. Our girl has been stolen, and we need to focus on getting her back."

The door opened, and Han, as naked as before, entered.

"Our satellites confirm the Protectorate search party has departed. However, we suspect they are guarding the gate."

Veena let out a long exhale as she returned to the couch.

This was exactly what she'd feared. She slumped further down. "I can't keep sitting around and doing nothing."

"We would like your party to depart." Han kept his expression neutral, but it was clear he'd made an order.

"Of course," Orin replied. "We'll leave right away. And again, thank you for your hospitality."

"Where in the bloody hell are we going to go?" Baker asked. "Hanging out on your tiny ship for any length of time sounds colossally unfun to me."

"We can direct you to a shortcut to Indigo Station," Han said. "Only if you will swear to keep it a secret. Like the knowledge of our city, its existence keeps us safe."

"There's a second gate in this system?" Veena raised an eyebrow. Another way out of the system was the solution they needed.

"Yes. Its anchor world disintegrated; however, the ring of debris still provides enough pull to support the gate."

Emiko stood. "An off-loop link. To Indigo Station?"

The elder nodded.

"Is it used for smuggling?" Emiko asked.

Han pursed his lips. "I can't say. I'll send someone to take you to your ship in a few minutes." He left.

Baker returned to the bar, stuffing more ration bars into her pockets while Emiko chugged another glass of the liquor.

"It seems our destiny is to go to Indigo Station." Hwicce entwined his fingers in Veena's. "We won't stay there long. I want to rescue Molly as much as you do."

Veena nodded. "I suppose you're right. The tanker will make a better disguise." She glanced up to where Baker and Emiko laughed while taking turns chugging from the bottle. "And, with those two, more space will be good," she said in a low tone.

Click dropped from the ceiling and onto her lap. They flushed a series of dark blue and pale pink stripes. Veena put a hand on the little alien's head as it wrapped a tentacle around her arm and relaxed. Warmth radiated from their little body.

"I guess you'll end up being a ship's captain before your big sister does," Veena said.

Hwicce snorted. "Selene's going to be pissed when she finds out Aunt Darla left the ship to me and not her."

Chapter Thirteen

Veena let out a soft sigh as she wrapped her hands around her mug of mint tea. It was no longer even slightly warm, but she took a sip anyway. They were back on *Buttercup*, but now Hwicce was there too. She could hear the shower running as he took his turn to clean off.

Despite being an old ship, *Buttercup* ran quiet—just the hum of the ventilation system above combined with giggles from Baker and Emiko from the airlock, where presumably they thought no one could hear them. Veena smiled.

"Click suggests altering your algorithm to include the possibility of overlaid messages."

"Hmm?" Veena shifted her focus to Nigel. The AI steward appeared to be sitting beside her on the banquet seat, studying the alien code with her. Above, Click hung from two tentacles from the ceiling, swinging back and forth while shifting through a rainbow of colours.

"Click thinks there might be more than one message in the code," Nigel said.

"Right." Veena stared down at the display on her datapad for a moment, then projected it into the air over the table.

Rows of symbols glistened, taunting her with meaning she hadn't yet deciphered. She'd received the same set of symbols twice. First through her DeepNet contact Theo65, then from Swa's minion, Dr. Greer. That Swa still wanted her to decipher them suggested that whatever the text said was important.

Finding the same symbols on the walls of the caves belonging to Click's ancestors' on the anchor world left no doubt who originally wrote them. But Click couldn't read the ancient language—like Egyptian hieroglyphics were unreadable to her.

She sighed as she sorted the symbols into groups. Some were clearly rotations of each other. Did that mean they were separate symbols, or did the rotation have meaning? She set up a brute force algorithm on her datapad, one that would take into consideration rotation. With a long exhale, she leaned back in her seat.

"Figure anything out?" Hwicce sat down on the other side of her.

She glanced over at her husband. Even freshly showered, the red hue of his beard didn't quite match his sandy blonde hair. She met his gaze and smiled. Having him with her made getting Molly back seem so much more possible.

"Everywhere I look, it's the same one hundred symbols...." Her words trailed off, and she sighed again. "No, I still have no idea."

Above, Click emitted a series of clicks.

"Click thinks you are making progress," Nigel translated.

"Can you ask them for ideas?"

Nigel cocked his head to the side, then it glitched back to upright. "They don't know. It's one of their kind's lost languages."

Veena ran a hand over her head and down her ponytail. "Yeah, we've established we're dealing with an ancient language."

No doubt sensing her frustration, Hwicce wrapped an arm

around Veena and pulled her in close. He smelled like generic soap.

"I thought the code would be a pleasant distraction, but I just can't focus." She let herself relax against him. "All I can think about is Molly and how we're going further away from her." Setting the projection back to the original code, she stared at the symbols.

"It's just a temporary detour. Once we have Aunt Darla's ship, we'll head out and find that off-loop link," Hwicce said.

Baker came into the common room and poured herself a mug of tea. She leaned against the kitchen counter and stared at the symbols. "Is it a hex?"

Veena sat upright and cocked her head. "You mean hexadecimal numbers? Like base sixteen?"

"Naw, I meant is it some curse meant to keep you distracted." Baker chugged her tea and put the mug in the sink. "We need to load up on coffee at Indigo Station. I don't know how much more fucking tea I can take."

"It can't be base sixteen as there are a hundred symbols; that doesn't divide by sixteen evenly." Veena bit her lip. What if it was just encoded numbers? She tweaked her decoding algorithm.

"We're coming up on the gate," Orin said over the ship's intercom.

"I gotta check that out." Baker headed towards the bridge. Click dropped from the ceiling and skittered after her, and Nigel winked out.

Now alone, Hwicce pulled Veena in close again and wrapped his arms around her. "I just wanted to say that I wish I'd been with you all along."

Veena swallowed as she nodded.

"And we'll get Molly back." He kissed the top of her head. "I missed you both."

Veena bit her lip and pulled slightly away from Hwicce. She

looked him in the eye. "Swa implied you left the army to have a tryst with Baker."

He let out a laugh that shook his entire body. "With Baker?"

"She resigned at the same time you did."

Hwicce put his forehead on hers. "We'd both had enough of what the Protectorate was asking us to do. That's all." He leaned in closer until his lips were right at her ear. "And she's way too rough around the edges for my tastes."

"Hmph. You're pretty rough around the edges too—you're lucky I'm willing to keep you around." She put her head back against his chest. She knew he wouldn't run off with another woman, but it relieved her to hear him say it. "Let's go see this gate."

As she put her mug in the sink, she made a mental note to catch Baker alone. She owed the other woman a thank you for her help to get Hwicce back.

The five humans and one alien crammed onto the bridge. Emiko sat in the co-pilot's seat, with Baker standing, slightly stooped, in the narrow space behind it. Click perched in the middle of the dashboard, and Orin was in the pilot's seat. Veena tucked herself into the space behind him as Hwicce stayed in the doorway.

Outside, floating rubble filled the view, reminding her of the asteroid belt from her home system, which hid Rock 13-A5. These asteroids appeared marbled grey and black, so matte they barely reflected any light from the system's star—the same colours as an anchor world.

"What if the greenies were just luring us into a trap?" Emiko consulted a side panel. "These rocks are creating so much interference in our sensors, there could be an entire Protectorate armada hidden in there, and we'd have no idea."

"If they wanted to sell us out, they had plenty of opportunity back on Smaragdos. I'm confident we can trust them—especially considering how they're trusting us with their secrets," Orin said. Veena leaned over Orin to get a better view. "I'd say it's a good sign there's interference—the anchor world we landed on created similar interference."

Orin kept his eyes fixed on the view outside the windshield. "Then how do we find the gate?"

Click slid down onto Orin's lap and clicked.

"Click has an idea," Nigel said.

"And he wants to take control again." Orin lifted his hands and relinquished control.

With two tentacles, Click took over. They angled *Buttercup* into the asteroid field.

"Is that wise?" Hwicce asked as he leaned into Veena.

Veena bit her lip. "Click got us away from Swa's forces before—piloting is clearly one of their skills."

Click smoothly dodged the floating hunks of rock, passing deeper into the debris field. Just as they rounded a larger asteroid, Click emitted a series of clicks and pointed with one tentacle.

In the distance, the shimmering surface of a gate came into view. It shone with the expected aqua hues on the debris field of the lost anchor world.

"I wonder what happened here?" Emiko asked as she worked through screens on a side panel. A moment later, green lines highlighted all the rocks between them and the gate.

Click clicked before setting a course directly for the gate, then jumped off of Orin's lap and back onto the dashboard.

"No wonder it stayed hidden. No one in their right mind would fly around in here," Orin said, taking over the controls.

Baker crossed her arms over her chest and frowned. "Damn right! Only a complete fool would try to fly through that mess. What kind of armour plating does this rust bucket have?"

Veena kept her gaze on the view outside and ignored Baker's question. "This is a hell of a lot better than facing down Swa's minions again."

As they approached, the shimmering surface of the gate appeared more and more like the surface of a liquid. A half-hour later, it dominated their view, masking the dark rocks behind it.

"I wonder what's powering it with the anchor world pulverized like it is." Emiko leaned closer to the windshield.

Veena frowned. "Pet theories on how the gates function crop up all the time. Most suggest the extra mass of the anchor worlds transfers energy somehow—and this anchor world is still here, even if it is in pieces. But no one really knows for sure what powers the gates."

Orin glanced her way. "Maybe the code you're working on will provide some insight."

"Or maybe it's just a boring shopping list reminding spacefarers to stock up on extra coffee," Baker said as Buttercup's nose touched the gate surface.

Veena snorted. "I'm sure an alien shopping list would delight Swa."

On the dashboard, waves of yellow and pink radiated down Click's tentacles—a colour scheme that suggested they were laughing. Veena smiled as they crossed the gate's threshold.

In the dark of the small sleeping cabin on *Buttercup*, Veena woke with a start. For a moment, she thought she was back in her small room on Rock 13-5A. Her heart raced as she remembered the day they took Molly and how she'd failed to stop them. Even though she needed a few more hours of sleep, it was clear she wouldn't get that.

From the bunk above her, she could hear Hwicce sleeping, his breathing mixed with the odd snore. She sighed. At least she had him back. Together, they would rescue Molly.

As quietly as she could, Veena got up and pulled on her standard cargo pants, t-shirt, and jacket. She grabbed her boots and nanite scarf before leaving the cabin.

No one was out in the common room. She sat and tied up

her boots, then wrapped the scarf around her neck. The silk-like fabric's current program displayed an abstract combination of greens that matched the khaki of her jacket.

She went to the cockpit. Orin sat slumped in the pilot's chair, fast asleep. Shining against the black of the void, Indigo Station was dead ahead. She checked the autopilot; they wouldn't be arriving until at least lunchtime. With a sigh, she went aft and put on the kettle.

Sitting at the table, she brought up the alien code. The symbols seemed to mock her. Maybe Baker was right, and the text was some alien ephemera, not worth her effort. The kettle squealed, and she got up and set yet another pot of mint tea to steep—Baker was also right about them needing to stock up on coffee.

A few minutes later, Hwicce emerged from the single cabin, pulling on his hoodie over his head. "Thought I smelled fresh tea." He smiled at her, and she handed him her mug before pouring another.

"I couldn't sleep," she said as she slid behind the table.

"I see you brought Molly's backpack." He pointed to the glittery pink bag.

Veena nodded. "I wasn't thinking straight and made some bad packing choices." She opened the bag and pulled out the stack of *Bubble and Click* comics, and set them on the table. "I even brought these. I would have been better served by packing more socks."

"Hmmm." Hwicce sorted through the pile. A single piece of paper slid out—Veena's ticket to the *Garden Princess*. He picked it up. "I know we didn't have enough in our savings to get a seat on this ship."

"Yeah, it just appeared with some comics at my door on Rock 13-A5."

Hwicce turned it over in his hand. "Any idea who sent it?"

"One of my old DeepNet contacts—Theo65."

"Theo65 was willing to spend a fortune to get you to Indigo Station?"

"Yep," she said, putting her chin in her hands.

"Why?" He handed the ticket to Veena.

The paper felt smooth under her fingers. It was thick and pulpy—the kind of thing made by hand. She looked at the printed side, running her fingers along the embossed text. Then she flipped it over and re-read the note.

Hwicce leaned in closer. "What does it say?"

"Meet me at Summer's End Thrift Shop, Theo65." Veena scratched the side of her head as she stared down at the text.

"I wonder what your contact has to say in person that they couldn't say over the DeepNet?"

"I don't know, but it has to be important," she said.

"Or a trap."

"Either way, we'll soon have the opportunity to find out."

Chapter Fourteen

Xander Horowitz zoomed in on his display to study the footage of an ancient survey vessel as it darted away, right under the nose of the battlecruiser *Defiant*. An explosion rocked the mighty warship, and the clip ended. He almost laughed at the bold move the little ship made but restrained himself as General Swa's projected face hovered over his terminal, glaring down at him.

"So, you think they got away?" He leaned back in his chair. Of course, she thought they got away. Why come to a freelance bounty hunter if the quarry had been reduced to a red mist somewhere in the void of space? But he wanted her to say it.

Swa frowned. Her expression suggested she'd rather be talking to a garbage compactor than him. "We received a tip the ship was spotted on Smaragdos."

Xander smiled. "*Ad astra per aspera*. I always thought the Protectorate's motto was a little pretentious, don't you think?"

She pursed her lips. "Stay focused, you moron. Will you take the job? I need solid eyes on Indigo Station."

He snorted. Her insults didn't matter. Instead, what he cared about were her credits. "What makes you think they'll come here? They'd have to pass through a hell of a lot of gates to get here."

"Intel suggests there are other ways." Swa stared him in the eye. "I hear you're the best."

"As much as I appreciate flattery, I prefer credits."

"We'll pay your retainer fee." Swa glanced down for a moment.

A ping alerted Xander to credits arriving in his account. He forced himself not to smile. Based on how unlikely it was Swa's quarry would come his way, he'd just earned a fat wad of credits for doing nothing.

"You'll receive further payment for undisputed intel of these two people's location."

Two headshots appeared on his terminal—a middle-aged man, balding with dark skin, and a good-looking woman with medium brown skin and black hair pulled back from her face. The names below the pictures were Orin Akton and Veena Oswiu, both with advanced degrees in mathematics from New Haven University. He scanned through the provided bio and laughed.

"These are two of your brainiacs. How in the hell did they slip through your fingers?"

Swa didn't answer his question. Instead, the projection of her dark eyes bore into him. But she didn't intimidate Xander— if someone like Swa was lowering herself to hire someone like him, she was desperate. He clasped his hands behind his head.

"What's the bounty if I capture them?"

"The man can go out the airlock for all I care. However, if you can provide the woman to me unharmed, I'll give you triple your normal rate." Swa pursed her lips together. "As always, I expect you to be discrete."

Xander nodded. "I'll contact you when I have news." He ended the call and rubbed his chin.

The Protectorate Army was offering a hell of a lot of credits for a single academic. He scanned Veena's profile a second time.

All he needed to do was grab her, and he could pay off his debt to Long Enterprises. He could stop doing the shit wet work they kept assigning him.

He hoped Swa's prey came his way—maybe she really did know of a shortcut from the Charlie system to Indigo Station. There had always been rumours one existed, but never confirmation.

He brought up the latest job Long Enterprises had sent his way. He studied the three people he was to terminate if they appeared on the station. Two former soldiers and one former employee. Completing the job would only pay off a third of what he owed. Something twigged in his head, and he grinned.

The woman Swa wanted was married to the man the Longs wanted—if he was really, really lucky, he might accomplish both jobs at once. He could pay off his debts and have enough to upgrade his ship, give it more range and better living space. A grin spread across his face as he pondered the type of bounties he could go after then.

After isolating an image of the ship Veena and Orin were on, Xander accessed his back door into Indigo Station's space-port control. He set his AIs to filter the incoming ships and compare them to the image. There were other ways to get onto the station, but he suspected his quarry wasn't savvy enough for that.

"Well… shit," Xander muttered to himself as he checked his feeds a few hours later. "Lady luck has smiled down on me."

The AIs he'd tasked to monitor Indigo Station's traffic feeds had found a 99.7% match. The ship was called *Buttercup*, and the captain had already requested a berth to land in the visitor's docking bay, Docking Bay 5, right here on Indigo Station.

With two fingers, he expanded the image of the ship approaching. It had a distinctive paint scheme, mostly black with random patches of yellow, and it didn't reveal any of its secrets to the scanners. For such an old ship, it surprised him it could block scans.

He noted Buttercup's assigned berth and dropped a note to Swa that the ship had arrived. Then he stood up. If he took the tram, he could be at the docking bay before the ship landed.

Home Brew—an overpriced coffee shop overlooking Docking Bay 5 designed to pull in travellers—would make the perfect place for him to observe who came off the ship. He'd have plenty of time to plan his next move. He didn't dare be hasty; this could turn into a huge payday for him—he couldn't afford to blow it.

He sauntered into his spare room/armoury and surveyed all his equipment laid out on the two walls of shelving. Everything was as state-of-the-art as he could afford, bought on the black market and mostly illegal.

He pulled on a dark jacket, then put a nanite knife in the pocket. The knife was new. It looked like an ordinary datapad until activated—then it would reform into a blade so thin he could almost split atoms with it. He clipped a set of binders on his belt along with a small blaster. Into the cargo pocket on his pants, he added a stun rod.

A second nanite knife got clipped to his left boot, and finally, he tucked his most powerful blaster into the waistband at the small of his back.

He regarded himself in the mirror. Nothing about his appearance stuck out. He'd blend in fine—just another anony-mous one of the masses. A wide grin split his face.

"It's payday," he said as he pulled on his dark grey cloak and left his apartment in the Delta Quadrant. The elevator to the main level wasn't working again, forcing him to take the stairs down the three levels to the lobby. As he exited the accommoda-tion block, he pulled up his hood.

Cooking smells wafted from the food kiosks near the tram station. The frying onions and crickets made him salivate—but he didn't have time to stop. He boarded the first tram that arrived at the station.

At Docking Bay 5, he pushed his way through the crowds to Home Brew Coffee Shop. After ordering a mug of their best roast and paying way too much for it, he sat at the bar overlooking the cavernous space. Neon signs advertised everything from gift shops to washrooms and even the way out. The bright colours augmented the cacophony of echos in the space.

People moved back and forth, some with the wide eyes of tourists, some hunting for newly arrived family. The port officials all wore black bands on their right arms in mourning for the lost *Garden Princess*. They were most likely really mourning the loss of revenue such a posh ship generated.

Opening up his datapad, he feigned interest in what was on his screen, all the while scanning the crowd and the ships arriving through the massive airlock at the far end of the port.

He was on his second coffee when *Buttercup* flew into the bay. It landed right where he expected, directly across from the coffee shop. The crowds prevented him from taking any action —plus, he wanted to stay off the station police's radar. It was time to cultivate some patience. He took a sip as he activated the camera mounted on the top of his cloak's hood. He watched the view on his datapad.

Up close, *Buttercup* looked in rough shape. The black was a patchy coating of some sort, while the yellow was the hull's colour underneath. A faint whiff of tar wafted in his direction from the ship as it powered down.

A few moments later, the door opened, and a tall, bald, Black woman extended the steps. Xander cross-referenced his targets and smiled. The woman was Fanny Baker, one of the three wanted by the Longs. As she stepped onto the deck, Hwicce and Veena Oswiu followed. Next came Orin Akton and Emiko Green.

Xander could hardly contain his excitement. He'd finally gotten his break—all his targets were travelling together. His big payday was almost here. He reminded himself to be patient—a rash move now could ruin everything.

The group milled around the door for a few moments. Then Baker, Hwicce, and Orin headed off towards the administrative offices while Veena and Emiko headed towards the tram.

Xander got up. Veena was worth the most. Getting her would be his top priority—then he would deal with the others. Staying well back, he followed Veena to the tram.

Chapter Fifteen

Hwicce took a deep breath as he stepped over the threshold from the docking tube and onto *Virdis*. After a morning spent signing paperwork in the magistrate's office, the ship was now his. Baker and Orin followed a few paces behind.

He entered the cargo bay and inhaled. The air smelled fresh, better than Indigo Station's docking bay—and it was spacious, big enough for a shuttle and plenty of cargo. Even though the space needed a fresh coat of paint, it was clean. So far, no red flags.

But the century-old water tanker needed an overhaul. From the windows in the docking bay, he identified sections of damaged hull he should address soon. He swallowed. He had no idea how bad the ship's problems were going to be. Would the ship be ready to go in short order? He didn't want to delay their hunt for Molly any more than necessary.

"Well, I have to admit, this ship is in slightly better shape than the *Shimmer* was," Baker spoke from behind him.

Hwicce frowned. Whether it was Boris Long's captaining or the poorly maintained ship, the *Shimmer* had always felt off. But here, someone had poured their love into this ship.

"*Virdis* is much older." He walked back and forth and couldn't detect any issues with the gravity—another good sign.

Orin frowned. "Odd that the ship's name isn't painted on the hull outside."

"Yeah, I noticed that too," Baker said.

Hwicce chuckled. "My sister used to rant endlessly about the anonymous water tankers. It seems the members of the Water Guild value their privacy so much, it's against guild law to make your ship identifiable."

"I'm surprised the Protectorate allows that," Orin said.

"They need the water." Hwicce shrugged.

Baker snorted. "In that case, water tanker crews must be full of criminals, smugglers, and pirates."

"Or people like us who need to stay under the radar," Hwicce added.

"The good news is *Buttercup* will fit into the bay with no problem. Especially since this ship doesn't have any shuttles," Orin said.

Hwicce stopped in his tracks—Virdis didn't have a shuttle because his aunt had died in it. He frowned, trying to picture the woman. In all his life, he'd only seen her a few times. Her water runs always seemed to take her to the far reaches of known space, especially at holiday times.

"Why did she leave this to me?" He gestured to the surrounding ship.

Baker shrugged. "Hell if I know, sir. This ship seems more like a curse than a gift. Maybe you pissed her off when you were a kid."

Orin smiled as he looked around. "I disagree. You could do a lot with this ship. Hell, with a bit of sprucing up, this would be a great place to live."

"Maybe…." Hwicce let his words trail off as he didn't know what to think yet. To the side, a set of metal grating stairs led up to a catwalk above. "That must be the way to the bridge," Hwicce said as he climbed the first step.

Before he took a second step, a door on the other side of the cargo bay clanged open, and a male greenie with shoulders almost as wide as he was tall barged through. With a firm set to his square jaw, the man strode over. The red of his jumpsuit, combined with his skin, made him appear wrongly festive.

Stopping a pace away from Hwicce, the greenie lifted his chin. "You the kid Darla talked about?"

Hwicce shifted back. He hadn't encountered a greenie this bold before. After wiping his right hand on his pants, he extended it. "Hwicce Oswiu."

"Max Celadon." Max gripped Hwicce's hand significantly tighter than necessary. Hwicce did his best not to wince. "I keep *Virdis* running. A big job, considering the vintage of this lady."

Baker snorted. "I think you mean beast."

"This is Baker." Hwicce cut in as Max's brow furrowed. "And this is Orin."

Orin stepped forward and extended a hand. "Your skill in keeping *Virdis* in such good shape is commendable."

Max continued to glare at Baker but shook Orin's hand. "I'm glad someone sees the value of my work."

"How quickly can we get the ship ready to go?" Hwicce asked.

"What's the rush? You rob a bank or something?" Max crossed his arms over his chest. "I was gonna meet up with a friend for dice this evening."

"I need to get to the Delta system as soon as possible." Hwicce stepped closer to Max and looked down at him. The greenie barely came up to Hwicce's mid-chest. "How quickly until this ship can be ready to go?"

Max stepped back and smiled. "We can go anytime, but you might want to stock the larder beforehand."

Hwicce turned to Orin and Baker. "I need the two of you to do some shopping."

"Yes, sir!" Baker's tone was more ironic than obedient.

"Get some cookies," Max said to Baker.

Hwicce cocked his head. "Didn't think your kind needed to eat."

"I don't, but I like cookies." Max looked again at Baker. "Get the chocolate chip ones in the green package."

Baker raised an eyebrow.

"Grab some cookies while you're out," Hwicce said. "And get at least a case of coffee...maybe two."

Baker shrugged before heading back up the docking tube with Orin in her wake.

Now that it was just the two of them, Hwicce turned to Max. "Can you show me to the bridge?"

"Sure thing, boss." Max pushed past him and started climbing the stairs. "Care to share where we'll be headed in the Delta system?"

"Umm." Hwicce scratched his head as he followed the engineer up to the catwalk above. He wasn't certain where they were headed but didn't want to let on. "Delve's Landing."

Max grunted in reply. Delve's Landing was a farming station under a dome on a rocky moon—the kind of place that would bring in water.

"How much water does the ship currently hold?"

"We're at about 50% capacity," Max said as he led Hwicce through a set of air-tight doors and down a long corridor. A waft of synthetic lemon scent filled the air—a cleaner, no doubt. As the only crew member, Max must have been busy anticipating their arrival. The floor, walls, and ceiling were spotless but with the same worn paint as the cargo bay below.

"Does Darla have any outstanding deliveries?" Hwicce asked just to keep the conversation going.

Max stopped and turned towards him. "I never worried much about the business side of things. You'll have to ask GRUB."

"GRUB?"

"The *Virdis'* AI. Darla confided in them more than any of the crew."

"Is that why the others left?"

Max shrugged. "This ship doesn't need a large crew." He turned and resumed his path down the corridor. They passed a closed door. "Kitchen and common rooms are through there. Crew cabins are in there too."

"Okay." Hwicce was tempted to look inside, but Max kept on going.

"In there are the ship's electronics and a workshop," Max said at the next set of doors. The corridor ended at a set of stairs, which Max ascended. "Captain's office is in here." He pointed to a door leading off to the right. Then he opened the door dead ahead.

"And this is the bridge?" Hwicce asked.

"Yeah." Max stepped aside. "GRUB will give you the low down. I'll make sure we're ready to go." Max turned.

"Sorry about messing up your evening plans, but we need to go," Hwicce said.

Max nodded and headed down the stairs.

"What a strange man," Hwicce whispered to himself as he watched Max disappear from view.

Hwicce stepped onto the *Virdis'* bridge. Actual windows filled the forward bulkhead, a change from the walls of screens he was used to seeing on the military ships he'd served on. Outside, the panoramic view of the side of Indigo Station and space extending out in front of him.

The three levels of the semi-circular design of the bridge felt old-fashioned. He strode forward to the shiny metal railing that circled the upper level. At each end were the three steps down to the middle level.

Directly below him on the second level stood the captain's chair. His mother had sat in such a chair before she had passed away, and his sister was focused on getting such a position herself. It had never been his goal. Again, he wondered why Aunt Darla left the ship to him.

There were two other chairs on the middle level; each had a

panel of controls arrayed before them. The bottom level had more workstations, all of which were currently powered off.

"Welcome, Captain Oswiu." A rich, androgynous voice reverberated from everywhere at once.

"Are you GRUB?" Hwicce asked.

"Affirmative. I have been awaiting your arrival. How many people will you be bringing on board?"

Hwicce listed off the humans in their group, deciding to keep Click a secret for now. Currently, the little alien remained hidden on *Buttercup* and might need to stay hidden. "Once everyone has returned from their tasks and we load our survey ship into the cargo bay, we'll be leaving."

"Affirmative. Fuel levels are at 87%, and oxygen is at 91%. Based on our current load of water, we can reach Delve's Landing in 18.21 hours."

"Great." Hwicce wandered around the bridge, studying the workstation displays as he went. He took his time, taking it all in. His sister was going to be so jealous—he was going to be a ship's captain before her. With a snort, he realized their next holiday gathering was going to be tense.

He walked down to the lowest level and stared out at the traffic around Indigo Station. Ships of all sorts were coming and going. He fixated on a gate-rated ferry, the kind an ordinary citizen might take—nothing like the luxury liner *Garden Princess*. He frowned. Had the liner completed its scheduled trip, it would arrive about now.

Hwicce turned back to the empty bridge. "GRUB, are you linked with the Station?"

"Affirmative."

Hwicce sat down in the captain's chair, half expecting someone to tell him not to. But *Virdis* was his ship now. He relaxed back for a moment and took a deep breath. There was something he needed to do before leaving Indigo Station.

"Can you locate the residence of Boris Long?"

"Searching." The AI fell silent.

Hwicce closed his eyes and pictured the captain of the cargo ship *Shimmer*. Boris loaded the ship full of explosives and aimed it right at the luxury liner *Garden Princess*. Then the coward fled, leaving Baker, Emiko, and Hwicce to near-certain death. A new round of anger flowed through his veins.

He brought up a holographic display and searched the news feeds on the collision. Relief washed over him as he saw reports that most of the crew and passengers on the liner escaped. Over three thousand of them. Only five remained unaccounted for. Their plan to divert *Shimmer* had worked. He let out a long exhale. At least they'd been able to do something.

"Boris Long's residence is not listed in the station archive," GRUB said. "However, I can provide you with an address for the main office of Long Enterprises."

"Okay, transfer it to my datapad." But then Hwicce realized he didn't have one. The military had confiscated his when he resigned. He let out a long exhale. "Are there extra datapads around?"

"The previous Captain Oswiu may have left one in her office," the AI answered.

Hwicce nodded as he played around with the displays next to the captain's chair. There was so much to learn about how everything worked. He ran a hand over his face and beard—but first, he had to confront Boris.

"Two of your group have returned." A screen on the console beside him flicked to life and displayed Orin and Baker entering the cargo bay.

"Send them up here," Hwicce said as he stood and went to the door of the captain's office.

The office was in chaos. Clearly, Darla's desire for a neat and tidy ship ended here. Hwicce let out a sigh. He didn't know where to look.

Piles of broken instruments lay on the floor; he recognized one as a music synthesizer, another as an old-school oscillo-scope. Then he realized this was Darla's collection—the one she'd told him about when he was a kid. Back then, she'd said it would all be his one day, but she'd never clarified what exactly she'd been collecting. Looking around, Hwicce still wasn't sure the collection was anything beyond a pile of random stuff.

He let out a long exhale. "Oh crap, she did warn me."

Surveying the stuff, he decided it was all just junk. He ran both hands through his hair. It was a pile of junk he was going to have to deal with. The entire ship was more than he wanted to deal with right now. Dumping the dubious treasures off one end of a couch, he sat down.

Veena was right—he should focus on getting Molly back. Was claiming the *Virdis* the best way to do that? Closing his eyes, he pictured Molly's face. How her curly dark hair framed her huge eyes.

"Yo, sir." Baker leaned against the door jamb. "It looks like a kit bomb went off in here."

Hwicce shrugged. "I have no explanation for all this." He gestured to the piles of stuff. "I guess Aunt Darla was some sort of collector."

"Or hoarder?" Baker strode across the room and slumped down on the couch beside him.

Orin followed her in and roamed around, studying the objects. Every now and then, he'd pick up an item, then put it back, all the while wearing an inscrutable expression. "Some of this stuff might have value."

"What do you suggest I do with it?" Hwicce asked.

"I can sort through it for you." He frowned and stared off into the distance, not focusing on anything. For a moment, all three of them were silent.

"Where'd you go, little man?" Baker asked in an uncharacteristically kind tone.

Orin sighed. "Just thinking about Mary."

"Who's Mary?" Hwicce shifted on the couch and focused on Veena's former boss. He still didn't understand why the man was here—his story of suddenly growing a conscience seemed a bit too convenient.

"My wife." Orin smiled. "And she would've loved going through all this junk."

Hwicce shrugged. "I'm sure we can just stash it for her."

"She was on New Haven when...." Orin's words trailed off.

"Oh," Hwicce stood. He'd been so worried for Veena and Molly when he heard the Nader Alliance had bombed New Haven. His family had been lucky, but clearly, not everyone's was. "I'm sorry."

Orin nodded. "She made sculptures out of found stuff like this." He gestured to the room. He picked up a metronome, then put it down. "But we need to focus on getting to the Delta System."

"Did you get supplies?"

"The outfitter is going to deliver the food this afternoon," Orin answered. "We ordered twenty days' worth of fresh rations, eighteen months' worth of ration bars, plus two crates of coffee."

Baker cut in. "And we got the damn cookies."

"I'm hoping that'll be enough," Orin continued. "If not, there are plenty of places to re-supply on route if we need."

"And we grabbed our gear from *Buttercup*," Baker added. "It's all on a trolly in the common room."

"I'll have to maneuver the ship into the cargo bay once we're underway, as it can't be done while docked."

"Are you sure *Buttercup* will fit?"

Orin nodded. "I think so. But it'll be tight. Hopefully, you aren't planning on taking on any cargo."

"Finding Molly is the focus for now." Hwicce strode over to the desk and started searching through drawers. "But while we're waiting around here, the ship's AI found an address for Long Enterprises."

"You wanna confront Boris?" Baker stood and frowned. "I'm in, sir. I'd love to rough up that asshole."

"Why not leave an anonymous tip with station police?" Orin suggested. "Leave it to the professionals to arrest him."

Hwicce ran a hand down his beard. "I need to ask him some questions first."

"If you want answers, you need to talk with his grandmother," Baker said. "That bitch is definitely the puppet master."

"True, she's the mastermind—but I suspect it'll be easier to corner Boris. I want to know why they rammed the *Shimmer* into the *Garden Princess* and what kind of experimentation the military was hoping to do on Hamber's Hole."

Baker crossed her arms over her chest. "You think these things have something to do with your little girl?"

"We overheard Mrs. Long mention a contract for human experimentation on Hamber's Hole." He ran a hand over his beard. "And there had to be an intended target on the *Garden Princess.*"

"You think they were after Veena?" Orin asked.

"No, I don't think she was a target," Hwicce said. "Veena told me there was a minion of Swa's on the liner. I think he was the same one who was supposed to move his lab to Mrs. Long's facility and changed his mind."

Orin nodded. "Dr. Greer. He was there when they took Molly."

"We don't have many leads." Hwicce pulled himself up tall. "So let's follow up on what we have."

Baker frowned. "I wish I had my combat armour for this."

"You don't need armour. Just give Boris the eye, and he'll crumble." Hwicce turned to Orin. "I need you to stay here and ensure we're ready to go."

Orin stood. "I'll head to the bridge and prepare for our departure. Don't do anything foolish out there."

"We won't," Hwicce said as he pulled up the hood on his hoodie. He turned and nodded to Baker.

"Let's go."

Chapter Sixteen

Veena couldn't help but count the people around them as she and Emiko crammed onto a tram already packed full of humans on the go. The bustling public transport forced everyone onboard to press up against each other with a complete disregard for personal space. A myriad of scents washed over her, from synthetic rose perfume to exceptionally rank body odour.

There wasn't an empty seat forcing them to grab onto a pole as the tram lurched away from the station. Veena glanced out the window as they picked up speed and plunged into a darkened corridor. Being jostled by strangers grated on her, and she had to remind herself to breathe.

"Why aren't there any windows in the tunnel?" she asked Emiko, looking for a distraction. The tram windows only showed an endless, graffiti-covered wall of the metal tube the tram ran in.

"Rich folks get the windows, and they don't take the tram," Emiko said as she scanned the crowd.

Veena followed her gaze. Most of their fellow passengers appeared to be labourers in well-worn work clothes. Some were dressed in 3D printed suits, the kind a low-end bureaucrat might wear. A few uniformed station workers were peppered throughout the crowd. By the doors, a mom struggled to keep control of her three kids. Behind her, a man in a black cloak stood like a statue.

Veena saw nothing to be worried about other than simply too many people in the small space.

"How do you know where this shop is?" Veena ran a hand over the pocket where she'd stashed the *Garden Princess* ticket with the note about going to Summer's End Thrift Shop on the back. When she'd mentioned it to Emiko, the other woman had known exactly where to go without consulting a map.

Emiko didn't take her gaze off the sea of people. "I used to work nearby. I passed it every day, but I never went in."

Veena nodded. What was waiting for her there? She used to interact with Theo65 all the time when she played with the codes on the DarkNet—but that was years ago. Out of the blue, they sent a ticket to her, a physical object that had come to her physical location. She swallowed and hoped following the note was the right thing to do. But she needed to keep busy while Hwicce did the paperwork to transfer the tanker to him—then they'd be on their way towards Molly.

Emiko remained silent as Veena kept her eyes on the limited view outside the tram's windows. Every now and then, a station broke the monotony of the tram's tunnel. As passengers flowed on and off, Emiko held her ground. Veena started to wonder if they were going to take the tram the entire circle back to where they started from.

"This is us," Emiko said finally as the tram pulled into another station.

This station was the same as the last three they'd passed. As soon as the doors slid open, they pushed through the crowd to get out. On the platform, food kiosks rose like pylons forcing the bulging crowds to flow around them.

A man in black walked into Emiko, nearly knocking her off her feet.

"Watch it, asshole!" Emiko steadied herself and glared at the man. He didn't look back as he wove his way through the crowd and out of sight.

"You okay?" Veena stayed close to her as more people surged past them.

Emiko straightened out her jacket. "I bet he did that on purpose. Let's get out of here." She pushed ahead, and Veena stayed in her wake.

By the time they reached the concourse outside the tram station, the crowd had mostly dispersed. Veena felt like she could breathe again and filled her lungs. Shops lined the walls, including the Space Chew head office and several mycelium suppliers.

The further they moved away from the station, the quieter it became. It also became dirtier with garbage brushed up against the walls beneath colourful and rude graffiti.

"This used to be your path to work?" Veena asked.

"Yeah, I had a job cleaning the algae tanks in this sector." Emiko turned a corner into a dead-end alley. Halfway down sat Summer's End Thrift Shop, the yellow lettering above the door peeling as though under a summer sun instead of industrial lights. "And here we are."

Veena pressed her hand against the pocket containing the ticket and took a deep breath. When she opened the old-fashioned hinged door, a bell above it announced their presence. A wave of musty, spicy air hit her as the proprietor of the shop turned towards them and smiled.

"Welcome," the proprietor said. Its olive skin was too even to be real, and its black hair shone under the store's overhead lights. Androids weren't common back on New Haven. Even so, this model she recognized. Usually, it was employed in security or as a bouncer for a bar—tasks that needed a little extra muscle. It was odd to see one placidly running a thrift store.

"Good morning." She smiled as though speaking to a human and stepped further inside. Emiko came in behind her and shut the door. "I received a message to come to this shop."

She bit her lip and surveyed her surroundings. The shop was the size of her bedroom on New Haven. Walls lined with shelves contained everything from assorted bucket-o-stuff toys to scientific equipment. Several used spacesuits hung from one wall with their helmets on the shelf above. There was a blue and white vase that could be a relic from Old Earth and a well-worn yellow tricycle. Someone had positioned every item just so and kept them entirely free of dust.

A large aquarium made up the shop's counter, which the proprietor stood behind. He stared at Veena for a moment. "My data banks tell me you are Veena Oswiu."

"That's correct." Veena made her way around a table displaying pulp books, including several issues of *Bubble and Click*. When she reached the counter, she leaned her elbows on its clear surface. "Why was I called here?"

The android slowly nodded. "The owner left a package for you. Please stand by." It turned and went into the back.

As Emiko browsed the shelves on the back wall, Veena glanced down into the murky water of the aquarium. Something big moved inside. When whatever it was moved a second time, she crouched down to get a better view. Placing a hand on the top for support, she peered in. Out of the murk on the other side, a brown nubbly appendage reached for her hand. She held her breath as her gaze followed the tentacle deeper in. A massive body filled the back of the tank, and two glossy eyes fixed on her.

Veena gasped and fell back onto her butt just as the android returned. "What's in there?" she asked, pointing at the water.

"Just the new animatronic Click doll," it said as it put a small box on the counter.

Veena stood, keeping her eyes fixed on the aquarium. A Click doll wouldn't look that rough or big. "It looked real."

"I don't see anything," Emiko said as she approached the counter.

"It was—"

"This is what Theo65 left for you," the proprietor cut her off.

A faint glow now came from the murky water in the aquarium below. It highlighted the box. Pushing her fear of what was in the water aside, Veena came closer. The box was the kind a fancy necklace would come in, made of sturdy pulp dyed a teal shade.

"What is it?" she asked without looking away from the box.

The bell at the door sounded. Another patron was here. Veena grabbed the box and slipped it into her jacket pocket.

Chapter Seventeen

As the echo of the door chime faded away, Veena, Emiko, and the android stared at the man in a black cloak who'd entered. Other than being tall, there wasn't anything out of the ordinary about him. Yet Veena's breath caught in her throat. It was the cloak—she'd spotted it on the tram. The man who'd bumped into Emiko.

With the same helpful expression he had used on Veena and Emiko, the proprietor said, "How may I help you?"

Emiko pulled Veena to the side and whispered in her ear. "I have a bad feeling about this."

"Me too."

The man stepped up to the counter an arm's length from Veena. He smiled at her, an expression that didn't reach his grey eyes, then he turned to the android. "I'm looking for issue 7 of *Bubble and Click*."

The proprietor nodded. "I have a pristine copy back here."

As the proprietor crouched down behind the counter, the man pushed his cloak off his right shoulder and raised a stun gun. The world slowed as he pulled the trigger. Emiko yanked Veena towards her as the gun flashed. The energy bolt grazed

Veena's left shoulder, and immediately her entire arm went numb.

In a single motion, the proprietor stood and grabbed the stun gun out of the man's hand. "I have notified station police." It squeezed, and the gun crumpled in its hand as if it were a toy.

The man smirked and reached out with a rod, contacting the android's neck. A flash of sparks leapt over the android's synthetic skin, and it collapsed forward onto the counter. The man then leveled the rod at the two women.

"Veena Oswiu, if you come with me peacefully, I'll let your companion go."

"Bullshit!" Emiko threw a child's spacesuit helmet at the man.

He dodged, and the helmet hit the side of the aquarium. A web of cracks radiated across its surface.

As Emiko continued throwing things at the man, Veena glanced around. If she could crack open the aquarium, the gushing water would knock the man down—maybe. She picked up an air filtration unit and threw it at the glass. More cracks radiated, but the aquarium's wall held.

"Crap." She searched for something else. She picked up a full-sized helmet with her right hand, her left arm still numb.

The man grabbed Emiko by the wrist and pulled her in close. He wrapped his other hand around Emiko's neck.

"Last chance before things get messy," he said while maintaining an unsettlingly calm demeanour.

Emiko flicked her eyes down. Veena followed Emiko's gaze. The other woman's jacket had lifted enough that Veena spotted a knife hilt sticking up out of her waistband.

"What do you want with me?" Veena took a step closer, forcing herself not to look at the knife.

"Put the helmet down." His tone could have been used to request a cup of tea from his grandmother.

Veena nodded and set the helmet down on the counter. She bit her lip and stared into the man's face. His expression remained neutral, as though it were ordinary to hold a woman's life in his hands.

With a burst of speed, Veena drew Emiko's knife with her right hand. At the same moment, Emiko dropped her weight, forcing him to let her go. As Emiko fell to the floor, Veena squeezed her eyes shut and slashed at the man's face. As Veena opened her eyes and saw what she'd done, she dropped the blade.

"You fucking bitch!" The man clamped a hand over the gash across his right cheek, blood pouring out between his fingers. He took a step back, blocking the way to the front door. "Now I'm going to hurt you." He pulled out a second blaster and pointed it at them. "I don't give a shit if you're worth less dead."

With a loud crack, the aquarium split open. A wave of water and glass sloshed across the shop's floor. The man's focus shifted. Veena and Emiko dove behind the counter where the android had fallen.

Out of the wreckage of the aquarium, a beast emerged. Its tentacles slapped the floor as it moved towards the man. It was more than twice the size of Click with nubby skin. It flashed red and emitted a deep groan that shook everything in the shop.

"What the hell!" the man shouted as he scooted backwards until he reached the front door.

Something touched Veena's leg, and she screamed.

"Veena," the proprietor said.

She took a deep breath and crouched down next to him. Most of its body remained unanimated.

"The back door." It reached out and pushed a hidden panel in the wall. A half-height door opened. "Go. Theo65 will buy you time."

"What? That's Theo65?" Veena stared at the beast. How could that tentacled monster be her DeepNet contact?

Theo65 thrust the man down and turned her way. Their

dark eyes met her gaze for the briefest moment. Then they turned back to their fight.

"You need to go," the android said.

"I can help." Veena lay her right hand on the damaged android's shoulder. It didn't feel right to abandon Theo65 and the android. She looked around for a weapon.

"Go," he said. "Don't waste this."

Emiko pulled Veena to her feet. "Let's go."

Even though it still didn't feel right to her, Veena relented and allowed Emiko to pull her out of the shop. The two of them darted through the door, and it slid shut behind them.

"What the hell came out of that aquarium?" Emiko asked as they jogged down the maintenance corridor on the other side.

"Looked like a bigger and meaner Click." Veena turned right at the first intersection. She'd been messaging Theo65 for years and had no idea they weren't human. She swallowed. "Maybe there are more aliens about than we realize."

"So your contact was an alien?"

"Turns out." A crash reverberated from behind them—the man had gotten past Theo65 and was on their tail. His footfalls sounded heavy on the floor behind them.

Emiko turned and sprinted down the corridor. Even though Veena was taller, she had a hard time keeping up. Emiko shouted over her shoulder as she ran. "We need to get back onto the public concourses. It'll be easier to lose him in a crowd."

The hall ended at a ladder leading up. Emiko didn't wait; she started ascending.

"Wait! I can't go up there," Veena said, shaking her left arm. It remained numb.

Emiko stopped and glanced down at her. Then she came back down.

"He wants me alive, so you can get away." Veena handed Emiko Theo65's package. "Get this back to Hwicce."

Emiko pursed her lips and didn't take it. "There's no way I'm leaving you."

"I don't see another option." Veena faced the way they'd come. "He'll be here any minute."

"Then get your ass up the ladder." Emiko glared at her before climbing.

Veena swallowed as she shoved the box back into her pocket. Time was running out. She opened and closed her left hand. Pinpricks now ran up her arm.

Ignoring the painful tingling, she grabbed onto the ladder and started climbing. She didn't trust her left hand to hold her weight, so her going was slow. Above, Emiko continued her ascent.

The ladder rose without an exit as far as Veena could see. The only break in their climb was the small platforms every few stories. More sensation returned to Veena's arm as she climbed; it went from tingling to flat-out throbbing. But she gritted her teeth and continued upwards. She kept glancing down, expecting to see the man gaining on them, but he didn't appear.

"Here we are." Emiko stepped onto the top platform.

Breathing heavily, Veena followed. She massaged her arm and glanced down. The shaft they just came up seemed to extend down forever. A wave of vertigo swept over her. She swallowed and forced herself to focus on Emiko.

The other woman went over to a door in the wall and put a hand on its doorknob. "Here's hoping we don't need a key."

A wave of relief swept over Veena when Emiko turned the knob, and it opened. Scents of charred vegetables and laundry soap rushed in. Veena leaned through the doorframe and looked around.

"We're over one of the habitat modules," Emiko said, glancing back.

Veena stared past Emiko at the catwalk that extended more than a hundred metres to the other side. Every twenty metres, there was a junction with a perpendicular catwalk. The metal mesh floor and single handrail seemed under-designed considering the height, but at least crossing it wouldn't require any more climbing.

"Let's keep going." Veena swallowed and walked out onto the catwalk.

Massive vents kept the air moving, creating enough of a wind that the stray bits of escaped hair from Veena's ponytail flew straight into her mouth. Her stomach lurched when she glanced down. Her boots on the mesh floor didn't hide the height. There were at least five stories up. Far below, tiny people moved about, unaware of what was going on above.

Emiko put a hand on Veena's back. "Just breathe. He was going to shoot us."

Veena took a deep breath and looked at Emiko. The other woman's eyes were wide, but she was holding herself together.

Veena nodded. "It was the best option I could think of."

She forced herself to keep moving with her eyes fixed on the door at the far end. Her feet clanked on the metal reassuringly.

"We should be able to get down at the far end. Then we can disappear into the crowd," Emiko said from behind her. "We got what we came for, right?"

Veena turned to respond. Instead, she gasped. At the door they'd just come out of stood the man. He raised his blaster. Veena grabbed onto Emiko's arm and pulled her down one of the perpendicular paths just as a blaster bolt passed through where they just were.

The two women sprinted. Their catwalk passed various ventilation equipment, preventing the man from taking another shot, but he ran after them, his boots thundering against the metal grill.

At the end of the catwalk, they came to a door. This time, it was locked.

"Fucking hell!" Veena cursed as she turned around.

The man was close behind. He slowed as soon as he saw his quarry was trapped. He'd put some sort of coagulant on the gash on his face, but crimson blood still coated his cheek and jaw. With a sneer, he raised his gun.

"Tell me you can pick the lock," Veena said. A lump formed in her throat as she kept her gaze fixed on the man.

Emiko knelt to get a better look. Then she frantically turned the knob, jiggling it one way, then the other.

"I should just shoot you." The man's calm demeanour had returned.

Veena glanced around. Unlike the thrift shop, there wasn't even an old boot she could use as a projectile. She glanced down. Rows of balconies extended below them. Some with brightly coloured lounge chairs, some with flowers, while others contained drying laundry—all of them out of reach.

Behind her, Emiko kept rattling the door.

Veena took a single pace towards the man. "You said I was worth more alive."

"You've proven yourself to be more trouble than you're worth." He raised his empty hand up to his damaged cheek.

Veena let her shoulders slump forward. "I'll come quietly now. Besides, where am I going to go?"

The man nodded, never taking his eyes off her. "Put these on." He threw a set of binders down at her feet.

Veena swallowed, staring at the rounded form of the hand-cuffs. Nodding, she took another pace towards the man and knelt. She picked up the metal restraints and wrapped one side around her left wrist without clipping it closed. As she took a deep breath, she analyzed the distance between herself and the man. She could do it.

Dropping her head, she launched herself forward. Her momentum drove her into the man before he could shoot. The railing groaned as his hip smashed into it, but it didn't stop him. His body pivoted over the bar as he lost a grip on the blaster. He fell, landing flat on his back on the nearest balcony, knocking over laundry hanging out to dry. The gun landed on the catwalk. Veena steadied herself by holding onto the railing with both hands.

"Holy shit!" Emiko came to Veena's side.

The two of them looked down. The man lay splayed out on a pile of colourful clothing. He didn't move.

"Did I kill him?" Veena's throat constricted as she stared at his inert form.

"Come on. Let's get out of here," Emiko said, dragging Veena away.

"Hang on." Veena bent down and picked up the gun. She powered it down and stuck it into her belt at the small of her back.

Emiko led them back to the junction. She turned away from the way they'd entered, instead heading to the far end, just like they originally intended.

Veena followed, her hands trembling.

Luck was with them; this time, the door opened. On the other side was a maintenance room. One worker looked up as they entered and scowled at them. "The catwalks aren't open to the public."

Emiko grimaced in a cute way. "Oops, sorry. How do we get down to the main level?"

"I have half a mind to call the station police and have the two of you arrested for trespassing." He frowned.

"No need for that." Veena used as calm as a voice as she could muster. "We just got turned around."

He stared at them for a long minute, then shrugged. "Letting you two go saves me a ton of paperwork. Just take the stairs through there." He pointed to another door on the far wall.

"Thank you," Veena said as the two of them headed to the door.

A few minutes later, they emerged down on the main floor. Veena stopped and stared up at the catwalks they'd just left. She half expected to see the man up there staring down at them, but the catwalks were empty.

A siren sounded, and Emiko pulled Veena out of the way. An ambulance passed by.

"We best get out of here and lie low for a while. I know a great place we can grab a piece of pie."

Veena stared at Emiko. "Pie?"

"Yeah, pie." Emiko turned and strode towards the tram station at the end of the habitat module. "Their apple pie is to die for."

Chapter Eighteen

Nigel paced back and forth between *Buttercup's* common room and survey room. For the first time in his existence, he felt trapped. The others had accepted him into their group as an equal—something he'd never expected. And now they were all out doing important things, and there was nothing he could do to help. He hoped the others were all right.

In a massive glitch, his pixels disintegrated and reformed in the airlock. He stared out into the port. People flowed through the area, past the other ships, in and out of the neon labelled shops. They weren't the finely dressed folks he'd served on the *Garden Princess*; even if he could, somehow, leave the ship, his period programming wouldn't help him much here. Plus, he didn't know the layout of the station, and his available memory couldn't fit a complete station schematic. Calculating the number of unquantified unknowns made him want to power down completely.

He rubbed his hands together, faster and faster as his algorithms tried to process his situation. With each motion, his fingers started passing through each other—a glitch that indicated an impending system overload. With a sigh, he turned back to the ship and went to the common room.

Click sat on the table reading the *Bubble and Click* comics Veena had left them. The little alien was engrossed in the stories; their colour changed each time the illustrated alien did. Without a word, Nigel sat down.

A chime sounded from the bridge. Both Click and Nigel glanced that way.

"What is it?" Nigel asked. He didn't have access to an inventory of the ship's sounds. He made a note to ask Veena for an upgrade—his systems seemed so inadequate now he was off the *Garden Princess*.

Click shrugged, then leaped down off the table and skittered to the bridge. Nigel followed, stepping onto the bridge just as Click climbed up onto the pilot's seat. They studied the display, and after a moment, they pointed to the comms screen and let out a sharp click.

"Oh, it's a message." Ignoring the seats, Nigel passed through them to view the screen. "Go ahead and play it."

Click started the message, and General Swa's head appeared above the dashboard.

"Veena, we received word that you have arrived at Indigo Station. Call me. I have news of Molly and would like you to reconsider my offer. If you can decode that alien message, I will make sure you and your daughter are reunited."

Flashing red and yellow, Click let out a series of clicks as the message ended.

"I agree," Nigel said. "That woman is lying."

Click climbed up onto the dashboard and rotated to face Nigel. They let out two sharp clicks.

"Yes, if Swa knows Veena is here, she might send a ship."

A green flush rose up Click's tentacles, then they went hot pink, emitting a long series of ping-like sounds.

"Oh…." Nigel shook his head. "No, you shouldn't do that."

Click made a loud pop.

"I'm sure there's another way to see if any navy ships are on their way without hacking into the station's system."

Click raised a tentacle and flashed yellow.

Nigel frowned. "You're right. I'm sure the others will appreciate any information you can find."

After making a popping sound, Click jumped back down onto the pilot's seat and started working through the screens on the display. Different views flashed by, from command lines to restricted displays. After twenty minutes, Click stopped and slumped down. A dark grey colour started at the end of their tentacles and rose until their entire body became the same dull hue.

"What is it?"

With a single tentacle, Click pointed at the screen. Nigel leaned down to look.

"The *Defiant* is in the system?" That was bad news; they'd only barely escaped the battlecruiser before. "We have to tell the others."

Click flushed orange with pink dots.

"Yes, I know they are busy."

As Click raised a tentacle, they let out a series of soft clicks reminiscent of a purr.

"You are correct," Nigel said. "They have been kind to us."

After flashing a rapid succession of cherry red and cyan, Click returned to working the screens.

"No. That's a bad idea." Nigel stepped closer to the alien and shook his head. "You've been reading too many of those comics."

Click emitted a series of clicks that sounded like an old-fashion internal combustion engine revving.

"No, I forbid it." Nigel's hands started glitching as he rubbed them together. "You and I are not equipped for that kind of thing. Rash action like that will spell our doom. We must continue to follow Dr. Oswiu's instructions and hide here."

Unfamiliar sensations washed over Nigel's code as he

watched Click send a message to the harbour master requesting permission for the *Buttercup* to depart. It was granted. The world inside the cockpit seemed to contract around Nigel. Without a connection to the ship, he was powerless to stop Click.

"We can't just leave without telling the others." Nigel put his hands on his hips. The alien was going to drive him to dematerialize all together.

Click ignored him and started the main engines. A low hum reverberated through the ship. Standing on a tripod of tentacles, they grabbed onto the controls. In a single maneuver, they smoothly lifted off and headed to the airlock.

Wishing he was somewhere else, Nigel threw up his hands. "You'll be the death of us both."

Click flashed a pale yellow with green dots and let out a series of long clicks.

"Why in the hell would Swa just let us go?"

Click made a pop sound as they exited Indigo Station and set a course towards the system's anchor world.

"Oh...." Nigel pondered the plan for a moment. He knew his processing power wasn't anywhere close to what was needed for such a complicated ruse, but Click's plan made sense. "So we create a diversion. Make the Defiant think Veena is heading somewhere she isn't."

Click nodded.

"But how do we get away?"

After three sharp clicks, the green dots on Click's skin changed to purple.

"We hide when they capture *Buttercup* in their tractor beam. They pull us on board, search the ship, decide it's empty, and jettison it. Then we rejoin the others." Nigel smiled. Yes, this plan might just work.

Chapter Nineteen

Standing on the platform, Hwicce tried to orientate himself on the map. Rush hour was long over, leaving the tram station mostly empty.

Baker glanced down at the datapad Hwicce held and raised an eyebrow. "Are you sure that ancient thing is going to keep a charge?"

"I'm sure it's fine." Hwicce held up Darla's old datapad and compared the map it displayed to the list of tram stations posted on the wall.

"Your aunt was a hoarder. That model of datapad came out when I was ten."

Hwicce frowned and rotated the datapad until the stations lined up. "So you're a connoisseur of electronics now?"

She snorted. "I'm going to grab a taco."

A few minutes later, a tram pulled into the station, its brakes squealing as it came to a stop. Baker, still eating her taco, boarded first, and Hwicce followed her in. Even though it was nearly empty, the tram car stank of sour body odour. Against the walls, glittering pieces of Space Chew wrappers shone amongst the layer of litter. Cleanliness didn't seem to be a priority on Indigo Station's public transport. After stashing his datapad in a pocket, Hwicce grabbed onto one of the loops that hung from the ceiling.

Still eating her taco, Baker raised an eyebrow as she leaned into the tram's motion when it departed the station. "So... what exactly are you planning on doing when we get there?"

"We wait for Boris to show up, then follow him until we can corner him." Hwicce scratched the side of his neck. It sounded like a bad plan. No wonder Baker seemed sceptical.

"Okay, sir." Baker nodded, then frowned. She crumpled up the taco wrapper and stashed it in a pocket. "Once we got him, then what?"

"We ask him to explain why he sent the *Shimmer* into the *Garden Princess*." He pursed his lips together—his plan sucked.

Baker met his gaze as she wiped her hands on her pants. "Why in the hell would he tell us anything?"

"We can threaten that we'll report him to the authorities."

She drew her eyebrows together. "He'd just shift the blame to us."

Hwicce tried not to sigh. "It's a bluff."

"Right."

The tram slowed for their stop and exited into a cleaner section of the station. So few people milled about the space, he could make out the curve of the station. Shiny windows on both sides of the main concourse reflected the daylight lights above. A line of planters ran down the centre of the concourse, each one harbouring a single perfectly groomed conifer tree. Cleaner bots scooted out of their way, picking up any piece of debris within range.

Baker put one hand on her hip as she turned to Hwicce. "Well, this place is fancy."

"Keep an eye out for unit 106." Hwicce continued forward down the concourse. His plan was sketchy, but he needed to do something.

Long Enterprises was easy to find. Above its double set of

doors, an elegant sign labeled it. Hwicce leaned against the nearest planter and watched the entrance. Well-dressed people filed in and out, but none were Boris or his grandmother.

Beside him, Baker sighed. "I think this might be a bad plan."

"Why do you say that?"

"Cameras." Baker tilted her head towards the building.

Hwicce let his gaze follow the direction she indicated. Sure enough, there was a camera, and it appeared to be pointing at them. "Crap. How about we just go inside?"

Baker scowled. "That's fucking nuts. I'd rather just go for a beer."

Hwicce didn't answer. Instead, he strode through the double doors of Long Enterprises. Keeping further complaints to herself, Baker followed.

Inside was fancier than the exterior. A massive crystal chandelier hung above, casting glittering light over everything. The gleaming white floors seemed to be made of actual stone from a land-based quarry. A counter split the space in two; behind it was another set of double doors. Hints of something floral wafted through the air.

Hwicce went straight to the counter and leaned against it as though it was a bar. An impeccably dressed woman approached with a frown on her face. Her black jumpsuit fit her precisely, and her black hair was pulled back into a perfect chignon.

"May I help you?" she asked, raising a perfectly drawn-on eyebrow.

"I'd like to speak with Boris Long. My colleague"—Hwicce gestured towards Baker—"and I were among his crew on the *Shimmer*."

"Hmmm." The woman brought up a holographic display.

On Hwicce and Baker's side, the Long Enterprise's logo popped up. On her side, Hwicce assumed there was more info. She stared into the hologram and occasionally swiped. Her neutral expression soon sank into a frown.

"I don't see any record of such a ship in our database." With a hand gesture, the holographic display vanished. "What I do see is that station police wants the crew of the *Shimmer* for questioning."

"Dumbass," Baker said under her breath before turning her back to him.

"I see." Hwicce frowned; Baker was right. He needed to become better at nefarious plans. Bold army tactics weren't going to work in his new world.

He grabbed Baker's arm and turned. The two of them sprinted towards the door as the woman shouted something after them.

Outside, Hwicce walked at a brisk pace back towards the tram station. "You think she called security? Or the local cops?"

"I'm fucking sure she called someone the instant we walked in. This way." Instead of going into the tram station, Baker turned down an alley leading away from the fancy concourse. "Why in the bloody hell did you tell her we were on the *Shimmer*?"

"I don't know."

"There's fucking targets on our backs now." Baker extended her strides, forcing Hwicce to keep up with her.

They emerged into a new sector that wasn't anything like the business area they'd just left. A crowd of people in rough clothes waited outside a double set of doors, and Baker pulled Hwicce into the middle of them.

Baker turned to a labourer standing next to her. "Excuse me. Is this the lineup for the job?"

Hwicce looked at her and raised an eyebrow.

"I hear the indigo is ready for harvest; they need as many labourers as they can get," he said. "Seems it's worth more if they can claim it's hand-harvested."

"Oh good, we're in the right place." Baker smiled at the labourer. "Got any tips for the harvest?"

He frowned. "They pay by weight, so you're going to have

to figure that out on your own." He turned and moved a pace away.

Hwicce glanced over his shoulder as a pair of station police officers exited the alley they'd just left. His gut clenched; his 'dumb ass' plan might result in their arrest. He should've stayed on the *Virdis*.

At the front of the line, the double doors to the farm slid open, and the crowd started pushing inside as an earthy smell wafted out. Baker kept her head bent down to converse with the other labourer as she went with the crowd inside. Hwicce could see the police officers in his peripheral vision. They were scanning the crowd. Just as he wondered why they weren't using drones, a swarm of apple-sized ones flew into the space.

"Oh, crap. They'll have facial recognition technology," he said in a low tone to himself. He pulled his hood over his head and allowed himself to be pulled along with the crowd through the doors.

On the other side, the multi-level farm extended up several stories. Bright light illuminated the space at a level much greater than anywhere else he'd seen in the station so far. Like a Ferris wheel, long troughs slowly moved in a circle that extended up several stories towards bright lights on the ceiling.

Indigo plants filled the troughs, their ladder-like branches of leaves flowing over the sides. The pink flowers gave no hint of the colour of dye the plants ultimately produced.

"Sir." Baker appeared at his side. "Apparently, there's an exit to another concourse down here." She gestured to a gap between indigo troughs leading away from the others.

"They have surveillance drones." He glanced back at the doors. So far, none of the drones had come through.

"Even more reason to get the hell away from here," she said before heading down the path.

Pursing his lips together, Hwicce followed. He didn't see any cameras inside the farm, so hopefully, they could evade the police. There seemed to be a wide divide between the different concourses, some with more security than others.

Instead of an exit, they ended up in another vertical farm. Plants with tiny blue flowers filled these troughs. Like rain, the blue flowers drifted down, coating the floor and all the irrigation pipes. It was almost pretty; Molly would have loved the sight.

In a flurry of motion, Baker stopped and turned towards him. She wrapped her arms around his neck and kissed him. Hwicce froze.

"Get a room," shouted a woman from a higher level.

Baker pulled away and smiled at the woman. "I'm sorry. We seem to be lost."

"Bullshit," said the woman. "Now get the hell out of here." She pointed to a set of double doors at the other end of the space.

Hwicce wiped his hand over his face as he followed Baker out of the farm.

"What the hell was that?" he asked as they exited the farm and ended up in a busy concourse full of shops and restaurants. "I'm a married man." Above, there were apartments with laundry hanging off their balconies. He didn't see any surveillance drones or cameras.

Baker shrugged. "I didn't want her thinking we were running from something." She turned and looked at him. "Don't worry; you're not my type."

He raised an eyebrow. "Do you remember if there were cameras in the tram stations?"

"I'd be surprised if there weren't," she said, walking over to a noodle stand. She ordered ramen while Hwicce tried to make sense of the station map on his datapad.

"Looks like we're in for quite a walk."

"I can slurp and walk," Baker said as she shovelled a mouthful of noodles in.

Shaking his head, Hwicce started walking. "That was a complete waste of time."

"Well..." Baker slurped up another wad of noodles. "We now know to stay clear of the entire sector around Long Enterprises. And that, when Boris finds out we came by, he'll be staying away from the office too."

Hwicce sighed. "That doesn't help us one bit."

Chapter Twenty

Even after an uneventful tram ride, Veena couldn't shake her feeling of unease. Swa had sent a bounty hunter after her! She mulled over options as she followed Emiko through the cheery market.

High overhead light levels mimicked midday. Flowering trees filled the planters running down the centre of the concourse, their pale pink petals drifting down on the pedestrians below. No drying laundry showed from the balconies of the apartments above. That and the general cleanliness suggested they were in a wealthier neighbourhood.

"This way," Emiko directed as they passed a kiosk selling brightly coloured knit hats. She wove between several other kiosks, past a taco stand, and into a restaurant with a neon sign declaring it 'Aunt Em's Pies.' Selecting a booth with views of both outside and the door, Emiko sat down.

Veena glanced around. The homey decor and jewel-toned booths gave off a cozy air. At the back, a display of pies made her mouth water. With a sigh, she slid into the booth across from Emiko. "This place is nice."

"And they make the best pie."

As Veena stared at the door, she expected the bounty hunter to waltz through at any moment. Instead, all she saw was the taco stand and a flow of people just passing by.

"There's no way he could have followed us…." Emiko leaned in. "Even if he survived that fall."

Veena swallowed. "What if there are others? There could be an entire team of bounty hunters after us."

"Let's hang out here a while. Make sure no one else shows up. Then we'll head back to the ship. Hopefully, by then, they're ready to go."

Veena nodded.

"What would you two like?" a pudgy man in an apron asked.

"Do you have any apple pie?" Veena asked.

"Not after the problem at Red Apple Colony. But our cherry pie is fantastic," the waiter said.

"Sure. I'll have that and a coffee." Veena couldn't keep her eyes off the door. She had to force herself not to count the people walking by.

"Same for me," Emiko said. The waiter left the two of them alone. "Just play it cool."

"No one would ever accuse an egghead like me of being cool." Veena leaned back into the seat and forced herself to take deep breaths.

"Hwicce said you broke codes for the army." Emiko's expression suggested this was a well-planned conversation.

"Yeah." She let out a long exhale as she studied the other woman—she knew almost nothing about Emiko, except that Hwicce seemed to trust her. "They seconded me to Rock 13-A5 after the bombing of New Haven. Molly came with me."

"I'm sorry they took her." Emiko pulled herself up tall, as though fortifying herself. "I lost my parents as a baby, and I've always wondered about them. I wish they would have come looking for me like you and Hwicce are looking for Molly."

The waiter brought two mammoth slices of pie and

steaming mugs of coffee. After setting everything on the table, he left.

Veena picked up a fork and took a bite. The sweet cherry flavour burst through her mouth—the pie was indeed fantastic. "Did family take you in?"

Emiko shook her head before she took a bite of her pie. "I grew up as a ward of Indigo Station. I don't even have a last name." Her tough demeanour suddenly seemed only a veneer.

"I'm sorry to hear that."

"You see.…" Emiko's words trailed off, and she sighed. She looked down at her pie. "Hwicce said you might.…"

Veena paused with her fork of pie halfway to her face and cocked her head. "What did he say I might do?"

"You see, they messed up the records where I was born. Maybe if you looked.…"

"You want me to see if I can find out if you have family?"

Emiko nodded.

"Sure, I can do that. Orin is also good at finding that kind of thing out; I'm sure he'd help too. If there's information out there, we'll find it."

Emiko grinned and put a huge forkful of pie in her mouth. "That would be great."

"A simple DNA test might also provide some clues." Veena finished her pie and picked up her mug, wrapping both hands around the ceramic surface. She was half-tempted to order more pie.

"I never could afford that. That's why I took work on the freighters."

"I wouldn't be surprised if the *Virdis* has the right equipment for that kind of analysis," Veena said.

"Now you're sounding like an egghead." Emiko smiled.

"I warned you." Veena smiled back. The problem of Emiko's identity was a welcome distraction—a nice solvable problem.

Emiko lifted another forkful of pie to her mouth, then froze.

"What is it?" Veena followed the other woman's gaze.

A short, fleshy man was ordering food from the taco stand. He didn't look threatening or even aware of their presence.

"Is he someone you know?" Veena slid a little lower in her seat, just in case.

"Boris Long." Emiko put her still-loaded fork back down on her plate.

"Your captain on the *Shimmer*?"

"That's him. That asshole tried to kill thousands of people and left us for dead." Emiko pressed her lips together as she kept her gaze fixed on Boris.

As Boris took his box of tacos from the kiosk operator, Emiko stood. Without a word, she left.

"Wait! Where…." Veena's words trailed off, and she frowned. Emiko wouldn't hear her now.

Veena watched as she trailed Boris. A moment later, the two of them disappeared into the crowd. She took a deep breath and glanced around the pie shop. She was alone now. Even if she followed, she was certain she wouldn't find Emiko.

She took another sip of her coffee and considered her options.

She couldn't go directly back to *Buttercup*. Likely she'd been reported as travelling on that ship. If there were other bounty hunters, they'd probably be keeping watch there. But it did not link her to *Virdis*.

First, she needed to obscure herself—not to hide from any facial recognition systems out there. She wouldn't be able to do that, but she might throw off any bounty hunters doing a visual search.

Removing her scarf, she interfaced it with her datapad. She changed the hue from abstract greens to a soft pink paisley pattern. Then she took her hair down from its ponytail and combed it out with her fingers. She tied the scarf over her head and under her chin. Next, she took off the khaki jacket she'd been wearing and turned it inside out. The lining was maroon. She put it back on.

Her stomach was quivering now; the thought of making her way to *Virdis* on her own when there might be bounty hunters out there looking for her left her nerves frayed. But maybe Emiko was right, and there had been only one, and they'd defeated him.

After paying for the pie and coffee, she left the shop.

***

Veena let out a sigh as she found *Virdis* was exactly where it was supposed to be. Without slowing, she went on board. Orin greeted her in the cavernous cargo bay.

"Just bringing on more supplies," he said as he moved a pallet of boxes with a pallet jack. He pushed the pallet next to another under the stairs before turning to her. "Made sure we're well supplied with coffee. So no more fucking mint tea for us."

Veena smiled as the tension drained out of her. She felt safe. "Sometimes, I just want a mug of mint tea to calm my nerves."

"In that case, I'll transfer some from *Buttercup*. We have enough for years of soothing frayed nerves." He put his hands on his hips and looked around. "This is quite the ship. It's going to take some getting used to having so much space. Here Baker and Emiko can have their own room and spare us from witnessing too much of their budding relationship."

"We won't have to hear them kissing."

"Exactly. Did you find what you were looking for? It was a thrift store you were going to, right?"

"Well...." Veena frowned.

"Your expression tells me you have a story to tell. How about we go to the common room?"

"Sure." Veena followed Orin up the stairs, down the very ordinary main hall, and into a large space.

She stopped dead in her tracks and gasped. A three-story garden dominated the space. It needed some work, but the bones were fantastic. A thick grove of bamboo filled one end, and a few trees were peppered around the rest of the space, leaving enough room for shrubs and plants between them. In the middle, a column with a circumference over three times her arm span rose to the ceiling filled with apple green algae, no doubt filtering their air.

Several rooms opened out into the garden, including a dining area and a space filled with a large sectional sofa in the shape of a U. With some work, this place would be nicer than her home on New Haven.

Orin gestured to the sofa, and Veena sat down.

"There are cabins on the level above." He pointed up as he sat across from her. "All of them need cleaning out and a coat of paint, but otherwise, they're pretty nice."

"I think we can make this place work," Veena said.

Orin nodded. "What did you find at the thrift shop?"

Veena relayed everything that happened, from receiving the artifact to escaping the bounty hunter and finally, how Emiko ran off after Boris.

When she finished, she pulled out the object the proprietor had given her at the Summer's End Thrift Shop and turned it over in her hands.

"Any thoughts on what that might be?"

"I have no idea," she said as she continued to stare at it.

The object was a dull grey hexagonal prism about the size of her palm, and it rose about two centimetres. Across all the surfaces, more hexagons were etched. It felt like metal, yet it was warmer than she would have expected.

"It could be an alien artifact," Orin said. "You could try asking Click."

Veena ran her thumb across the surface. "I saw something at the thrift store." She bit her lip. "I think it was another alien, but this one was much bigger. And kinda scary—yet I think I've been corresponding with them for years."

Orin stared at her. "Were they the same type as Click?"

Veena shrugged. "Maybe." She licked her lips. "There can't be too many types of tentacled aliens around, can there?"

"I suppose not. And they gave that to you?"

"Yes. Then when the bounty hunter attacked, they bought us enough time to escape." She continued flipping the object in her hand. Veena frowned. "I feel guilty for leaving them behind. I really hope they're okay."

"Can you just message them and ask?"

Veena nodded as she set down the object on the coffee table.

Orin leaned in to get a better look. "I assume this object is important."

"Yeah, but I don't know what it is."

Orin picked it up just as Hwicce and Baker came in with frowns on their faces.

"Any luck?" Orin asked as Hwicce sunk onto the sofa beside Veena.

"No," Hwicce grumbled.

"It was a fucking waste of time." Baker paced for a moment, then stopped. "Where's Em?"

"She…." Veena paused as Baker turned on her. "She spotted Boris Long at a taco stand and followed him."

"She went alone?" Baker raised an eyebrow.

Veena shrugged. "She just left."

"Great." Baker slumped down on the sofa. "What the hell do we do now?"

A chime sounded from Veena's datapad. She opened the device. "It's from Emiko." Baker and Hwicce leaned forward. "It's an address."

Chapter Twenty-One

Nigel stared at the *Defiant* looming off their bow, like a whale about to devour them. The sharp lines and clean angles gave the battlecruiser an angry look. To make matters worse, the matte grey of its hull didn't pick up reflections from the system's suns. The ship lacked any hint of elegance. He frowned while forcing his pixels to stay together.

"You sure this is a good idea?" He looked down at Click.

Click made a pop sound, then flushed the same grey as the ship's hull.

"Right, I guess we can't escape their tractor beam." Nigel bit his lip and ignored how his hands glitched in and out of view. "It's too late then. We have no choice but to go through with your plan."

The *Defiant* pulled *Buttercup* into its massive hangar. Click extended the landing gear just as their ship was set down. This time, a platoon of armed guards greeted them with their weapons at the ready.

Click changed to the same yellow of the ship's interior.

"Right, we're hiding." Nigel released his pixels and went invisible.

Moments later, soldiers stormed the ship. Their boots clunked on the metal deck as they searched every nook and cranny. One of them shouted all clear, and General Swa strode in.

As she looked around, she held her nose high as though she'd detected a foul odour. The rich indigo of Swa's uniform made *Buttercup's* yellow interior appear dingy. She picked up a *Bubble and Click* comic from the table and stared at it for a moment before tossing it down. She put her hands on her hips and turned to the waiting lead soldier.

"This is definitely their ship."

"That's correct, ma'am," the lead soldier said, her face invisible beneath maroon combat armour.

"But no one's here."

"Yes, ma'am."

As Swa slowly turned around, Nigel noted Click had fixed themselves to the ceiling directly above Swa's head.

Swa glared at the soldier. "Have you scanned the ship for life forms?"

"No, ma'am," the soldier said. "We'll do that now."

Two other soldiers entered the space with what looked like long wands. One proceeded to the bridge while the other remained in the common room and waved their device around.

Nigel clenched his invisible hands together and considered turning himself off altogether. His algorithms weren't designed for this level of stress.

As one soldier waved the wand along the common room ceiling, Nigel put all his processing power towards figuring out how to create a distraction. If only he had access to the ship's system—but he didn't. He almost called out when the soldier with the wand shifted position.

The soldier swept the wand across the ceiling right under Click. A light on the side of the instrument flashed red. Click flushed the same red as the soldier jammed the wand their way.

Click cried for help over their link with Nigel, and Nigel's code nearly crashed. Tendrils of blue light extended from the wand into Click, and the little alien lost their grip on the ceiling and fell to the deck.

Unable to figure out a better solution, Nigel reformed the image of himself. "Don't hurt them!" He approached Swa.

"Interesting." Swa cocked her head as she studied Nigel. Then she bent down to look at the now inert form of Click. "Looks like I've found Greer's missing subject." Swa poked Click.

"Please don't." Nigel clasped his hands together. "They're a sentient being."

Swa stood. "And what kind of code are you?"

Nigel took a step back and adjusted his cravat. "Nigel 378, formerly of the *Garden Princess*."

"A steward AI?"

"That was my original function."

"Interesting." Swa looked him in the eye. "But Dr. Oswiu reprogrammed you."

Nigel didn't want to answer, but he saw no other choice— besides, lying and deception were not part of his base algorithms. "I've been functioning as the alien's translator."

"Hmmm." Swa glanced down at the alien and licked her lips. "Dr. Greer is going to be very interested in meeting you. Is your code in this ship's system?" She gestured upwards.

"No, madam. My entire code is in Click's band."

Swa bent slightly and studied the band metal band around Click's neck. "How convenient."

"Yes."

Swa turned to the soldier. "Load the alien into a box, then jettison this hunk of junk." She gestured to the ship they were in. "Better yet, booby trap it."

"Yes, ma'am," the soldier said.

Swa smiled as she watched the soldier transfer the alien into a box.

"What did they used to call those things?" Swa asked. "When fried up as a dish on Old Earth."

None of the soldiers answered her.

"Calamari," Nigel said in a flat tone.

Swa smiled. "Yes, that's it. I heard it was tasty." She turned. "I'm going to call Dr. Greer."

Chapter Twenty-Two

Wearing a new set of clothing scrounged from one of the cabins on *Virdis,* Hwicce consulted the datapad's map to confirm where Emiko waited for them—so far, every station had looked the same to him. A few minutes later, their tram pulled into the next station, and the other passengers disembarked.

Beside him, Baker wore a long blond wig and a red jacket. The light hair made a sharp contrast with her dark skin. Somewhere she'd found lipstick the same shade as her jacket. The overall effect was rather garish. She glared at anyone who even looked her way.

Hwicce glanced down at himself and realized he didn't look any less foolish. Veena had dyed his hair purple, and he'd shaved off his beard. The clothing he'd found was the same purple, making him look like a comic book villain. They may not be recognized for being wanted, but they would get noticed. And his shirt itched.

"This has to be our stop."

Baker nodded, and they left the tram. Outside the station, they entered a posh residential area.

Emiko materialized out of the crowd and smirked. "You two look ridiculous. Your outfits are so bad, they're great."

Baker held out a bright yellow trench coat. "I thought you should match."

With a snort, Emiko took the coat and put it on. "Boris' apartment is just down there." She pointed to the left side of the concourse. "Unit 151."

"And he's home?" Hwicce ran a hand over his cleanly shaved face, noticing the smoothness of his skin.

"Unless he has a backdoor," Emiko said in a flat tone. "Can your wife hack his locks?"

Hwicce frowned; Veena would hate doing that—except that it might get them clues to where Molly was. "I'll ask." He sent her a message over the datapad. A few moments later, she responded. "She added my thumbprint to the biometric lock."

"Then let's go." Emiko headed down the concourse, and the others followed.

At the door, Hwicce held his breath as he let the lock scan his thumb. A light flashed green, and the door slid open. The three of them hurried inside.

Boris' apartment was a multi-story luxury affair. In the foyer, the floor appeared to be made of stone, and a glittery chandelier hung from above as though the same designer who had worked on the Long Enterprise's office had designed this space too. Directly in front of them, a curved set of stairs led to the second story, from where an off-key song occasionally rose above the sound of running water.

Taking care to not make a sound as he crossed the floor, Hwicce gestured the others to follow him up the stairs. On the second story, he followed the sound of running water to a bedroom. The door stood open, so he slipped inside.

The expensive decor had been overlaid with dirty clothing and half-eaten takeout food—reminiscent of Boris' cabin on the *Shimmer*. Hwicce focused on the open ensuite door; steam from the shower billowed out, along with more terrible singing.

Emiko tapped his arm and pointed at the bedside table. A pistol sat beside an open taco box. After gesturing for Baker to guard the door, Hwicce walked over, picked up the pistol, and checked its status. The weapon only had a half-charge, but it would do.

The shower stopped, but the singing continued. Hwicce handed the pistol off to Emiko, then moved over next to the bathroom door. Wearing only a towel wrapped around his hips, Boris waltzed out of the bathroom. He froze when he spotted Emiko levelling a pistol at him.

"Remember me?" Emiko spoke through clenched teeth.

Boris' jaw dropped open. His eyes darted between Hwicce and Emiko.

"You left us to fucking die." Emiko took a step towards him.

Boris raised his hands, shaking his head. "No, no, no, that's not how it happened at all."

Hwicce stepped forward and slapped Boris on the shoulder. "We have proof, Boris." He hoped Boris wouldn't call their bluff. "We can prove you set a collision course with the *Garden Princess* on purpose. If that gets to the authorities...."

"No. No, please don't."

"Even your grandmother wouldn't be able to keep you out of jail," Emiko said.

"I can't, can't go to jail." Boris bit his lip and looked from Emiko to Hwicce. "I just can't."

"Then we need you to answer some questions," Hwicce said.

"Okay."

"What kind of facility was your grandmother building on Hamber's Hole?"

"I don't know...."

"Emiko, send the files to station security," Hwicce said.

Emiko gave a curt nod and pulled out her datapad with her free hand.

"No, you can't do that. Please...." Boris went redder than before. "I'll tell you what I know."

"Go ahead," Hwicce said.

"Long Enterprises set up that facility to work on genetic engineering of humans."

Hwicce frowned. "But that's against the GenEn protocols."

"I know, but.…" Boris grimaced. "I shouldn't tell you this, but new information has come to light about enhancing humans using some ancient alien technology."

Hwicce cocked his head.

"Sounds ridiculous, I know. But the scientists on Vortex View have done it." Boris took a deep breath. "Someone with the right base genetics can be turned into a super-soldier."

Hwicce said nothing; he'd faced one of those soldiers on the battlefield at Candy Cane Lane and barely survived. Dread filled him as he realized that might be why they'd taken Molly—Did she have the right genetics to be turned into a super-soldier? He swallowed.

"I really don't know how it all works," Boris said, filling the silence.

"Where else are they doing this work?" Hwicce asked.

"I don't know." Boris bit his lip. "Honest, I don't."

Baker stuck her head back into the room. "We should get out of here."

Hwicce nodded. Something wasn't sitting right with him. Long Enterprises was aiming to get rich off some alien technology, and human gene editing made sense in a corrupt-capitalist-kind-of-way. But what did that have to do with a luxury liner?

Hwicce met Boris' gaze. "Why destroy the *Garden Princess*?"

Boris opened and closed his mouth like a fish. He looked from Hwicce to Emiko, then to the door where Baker stood. "I...I... never asked."

Emiko stalked forward and poked Boris in the chest. "You were willing to murder thousands without question?"

Boris backed up a pace and lost his grip on his towel. It fell to the floor, and he didn't seem to notice. His lower lip quivered.

Hwicce cocked his head. "You truly don't know?"

Boris shook his head.

"He doesn't know shit." Emiko turned to Hwicce. "Let's get out of here."

"Boris, where can we find Pam Long?" Hwicce put a hard edge to his words—the kind of tone that had made his soldiers rush to comply.

"Grandma left for New Venus this morning," Boris said. "There's an auction.…"

"Auction?" Hwicce ignored Boris' nakedness and stalked towards him.

"Yes." Boris licked his lips as he looked up at Hwicce. "At the Department of Curiosities. They're auctioning off some alien artifacts, and there's one Grandma wants."

Hwicce crossed his arms over his chest. "Do you know what she's after?"

"I don't know. I never thought she was interested in alien archeology." Boris shrugged.

Hwicce turned away from Boris. "Let's get out of here,"

Emiko nodded and backed towards the door, keeping the blaster levelled at Boris.

Hwicce turned on Boris. "Go back into the bathroom and lock the door."

Boris grimaced. He turned and bolted inside; the door slid shut behind him.

"There'll be a comms terminal in there," Baker said from the door. "No doubt there's a security station nearby."

"Right, let's go." Hwicce started walking.

Emiko stashed the blaster in her coat. "We'll be easy to describe."

"So we should've brought a second disguise?" Hwicce's gut churned as it dawned on him that they might not get away.

"Good plan, sir." Baker stripped off her blonde wig and red jacket. Emiko nodded and removed the yellow trench coat. As quick as he could, Hwicce stripped off the purple suit and dressed in a tracksuit out of Boris' drawer. Emiko found a hoodie with a kangaroo pocket and pulled it on. She stashed the pistol in the front pocket.

The three of them left the apartment and started walking briskly towards the tram station just as a wave of surveillance drones came down the concourse from the tram station.

"Crap." Hwicce started glancing around to see if any of the other apartment doors were open.

"We can't outrun them, but maybe I can shoot them down." Emiko pulled out the pistol before Hwicce could stop her.

Baker grabbed the weapon out of her hand. "You two, run. I'll be the distraction."

Hwicce froze. He weighed the distance between the nearest drone and the tram station. "That's nuts. We have to surrender." Veena was going to be mad at him. His gut continued to churn.

"No, the two of you can still get away. Go now."

"That's crazy hero shit." Emiko gazed up at Baker, her eyes wide.

Baker grabbed Emiko around the waist and pulled her in close. "That's what I do, sweetheart."

As soon as it looked like the two of them would kiss, Hwicce averted his gaze.

"No, go." Baker released Emiko and pushed her away.

Hwicce turned to Baker. "You're not going to escape."

"True, but they won't shoot to kill. I'll just get arrested. I expect you to bail me out."

Emiko cocked her head slightly. "I expect to see you later."

"It's a date." Baker grinned as she took a pace towards the approaching drones.

Hwicce pursed his lips, then turned and started walking in the opposite direction. Emiko fell into step beside him. Behind, weapons fire sounded, and drones hit the ground. He wanted to turn and help his friend, but he followed her wishes and kept walking.

Chapter Twenty-Three

Veena paced back and forth across the common room. Mulling over the possibilities of the garden space no longer kept her distracted. Hwicce, Baker, and Emiko weren't back yet, and it had been at least an hour since she'd helped them get through that door.

She headed into the apartment she'd selected for Hwicce and herself and, ultimately, Molly. The previous occupant's odd collection of abandoned belongings were strewn around the series of three rooms. In the living room, Veena stopped and put her hands on her hips.

"I should start organizing." She picked up a pair of men's pj pants and held them up. They would probably fit Hwicce. With a sigh, she sunk down onto the nearest chair. Cleaning up their quarters was only a distraction—and the distraction wasn't working. Out there somewhere, Hwicce was chasing down the guy who'd destroyed the *Garden Princess*.

"What if he needs my help?"

Dropping the clothing on the floor, she headed up to the captain's office. Head bent over a screen, Orin sat behind the massive wooden desk. He glanced up when Veena flopped down onto the now cleared-off sofa.

"What's on your mind?" Orin asked.

"They're overdue, and I'm worried."

He scratched his head. "Yes, of course. They should've been back by now. But I'm sure they're fine. Otherwise, they would've called."

Veena nodded as she counted the scattered takeout ketchup packs on the floor under the coffee table—thirteen. She took a deep breath. "You're right—they would've called."

"The good news is, our departure permit came in. We're all set to go as soon as they get back."

"That is good news."

"Why don't you have the ship's AI scan that artifact Theo65 gave you? There might be a record in a public database somewhere."

Veena pulled out the artifact and set it on the coffee table in front of her. "I'll link through my datapad." She used a subroutine to scan *Virdis'* computer system just to get an idea of what she was working with. The memory banks were just as messy as the office she sat in. She scratched her head as she tried to make sense of what she was looking at.

Orin stood and came around the desk. He sat on the sofa next to her. "You look perplexed."

"I can't find anything on the ship's computer beyond an autopilot sub-routine. That's odd."

Orin raised an eyebrow. "Odd how?"

"There's no level three AI on this ship."

"Hwicce said its name was GRUB. Even Max referenced it," Orin said.

"I don't see any sub-routines for it. They must have been mistaken."

"A ship this size can't run without one." Orin's expression became more serious. "If we can't install one in short order, we'll have to have someone with the 'right' qualifications on the bridge at all times—and I suspect none of us have the 'right' qualifications."

Veena snorted. "Plus, I don't think we have the funds to purchase that kind of AI." She gestured to the room. "Unless we can sell some of this junk."

"I'm sure there are some gems in here, but selling would take time," Orin said.

"Ugh, why do things keep getting more complicated?" Veena forcefully exhaled and put her hands over her face. "I don't want Molly to wait."

"I have an idea. How about you install Nigel to run the ship?"

Veena shook her head. "Nigel is only a level 2 AI. His algorithms aren't sophisticated enough to run a ship."

"GRUB?" Orin glanced up.

"How may I help you, Dr. Akton?" an androgynous voice answered.

Orin and Veena exchanged a look.

Veena stood and started pacing across the office. "What is your AI classification?"

"I am a level 5 shipmaster," the voice said. "My algorithms are authorized to autonomously run this ship. I have the 'right' qualifications."

She ran a hand over her head and down her ponytail. "Why can't I see you when I look at the ship's computers?"

"My base code is behind a firewall as a protection against malevolent cyber attack."

Veena scratched her head. "That doesn't seem right." She looked at Orin, who shrugged.

"I have analyzed your object," the AI said. "It is an alien data-drive collected on the anchor world in the Juliette System."

Veena sat back down and picked up the brassy hexagon plate. She turned it over in her hands. "I've never heard of alien objects like these. All I've seen are the rock carvings."

"The Juliette System is part of the Nader Alliance," Orin said, leaning in to get a closer look at the object. "How did Theo65 get their hands on it?"

"Theo65 is resourceful," GRUB said.

"Wait a minute. GRUB, did you just suggest this is a computer?" She held it up as if GRUB needed to see it again.

"Affirmative. However, it is incomplete."

Veena studied the object and didn't see any place another object could connect to it. She didn't even see any hint it was a computer. "I don't see how this is going to help us." She put it down on the coffee table and leaned back into the sofa's cushions.

"The missing component is going on auction at the Department of Curiosities on New Venus in two days," GRUB said.

"Is that on one of the Seven Soaring Swans islands?" Orin asked.

"Affirmative."

"Mary always wanted to have one of her statues on display there."

Veena nodded as she pondered GRUB's suggestion. Getting their hands on the other component of this supposed 'alien computer' could give them a bargaining chip.

"GRUB, what does this computer do?"

"I don't know," GRUB said with a slightly sad twinge to their voice. Veena shook her head—she shouldn't apply emotion to the AI.

"Could it decode the alien text you've been working on?" Orin asked.

"Which text is this?" GRUB asked.

Veena felt her forehead wrinkle as she tried to work out if going for the second piece of the supposed alien computer was a good idea or not. A niggling sense in the back of her mind told her it was all connected, but she couldn't prove it. She sighed.

"I have copies of text found on at least two different anchor worlds."

"And you wish to know what the text says?" GRUB seemed overly curious for a computer. Veena pursed her lips and considered if she should answer.

Before Veena said anything, Hwicce and Emiko burst into the office. Veena stood at the sight of her husband. He looked so different without the beard—younger, more like the man she met in university.

"They got Baker," Hwicce said between breaths.

Veena cocked her head. "The Longs? I knew getting you into that apartment was a bad idea."

Shaking his head, Hwicce sat down. "No, no, no. She's been arrested." He ran a hand through his hair. "But you're right. Breaking into that apartment was a bad idea."

"We need to bail her out." Emiko crossed her arms over her chest and leaned against the wall beside the door.

"Right. Have they posted bail?" Orin asked as he returned to the chair behind the desk.

"Hang on," Veena pulled out her datapad. "Let's start by confirming they got her." She accessed the station police public network.

It listed the names of everyone in holding. Baker's name was there, and the pending charges were breaking and entering, assault, and damaging station police equipment.

Veena's heart sank. "She's got an appointment with a judge tomorrow."

"Our departure window is this afternoon," Orin said. "If we miss it, there's a penalty."

Emiko stood up straight and clenched her fists at her sides. "We can't just leave her."

"No one's suggesting that," Hwicce said.

Veena set her datapad down and looked at Emiko. "Baker's entitled to see her lawyer."

Emiko groaned. "I don't know any lawyers here."

"I think Orin would make a believable lawyer," Veena said, and Orin groaned. "I can forge some credentials."

"Okay, say I get in to see her, then what?" Orin asked.

"Then you break her out."

Chapter Twenty-Four

Orin swallowed as he left the *Virdis*. His route to the police station was already mapped on his datapad. As he wound his way through the crowds heading to the tram, he went over the plan. First, he needed to plug Veena's the datapad into a direct port within the station—that should get her access behind the firewall. That he could do. The rest of the plan terrified him.

It was the afternoon end-of-shift rush now—meaning their departure window closed in less than an hour. Time was running out. *Virdis* would leave as scheduled. He and Baker would take *Buttercup* and catch up. It could work, except....

He tried not to think of all the ways his plan could go wrong as he stepped onto the tram. He would rescue Baker, and that would be that.

Tucked into a corner of one of the middle-class residential concourses right outside the tram station sat the single police station. The home-going crowd flowed past him as he stopped to stare at the entrance. Nothing about the police station appeared fortified—a good sign. He licked his lips and strode inside.

No one even checked his credentials. Instead, a uniformed police officer showed him right to Baker's the holding cell.

Baker came to the energy barrier separating her cell from the corridor. "Orin?"

"You have ten minutes," the police officer said.

"Thank you, Officer," Orin said as she left him alone with Baker.

"Tell me you have a plan, little man. I can't stay trapped like this."

Orin looked around. Cells similar to Baker's lined both sides of the corridor, their shimmering translucent blue walls keeping the criminals inside. Closed doors blocked both ends of the corridor.

He met Baker's gaze and shrugged. "It's not so bad here."

"One cop came by with homemade cupcakes," she said through clenched teeth.

"The horror." Orin continued to scan for a data access port but didn't see one.

"I had to play nice and accept his bloody chocolate banana creation. He'd even decorated it with icing." Baker sat back down on the cot as though traumatized.

Orin frowned. His rescue attempt was going to fail without a port. "I'll be right back."

He turned and headed back the way he'd come. Past the security doors, he found the entrance to a break room. Inside, three plainclothes police officers sat eating cupcakes.

"Excuse me," Orin said as he stepped inside.

The three police officers' heads swivelled to stare at him. A short man with wide shoulders stood and approached with a smile.

"Aren't you Miss Baker's lawyer?"

"That's correct." Orin ran a hand down his pants to wipe the sweat off his palms. "I've encountered a technical glitch in recording her plea. Do you have a data port where I can plug in my datapad so my assistant back at the office can troubleshoot?"

"Sure thing." The cop pointed to a port in the wall beside a table filled with colourful cupcakes.

Orin nodded and walked over. As the cops watched, he plugged the datapad.

"What was Baker thinking when she broke into Boris Long's home?" asked one of the cops still sitting.

Orin's hands shook as he started at Veena's code. "It's best I don't discuss my client's motives."

"Sure," she said. "I hear Long Enterprises' lawyers are going to throw the book at Baker and not even offer her a deal to give up her accomplices."

A progress bar appeared on Orin's screen.

"That's interesting," said the standing cop as he looked over Orin's shoulder at his screen. "I don't recognize your diagnostic software."

Orin could feel sweat forming on his brow. "Um… it's custom software my assistant wrote."

"Cool. Do you want a cupcake?" The cop lifted a plate of cupcakes and offered it to Orin. "I made them this morning."

The progress bar reached 100%.

"Those look great, but no, thank you. I need to get back to my client."

"Sure thing." The police officer took a cupcake and devoured half of it on the way back to his seat.

With his gut churning, Orin retreated out of the break room, closing the door behind himself. "How long will this take?" he asked himself as he stood alone in the hallway.

With a pop, all the lights went out, plunging Orin into inky darkness. A moment later, emergency lights running along the floor blinked to life, giving off barely enough light to see by.

Orin scratched his head. "Is this part of the plan?" Veena hadn't mentioned a power outage.

Pounding from the break room door drew his attention. He turned and stared at it. The lock had activated, trapping the three cops inside. He reached forward to unlock the door, then stopped himself. This had to be Veena's doing.

"Come on, little man," Baker said as she grabbed his upper arm and pulled him along.

"What?" Orin turned to stare at Baker—then he realized they weren't alone. A crowd now surrounded him. "We've let everyone out."

The escaping prisoners hooted and cheered as they pushed their way through the police station. Baker pulled him along.

"This isn't good," Orin said as they passed through the waiting room and out of the station.

"We gotta keep going before the cops start rounding folks up." Baker kept dragging him on.

"Did we really let everyone out?"

"Hell yeah. It's a full-on prison break." At Baker's words, a bear of a man beside her let out a cheer.

Once outside the station, the prisoners dispersed into the crowd of passing pedestrians. Orin and Baker walked down the concourse at a brisk but not-too-brisk pace.

"We need to get to *Buttercup*," Orin explained as they got on the first tram that arrived.

"Right." Baker nodded. "Once the cops get their shit together, they'll use facial recognition technology to hunt for me, and now probably you."

"Then we keep moving." Orin tried to sound more confident than he felt. "And hope we get there before we're recognized."

Orin and Baker stayed near the doors as the tram smoothly pulled away from the station. Orin couldn't help but study the crowd, looking at each face and wondering if they were on to him. He and Baker needed to stay on the tram to go halfway around the station to reach *Buttercup's* berth.

At the first stop, a flow of people got off, and new people got on. They pulled away again without incident. Orin released a breath he didn't realize he'd been holding.

"We're going to make it," he whispered in Baker's ear.

She just looked at him and raised an eyebrow.

They passed the next three stations with no issue. The tram was more crowded now, standing room only. People jostled and pressed against them as the tram continued on.

When Orin thought his nerves were frayed to the maximum, they pulled into the public harbour station—their stop. Baker strode off the tram as though no one was after her, and Orin followed in her wake. He envied her confidence as he continued scanning the crowd with every step. His worry was making him sick to his stomach. Would the station police be waiting for them at *Buttercup's* door?

"Well... shit." Baker stopped.

"What?" Orin's heart thumped in his chest. He swung around, looking for approaching cops. "What?"

"*Buttercup's* gone." She pointed to the berth where they'd parked his little ship. It was empty.

Orin's jaw dropped. How could it be gone? They'd paid their berthing fees for twenty-four hours.

Baker scowled, then grabbed his arm. "No use standing out in the open." She pulled him with her into the Home Brew coffee shop across from where they'd parked *Buttercup.* She took him to a seat in the back and ordered a full breakfast from the server drone.

Orin slid into the seat across from her and messaged Veena. The *Virdis* had already slipped its docking clamps—and they didn't have any shuttles to send back for them. His hands trembled as he studied his datapad.

As Baker's food arrived, Orin tracked the *Virdis'* most logical path around the station. The behemoth would still be going slow.

He scratched his head as he stared at the nearest airlock. They wouldn't have much more time until the police found them. Commandeering a spacecraft wasn't an option. No doubt, the police would watch the passenger queues at the ferries and passenger liners. But even if they got on a passenger ship, then what?

His gaze remained on that airlock. He had a bad idea—a very, very bad idea.

"Cops," Baker said between mouthfuls. "They've just gone to where *Buttercup* was parked."

Orin craned his neck to look. Two uniformed officers were talking to a harbour official at the berth. Above, a swarm of police drones fanned out and started scanning the crowd. It was only a matter of time before they were spotted.

"I have a bad plan," Orin said.

Baker wiped her face with her sleeve. She met his gaze and grinned. "I love a bad plan."

"We go out the airlock here." He pushed his datapad into the centre of the table and pointed. "And have the *Virdis* do a second rotation around the station and pick us up."

Baker frowned. "I think you're missing a few steps, but we gotta get going." She paid for her food and stood.

Orin messaged Veena and told them of the plan. He stood, keeping his eyes fixed on the cops outside. So far, none of the drones had entered the diner. "Is there a backdoor?"

"Follow me." Baker headed for the kitchen door, and Orin stayed right behind her.

"You can't be in here," a cook said, looking up from the grill.

Baker ignored him and pushed past, heading to the back door. On the other side was a utility hall running parallel to the docks on the other side of the shops.

Orin checked his map. "This way," he said as he started walking.

The utility hall let them out right next to the tram station. Orin looked both ways. No police were on the platform, but in the distance, a drone systematically scanned the passing people.

"How far to the airlock?" Baker asked.

Orin glanced down at his datapad. "The public access one is at the next station. Otherwise, there are only the escape pods."

"So, we ride the tram." Baker strode out onto the platform.

Stifling a groan, Orin followed. "We can't stay here," he said as he reached her. "They'll find us for sure. And we can't take the tram; they'll be scanning those."

"Shit," Baker said as a tram raddled to a stop at the platform. People pressed on and off, then a warning bell announced the tram's imminent departure. "How far to the next station?"

"About 500 metres," Orin answered as the tram pulled away.

"Then we run." Baker jumped down off the platform and onto the tracks. She started running in the direction the tram went.

"Damn," Orin said as he hopped down, ignoring the bystanders' comments of concern. He ran after her—the first time he'd run in years.

Chapter Twenty-Five

Emiko paced back and forth across the common room. From the sunken U-shaped sofa to the kitchen and back, then back and forth again.

"Fucking hell, I can't just stay here and do nothing." She clenched her fists at her side as heat rose up her face. "I can't believe I just let Hwicce leave B behind. She's...." Her words trailed off as she stopped and scrunched up her face.

What was B to her? She put a hand over her heart and sighed. B was someone she hadn't expected to meet, and she could be everything. Her place could be here with B. She surveyed the untended garden space and let her eyes land on the door to her apartment.

"And here I am doing nothing."

"What do you mean, doing nothing?" a male voice said behind her.

Emiko spun around. Max, the engineer, stood in the open door to the hall. He smiled at her, a smile that contained hints of a sneer.

"Is that what you do? Lurk?"

He shrugged. "This is the common room; I have every right to come in here."

"Don't you have engines to check? We'll be leaving at any minute."

"Why are you stomping about talking to yourself?"

She snorted and looked him up and down. The green hues of his skin looked out of place. "None of your damn business."

"Right then, your majesty, I'll grab my snack and get out of your hair." Max sauntered into the kitchen and started rooting through the cupboards.

Emiko glanced back at the door to the apartment she'd selected. All she had to do now was invite B to share it with her. At the thought, her heart raced. It was a bold move, living together—especially since they'd only known each other for a few days.

"By the way, if you're really doing nothing, I could use a hand—assuming you'll lower yourself to get your hands dirty," Max said from the kitchen. "Also, I saw cookies in the supplies. Where'd they get stashed?"

Emiko took a step towards him. He was the ship's engineer —a role she'd always pictured taking on, especially since she'd left Indigo Station. If there really was a place for her on this ship, she should make sure she could be useful.

"They're in the top right cupboard," she said.

He opened that cupboard, and a box of cookies fell out and hit him on the head. "Ah, excellent!" He picked up the package and turned towards her without bothering to close the cupboard door.

He met her gaze and raised an eyebrow. "So, are you coming with me or what?"

"Sure," she said.

With a curt nod, Max left the common room and headed aft. Emiko followed.

In the engine control room, Max tossed the cookie package onto a workbench already covered in food packages. Emiko bit her lip and tried to ignore the mess. Instead, she wandered to the far side of the room. Floor-to-ceiling windows gave her a view of the massive engines on the other side.

"How do you keep this place running alone?" she asked without taking her eyes off the twin engines.

"Well… first, I'm a genius. Second, I practically live down here. For some reason, the crew never seems to like me." He shrugged.

She turned away from the windows and crossed her arms over her chest. "That's not really surprising as you come off as an arrogant asshole—also, you're pretty condescending."

He laughed, a belly laugh that reverberated through the room. "You might be the first crew member that I've ever liked."

Emiko shook her head and walked over to the nearest control panel. "So, what do we need to do?"

"Gotta love a girl who's all business." Max strode over to her and swiped to a new screen. "This shows the engine stats."

"Do we need to warm them up before departure?"

"Nah, the previous captain put a lot of cash into engine upgrades. Those beauties out there…." He gestured out the floor-to-ceiling windows. "Need less than a minute from turn on to full speed."

"Cool." Emiko swiped to the next diagnostic screen. It was a schematic of the gravity plating. "Did Darla update this system, too?"

He nodded. "Our gravity system is solid." He laughed like he'd told a joke. "Hull integrity is typically good too. The old captain was planning on updating the hull plating, but died before she could. That's why from the outside, *Virdis* looks like shit."

"Maybe not looking fancy isn't a bad thing. I hear there are pirates out there, and we don't look like a target."

He snorted. "Pirates never bother with water freighters."

Emiko felt her cheeks flush. She focused back on the diagnostic screens. Next up was the water tank system. The massive tanks took up most of the ship's interior. Currently, they were a third full.

"How about this system?" she asked.

"It needs work. There are near-constant water leaks. I'll get to it." He swiped onto the ship's electrical systems.

"Once we've rescued B and are on our way, I'll help you with the water system. I've done a lot of that kind of work on other ships."

"Ah, you're an expert then." He put a hand on her forearm.

She moved her arm out of his grip; he didn't seem to notice.

"I wouldn't call myself an expert. It's just a way to make myself useful."

"Well, doll, there's no doubt in my mind you're the most useful person this ship has taken on in some time."

"We'll be leaving in five minutes," Hwicce said from the door.

Both Max and Emiko turned to him.

"Did Orin break out B?"

"Yeah, the two of them are on the run. They're going to take *Buttercup* and dock with us once we're away from the station." Hwicce scratched his head.

Emiko couldn't help but grin. "B's an expert on that kind of action-hero shit."

"I hope so," Hwicce said before focusing on Max. "Is this ship ready to go?"

"Yes, sir!" Max gave Hwicce a salute.

Hwicce frowned. "Right, just be ready. I'm not sure what kind of maneuvering we're going to have to do." He turned and vanished down the hallway.

"You like him?" Max asked.

"Hwicce?"

"Yeah. He strikes me as more of a goon than a ship's captain. I have no idea why Darla left the ship to him."

Emiko stared at the doorway Hwicce had just left. "B thinks he's great. I've only known him a few days, but I'm starting to agree with B."

"Well, I hope he doesn't kill us all with this 'maneuvering' he's planning. This is a water tanker, not some sort of combat ship." Max turned back to the diagnostic screens.

Emiko cocked her head and stared at the engineer. "Were you and Darla close?"

He shrugged. "We got along well enough."

"What happened to her?"

Max froze for a moment as his gruff demeanour vanished for a moment. "The shielding on the shuttle was old. I should've replaced it."

Emiko stayed quiet, watching as he rubbed the back of his neck.

"She shouldn't have gone down to that planet."

"What planet?"

Max shook his head. "It doesn't matter. A fist-sized meteor punched a hole through the shuttle. She would've suffocated before crashing."

"I'm sorry you lost a friend."

He snorted. "Come on, doll. I'll show you how to get the engines running."

Chapter Twenty-Six

Away from the platform, faint green lights barely illuminated the tunnel. Evenly spaced, they created a halo of light in their immediate vicinity and pools of near pitch blackness between them. A sour scent of urine combined with hints of mould made the tunnel seem like a threshold to a different, more sinister world.

Baker didn't slow, and Orin could barely keep up. He panted with each step, struggling to get enough oxygen to support his sprint. His legs burned, and a stitch formed in his side, forcing him to slow down. He let his pace lag as Baker zoomed ahead. With one hand clamped to his side, his gait became a walk.

"Baker." Short on breath, his words came out cracked and too quiet for her to hear.

Orin stopped, wondering if the brightening of the surrounding tunnel meant he was about to pass out. His shadow danced on the tracks in front of him. With each breath, the walls became brighter and his shadow darker. No, he wasn't about to pass out.

He turned, and his mouth went dry. A tram sped towards

him. In a single motion, he rotated and picked up his pace to a sprint. Ignoring his burning muscles and lungs, he focused on the tunnel ahead. He could see the next platform. Baker would reach it in time, but it was out of his reach—he wasn't going to make it.

"Damn it." He skidded to a stop, his blood thundering through his veins. He had seconds. With a lunge, he flattened himself out against the metal wall and squeezed his eyes shut.

The rattle of wheels against the track was the only sound the approaching tram made—there were no fancy magnetic levitation devices here. He closed his eyes as the tram zoomed towards his hiding spot. Was there enough room? He swallowed.

With a whoosh of air, the tram passed him by. As soon as it cleared him, he leapt away from the wall and resumed running—but now at a slow jog.

"I'm not cut out for this action hero stuff."

A faint humm of propellers approached from behind. He turned to see a police drone approach.

"What the hell?"

With a beam of red light, the drone scanned his face.

"I just can't catch a break."

With renewed urgency, he sprinted towards the platform ahead. The tram had already pulled away, giving him a clear view of Baker frowning at him.

When he got close enough, she reached down and hauled him up by his upper arm. "I thought you were going to be pancaked."

"They've spotted me. We got to keep going." Orin could barely get the words out between heaving breaths.

"Where's the airlock, little man?"

"This way." From memory, Orin headed away from the platform and down a corridor. He walked fast, but hopefully not so fast as to draw unwanted attention. Sweat dripped down his head, which he mopped up with his handkerchief. "I should've stayed on the ship."

Baker grunted in reply. He glanced over at her, and it didn't look like she'd even broken a sweat.

The corridor opened up into a large room full of automated drones moving shipping boxes. A waist-high barrier separated them from the workspace. Suspended from above, a shipping and receiving sign marked the space. A note stuck to the bottom said that all visitors had to report to the main office.

Orin glanced over at the office. A row of tall windows over-looked the room. Inside, three staff members hovered around a table playing dice. No one even glanced their way.

Along the back wall, the industrial size airlocks surrounded by fluorescent yellow warning bars stood out. Presumably, smaller cargo ships could pull up on the other side of the hull and transfer their cargo using the airlocks. That was where they were headed.

On the other side of the barrier and off to the side was a door labeled 'space suits.'

"That's our first stop," he said, pointing.

Baker nodded and stepped over the barrier. Orin followed, fearing alarms—but none sounded. They walked through the door and into the room of space suits like they were meant to be there. Inside, rows of colourful suits hung from pegs along the walls, with matching helmets sitting on a shelf above.

Orin grabbed an orange suit labelled size medium and started putting it on. "The comms are likely keyed to a common frequency, so don't say anything until I get us on our own frequency."

"Good thing I'm not a fucking chatterbox," Baker said as she began putting on a sinister-looking black suit. "For the record, this is a bad plan, but it's going to be fun."

Orin sighed. "Our ideas of fun might not be the same."

"Buck up, little man." She slapped him on the shoulder before putting on her helmet.

Orin put on his helmet and checked his suit's integrity—it was good. He set up a direct link to Baker's suit. "Okay, we can talk now. First, we need to go to the closest airlock and call the *Virdis*."

Baker gave him a thumbs up. He led the way back out into the main space. A quick glance confirmed the staff remained engrossed in their dice game, so Orin turned and headed towards the closest airlock.

A single jet pack sat in a rack next to the airlock doors. Without a word, he picked it up and slung it over his air pack, and buckled it into place. The jet pack made the suit cumbersome, but he continued trying to look natural.

They stepped inside the airlock, and no one tried to stop them. Orin let out an exhale as Baker closed the door behind them. Then the comms crackled to life.

"State your ID code," an androgynous voice demanded.

Orin pursed his lips. He needed to say something, or they'd lock out the airlock and trap them. He took a deep breath. "This is AM-14567." He made up the code. "We have an emergency situation here. We need to immediately exit this airlock and provide assistance."

"Stand by," the voice said.

"We don't have time for this shit," Baker said on their private channel.

Before Orin could stop her, she hit the emergency release button. Explosive bolts blew the outside doors off, and the contents of the airlock were blown out into space.

"What do you mean *Buttercup* wasn't there?" Hwicce didn't look up from his console as he spoke. *Virdis'* undocking procedure was more complex and manual than he'd expected. He gritted his teeth as he went through and confirmed the ship's airlocks were sealed. The main engines were running, the ship's gravity was at 1.03g, and his navigation path through the local traffic was plotted. Everything looked good.

Veena sat on the seat beside the captain's chair. "Orin said it was just gone—along with Click and Nigel."

"It's too late to turn back. We've got to pull out of our berth." Hwicce released the docking clamps. "The tug already has a hold of us."

As if on cue, the ship lurched as the tug pulled it free of the dock. The view through the bridge windows shifted from just the side of Indigo Station to a clear panorama of stars. Hwicce swallowed—this was exactly what his mother, sister, and Aunt Darla lived for, the freedom of running a ship in space. Yet, he didn't feel ready. A knot tightened in his gut.

He opened up a link to the engine room, and the camera feed blinked on in a side terminal. Emiko sat next to Max, both of them working through diagnostic screens.

"Is everything all right down there?" Hwicce asked.

The two of them looked into the camera.

"Aye aye, Captain." Max wore a smug look. "Emiko here is providing great help."

Beside him, Emiko smiled.

"Right. Let me know if there are any issues." Hwicce turned off the link.

"The tug is signalling they are ready to release us," GRUB said, their voice coming from everywhere.

"Are we all set?" Hwicce asked.

"Affirmative. The automatic pilot is engaged on a course circling the station." As the AI spoke, a map of the station appeared above the nav console, showing their projected route as an orange line. More lines showed other traffic, ranging from other supply ships to ferries to pleasure craft. All together, it looked like wasps circling a hive.

He leaned back into his chair. "Signal the tug to let us go."

"We're going to need to take a second orbit of the station," Veena said.

"Why?"

"Orin is going to use this airlock." She projected a hologram of Indigo Station into the air in front of them.

Hwicce frowned, leaning forward to get a better look. "Are they sure *Buttercup* is gone?"

"Yeah."

"Crap." Hwicce scratched his head. "GRUB, we need to plot a new course."

"A new course past the indicated airlock has been set," the AI reported.

"Good." Hwicce leaned back in the captain's chair. The sheer mass of the water tanker was creating a knot in his gut. The *Virdis* wasn't maneuverable, and yet he needed to maneuver close enough to the station to pick up Orin and Baker.

Hwicce and Veena sat in silence as *Virdis* followed the curve of Indigo Station's hull. The knot in Hwicce's gut writhed. This wasn't the course he should take the tanker on for his first time. With one wrong step, they could crash into the station, killing thousands.

"What's our distance to the station?" Veena asked, pulling Hwicce's thoughts back to the present.

"1.2 kilometres," GRUB said.

Hwicce nodded. He needed to focus on the issue at hand. "We're going to need to get closer."

"There is a no-fly zone starting at 1km around the station. Unless we are docking, we need to stay further out," GRUB said.

Veena leaned towards him. "Orin and Baker will not reach us that far out."

"I know." The knot in Hwicce's gut squeezed tighter as he looked down at the comms display. Station Traffic Control was calling. "Crap!"

Veena glanced over at the screen. "Can we just ignore them?"

"There are hefty fines for ignoring Station Traffic Control." GRUB's tone was flat.

"Right. What do we tell them?" Hwicce looked to Veena.

"Tell them we are having an issue with our port side thruster," GRUB said. "We have a maintenance crew working on it to determine if we need to call a tug and return to dock."

Veena drew her eyebrows together. "GRUB, is there really an issue?"

"Negative. However, reporting such an issue will explain any wobbles in our course."

Hwicce cocked his head. "You mean we can use this excuse to get in closer to the airlock?"

"Exactly," GRUB said.

"That's a creative solution." Veena spoke in the same tone she used when Molly tried to explain away something she'd done.

He answered the call from Station Traffic Control and gave them GRUB's excuse. They bought it.

"I didn't think a level 5 AI could lie," Veena said.

"The previous captain made some adjustments to my base code," GRUB said.

"Unauthorized adjustments." Veena crossed her arms over her chest.

Hwicce glanced at the holographic display showing their position relative to Orin's airlock. It was fast approaching. "Um, Veena, we need to focus on the rescue. Can you confirm they are in position?"

Veena nodded and activated a comm link to the frequency she and Orin had agreed on. "Orin, are you there?"

A lump formed in Hwicce's throat as only static filled the link. He stood and paced forward to stare out the window.

"Orin, are you there?" Veena paused. "Come in, Orin."

"The emergency release has been used on the airlock," GRUB said.

"Right." Hwicce squinted at Indigo Station but couldn't see the airlock. "Time to bring us in closer."

"Affirmative." At GRUB's words, the ship altered course towards the space station.

"Orin, please come in," Veena said.

Virdis swerved towards Indigo Station as Hwicce kept searching for Baker and Orin.

"Veena, Hwicce, are you there?" Orin's voice came over the radio.

"They are here." GRUB highlighted a section of the station's hull. "I can maneuver us to about 200 metres along their current trajectory and slow to match their rotational velocity."

Hwicce looked up. "How are we going to get them on the ship?"

"There are too many variables to predict if their current trajectory will line up with our airlock."

"Crap."

"Well, shit." Veena bit her lip. "What should I tell them?"

Orin reached out and tried to grab Baker, but just missed her. As the air raced out into the void of space, he started spinning. The little rectangle of the open airlock door got small at an astonishing rate.

He waited for his velocity to slow, then realized it wouldn't. He tried to spot Baker in his tumbles. It took several rotations until he spotted her dark suit. She was tumbling like him about one hundred metres away.

"AM-14567, you are not authorized to use the airlock," the voice in his comms said as if it wasn't too late.

Instead of responding, he turned it off. That's when he remembered he was wearing the jetpack. Gingerly, he put his hands on the controls. He flared the right thruster a tiny bit, and his rotation slowed. He did it again and again until he was maintaining a stable position.

Even though he was still receding away, he now faced the rings of Indigo Station. Its dark hull was punctuated with thousands of windows, each shining from light within. From his distance, the station's rotation became visible. The little rectangle of airlock he'd exited was now moving towards the edge of his view and would soon rotate out of sight.

"Okay, little man, you need to grab onto me," Baker said.

Using his thrusters on minimum, he started rotating. All he could see was the blackness of space. "Where are you?"

"Behind you, doofus."

Orin changed his rotation. He tried to keep his motions slow and deliberate while the adrenalin of their escape still raged through his system. "I'll find you," he said, more to himself than to her.

Once his back faced the station, he spotted her dark suit. She hung in the vacuum only a few meters away in a slow rotation. Orin hit his forward thrusters, and as soon as he was close enough, she grabbed on.

With one hand, he reset his comms to the *Virdis'* frequency. "Veena, Hwicce, are you there?"

There was a disturbingly long period of static.

"Orin," Veena came on the radio. "We've pinpointed your trajectory. Is Baker with you?"

"We're together," Orin said.

"We're coming around the station now. We should pass within two hundred metres. Can you move on your own?"

"I have a jetpack." Orin looked around for the hulking ship. The worn, grey hull of *Virdis* came around the station on a course towards them. "What will your velocity be?"

"We can slow to near stationary," she said.

With Baker holding on around his neck, Orin watched the ship bearing down on them. No one would accuse the *Virdis* of being sleek or stylish or even modern, but it appeared sturdy, like a block of metal. The massive ship fired its thrusters and decelerated. Orin swallowed, still thinking it might run them down, but it didn't. Instead, it glided up beside them, blocking the view of the station.

With Baker still holding on to him, Orin used the jetpack to maneuver them towards the cargo hold airlock. The exterior door opened as they approached, and Orin smoothly navigated inside.

As the exterior door closed, gravity engaged, pulling them to the ground.

Chapter Twenty-Seven

As Xander worked through the start-up sequence, he wanted to stop and scratch his back. Even though he knew they shouldn't, the nanites at work repairing his spinal damage itched. The doctors directed him to take it easy for a few days while the little robots fused the bones back together, but he didn't want his quarry to get away. His reputation needed maintaining, after all.

It hadn't taken too much for one of his AIs to find where Veena had gone. The entire group had taken over an old water tanker. Even though they'd already departed, the fools had submitted a flight plan.

The downside was, he had to call in a favour and borrow a shuttle from Long Enterprises. The little ship was a piece of crap—more appropriate for the junkyard than an interstellar chase.

As he continued to power the ship up, a fit of giggles overcame him. He'd outsmarted his math-genius prey. His redundant plans meant that even if she thwarted one method, he still had two more ways to hunt her down.

"The game is fixed," he said as he activated the tracking

device he'd slipped into Emiko Green's jacket at the tram station. "All I need is to be in the same system."

He tapped the display to his right, and the beacon's signal flashed red. *Virdis* had slipped the dock and was orbiting the station—he had plenty of time. He opened a shiny green package of chocolate chip cookies and set them on the dashboard in front of him. With his snack at the ready, he called Station Traffic Control and requested a departure window—no big deal for a ship as small as his. Within ten minutes, he was on his way.

As he piloted his ship away from Indigo Station, a flashing light announced an incoming message. It was Swa. With a sigh, he answered it. Swa's head appeared above the cookies—it was almost comical, but Xander forced his face to stay neutral.

"How may I help you?" he asked.

Swa scowled. "You promised me results."

"And you will have them." Xander set an AI to project the *Virdis* flight path.

"My sources tell me that a mere mathematician slipped through your fingers, leaving you broken in her wake." The set of Swa's chin made her look smug, which she probably intended.

"A minor setback, that's all." He altered course to follow the water tanker's projected path without getting too close. "I'll have your target in custody shortly. You just need to be patient and trust me."

Swa pressed her lips together. "Trust you?"

"That's how this is going to work."

"You are a low-life goon barely one step up from a criminal." Her eyes bore into him.

Xander reached through her projection and grabbed a cookie. "I'll get your mathematician. I always get my target." He shoved the entire cookie into his mouth.

"You'd better. Failing might damage your reputation beyond

recovery." Her face blinked out of existence as she cut the line at her end.

Xander frowned as he reached for another cookie. Dealing with Swa was always more trouble than it was worth. Dealing with one of the syndicates, like Long Enterprises, was so much easier. Too late now. He'd accepted Swa's job.

Swa leaned back from the comms unit and smiled. As much as she despised dealing with the low-life bounty hunter, she knew he would deliver. She gazed out her office windows at the starfield beyond. Her new home base on the battlecruiser *Defiant* kept her in the action—the perfect place for her to make her mark. Her mother would've approved.

If only she didn't need Veena. That woman was nothing but trouble. But Greer promised that decoding the alien texts would provide the insights he needed to finish his work.

Swa closed her eyes and let her head tilt back onto the headrest of her seat. She could almost hear her mother chiding her. No matter how successful she'd been as a kid, her mother always insisted she could do better. Swa sighed. From beyond the grave, her mother could still make her feel like shit.

Opening her eyes, she brought up the comms link to Greer and called him.

When a projection of his head appeared, he had the audacity to frown at her. "I'm in the middle of something."

"Do I need to remind you who you work for?" She raised an eyebrow.

Greer's smug expression drained from his face. "Of course not."

"Good. Now, I have a few things that may interest you." She leaned back in her chair. Even though her mother still seemed able to manipulate her, Swa knew she had the power to manipulate others.

Sitting on the side of her desk was a clear box holding the alien—the one Greer had lost on the *Garden Princess*, the one he'd called Subject 33. It pushed at the walls of their cage while alternating between flushing red and grey. The clear sides insulated her from the incessant train of clicks and pop the little monster emitted.

Swa picked up the band that Subject 33 had worn around their neck. Veena's clever use of memory space had fit a level 2 AI translator in the little device. A handy way to talk to the alien, something—Greer would appreciate.

She smiled and turned back to where his head was projected.

"First, I have a present for you." Swa expanded her view to show off the alien.

"You found Subject 33," Greer said. "Having it back will expedite my experiments."

"And I'll have Dr. Oswiu back in my custody shortly." Swa didn't share her concerns about working with that bounty hunter—at least he wasn't the only one she'd hired.

"We should have taken her with the child." Greer's eyes seemed to judge her. "This entire process would have gone smoother."

"Perhaps," Swa said, wishing she had someone to replace the arrogant Greer—he was as annoying as the bounty hunter. "Or perhaps she would have taken her child and escaped." She sneered. "And then you would have nothing."

He said nothing in response.

"Dr. Oswiu needs to decode that alien text, and having her daughter is the carrot I need to make her do it."

"That threat didn't work before," Greer said.

The skepticism on his face enraged Swa. If she didn't need him so much….

Pulling herself together, she fixed her gaze on Greer. "You need to focus on providing me with results. Molly Oswiu's parents—"

Greer cut her off. "Call her Subject 34."

Swa pursed her lips together and made a mental note to cut off all of Greer's 'luxury' supplies. He could sit on the icy moon forever as far as she cared—as long as he came up with a way for the Protectorate to make supersoldiers of their own.

"Focus on results Greer, before I find your replacement." She cut the line and his image winked out just as he opened his mouth to retort.

She let out a long exhale. She'd have to schedule a call back in a day or so to get another update. Short of heading out to the X-Ray system in person, all she could do was keep harassing him.

"That putz better start providing results soon," she said as she stalked over to the floor-to-ceiling windows. She could almost hear her mother chiding her, telling her Greer was the weak link in her plan.

Chapter Twenty-Eight

Veena sat at the table facing the common space. Green leaves graced a single tree—on the rest, nude branches forked towards the ceiling. Beneath, occasional dead flower heads punctuated the carpet of overgrown shrubs. A grove of bamboo against the back wall was the only section that seemed lush and thriving.

With a deep breath, she savoured the freshness of the air. Neglect made the garden what it currently was, but that could be turned around. A lot of work, but worth it.

She pictured Molly running along the path, her midnight curls bouncing with each step. Veena could almost hear her little girl's laughter. And Click—a smile crossed Veena's face as she pictured the two of them playing together. It would be chaos in the best kind of way.

Her gaze settled on the pillar of an algae tank in the centre of the space. Its central location seemed an odd design decision, and it was clearly an add-on—most likely done while Darla was captain. As she stared at the murky interior, a shadow of something crossed the light. For a moment, she thought she saw tentacles, but more likely it was just her mind playing tricks on her. She shook her head.

"I must be thinking about Theo65," she said to herself. But from the kitchen, Orin heard her. He set down the coffeepot he'd been cleaning and approached.

"Theo65?" He sat down beside her. "Did you get word that your contact is okay?"

She smiled. "I haven't heard anything and I'm still pondering this." She pulled the alien device out of her bag and put it on the table. "This."

"Still no idea?" He leaned in closer to the bronze-coloured, hexagon-shaped device.

"GRUB said it's an alien computer." Veena ran her finger along the honeycomb pattern on the top. "But it's missing a piece."

"Why did your contact want you to have a part of an alien computer?" Orin asked as she handed him the device. He turned it over, studying it from every angle.

"I didn't have time to ask." Veena rubbed a hand on her chin. Even though she'd sent him several messages, she didn't know what had happened to Theo65. "GRUB?"

"Yes." The AI's voice seemed to come from anywhere at once.

Veena's gaze drifted to the algae column. A shadow moved again. Probably just cleaning drones in the water tanks.

"You summoned me?" An edge of annoyance laced GRUB's voice.

"Do you still have access to the public news feeds from Indigo Station?" she asked.

"Affirmative."

"Great. Search for Summer's End Thrift Shop. The proprietor...." She frowned. Was Theo65 the proprietor? A pet? Actually, she didn't even know what Theo65 was? Maybe they were another alien like Click, except way scarier.

"Stand by."

Veena turned back to Orin, who was still studying the object. "Any ideas?"

He shrugged. "Maybe——"

"I found the information you requested," GRUB cut Orin off.

A holographic display appeared over the table. News reports from various sources flashed up. The incident had been reported as a robbery of the shop; the only injury reported was of the android that ran the store.

"Are there any photos of inside the shop?" Veena asked.

The feeds changed to several still shots. All of them showed the burst aquarium/counter, but none showed the thing she saw. With a swipe, she zoomed in on each one. Then she sighed.

"What are you looking for?" Orin asked.

She pursed her lips. "This might sound crazy, but Emiko saw it too." She took a deep breath. "Something came out of the water. They were probably three times the size of Click and had much more nubbly skin, but they had eight tentacles."

"Another alien?"

Veena ran a hand over her ponytail. "Maybe a larger version of the same type as Click, or maybe a different type of alien altogether."

"Click is a cartoon," GRUB said in a condescending tone.

"Yes, but I found a little alien on the *Garden Princess* that had been captured——" A loud thump from the algae column drew her attention.

The dark shadow had returned. A flutter formed in Veena's gut as she stood and started approaching the column.

"What is it?" Orin asked as he followed.

"GRUB, what's in the algae tank?" Veena approached the clear surface and peered inside. "GRUB?"

A shape materialized on the other side of the wall.

"Oh!" A breath caught in Veena's throat. She took a step back, tripped over a dead bush, and fell onto the soil, landing on her butt.

"It's me," they said, waving their tentacles, yet their voice came from the ship's system. They were another life form with the same shape as Theo65. "I didn't mean to alarm you."

"Are you Theo65?" Veena asked, her curiosity overcoming her initial shock. Her heart rate slowed back to normal.

"No, I'm GRUB." They continued waving their tentacles and flashed pale yellow. "Theo65 was injured, but they are okay."

"We've been interacting with you all along." Veena looked to Orin.

"Are there many of your kind among us?" Orin asked as he helped Veena back up onto her feet.

She wiped the dirt off her pants as she stared at the alien— no, at the unfamiliar organism—humans were the aliens here. The curved wall of the column distorted their shape, but she could still make out their eight tentacles and two gigantic eyes.

"So, you masquerade as a ship's AI?"

With three tentacles, they made a motion like a shrug. "It makes sense." Then they flashed black. "If you saw one of us that looks like the cartoon, then you saw a child."

"A child?" Orin said.

A knot formed in Veena's gut. "We didn't know they're a child." She swallowed. "They took our other ship. We've picked it up on long-range sensors, but no one is answering our hails."

"I will pick up speed. Our spawn are precious." GRUB flushed a fire engine red.

"Of course," Veena said.

From deep in the bowels of the ship, a grumbling sound came. Briefly, the acceleration overcame the artificial gravity, and Veena had to compensate to stay upright. GRUB sloshed back and forth in the column.

"How many of your kind are there?" Veena asked, putting a hand on the column to steady herself.

"Not many since the Slip," they said.

"The Slip?" Orin asked.

"We were over-ambitious, made a mistake, and lost our

homes." GRUB de-saturated to a dull grey. "I don't have time to explain right now. We must discuss the one you named Click. Where are they from?"

Veena scratched her head. "Um." Click had never been talkative. "I don't know. A military scientist named Dr. James Greer had them in a box. I don't know where they were captured."

GRUB flashed orange.

"They mentioned wanting to get to the seventh world," Veena continued.

GRUB went pale pink and put two tentacles against the clear surface.

"How did one of your children end up in a comic that's so popular with our kids?" Orin asked.

"Theo65 believes they can teach our younger generations to be friends." A dark green started in GRUB's tentacles, then expanded to cover his entire body. "Theo65 pictured a future where our kinds can live together in harmony."

Orin snorted. "Humans can't even get along with themselves."

"I have warned Theo65 of the dangers of their utopian ideas." The tips of GRUB's tentacles went orange.

"There's nothing wrong with Theo65's optimism. My daughter would love to meet Click; I bet the two of them would end up friends just like in the comic." Veena hugged her arms around herself, wishing she was hugging Molly.

GRUB shifted until they were right on the other side of the column's wall. "This is the girl who is missing?"

Veena nodded. Just thinking of how alone Molly must be feeling created a knot in Veena's gut. Even though it had only been a few days, it felt like Molly had been on her own forever.

"We will find the children," GRUB said. They turned a steel blue before they pushed off the wall and shot like a torpedo up the column.

Chapter Twenty-Nine

Now that Baker was safe on the *Virdis*, her thoughts ranged to Emiko. Bent over the workbench across the engineering bay, Emiko worked, checking out the jetpack. The inner workings of the device captivated her, drawing in her entire focus. She made cute sounds as she worked.

Baker still couldn't get over how hot Emiko was. From her pixie haircut to her shapely ass. Better yet, Emiko got Baker's humour. Baker hadn't thought she'd want a serious relationship with someone—especially so soon after leaving her first love, the army. Hell, she'd only known Emiko a few days. Despite that, she knew. Butterflies welled up in her gut as she considered admitting her feelings to Emiko.

Just as Baker opened her mouth, Emiko looked up from the jetpack. "This is quite a score. Industrial grade and in good working order."

Baker smiled. "I'm glad you like it." Then her mouth went dry. "I...." She wanted to say it, but the words weren't coming out.

"What's on your mind?" Emiko met Baker's gaze, her perfect face waiting for Baker to say the right words.

"I was thinking…." The butterflies in Baker's gut fluttered harder.

"Yo doll, is that the jetpack?" Max asked as he strode into Engineering with two coffee mugs. He handed one to Emiko before noticing Baker. "Sorry, I didn't know you'd be here, or I would've taken your coffee order."

"No worries." Baker suddenly felt very out of place. Mechanical things weren't her domain. "I didn't need any more coffee today, anyway."

Without another word to her, Max turned back to the jetpack. "This is great. I've never had a chance to check out one of these models."

Baker took a step back as Emiko and Max engaged in a technical chat that could've been a foreign language. Baker bit her lip as she noticed the way Emiko gazed at Max. He smiled back in a way that didn't seem innocent.

Baker's heart sank as she realized she had competition for Emiko's affections. Why would Emiko want to be with a goon like her? Without another word, Baker turned and left. She headed up to the bridge with the hope there was something useful she could do there.

Grumbling to herself, Baker strode into the common room. She wasn't needed anywhere—she didn't know how to maintain a ship or even fly it. The cleaning bots did a good enough job, there wasn't even any need for her to pick up a mop. With a sigh, she headed to the coffee maker—but someone had already made fresh coffee.

Baker snorted.

"You look like things aren't going your way," Orin said with a yawn.

She turned to where he was working at the table. She'd been so focused on her fucking love life she hadn't even realized the little man was right there. As she stared at him, he took a sip out of his mug as though he expected her to make conversation.

"I fucking broke into someone's house, got arrested,

escaped, and then blasted out of a bloody airlock." After pouring herself a mug of coffee, she sat down across from him.

Orin smiled. "I'm guessing none of that stuff phases you."

Baker pursed her lips together and gazed past Orin into their sad garden. At least the lights had cycled down to the low setting, so she couldn't see how bad it was. She shifted her gaze back to Orin. "What are you working on, little man?"

He glanced down at his datapad. "I'm trying to make sense of the economics of running a water tanker. I've accessed Darla's books, and I have to say her accounting was rather unconventional."

"Is delivering water lucrative?" Baker didn't care, but she just wanted to chat with someone. Yet her question sounded just like something her brother would ask.

Orin shrugged. "This ship needs an overhaul. But lots of places need water. Customers won't be hard to find."

"Hmmm." Baker took a sip of coffee. "Have cabins been assigned yet?"

"Not yet, but Hwicce asked me to look after it. Will you be sharing with Emiko?"

Baker groaned and slumped over her coffee. "Best not," she said. Then she pulled herself up tall and looked Orin in the eye. "I think I'd like some space to myself."

"There are plenty of cabins." Orin cocked his head as he stared at her for a moment. "It's not my place to ask, but did the two of you have a falling out?"

"You're right, little man. It isn't your place." Baker chugged the remains of her coffee, then made to stand up.

"Did I ever tell you about how I met Mary?" Orin asked.

"I've known you all of two days, so basically, I know nothing about you." Baker sat back down. "Who's Mary?"

"My wife." Orin closed his datapad. "I was a shuttle pilot back then, based out of Jupiter Station. While wandering around the station, I stumbled on a sculpture exhibit in one of the galleries."

"I never get what passes for art," Baker said.

"These sculptures were something to behold." Orin smiled. "And not in a good way—which I said to this pretty woman standing near the door."

Baker snorted. "You were flirting."

"It was my hope. I was young and full of myself," he said. "The woman wasn't impressed; she just walked away."

"Was she the sculptor?"

"I found out later that she was Mary Crane, and it was her first show."

"But if she walked away from you, how..."

Orin smiled. "I went back the next day, and the next day, and the next day. Eventually, my persistence paid off, and she went for a coffee with me."

"I suspect there's a moral to your story," Baker said.

"Even after two decades of marriage, I still never got her sculptures. But her fans loved them. I remember how jealous I'd get when I accompanied her to gallery openings and her fans would gather around her."

Baker nodded.

"But here's the thing." Orin put his mug down and leaned forward. "She'd smile and engage with them, but at the end of the night, she'd always come home to me."

Baker sighed. "Emiko and Max have hit it off."

"That makes sense, as they're both technical-minded."

"You're right. It makes sense," Baker said.

"Don't jump to any conclusions," Orin said. "I think you and Emiko have potential together. If that's what you want, then be persistent. Play the long game."

"And there's the moral of your story." Baker took her now empty mug over to the sink.

"That's the best I can do with relationship advice," he said.

A crackle came over the ship's comms. "We are approaching Buttercup now," GRUB announced over the intercom. "Everyone is required on the bridge."

"I'm guessing your skills will be needed soon," Orin said as he stood. "Hopefully, Click is over there just waiting for us."

Baker smiled. "I'm always up for some hero shit."

Chapter Thirty

Hwicce sat on the forward edge of the captain's chair, staring out the front windows at the yellow and black hull of *Buttercup*. The survey vessel was dark, and the sensors said someone powered it down. He ran a hand over his head as his gut churned.

"I've been calling them for hours, and no one has answered." Orin sat at his post at the middle console, one level down. "The *Virdis'* system is fine, so the problem has to be at their end."

Hwicce stood and scratched his head. "Does that mean no one's there or that the comms are down?"

"*Buttercup's* communication system is functioning within acceptable parameters," GRUB said.

"However, their life support and gravity are down."

Orin turned and looked at Hwicce. "That's not good news. I mean, maybe Click and Nigel got off somewhere?" Orin bit his lip. "I hope."

"GRUB, what kind of atmosphere does your kind require?" Hwicce squeezed his eyes shut as he tried not to picture Click's corpse floating around over there.

"We require oxygen, though we can tolerate a wider range of conditions than a human. However, based on the lack of activity on the other ship, combined with the fact the ship was manually powered down, my hypothesis is that no one is there."

Opening his eyes, Hwicce nodded. He still couldn't believe that GRUB was an alien masquerading as an AI. But they had legitimate AI qualifications and, better yet, actual experience running the ship. If his aunt had trusted them, so would he.

"Can we open the doors and maneuver *Virdis* to get *Buttercup* into our cargo bay?" Hwicce ran a hand over his face before staring out the front windows.

"That ship is near the maximum size that will fit," GRUB said. "I would advise against trying to do that. One wrong move could cause us a lot of damage."

"Right." Hwicce crossed his arms over his chest and tried to ignore the sour taste in his mouth. "That means someone needs to go over there and fly *Buttercup* into the hold?"

"Affirmative."

Hwicce let out a long exhale. Getting *Buttercup* would require the risk of an untethered spacewalk—but even if Click and Nigel weren't there, they could use the smaller ship like a shuttle opening up access to locations the *Virdis* could never reach. "I'll go." He met Orin's gaze. "You're going to have to come with me."

Orin's eyes widened. "Me? I barely survived my last spacewalk. Twice in one day is tempting fate."

"If it's going to be a tight fit getting *Buttercup* in the hold, it's probably best that you fly."

"Right." Orin nodded and stood. "I guess I'll suit up." He didn't look the least bit confident to be going on yet another spacewalk.

Hwicce smiled and tried to look casual. "Don't worry. You won't be alone out there, and I have training for this kind of thing." His hundreds of hours of spacewalks were with state-of-the-art combat armour, not a single ancient jetpack, though—something he didn't think was a good idea to mention.

Twenty minutes later, Hwicce checked over Orin as the two of them stood in the port-side airlock wearing ancient space-suits. Max had assured them he'd kept on top of maintaining them and that they were the best suits they had. Hwicce sniffed the air inside his suit—there wasn't even a hint of body odour, meaning at the very least, the suit was clean.

After he was done with Orin, Hwicce double-checked his own suit's integrity. It held air perfectly. There was no more reason to delay.

"You ready?" he asked Orin as he clipped a tether between the two spacesuits. Emiko had assured him the jetpack was in working order, but he double-checked it anyway before swinging it onto his back.

Orin's comms crackled to life. "Yes."

Hwicce took the other man's uncharacteristic single-word answer to mean Orin was struggling to keep it together.

"All right, all we need to do is get out there and fly that ship into the cargo bay—easy stuff."

"Yes, yes, of course," Orin said, shifting from foot to foot.

"We'll stay tethered together until we get into *Buttercup's* airlock."

Orin nodded in response.

For no good reason, Hwicce looked up at where he thought the camera was. "Okay, GRUB, are we in position?"

"Affirmative. We are as close as regulations allow for this type of operation," GRUB said.

After patting Orin's shoulder, Hwicce cycled the airlock. Once the light by the outside door flashed green, he opened it. The black void on the other side extended probably forever. He felt its pull. As always, he wondered about his ancestors who'd ventured out into the infinite unknown. Then he forced his thoughts back to the task at hand.

Buttercup's marbled black and yellow hull floated dead ahead

—less than fifty metres away. GRUB certainly knew how to maneuver a ship. They'd matched *Buttercup's* spin perfectly, making the survey ship appear stationary. But the little ship seemed lifeless, its dark windows as black as the space around it. What had Click been thinking when he flew away from Indigo Station? Knowing that Click was a child changed things—they shouldn't have left them alone.

"Heading out now," he said over their open comms channel. He turned to Orin, who gave him a thumbs up.

Feathering the controls on the jetpack, he maneuvered out of the airlock door. Ten meters out, he rotated to confirm Orin's tether had held. "You okay?"

"Yes," Orin said with the same tension in his voice.

"This is nothing like your last spacewalk. It'll just take us a minute to get there." Hwicce continued towards *Buttercup's* airlock, towing Orin behind him.

They reached the other ship without incident. The airlock door was not locked, so they slipped in. Inside, the lack of gravity forced them to activate their magnetic boots.

"This isn't a good sign," Orin said as he closed the outside door.

"We knew the gravity was off." Hwicce removed the cumbersome jetpack and clipped it to the wall so it wouldn't float away. After cycling the air, he opened the inside door.

Hwicce shone his helmet light into the dark interior. Shiny floating objects glinted in the light, from a wrench to a metal teacup to the glitter text on a *Bubble and Click* comic. "Let's keep our suits on until we figure out what happened."

"I'll get the power on." Orin passed Hwicce and headed to the cockpit.

A moment later, the lights came on, and gravity returned.

As stuff of everyday life plummeted down to the floor, Hwicce deactivated his magnetic boots. *Bubble and Click* comics settled across the kitchen and dining table, while the dirty coffee mugs left in the sink missed it on their descent and crashed to the deck. Other than the mess, everything was as he expected it to be.

After activating his suit's external speaker, he called out. "Click? Nigel?" There was no reply. As the knot in his gut twisted, he reminded himself he wasn't expecting them to be on board.

On the floor in the corner sat Molly's Click stuffy, its faded pink colouring nothing compared to the real Click. Hwicce knelt down and picked up the toy and turned it over in his hands. Molly loved the stuffy—refusing to sleep unless she was cuddled up with it. He let out a sigh as he set the stuffy on the kitchen table and vowed to make sure his little girl was reunited with her favourite toy.

He checked the washroom and single cabin, but the little alien wasn't to be found. He pursed his lips as he wondered if Click was hiding somewhere in the ventilation ducts.

"Hwicce, you need to come see this," Orin called from the cockpit.

Trying not to step on the debris littering the floor, Hwicce went forward.

"This is where they went." Orin played the last recording the ship's external cameras had recorded.

Hwicce recognized the inside of the *Defiant's* main hangar, he used to serve on that ship and had spent hours training in the hangar space. He even recognized the dent where Baker had thrown him in full armour against the bulkhead.

"Crap! Why would they go there on purpose?" He slipped into the co-pilot's chair and checked the comms logs. He found a message from General Swa and played it.

"Veena, we have received word that you have arrived at Indigo Station. Call me. I have news of Molly and would like you to reconsider my offer. If you can decode that alien message, I will make sure you and your daughter are reunited."

Watching Swa's holographic projection made him shiver. She was the one who'd taken his little girl.

"That woman is tenacious," Orin said when the message finished. "She really wants those alien codes translated—and I don't believe she'd follow through on her promises."

Hwicce wished his helmet wasn't blocking him from running a hand through his hair. He sighed. "It appears Click bought us time to escape Indigo Station."

"And now Swa has them." Orin's tone was flat.

"Let's get this ship into Virdis' cargo hold. Then we'll figure out our next step."

A high-pitched whine reverberated through the ship as Orin engaged *Buttercup's* main engines. With each second, the sound increased in intensity.

Orin started swiping through screens on his display as red lights started flashing. "This isn't right."

"What's going on?" Hwicce asked.

"No, no, no." Orin's hands started moving faster and faster through the diagnostics.

Hwicce stood and put a hand on Orin's shoulder. "You gotta tell me what's going on."

"I can't shut the engines down. They're going to overload."

"Crap! GRUB, we have a problem." Hwicce grabbed the smaller man's arm and pulled him out of the pilot's seat.

"Confirmed. Evacuate now," GRUB said as the ship shuttered.

Orin started running to the airlock. "Rosie's going to be pissed. I promised her I'd take care of this ship."

"GRUB, how big is the explosion going to be?" Hwicce asked. His heart hammered in his chest.

"*Virdis* is within the blast radius. Moving now, but we will still be impacted."

Hwicce looked down at the controls before him. "Crap!"

Veena was on Virdis. He grabbed the thruster controls and rammed them up to maximum. The engines flared, and more red lights flashed. A moment later, the little ship lurched and began accelerating away.

"Get out of there now," GRUB ordered in his ear.

Hwicce turned and sprinted into the common room. Without stopping, he grabbed Molly's Click stuffy off the table and shoved it into the webbing of his airpack.

Sparks cascaded out of the door to the engine room when he passed. The lights began flickering, then gravity failed.

"Blow the airlock," Hwicce shouted as he lifted off the floor —there wasn't time to activate his magnetic boots.

Orin must have followed his order, as the air suddenly started moving. It swept Hwicce along with everything else inside the ship out into space. Outside, he tumbled in relation to *Buttercup*, surrounded by the flotsam of everyday life.

Buttercup continued to accelerate away until it was a yellow speck. Then the engines overloaded. A ball of flame extended out from the speck as an expanding sphere—a sphere filled with metallic fragments moving exceptionally fast.

"Crap!" Hwicce cursed when he realized he didn't have the jetpack. There was no way to avoid the shrapnel—all he could do was hope his suit would hold. He rotated his back to the approaching wave of debris to protect Molly's Click stuffy.

Shards of metal peppered his airpack and the back of his suit and helmet, pushing him as they unevenly transferred momentum to him. He started spinning on three axes as alarms sounded in his suit.

He could feel air moving across his face, and his mouth went dry. The bubble of air in his suit was venting into space.

"GRUB?" His voice cracked as he spoke. "Orin?" When no one answered, he checked the suit's diagnostic panel on his left forearm. His comms were down, and he was losing air at a rapid rate. Before he could get his bearings, he smashed into something solid. The impact knocked the wind out of him.

"Crap!" He squeezed his eyes shut. Then it dawned on him; his back was up against something big and stable.

As he turned over, he opened his eyes and gasped. The grey

of *Virdis'* hull extended off almost as far as he could see, as though he was an ant dwarfed by a massive structure.

"How?"

GRUB was moving *Virdis* out of the blast radius. How could the ship be here?

He activated his boots and stood. About three metres away, a ladder-like structure ran the length of the ship—a maintenance path for spacewalks. He walked over clipped himself in before deactivating his boots.

"Air at one percent," an automated voice in his spacesuit informed him.

"Crap!"

While keeping his grip on the handhold, he tried to get his bearings. One end of the ladder would be an airlock, but which way did he need to go? He let himself float away to the end of his tether and looked around. To his right, he could see the bubble-like structure of the bridge—that meant he had to turn left. After pulling himself back to the ladder, he traversed to where he hoped he'd find the airlock.

As the air in his suit got thin, he started gasping. Nausea swept over him and his head started to spin, but he kept going.

"Keep your ass moving!" His basic training drill sergeant loomed over him.

"I can't..." Hwicce's words trailed off as his pace slowed.

"I've never seen a sorrier recruit in my life," his drill sergeant said as she went red in the face. "Keep your ass moving. Hand-over-hand until you get there."

Hwicce swallowed and grabbed onto the next rung.

"Did you come from some pansy-ass utopian colony? You useless piece of shit."

Hwicce focused on the ladder ahead and forced himself to keep moving.

"At this rate, I'll be sending home a corpse to your momma."

"No," Hwicce said, gasping for what little oxygen remained

in his suit. His peripheral vision faded to black. Soon, all he could see were his hands and the next rung. As he reached out, everything went black.

———

"Hey, dumbass."

Hwicce opened his eyes. Behind her own helmet, Baker's face hovered above him. Above her were bright lights. He took a deep breath—and realized he was breathing.

"Is he okay?" Orin's voice came from somewhere out of sight.

"I plugged him into my air," Baker said. "He's just malingering now."

Hwicce started to chuckle. He reached down and pulled out the undamaged stuffy from his webbing. "Molly would never forgive me if I left this behind."

Baker frowned. "You risked your life for a stuffed toy?"

"If you had a kid"—Hwicce pushed himself up to sitting —"you'd do the same."

Chapter Thirty-One

Veena frowned as she stared up at Hwicce from her perch on the edge of the bed. He'd just come out of the shower and was dripping wet with only a towel wrapped around his hips. Finally, they were alone in their quarters.

"You almost got yourself killed!" She paced over to the windows overlooking the ship's rather dishevelled garden and took a deep breath. What she didn't say was how much fear had gripped her until Baker reached him. Nor how improbable it was his suit had only sustained minor damage considering his proximity to the explosion. She let out a long exhale and sat back down on the bed.

"I know." He ran a hand over his head as he sat down beside her. "I didn't expect that Swa would stoop to booby trapping *Buttercup*."

"I can't lose you a second time," she said, her mouth dry. "And Molly needs you as much as I do."

Hwicce nodded and took her left hand into his.

"Hell, while you were out there, and I thought I might lose you, I resorted to counting each breath I took just to keep my shit together."

He let go of her hand and wrapped his arm around her shoulders. "I'm sorry. We need to figure out our next step, and we'll do it together."

Veena nodded as she rested her head on his shoulder. Even though he was still damp, warmth radiated off him. His proximity was reassuring. "We need to find the off-loop link to Greer's lab—that's where Molly is."

"What about the alien artifact being auctioned on Seven Soaring Swans?" Hwicce said. "We know Pam Long is going to be there, and she knows about the off-loop link we're looking for."

"New Venus is in the Foxtrot system. Five gates from here," she said, counting out five fingers. She pulled away from him to look him in the face.

Hwicce ran a hand over his stubble where his beard used to be. "The auction is the only genuine lead we have."

"The off-loop link to where Molly is being held is in the Delta System. We need to go there and look for it." Tightness gripped Veena's chest. It took her a second to realize it was uncertainty that she couldn't quantify what their next step should be. There were two good reasons to go to New Venus— both might lead them to clues, yet the off-loop link might lead them directly to Molly.

"Do you know how to find a secret off-loop link?" Hwicce asked in a gentle tone.

Veena filled her lungs and closed her eyes. She slowly exhaled. "I have no idea. We could end up looking for days and find nothing." She stood and paced over to the window again. Down below, Baker wandered through the garden, kicking at the ground.

Behind her, the bed groaned as Hwicce got up as well. "I can send a note to Selene and ask if she knows."

Veena turned to her husband. "Your sister never gets back to us quickly, and I doubt she'd know."

"Yeah."

"But if we go to the Foxtrot system and Pam Long doesn't show up or the alien artifact turns out to be some cheap knock-off, we'll have to go all the way around the loop to get back to the Delta System. We'd waste a lot of time." Veena gulped. "Molly's out there somewhere alone."

Hwicce frowned. "I know. Where did your intel about a secret gate in the Delta system come from?"

Veena bit her lip and hung her head. "Gloria. And she was probably playing me all along."

"Given her willingness to betray you, do you trust her information?" Hwicce's tone wasn't accusatory, but Veena felt like an idiot.

She shook her head. "No. All Gloria really wanted was for me to decode the alien text."

"So she probably would have told you anything to get you to do that work."

"I don't know." Veena paused, and a silence fell between them. "Going to the Delta System seems so right. A direct solution."

"But you have no credible evidence to back that up."

Veena ran her hands down her pants.

"We'll find Molly," Hwicce said. "We won't stop looking for her until we do."

"I know." Veena took a deep breath, hating that there wasn't a simple solution—but Hwicce was right. Hunting for an off-loop link was a waste of their time. She swallowed. "We should go to New Venus."

"Let me get dressed, and we'll head up to the bridge," he said as he released her hand.

Ten minutes later, Veena and Hwicce walked onto the empty bridge. Veena ran her hands down her pant legs as she stopped on the top level. The starfield out the windows seemed more expansive than usual—and somewhere out there, Mol waited.

"GRUB, how long until we reach the Foxtrot system?"

Hwicce asked as he continued down to the captain's chair.

"Based on our trajectory, we will reach the spaceport above New Venus in 27 hours."

"Are we on the wanted lists there?" Veena asked as she moved to the railing directly behind where Hwicce now sat.

"I have searched the public feeds and have found none of the crew's names listed as wanted," GRUB said.

Veena wrapped her fingers around the bar and tightened her grip. "Is that because they have not reported us or because we got away without notice?"

"Unknown."

Turning to look at her, Hwicce said, "We have to assume at least Swa is still hunting us and perhaps some bounty hunters. But the civil authorities, probably not."

"At least not yet," Veena said. "We should still keep a low profile."

"Captain Darla always kept a low profile," GRUB said.

Veena cocked her head. "Why?"

"She upgraded the hull on our last retrofit, adding a coating that, when activated, obscures our hull to other sensors."

"The *Shimmer* had something like that," Hwicce added. "But why did Darla need to hide?"

GRUB was silent for a few moments—long enough, Veena started counting each breath. "Captain Darla took on other delivery jobs. Nothing illegal, but the work required discretion."

"Humph." Hwicce shifted in his seat. "I didn't know Aunt Darla lived that kind of life. Does that mean you're skilled at forging docking documents and crew manifests as well?"

"That is correct."

Veena released the bar and crossed her arms over her chest. "We can evaluate Darla's affairs later."

"Right," Hwicce said.

"GRUB, are you sure you can't find a secret gate?" Veena glanced up towards the speaker.

"Even though my ancestors created the gate system, we lost most of our cumulative knowledge in the Slip."

"You didn't explain what the Slip was before," Veena said.

"Historians say there were signs before it happened. The gates were hungry and became more so with each new one created."

"Are the gates living?" Hwicce stood and paced forward.

"In a way, yes, but not how you and we consider," GRUB said. "The gates provide portals to a place outside this universe, where the laws of physics are different. Distance becomes an irrelevant parameter."

Veena cocked her head. Human physicists had been trying to figure out the gate system since the first generation ships stumbled upon them. But so far, no theory fully explained them.

"Are you saying there are no special dimensions within the gate?" Veena scratched her head.

"Not how we experience them," GRUB said.

Hwicce rubbed his chin and glanced up. "I'm confused. What exactly was the Slip?"

"An error was made. A misjudgement perhaps, or a bad calculation. A gate was created too close to one of our worlds." GRUB paused. "Once, my kind lived on hundreds of beautiful water worlds. The gates swallowed our oceans in one big gulp— our aquatic cities and most of our population just slipped into the gates." There was no detectable emotion in GRUB's voice, but it was computer-generated after all.

Veena and Hwicce looked at each other.

"The anchor worlds…." Veena ran a hand down her ponytail as her mind raced. "Are you saying the barren, rocky anchor worlds were once water worlds?"

"It was convenient to have the gates close," GRUB said. "Only a handful of my kind survived the Slip."

"But what happened to those pulled into the gates?" Veena asked.

"We assume they died." GRUB's tone was flat.

Veena and Hwicce fell silent.

"This history lesson will not help us get our children back." GRUB changed the topic. "I concur with Captain Hwicce's assessment that we need to go to Seven Soaring Swans. An additional reason is that the location is not where your enemy expects you to go."

Veena inhaled until her lungs filled completely, then slowly let out the air. "Swa might think I'm going to hunt for Gloria's gate."

"And she might set up an ambush there," GRUB said.

"Then let's go to that auction." Her chest felt tight. She wasn't sure this was the best option, but GRUB was probably right. Swa probably was waiting to capture her in the Delta System.

Chapter Thirty-Two

"Oh dear, oh dear, oh dear." Nigel examined the corridor he'd appeared in. Clinical white walls extended both directions, with clear doors running along one side. He searched his memory banks, but nothing seemed familiar. Where was he? He rotated as he rubbed his hands together, his fingers glitching through each other.

Behind the closest glass door, Click sat in a shallow pool of water. They flashed green and waved with three tentacles as soon as they made eye contact.

"You want me to look around?" Nigel ran one of his smaller sub-routines to control his glitching. With both hands, he adjusted his cravat.

Click maneuvered up to the door, flashed orange, and put a single tentacle on the glass.

"Of course, I'll keep myself together." Nigel bent down to be eye-to-eye with Click. "I'll look. But I can't go far without extending past the projector."

With another orange flash, Click fixed their gaze on Nigel, their big, liquid eyes boring into the AI.

Nigel stood and glanced both directions down the hall for a

second time. Closed doors capped both ends. He turned right and went to the next clear door. The cell was empty. As he continued to the next one, he glitched and reappeared in front of Click.

"See, I told you I couldn't go far."

Click put half of their tentacles against the glass, leaving moist smears on the surface. They flashed yellow and let out three clicks.

"Right. I can go the other way." Nigel turned left, took three paces, and peered through the glass door.

Inside, a little girl sat on a cot facing the door. She hugged her knees into her chest. Dark, unkempt curls hung over her face.

"Hello." Nigel used a gentle tone as he searched his limited data banks for reasons they might hold a child prisoner. He found no good reason.

The girl lifted her head and wiped the hair out of her face. Her big, dark eyes bore into him the same way Click's did as she met his gaze. Emitting a snarl, she exposed her missing two front teeth.

Something in Nigel's code clicked. He compared an image of Veena with the little girl's face, mapping the features together —they were a close match. It had to be her. Veena would be so happy!

"Are you Molly?"

With a snort, she buried her head in her knees. Her hair fell forward again, obscuring her face.

"I'm a friend of your mom," he said as he knelt down to her level.

Molly lifted her head and blew the hair out of her face. "My mom is coming for me... and my dad, too."

"Yes, absolutely. They are on their way. Finding you is their top priority."

Biting her lip, Molly slid forward off the cot and came to the door. She cocked her head as she studied him. "You're dressed funny."

Nigel nodded. "Yes. You see, I'm an AI designed to help people on a fancy ship." He adjusted his green silk cravat and smoothed his tweed suit. "I had to look fancy to fit in."

Molly pursed her lips, then nodded. "My mom would make friends with a silly AI. What's your name?"

"My name is Nigel."

"Why aren't you in a cell like me?" She mimed the shape of a cube with her hands. "Or some sort of computer program box."

"My current job is to be a translator for an alien," Nigel said. "They are in the next cell."

"An alien?" She perked up as she tried to catch a glimpse into the cell beside hers. "My best friend, Click, is an alien."

The real-life Click overheard and emitted a series of clicks while flashing pink, bright enough they illuminated the hall.

Molly started bouncing. She glanced back and forth between Click's light show and Nigel. "It's them, it's them," she chanted.

Nigel couldn't help but smile.

Molly stopped jumping and looked at him with her wide eyes. "Can you let me out?"

Nigel hung his head for a moment. "Sadly, no. I'm a hologram and not connected to the computers in this place." He waved a hand through the door. "I am unable to impact physical things."

She stomped her foot. "But I want to hug Click." She balled her hands into fists.

Nigel took a step to the side and glanced down at Click. He cocked his head as Click communicated with him. "I don't know if her nickname is Bubble. Fine, I'll ask her." He looked back at Molly. "Do you ever get called Bubble?"

Molly put her hands on her hips, assuming a superhero pose. "I am Bubble, space explorer extraordinaire."

Click let out a series of clicks and flashed blue and yellow.

Nigel smiled. The two of them were clearly on their way to becoming friends.

Nigel swallowed, wishing he could contact Veena and tell her Molly was fine. Rubbing his hands together, he watched his fingers glitch through each other. A realization dawned on him —it was now up to him to keep both Molly and Click safe, a near-impossible task considering he couldn't impact much of the world around him.

Nigel backed up enough that he could see both Molly and Click at the same time. "Right-o, we need to think about escaping."

"Like a full-on jailbreak?"

Click flashed green and yellow and let out a popping sound.

"Like Bubble and Click did in volume three?"

Nigel didn't know what the comic characters did in volume three. He focused his limited processing power on studying their surroundings. "We'll have to wait until we see an opportunity. Until then, both of you, please cooperate with our captors."

Molly nodded. "That way, they won't suspect a thing."

In the cell next door, Click flushed solid maroon and emitted three clicks.

Chapter Thirty-Three

An incessant ping pulled Hwicce from his slumber. He rolled over and found the bed beside him cold—Veena wasn't there. He sat up and rubbed his eyes. It took him a moment to recognize his unfamiliar surroundings in the dim light. He was in his and Veena's new quarters on a water tanker he'd inherited, headed towards the best lead they had to get Molly back.

The intercom pinged at him again. He'd set up their cabins as off limits to GRUB's sensors so everyone could have privacy. Why his aunt hadn't done that baffled him. The ping sounded again.

With a sigh, he pressed the comms button. "This better be good."

"I have detected an anomaly," GRUB said.

Hwicce yawned and scratched the stubble on his chin. "What kind of anomaly?"

"Someone is following us. It's a small ship, barely detectable."

"We're in the main shipping lane now. Are you certain it's following us?" Hwicce stifled a second yawn and checked the clock. It was the middle of his sleep cycle. No wonder he felt so discombobulated.

"The ship is communicating with a device on this ship," GRUB said.

"What kind of device?"

"It is not connected into the onboard network, so I do not have information on it, but it has to be a transmitter of some sort."

Hwicce got out of bed and pulled a t-shirt on. He ran a hand over the red flannel pyjama pants he'd found in the closet and decided to leave them on—it was the middle of the night, after all.

"Can you pinpoint where the signal is coming from?" Hwicce asked as he headed to the door.

"Negative. You'll need to use the XRT scanner from Engineering."

"We have an XRT scanner? That's ancient technology."

"Nevertheless, it is the tool you will need to pinpoint the source of the signal." GRUB's synthesized voice held a hint of annoyance.

"Okay, I'll go get it. Keep the external sensors on the other ship and tell me if it gets any closer."

"Aye aye, captain."

Hwicce cocked his head. GRUB's tone had shifted to sarcastic—maybe the alien had personality after all.

He trundled down the stairs from his and Veena's apartment and out into the common room. Veena looked up from where she was working on the alien code at the long table. Her messy ponytail left wisps of liquorice curls haloing her head.

"I couldn't sleep. Coffee's on." She yawned as she pointed to the coffeepot.

"GRUB woke me up." He poured himself a mug. "Apparently, someone is following us."

Veena's eyes went wide.

"I'm sure GRUB is over-interpreting the data." Hwicce downed the contents of his mug.

"I am not." GRUB's computer-synthesized voice now sounded indignant.

"I'll get that instrument and find the source of the signal," he said, putting a hand on Veena's shoulder.

"Do you need my help?"

"No," he said. "You should get some rest."

"Yeah," she said, making no move to get up. "Let me know if you decide you need help."

"I will."

Leaving his mug in the sink, Hwicce headed aft to Engineering. He knew she would be at that table when he returned, still working on making sense of the alien symbols. He took the catwalk around the cargo bay and entered the Engineering workshop. Lights came on as he went.

"Okay, GRUB." He surveyed the neatly ordered workbenches. "You're going to have to tell me what I need."

"The XRT scanner should be stored on the middle shelf in the red cabinet."

Hwicce turned around until he spotted a red cabinet on the far wall. He walked over and opened the door. The middle shelf stood empty. "Where else might it be?"

"It should be there," GRUB insisted. "I have no record of it being moved."

"Crap." Hwicce ran a hand through his hair as he looked around the room. "Do you have cameras in here?"

"I am filtering through those feeds now. Stand by."

While waiting, Hwicce wandered over to the clear wall that gave a view of the four great engines driving his ship.

"I am missing three hours of video feed just before our departure from Indigo Station."

"You mean the camera in here was turned off?" Hwicce asked.

"The cameras were turned off in this room, the main corridor, the cargo hold, and at the gangway to the ship," GRUB said.

"And you didn't notice?"

"I was focused on other issues."

"Who was on board at that time?" Hwicce asked.

"You and Emiko had just returned. Orin and Veena were also on board. Max was working on the seal to the forward airlock."

Hwicce nodded. "That was when Baker had been arrested. I don't know Max. What's his history?"

"He worked for your aunt for almost a decade. He was the most solid human she ever had on her crew."

"So, you're saying we can trust Max," Hwicce said.

"Since Captain Oswiu did, I would say yes."

Hwicce understood GRUB was referring to Darla and not himself.

The knot in his gut tightened at the thought that someone on the ship was secretly in communication with the unknown craft following them.

He pointed to the empty spot where the scanner should be. "Is this an act of sabotage, or just some missing gear?"

"It is the only piece of equipment we have that can track down the signal within the ship," GRUB said.

Hwicce scratched the back of his neck, and he regretted drinking the coffee so quickly. His gut was churning now. "Any unusual comms activity while the cameras were down?" It was a long shot.

"Checking."

With long strides, Hwicce headed up to the bridge. As he passed the common room, he debated stopping to check on Veena. Instead, he hoped she followed his suggestion to head to bed. On the bridge, he slumped down into the captain's chair.

"Okay, GRUB, what do you have?"

"There were several messages during that time frame. Most

were from Orin to port officials to obtain the appropriate paperwork for our departure."

"I asked him to do that." Hwicce scratched his head. Solving puzzles had never been his strength. Veena was good—no, fantastic—at that kind of thing, but confronting a potential saboteur was a captain's responsibility.

"Veena made several queries to Indigo Station archives."

"Ignore all of her traffic," Hwicce said. Veena was as focused, or more, on getting Molly back as he was.

"Emiko received a message," GRUB said. "Then she sent a reply just as we left the docks."

Hwicce let out an audible exhale. What did he know about Emiko, really? She had been an employee of Long Enterprises when he met her on the *Shimmer*. It seemed very convenient that she knew a way off the ship when a collision was imminent. Then the bounty hunter showed up at the shop when Veena was there. The coincidences were starting to add up to something in his head.

"Crap," he said under his breath as he stood. Emiko had seemed so genuine, so willing to be part of their group. Then there was the issue of her blossoming relationship with Baker. He needed to go to Baker first. "She just might kill me."

Before GRUB could ask what he was talking about, Hwicce strode off the bridge.

Standing in the door to her quarters, Baker crossed her arms over her chest as Hwicce explained the situation to her. "No. Absolutely not."

"I'm just saying, she's only been connected to us for a few days," Hwicce said. "There's just too many coincidences for us to ignore."

Baker just glared at him.

"I know the two of you have something going on." Hwicce

shifted his weight from foot to foot. "I like her too. I wish I didn't have to suspect her."

"What about Orin? Isn't it a little strange Veena's boss followed her with an offer for help?"

"True. But why would he be so quick to rescue you from jail? He risked his life for you—which he didn't have to do. Plus, he wasn't on board at the time."

Baker pursed her lips together. "What about the engineer? He seems a little shifty."

"Max has been with this ship for a decade." He ran a hand over his face. "My aunt trusted him and so should I."

"Emiko wouldn't sell us out."

"You've only known her a few days. There might be more to her story than she's let on."

Baker let her head drop. "I want to trust her."

"I know." Hwicce put a hand on Baker's arm; he'd never seen her so vulnerable before. "If she doesn't have the transmitter, we'll know it isn't her."

Baker nodded.

"Is she in your quarters?" Hwicce asked.

Baker sighed. "We decided not to share."

Hwicce checked the time. It was still early, but not ridiculously so. He looked Baker in the eye. "Do you want to come with me? It's okay if you just stay here. You don't have to be involved."

"Fucking hell, I hate this kind of shit, but I'll come."

Hwicce rang the bell on Emiko's quarters. A few moments later, she opened the door and rubbed her eyes.

"Is something going sideways?" Her gaze darted between Hwicce and Baker.

"There's no easy way to say it." Hwicce regretted he hadn't put on proper pants; his pyjama pants weren't particularly captain-like. He glanced from Baker to Emiko and for a moment wished he could be elsewhere. "We need to search your things. Someone onboard has a transmitter signaling a ship that's following us."

Emiko's eyes widened. "I don't know anything about that."

"We need to look." Hwicce felt like a monster for insisting. He wanted to trust Emiko almost as much as Baker did.

Emiko scowled and crossed her arms over her chest. She glared at Baker. "I expected more from you."

Baker hung her head. "Sorry, but we need to search."

Emiko moved out of the doorway and gestured Hwicce and Baker to enter.

On the first floor, there was a small sitting area complete with a kitchenette with enough counter space to accommodate a coffee maker. The single sofa was so ratty, it was impossible to determine the type of flower highlighted on the upholstery.

Hwicce circled the two-seater sofa and determined there was nothing to see in this room. A door led them to a storage area which was empty except for a thick layer of dust on the floor.

Hoping he was wrong, Hwicce climbed the stairs to the second level. A sleeping bag was laid out on the queen-sized bed. On the other side of the bed, floor-to-ceiling windows separated the bedroom from a small deck overlooking the garden.

Emiko's jacket sat on the floor at the foot of her bed. With a sigh, Hwicce went over and picked it up. He systematically put his hand into each pocket. At the bottom of the right front pocket, he found the transmitter. It had been too easy to find, yet he had no other suspects.

"Found it," he said, holding it up for the others to see.

Baker's jaw dropped.

Emiko's eyes widened. "That's not mine! I've never seen that before in my life!" She looked between Baker and Hwicce. "You have to believe me."

"I don't know what to think." Hwicce frowned as the knot in his gut tightened. He took a moment to turn the transmitter over in his hands. "I think it best you remain in your quarters for now."

Emiko turned to Baker. "You believe me, right?"

Without a word, Baker turned and went down the stairs.

Hwicce put the transmitter into his pocket before surveying the spartan bedroom. There was one more thing he had to find, and the closet was the only hiding place. He went over and opened the door. On the floor sat the XRT scanner.

"Did you take this from Engineering?" He pointed to the scanner.

"No, I swear." A tear dripped down her cheek as she stared at her feet. "I didn't betray you."

Hwicce pursed his lips together as he watched her. "Who's following us?"

Her head snapped up, and her gaze met his. "Someone is following us?"

"So you're not going to say?"

"Fuck you. After all, we've been through together, I deserve your trust."

Hwicce didn't know what more he could say. He turned and walked away.

"Do you think this is it?" Hwicce asked GRUB as he walked towards the side airlock.

"I would think so," GRUB said. "We'll know for sure once you jettison it."

Hwicce nodded. He hated that he'd been forced to confront Emiko, and he wanted to believe she wasn't involved. He sighed. After they finished their business at New Venus, he would leave Emiko behind. Baker would get over her, eventually.

Inside the airlock, he set the transmitter down next to the outside door. Then he went back into the hall and closed the inside door. Instead of cycling the airlock, he hit the emergency override. The outside door opened, and the transmitter, along with the airlock's air, was blown into space.

He closed the outside door and cycled the air. Then he put his head against the inside door's clear window, hating how he'd treated Emiko. But, all the evidence he had suggested she turned on them.

Chapter Thirty-Four

The next morning, Nigel took to projecting *Bubble and Click* comics on the wall so both Molly and Click could see them. Molly bounced as Click flashed the different colours their namesake in the comic did.

"My mom didn't believe Click could do that," Molly said, pointing at the cartoon Click floating through space without a spacesuit.

Nigel took a step over to her cell and knelt down. "I suspect they couldn't either," he said in a whisper.

From the other cell, Click emitted a series of clicks and flashed yellow.

"That confirms it," Nigel said. "Click would need a spacesuit."

Molly nodded solemnly, her big dark eyes dominating her face. "I'll keep that in mind." She came right up to the cell door. "We need to plan an escape."

Nigel cocked his head. "What do you mean?"

"When the guards bring lunch, can you distract them?"

"What are you going to do?" he asked.

Molly stared at him with her big, dark eyes. "I need to find my mom and dad. They must be so worried about me."

"You need to be patient; they're coming for you. It's just that they are in a different system and…" Nigel's words trailed off as he realized Veena and Hwicce still didn't know where to look. "They'll find us. I'm sure of it."

Molly scrunched up her face and balled her fists. "We need to escape by using a distraction. It's what Bubble and Click did in issue 7."

In the next cell over, Click emitted a series of clicks.

Nigel cocked his head and frowned. "You agree with her?"

Click clicked again.

Just then, the door at the end of the hall clanged open, and one of the staff pushed a cart through. Nigel set his pixels to transparent.

"Don't forget," Molly whispered as she pressed her face against the glass of the door and watched the cart approach.

The man pushing the cart wore the same grey uniform that everyone else in the facility wore. Even though Nigel's deductive thinking algorithms were rudimentary at best, he'd concluded they were in a secret military facility—there was no guarantee there was anywhere to escape to.

The man stopped at Molly's cell and looked in. "Are you going to try rattling things on me again, little monster?"

Molly bared her teeth and snarled.

"Back up next to the bed if you want your lunch," he said as he swiped an access card over the panel beside her door.

Molly complied, keeping her eyes fixed on the man. He slid the door open and took a tray off the cart.

"Kind, sir, do you have my lunch order?" Nigel materialized in the corridor behind the man.

"Huh?" He turned. "Who in the hell are you?"

Molly darted into the hallway, grabbing the keycard out of the man's hand as she passed. She turned, scrunched up her face, and the man fell backwards into her cell. Then she closed the door.

"I did it! I did it!" She bounced up and down, holding up the keycard. "I did it!"

The man's face went red as he stood and banged on the other side of the clear door. "Bad little girl! You let me out right now."

Molly stuck out her tongue at him.

"May I suggest we release Click and retire to a different area of this facility?" Nigel said.

Click placed three tentacles on their glass door and flashed pink. Molly swiped the keycard over their lock, and the door slid open. Click launched themselves into the air and hugged Molly. With a squeal, Molly returned their squeeze. Nigel glanced back and forth between the man in Molly's cell and the door he'd entered through. "We need to go. I suggest we try this way." He pointed to the door at the other end of the corridor.

The three of them proceeded down the hall. Nigel noted that all the cells they passed were empty. The keycard worked on the door, and it opened without issue. On the other side was a large, empty lab. High-tech devices surrounded several tables large enough for a human, complete with restraints.

Click pointed to a tank large enough to contain one of their kind, but it was empty. Molly's eyes were wide as she continued to hold on to Click.

There were two other doors out of the lab. Nigel chose the one on the right at random. The other two followed him.

"Click, can you fly any spacecraft?" Nigel asked.

Click flashed pink and red.

Nigel nodded. "I thought you'd say that."

Molly swiped the keycard, and the door opened. Inside was an office with floor-to-ceiling windows on the far wall—their first view of the world they were on.

Outside, the world was dark. Occasional flashes of lightning illuminated jagged rock formations in the distance. In the sky, a gas giant hung large. They had to be on a moon, Nigel concluded.

He studied the swirling yellow and blue storms on the gas giant, comparing it with the worlds in his database, but nothing came up.

"That looks like Drax." Molly stared at the gas giant.

"That's a fictional world from a comic," Nigel pointed out. Footsteps in the hall outside drew his attention. "Someone's coming. Hide."

Without a word, Molly darted under a desk near the door. Nigel turned off his projection, and Click stuck themselves to the ceiling.

Dr. Greer walked in and activated the holographic comms. Swa's head appeared.

"Did the girl's blood give you the information you need?" she asked.

Greer crossed his arms over his chest and paced over to the window. "My analysis has been inconclusive. I may need to resort to more invasive procedures on Subject 34."

Swa nodded her head. "You have full authority to do what needs to be done."

"About the alien code," he said, turning back to Swa's projected head.

"The bounty hunter on Indigo Station failed to capture Dr. Oswiu." Swa's tone dripped with disapproval. "She has left the station."

Greer slammed his hand against the wall. "Deciphering the code may be the key to everything."

Swa frowned. "Watch yourself," she said in a flat tone. "Your primary role is to isolate the genes that can create telekinesis. Your alien side project is just that: a side project."

"You just don't understand," Greer said. "Subject 34's telekinesis powers spontaneously emerged just like the others. The only common denominator between the subjects was multiple gate trips shortly after a traumatic experience."

"What are you getting at?"

"The aliens made the gates. Maybe they do more than just transfer ships from one solar system to another. What if they can also imbue these powers under the right circumstances?"

Swa raised an eyebrow. "You're saying the gates gave Molly telekinesis?"

"Call her Subject 34. And yes, that's my working hypothesis," Greer said.

Swa frowned. "Then using the gates is against the GenEn protocols. That knowledge would shatter our society."

"Look, I don't care about that," Greer said. "What I need is a way to translate the alien texts. They must have known more about how the gates work."

"There is something…" Swa's voice trailed off.

"What? What?" With each word, Greer moved closer to the projection of General Swa.

She smiled. "There's an alien artifact coming up for auction. My agents tell me it is a computer component."

"Well, I need to get my hands on it. It might give me the clues I need. Where's the auction?"

Swa's face took on a smug expression. "On Seven Soaring Swans."

"I have a shuttle ready to go. We'll leave right away."

"No, you have work to do. I need you to produce results."

Greer took a pace backwards and rubbed his chin.

"I have people on Dr. Oswiu's tail. She'll be in our custody soon. And, if everything goes according to my analysis projections, she'll have the alien artifact."

"I still think it's best I go to Seven Soaring Swans," Greer said.

"You just want to get off your rock and enjoy the luxury of that place."

"There's nothing wrong with mixing some pleasure with my business."

"I need you to produce results—or I'll find a jail cell for you." With a flash, her head vanished.

With a sigh, Greer shut down the comms and paced to the window. For a moment, he stood still, as though he was considering the view beyond.

He strode over to his desk and activated the intercom. "Bring the girl to the lab," he said. Then he left the office.

Nigel reappeared. He bent down to see into Molly's hiding place. "You made the right call. We need to get out of here."

Molly nodded and crawled out from under the desk. "My mom and dad are going to be trapped."

Click dropped from the ceiling, landing on the desk. They flushed a pale pink.

"We have little time until they discover we've escaped," Nigel said. "Click, we need to find you a ship."

Click flashed red before returning to pink.

"Good. Now we need to find their dock or hangar or wherever their ships are," Nigel said.

Molly went over to the ventilation duct. "How about we go through here?"

Click skittered over and unclipped the vent from the wall. The duct behind was just big enough for Molly to crawl through. After taking a flashlight from the clutter covering Dr. Greer's desk, she went right in.

Click followed, pulling the vent grating closed behind them.

Chapter Thirty-Five

Full daylight streamed through the bedroom windows with enough intensity, Veena thought, for a moment, she was back in her bed on New Haven. She sighed. Bombs had reduced her old home to rubble—it was a place she could never go back to.

"Hwicce?" She rolled over and realized he wasn't there.

Frowning, she sat up, her melancholy longing for the home she'd lost replaced with concern for her husband. He'd seemed so distracted the night before—like something big was on his mind. She stared at the spot she'd expected to find him sleeping.

"I should've asked what was going on," she said to his pillow, then bit her lip. "I've been so damn distracted by that alien text. But I'm so close to figuring it out. So close. A few more hours, and I could have it."

She yawned and stretched her arms overhead before surveying her room. The captain's cabin extended above the kitchen and dining area. It consisted of two spacious bedrooms on either side of a sitting room, along with a small study off to one side.

In the bedroom she'd chosen to sleep in, Aunt Darla's stuff remained scattered everywhere. The piles of what seemed to

Veena to be junk must have mattered to Darla and taken her years to collect. Veena spent a couple of hours the day before clearing enough space for them to sleep. She'd washed the bedding and towels and piled most of the junk up in the sitting room. It would take time to make this space into a home, but it would get there, eventually.

The glittery, purple mass of Molly's backpack caught her eye. Sitting on top of the bag, the stuffed toy version of Click stared back at her. Its time in the vacuum of space hadn't damaged it. Molly would want her toy back—and they now needed to rescue Click and Nigel as well.

"I can't just lounge in bed all day." Decoding—rather, translating—all that text still drew her. While in transit, figuring out what the text said was the most help she could be to their missing ones. Solving the puzzle of the text would give her leverage. Plus, she really needed to check in with Hwicce. Her stomach grumbled, a reminder she needed to eat something, too.

After getting up, she brushed her hair, pulling it back into her usual ponytail. Other than her green nanite dress, the only clothes she had were the same ones she'd worn the day before and the day before that. She paused for a moment to consider the pile of clothes strewn in front of the closet from the previous occupant of this cabin. The clothes seemed random, from beige sweat pants to a magenta sequin dress—even plaid pyjamas that fit Hwicce. There had to be something there she could wear—but hunting through the mess was a problem she could put off for now. Turning her back on the pile, she went down to the kitchen.

Also in the same clothes as the day before, Orin leaned against the faux marble counter next to the coffeepot. On seeing her, he filled a mug with coffee and handed it to her. "Good morning. Did you get any closer to a solution last night?"

Taking the mug, she sat at the table. "I'm getting close. Even though there are so many symbols, I'm not convinced they're going to translate directly to our words."

"Do you think it's written text or something else?"

Veena took a long sip of her coffee. "I don't know. The best I can say right now is that the text is not random garbage. There's a pattern there—more specifically, patterns within patterns."

"Patterns within patterns sounds interesting." Orin refilled his mug.

"And incredibly complicated."

"Some of the double encrypted Nader Alliance codes were complicated. And you managed to get us readable text."

"None of that was like this." She pointed to the text filling her screen. "There are the symbols, which I assume each have meaning. Then, each symbol is rotated in six different ways, as though orientation provides additional meaning." She scratched her head. "I'll keep working on it until we get to New Venus."

Orin sat down across from her. "That'll give you most of the day."

"I'm so close. It's like the solution is right in front of me, staring me in the face." Veena sighed. "Yet, still so far away."

"You'll figure it out." Orin smiled. "You have a knack for this kind of thing. Maybe that artifact on New Venus will hold the final key."

"Speaking of New Venus, did you get a hold of your contacts there?"

"I've left messages for everyone I know who might be in the area." Orin paused and glanced out at the garden for a moment. "No replies yet. Hopefully, someone gets back to me. But, my contacts are all on the spaceport. What we really need is some inside intel from down on Seven Soaring Swans."

"I know someone in the city," Baker said.

Veena turned; she hadn't even heard Baker come in. The ex-soldier stood next to the coffeepot as though she'd magically materialized there. A slump now replaced her normally erect posture. Her dark skin had lost its lustre, leaving a grey hue, and her eyes were red.

Veena almost asked what had happened, but hesitated. Her relationship with Baker hadn't warmed to that level, but Veena had to say something. "Um... I just want to say thank you for helping us. "

Baker sighed and poured herself a mug of coffee. "My contact probably has good intel," she said, ignoring Veena's comment. "He lives and works on the Island of Gold."

"Any information we can get from the surface—" Orin cut himself off. "Sorry, not the surface—we sure as hell don't want to be crushed on the surface—from the floating islands could be the clue we need. Someone from the Island of Gold probably has access to a lot of information. Give your contact a call."

With a nod, Baker pulled out a datapad. She set her mug down and typed out a message, scowling the whole time.

Orin continued, "My contacts are all up in orbit. The more we know, the better chance we'd have of actually pulling off a heist." He frowned. "Getting that artifact is not going to be easy."

"Don't forget: we need to find Pam Long as well," Veena said.

"Yes, your husband seems to think Mrs. Long might know where that secret lab is. She's going to the auction, right?"

Veena leaned back in her chair. "As far as I know."

She shifted her attention to Baker and cocked her head. The islands that made up Seven Soaring Swans were exclusive, mostly inhabited by the ultra-rich—and the Island of Gold was the kind of address only the elite of the elite might have. The fact that a former grunt knew someone living there was unexpected. "Who's your contact?"

"My big brother. He works at one of the banks." Baker spoke without looking up. She sighed again and put away the datapad. "He's always been a fucking goodie two shoes, so he's probably not going to be much help in stealing something."

"This ship is full of artifacts that one might want to auction off." Orin gestured to the surrounding ship. "Let's pick out a few that might be worth something. Hell, it would even make sense for a new captain to sell some stuff off to fund repairs."

Veena nodded. "Aunt Darla did like to collect things."

Baker scratched behind her left ear. "I'll ask my brother if he can make arrangements to put something in the auction."

"Excellent! That's a step in the right direction. I feel that we've made some progress." Orin smiled. "Now, back to the code. Has GRUB been able to provide much insight?"

"The symbols are ancient. I don't know the pre-Slip languages," GRUB said from the speaker above. They'd probably been listening all along.

Veena cocked her head and glanced up at the nearest speaker. "GRUB, do you have any contacts on New Venus, either in orbit or down in the city?"

"Captain Darla collected many items from the curio shops on Seven Soaring Swans," GRUB said. "As her successors, it would be logical for your captain to take some of her finer objects down for appraisal."

Orin grinned. "That's exactly my thinking."

"I heard your plan," GRUB spoke in a flat tone.

As Orin opened his mouth to retort, Veena cut in. "At least it would give us an excuse to look around. I've heard getting down to the floating islands can be difficult without prior appointments."

"I'll make us some appointments with several of the prominent curio shops on the Island of Silver," Orin said.

"Island of Silver? The metal names are a bit much." Veena rubbed the back of her neck.

Orin nodded. "Oh, they use non-metals too, like the Island of Crystal and Island of Dreams."

"It's all pompous ass shit," Baker said. "Seven Shitty Swans is just a fancy hellhole."

"True, true." Orin gazed up at the ship's speaker. "GRUB,

can you identify a few objects that are worth getting appraisals on?"

"Acknowledged." GRUB's tone had returned to their normal, synthesized cadence.

Veena turned and met Baker's gaze. "Have you even been down to the floating islands?"

Baker's brow wrinkled, and she frowned. "Yeah. I visited my brother once about a year ago. My ship was in dock at the spaceport, and I took a few days of leave."

"What was it like?"

"Stodgy as hell and full of pompous morons." Baker took a gulp of coffee. "They designed the place to be over the top, as though aesthetics were the only thing that mattered."

"I've seen pictures; the place is stunning," Veena said.

Baker shrugged. "If you like buildings with pillars and everything the colour of this counter." She gestured to the faux marble countertops. "Oh, and the endless sunset—it makes everything so picturesque, I could puke."

"Right." Veena had seen plenty of images of Seven Soaring Swans and its endless sunset—the result of attenuated light through the thick clouds of the Lid. Sure, the place felt contrived, but the Grecian-inspired buildings added a solid base to such a magical place.

"Don't forget the public art," Orin said in a wistful tone. "My wife's biggest dream was to have one of her sculptures on display there."

Baker snorted. "And my brother wants me to move there. He seems to think I should work in the family business. The nerve of him." She put down her mug and crossed her arms over her chest as though living in such a refined place was a fate worse than death.

Veena cocked her head. "Your family business is banking?"

"Ever heard of Baker, McBride, and Associates?"

"You're one of those Bakers?" Orin raised an eyebrow as he leaned back in his seat.

"Yeah." Baker looked down at the table.

Orin turned to Veena. "Baker, McBride, and Associates have satellite banks all over the Protectorate. I think they even have branches on the Nader Alliance side too. Is that right?"

Baker nodded.

"Then why join the army?" Veena asked.

Baker shrugged again. "Rebellion." Then she laughed. "More accurately, I wanted to escape that stodgy shit and have an adventure."

Chapter Thirty-Six

Orin itched to take manual control as they came around New Venus. Below, the deep gaseous atmosphere swirled in golden weather patterns worthy of being jewelry. New Venus wasn't a gas giant. Somewhere at the bottom of the atmosphere lurked a rocky core—but no one had ever survived going down there due to the extreme pressure and toxic gases.

For the millionth time, he checked their flight path. GRUB was keeping the ship in their assigned approach lane, leaving Orin with nothing to do.

"There the hell hole is," Baker said as the spaceport came into view—but she wasn't looking at it. Instead, her gaze remained fixed at the spot where Seven Soaring Swans floated beneath a thick layer of clouds—'the Lid', as the locals called it.

A message from the Water Guild came in, pulling Orin's attention. He smiled as he read the text. He turned to face Hwicce sitting in the captain's chair. "Just heard from the Water Guild, and it's good news."

Hwicce met Orin's gaze. "In that case, spill the beans."

"The military diverted the port's water shipment. They're willing to buy every ounce of water we have."

Hwicce stood and strode closer. "Will that earn us enough credits to get through Max's list of needed repairs?"

"That and some."

Hwicce frowned. "But our tanks will be empty, and we'll have to refill them at our next stop."

Baker turned to Hwicce. "On that note, how do we fill this hulking beast?"

"We will have to make a stop at a water world," GRUB said. "And dip low enough into its atmosphere that our proboscis can reach the water and pump it on board."

"That'll require some fancy-ass flying." Baker crossed her arms over her chest.

"According to the guild rules, we'll need to fill our tanks at the nearest water world," Orin said.

Hwicce scratched his head. "That'll be one more delay. Veena won't like that."

"Complying with the Water Guild's requirements will provide us with the ongoing anonymity we need to stay out of General Swa's grasp."

"I know." Hwicce crossed his arms over his chest. "Well, we need to dock, and we sure as hell need the money. Go ahead and make arrangements."

"Yes, Captain." Orin licked his lips, knowing what he was about to suggest may not go over well with Hwicce and Baker— but they needed to look less like people on the run and more respectable.

"One more thing…."

"Yeah," Hwicce said without looking away from the view outside.

"May I suggest we invest in high-end clothing for our excursion down to Seven Soaring Swans?"

Baker snorted. "What the fuck for?"

Orin smiled at Baker to smooth things over. "We need to look the part to be taken seriously." He shifted his gaze to Hwicce. "It's worth the investment."

Hwicce frowned. "Maybe."

"Humans do seem to be particular about what you adorn your bodies with," GRUB interjected. "The previous captain always wore her best clothing when she visited the islands."

"Fine. First, we'll get ourselves some fancy clothes."

Baker snorted, but didn't say anything further on the topic.

After the ship was docked and the water transfer had begun, Orin took a moment to stop by the kitchen and pack a meal for Emiko. Even with the evidence Hwicce found, he couldn't believe the young woman betrayed them. Yeah, she was rough around the edges, but she'd seemed genuinely one of them during the short time he'd known her.

Orin found a box of chocolate cookies and a lentil stew meal pack in the kitchen. Just as he turned, Max stepped into the common room.

"I couldn't find the captain," Max said as he came closer. The sheen of sweat on his forehead glistened under the bright lights of the kitchen.

"He's still on board. I'm sure GRUB can find him for you. If you need him, make sure you find him soon, as the captain, Veena, Baker, and I are all about to head off the ship."

Max put his hands in his pockets. "Well… when you see the captain, let him know the pumps are working at 93% efficiency. It'll take about two hours for us to fill the port's tanks."

"That sounds good." Orin could feel his forehead wrinkling. Why wouldn't Max just find the captain and tell him this himself? The living areas of the *Virdis* weren't that large.

"What should I do in the meantime?"

"Hwicce wants you to get the supplies on your list and start with the needed repairs."

Max nodded. "Is that girl… Emily…"

"Her name is Emiko."

"Yeah, that's it. Is she staying behind?"

"Yes. The captain has confined her to her quarters for the

time being. I'm bringing her some food." Orin held up the meal pack.

"I could use her help with the repairs."

"You're going to have to ask the captain about that," Orin said. "But I'd support that idea, especially since GRUB could keep tabs on what's going on."

"GRUB likes to stick their nose into everything. We can't do anything around here without them cutting in and offering an opinion."

Orin just nodded, as he wasn't sure exactly what Max wanted. This seemed more of a conversation for Hwicce. Besides, didn't GRUB have microphones in the common room? And wouldn't Max know that?

Max leaned against the kitchen counter. "Are the four of you headed down to Seven Soaring Swans?"

"Yes. Baker has family down there."

Max pursed his lips together. "Hmmm. That one doesn't seem to be the sort that would come from such a swanky place."

Orin smiled. "It surprised me when she admitted it."

"So, you're all heading down for a social visit?"

"Yes." Orin swallowed as he wondered if his lie was written across his face.

"Interesting."

Orin held up the food for a second time. "I'm going to drop this off with Emiko." He turned and started walking towards the door to her quarters.

"One more thing," Max called.

Orin stopped and looked over his shoulder.

"Do you know when we'll be leaving?"

Orin cocked his head.

"Cuz I need to make us an appointment to refill our water tanks —this port is going to take everything we have." Max still leaned casually against the counter, but his gaze made Orin's skin crawl.

Orin shifted on his feet. "The captain has asked that I take over the water supply logistics. I'll make arrangements for our refill. I've already been in touch with the Guild."

"Is that so?" Max frowned and crossed his arms over his chest. "Well, I still need to know when we'll be leaving, considering you are all heading off for a 'social visit.'"

"I don't know. You'll have to ask the captain," Orin said as he resumed walking to Emiko's door, glad that Max had no more follow-up questions.

At the door, he glanced back. Max had already left. Orin exhaled, released the lock on Emiko's door and rung the buzzer. A few moments later, the door slid open.

"Is it just you?" Emiko asked as she looked past him.

"You don't need to worry; it's just me," he said with a smile. "We're heading off-ship for a bit, and I wanted to make sure you had something to eat while we're away." He held up the tray.

She bit her lip and nodded.

"How are you holding up?"

With wide eyes, she stared right at him. "I didn't betray anyone. I don't know how that stuff got in my room."

"I know. When we get back, I'll go through all the camera feeds and any other sensors that might help to see what really happened. Don't lose hope; I'm sure there's proof you did nothing wrong."

"Did…" Her words trailed off, and she bit her lip again.

"Is there something else you need?" He handed her the tray of food.

"Did…" She sighed. "Did you see B?"

"I did. She seemed really upset."

Emiko glanced down at the tray. "Thanks." With her elbow, she pressed the door button, and it slid shut.

Orin pressed his lips together as he stared at the closed door. With a sigh, he locked it again. He was certain that Emiko was innocent, but didn't have time to prove it right now.

Chapter Thirty-Seven

Veena ran her hands down the smooth fabric of her green nanite dress, reformatted into a pants suit. The deep green fabric suited her, but the shine and figure hugging cut left her feeling conspicuous—like everyone around her suspected she was pretending to be someone she wasn't. She was the only one in their group who hadn't needed to purchase new clothes, but she splurged on a pair of glittery green shoes that were actually comfortable.

Resisting an impulse to futz with the nanite scarf around her neck, she smiled as Hwicce took her hand. The steel blue suit he wore made him look more like a banker than water tanker captain. But it also made him handsome in a more refined way than usual. She squeezed his hand as she glanced back over her shoulder.

Orin and Baker followed a pace on behind. Orin stood tall in the brown suit he'd chosen for himself, giving him an air of confidence Veena had never seen in her former boss. In his right hand, he held the case of artifacts GRUB deemed worthy of appraisal.

Beside him, in head-to-toe banana yellow—a colour that

actually worked on her—Baker strode as though heading to an execution. She held her face in a grimace announcing she dreaded something, whether it was that she was about to face her brother or related to her relationship with Emiko, Veena didn't know.

"Does everyone have their comms device?" Veena asked as they stopped in the waiting lounge for their shuttle trip down to the floating islands somewhere below. She kept a hand on the found messenger bag containing her comms device and datapad as she looked around.

The sleek spaceport was several steps nicer than Indigo Station had been, with a ubiquitous scent of lemon cleaner rather than stale urine.

"They're going to work like shit down there," Baker grumbled.

Orin nodded. "All that metal in the atmosphere layer below the islands, the Shimmer I think it's called, can cause interference."

"Shimmer. Just like that bloody ship," Baker muttered. "Everything has gone downhill since we set foot on that shitty cargo ship."

Hwicce turned to Baker. "Hey, we dealt with that cargo ship, just like we'll deal with what's down on Seven Soaring Swans."

"I think you mean Seven Shitty Swans." Baker turned away and started studying her cuticles.

"Focus, Baker," Hwicce said.

"Yes, sir!"

Veena grimaced, but said nothing. Baker was probably lashing out because of Emiko's betrayal. She ran her hands down the smooth fabric of her pants and vowed to reach out more to Baker once they got back to the ship.

"When we get down there, Baker and I will call on her brother." As Hwicce spoke, Baker's frown increased.

"And we'll look around," Veena said, forcing her focus back

to the plan. "If we're lucky, Orin and I'll spot Mrs. Long. I have that image capture you sent. And she shouldn't recognize us."

"If you find her, message us right away." Hwicce squeezed Veena's hand. "And don't get too close. I don't want you taking unnecessary risks."

"That bitch will have muscle with her," Baker said in a growl that made other passengers in the waiting room turn and stare at them.

Veena nodded. "Don't worry—we'll stay well clear of her. And we'll call if we spot her."

"Sir, what's your plan if we spot Mrs. Long?" Baker asked.

Hwicce drew a deep breath. "I just want to corner her and ask a few questions."

Baker nodded. "So no abductions?"

"Hell no," Veena cut in. "I don't want anyone to get arrested. The Water Guild won't protect our anonymity if we start doing that kind of thing."

"We won't do anything that'll get us arrested. The auction is scheduled to start at 1800 hours. Do you have your tickets?" Hwicce asked.

"Yes," Veena said.

"You'd better take this." Orin held out the case, and Hwicce took it from him.

A chime sounded, and an androgynous voice came over the speakers. "All confirmed passengers for shuttle 1701, please proceed to gate 1."

"That's us. We best get going." Orin turned towards the gate.

After showing her ticket, Veena followed Orin onto the shuttle. The cream upholstery and dark wood interior a clear sign their ride wasn't standard public transit. Veena swallowed and tried not to think about the cost of their four tickets.

"This side trip better be worth it," she whispered to herself as she sunk down into the upholstered seat.

Hwicce sat down beside her. "We'll find the clues we need. I'm sure of it."

Veena turned to him as Baker and Orin took the seats across from them. "Molly must be so scared, out there alone, wherever she is."

"I suspect she's more resourceful than we know. She'll be okay, and we'll get her back soon," Hwicce said.

"Excuse me." Both Veena and Hwicce turned to the glossy white server drone that hovered in front of their seats. "Would you like a drink?" It held out a tray of crystal tumblers filled with greenie liquor. The glass and the liquid caught the light, creating a constellation of pale green light spots on the cabin around them.

"Yes, please." Veena hoped the liquor would soothe her nerves. Hwicce took a tumbler as well, then the drone rotated to Baker and Orin.

"This is the captain speaking," came a voice over the speakers. "Please buckle your seat belts. We will depart momentarily. We expect turbulence when we pass through the Lid."

Their ride down into the atmosphere of New Venus was smoother than expected; the predicated turbulence never manifested. Veena sipped her drink as she stared out the window.

A rocky core was down there, somewhere far below, but all Veena could see was the thick cloud cover New Venus was famous for. At their level, pinks and yellows from the system's sun highlighted the clouds—a light that was attenuated across the Lid, creating a perpetual sunset no matter where the actual sun sat in the sky.

As they descended, bands of different coloured gaseous clouds passed by the windows. All were pastel colours ranging from yellow to lilac to puce. They even crossed through an iridescent band filled with rainbows. Even though it had been mineral mining that made New Venus rich, it was a beautiful place.

After nearly forty-five minutes of descent, the clouds

abruptly ended. A transparent atmospheric layer extended out as a horizontal buffer between the Lid and the Shimmer. This layer contained naturally floating islands and the right oxygen content and pressure for humans. The shuttle levelled off, heading directly towards the cluster of floating islands.

Farther below, the atmosphere shimmered as though liquid—no wonder it had been named the Shimmer. But it was still gaseous, just heavily laced with tiny metallic particles. One only had to dip a net into the layer to mine the metals—as a result, most of the inhabitants of the floating islands were ridiculously rich.

With the sepia sky above and a glittering ocean of metal below, the shuttle levelled off. Ahead, Seven Soaring Swans—the only publicly accessible group of the planet's floating islands—hung suspended. The white buildings reflected the sunset hues of the sky above. The islands seemed impossible—as if they would sink into the Shimmer at any minute—yet exotic matter in the rocks held them up.

Surrounding the islands, dirigibles of all sizes swarmed the airspace while hover cars darted about. Far in the distance, industrial mining platforms hovered above the massive nets used to pull up the metals from the layer below.

"It's quite something." Hwicce leaned closer to her to look out the window. He smelled of cedar soap and new clothing. Veena smiled and took his hand in hers.

"It's almost like physics doesn't apply here," she said.

The shuttle's landing was as smooth as the rest of the trip. At the port, they disembarked without incident. On the other side of the port, they entered Cygnet Square—the bridge to the first floating island. A gentle breeze greeted them, carrying a slight metallic scent.

Above, the perpetual sunset shone warm tones down onto everything, including Hwicce's face. Veena smiled at him before noticing the floor. She gasped and froze.

The floor beneath their feet was clear, giving a stunning,

vertigo-inducing view of the metallic layer underfoot. The Shimmer seethed as though a storm raged below. Eddies of silver, turquoise, vermillion, and gold spun about, creating fractal patterns of spirals within spirals threatening to pull her in.

"It's beautiful." Hwicce squeezed her hand.

Veena swallowed and forced her gaze up to her husband. "I didn't expect this." She surveyed her level. Circling the square were abstract sculptures that hinted at tree inspiration. However, there wasn't a spec of foliage anywhere.

"Mary's dream was for one of her statues to be featured here," Orin said.

"It's just fucking ugly public art. My brother's office is this way," Baker said as she headed towards the footpath leading to the Island of Gold without checking anyone was following.

With a sigh, Veena set off after her, relieved that Cygnet Square was the only place with a clear floor. Hwicce and Orin fell into step beside her. The crowds weren't thick, making it easy to move past the outdoor cafes and luxury shops.

After the group passed through two other expansive squares, Baker veered right into a jewellery shop. The others followed.

"I just spotted Pam Long," Baker said in a low tone as she looked at the items on display in a case.

"Where?" Hwicce asked, craning his neck to see out of the shop's windows.

"She's at a cafe across the street." Baker pointed.

Veena spotted the elderly woman sitting with a woman in a grey suit on a patio separated from the street by an intricately patterned metal fence. Emptied plates filled the table, suggested the pair had finished their meal. Both the patio and green with gold-trimmed interior space of the restaurant sat mostly empty —a perfect place for secret conversation. And Mrs. Long and the woman were deep in a discussion.

"She's eating with one of Swa's grey suits, like the uniforms the group that took Mol were wearing." Veena tried and failed to place the woman back on the Rock. "But I don't recognize her."

Hwicce gestured to himself and Baker. "Mrs. Long will recognize us."

Orin moved so he stood between Hwicce and Baker and the shop's windows. "Right. We've got six hours until the auction. Now might be a good time to split up."

Veena nodded. "Orin and I will follow Mrs. Long. We can meet inside the auction hall."

Hwicce pursed his lips together as though about to argue. He met Veena's gaze. "Mrs. Long is a dangerous woman, and don't forget, she probably has a security detail. Just try to figure out where she's staying so Baker and I can find her after the auction."

"Since she might know where Molly is, she's more of a lead than the auction." Veena stared at Mrs. Long. The wizened old woman didn't appear to be a danger to anyone.

"Promise me you won't approach her."

Veena turned back to Hwicce. The lines across his forehead betrayed his worry. "I promise I'll be careful."

Hwicce frowned. "That'll have to do. Come on, Baker. Let's go find that brother of yours."

Chapter Thirty-Eight

White marble buildings lined the street, each one more substantial than Hwicce would've expected on floating islands. Pillars and carved facades added to the ancient look. Even walking down the centre of the boulevard, he felt dwarfed by his surroundings.

He craned his neck to look up as a gigantic shadow darkened the sky. Above, a sepia and maroon toned airship coasted past. Its rigid balloon and cabin beneath were sleek and aerodynamic, as though it could travel great distances.

"This fucking way," Baker snarled. Her attitude had taken an even more sour turn since they'd arrived on Seven Soaring Swans—or Seven Shitty Swans as she liked to call the place.

Hwicce shifted his attention to where she pointed. Ahead, a gently arched stone bridge connected to the next island. He glanced back up at the passing airship, then realized Baker hadn't waited. She was already on the bridge and would soon disappear into the crowd on the other side—if disappearing was possible in her banana yellow pantsuit.

After dodging a swarm of uniformed children out on an

excursion, he ran to catch up with her while holding the case awkwardly at his side.

"So, your brother—"

Baker held up a hand to cut him off. "I don't want to talk about the dimwit."

"Right." Hwicce didn't press further as he transferred the case to his right hand.

He snuck another glance at the sky as they reached the apex of the bridge. The airship was already past the island, leaving the view mostly unobstructed. The churning mass of thick clouds of the Lid reflected yellow hues back down. A gust of wind ruffled his clothing and brought a whiff of sulphur.

In the city layer, the air remained transparent, allowing him to see far-off metal refineries sitting on top of billowing nets trailing into the layer below. He stared down into the mass of glittering confetti of metals—calling the layer 'The Shimmer' now made sense, even if the word made him think of that crappy cargo ship.

Baker didn't take her eyes off the street, as though the stunning vista wasn't worth a moment of her time. With a sigh, Hwicce ran again to catch back up with her.

The streets on the other side of the bridge changed to a golden colour—they'd reached the Island of Gold, also known as Banker's Island. Baker crossed the public square, heading directly for a particularly pillared building on the far side. Like the Shimmer below, this building glittered. Gold leaf encased its carved facade like paint covered the buildings back on New Haven.

Baker didn't hesitate at the threshold. With a clenched jaw, she forged on through the open doors. Hwicce followed in her wake.

Inside the solid edifice, soaring ceilings and more gold leaf greeted them. Impeccably dressed people moved around the space in dignified manners, only talking in hushed tones. Hwicce couldn't help but feel out of place as he followed Baker to a desk set off to the side. Her scowl drove everyone to give them a wide berth.

"I'm here to see Joseph Baker," Baker said to the startled receptionist. "He's expecting me."

"Who shall I say is here?" The receptionist smiled, an expression that didn't reach his eyes.

"His sister."

Hwicce barely had time to get comfortable on the waiting room sofa before the receptionist came to collect them. They were led up an opulent set of stairs, down a hall, and into an office that felt like a hotel lobby.

"Fanny!" Joseph grinned and came around his desk. Although he was at least a decade older, he was the same height as his sister and moved with a similar predatory confidence. He enveloped a rigid Baker in a big hug, leaving Hwicce surprised she didn't respond with a punch.

"This is my friend Hwicce." Baker pointed at him with her thumb.

"Ah." Joseph shook Hwicce's hand. "Always nice to meet my little sister's friends."

Hwicce smiled.

"Sit, let's have some coffee." Joseph gestured to the two sofas across the room from the massive desk. As Hwicce and Baker settled into one, Joseph snapped his fingers in an exaggerated gesture.

From a side door, a young woman entered with a tray of coffee mugs and pastries in one hand and a coffee carafe in the other. As she set down the tray and started filling his mug, Hwicce studied Baker's brother.

Joseph met his gaze. "Fanny tells me you've inherited some artifacts."

"Yes, my aunt left me a number of things from Old Earth." Hwicce put his case on his lap and opened it.

He put a taxidermy rabbit from old Earth on the table. The white rabbit was posed up on its hind legs, and its mouth gaped open, showing off its teeth as though about to attack. It was so hideous, Hwicce had to suppress a shiver. Beside the rabbit, he put an egg larger than his hand. Orin had identified it as an ostrich egg, also from Old Earth.

"I'd like to auction these off." Hwicce gestured to the two items that to him seemed more ready for the trash bin than a fancy auction.

"Hmmm." Joseph picked up the egg and turned it over in his hands, then he leaned in close to get a good view of the rabbit. "These are interesting. Are you sure you want to part with them?"

"The ship my aunt left me needs repairs."

Joseph nodded. "Just happens there's an artifact auction this evening."

Hwicce held his breath as Joseph picked up the rabbit.

"Have you had these items authenticated? If they came on the generation ships from Old Earth, they would be in high demand." Joseph met Hwicce's gaze. "You could stand to make a fortune tonight."

"I had an expert confirm they were both from Old Earth. I also have records showing the line of ownership from Generation Ship 5."

Joseph steepled his fingers together as he nodded. "In that case, we should proceed. I know the owner of the auction house. Let me call them." He stood and left the room.

Hwicce exhaled and looked to Baker. "Do you think he can do it?"

Baker shrugged, then slumped lower on the sofa. She put her yellow boots up on the coffee table.

Hwicce frowned. "What's with you and your brother? You never even mentioned him before. Or that your family owns a bank. Or that you have a first name."

"The family business is boring," she said, just as Joseph came back in.

"Good news." Joseph grinned. "The Department of

Curiosities will include your objects in the auction this evening on the Island of Silver. I'll forward you all the information you need. And since you have several hours to kill, I took the liberty of reserving us a place at the Basement for lunch."

"Fucking hell," Baker said under her breath.

Joseph's expression faltered, and he frowned at his sister. "Fanny, you are more than a low-brow grunt. Mom and Dad would be horrified—"

Baker put up a hand and cut him off. "Fine, I'll go to your fancy ass upside-down restaurant and play nice."

A pleasant expression returned to Joseph's face. "Excellent. I'll have my assistant send your items to the auction house. Let's go."

Uncertain if he wanted to be caught between warring siblings, Hwicce followed, hoping Veena's afternoon was less eventful.

Chapter Thirty-Nine

Emiko paced her bedroom for the ten billionth time. How could they believe she would sell them out? She swallowed. How could B believe such a thing? B and she had something special, at least it looked that way.

"I should have told her how I feel," Emiko said to herself, and she ran her hands over her head. She knew letting people in was not her strength.

She stared out at the ship's garden. The fractal pattern of the tree branches, occasionally punctuated by leaves, was the only part of the garden she could see. At the centre, the pillar of absinthe-green water passively filtered their air. Above, full daytime light shone down with nearly blinding intensity. Emiko looked away, blinking. She bit her lip. It was the garden of her dreams—one she wanted to nurture back to its full potential.

What if she could prove her innocence? Could GRUB stop her if she climbed down off the balcony? She still had her tool kit, so she could override doors if need be. She slung the tool kit strap over her shoulder.

"I'm done waiting around."

Stepping out onto the balcony, she looked down. It was

farther than she could jump, and the nearest tree was too far away to grab onto. Even if she could reach, there was no way it would hold her weight.

With a huff, she put her hands on her hips. "What I don't have is a bloody rope."

She slowly turned and surveyed her room. A pile of pink, polka-dot fabric in the corner caught her attention—the sheets she'd stripped from the bed the night before. She retrieved the sheets and tied the top and bottom sheet together, then tied an end to the deck railing.

"Try to stop me," she said, imagining GRUB in the algae tank watching her.

Using the sheet rope, she climbed down to the garden. When her feet touched the moist soil, she froze in a low crouch and held her breath. Moving only her eyes, she scanned the common room and kitchen. No one was there. Slowly exhaling, she checked the other balconies—all empty. As she rose to her full height, she let go of her pink sheet rope. The vivid colour would signal to anyone who passed that she had left her room, but there wasn't anything she could do about that.

She strode over to the main doors to the hallway, and they opened. Sticking her head through, she looked both ways. GRUB should stop her, or at least remind her she should be confined to her quarters. A knot started forming in her gut. Where was GRUB? If they controlled the computer systems, why weren't they stopping her? She headed towards Engineering. No one was around. Everyone must have had already left for the floating islands.

The main doors to the engineering workshop were closed. She took a deep breath and opened them. The room had changed dramatically since her last visit. A large, clear tank of water sat in the middle of the room. Inside, a dark shape with tentacles reached around. She took another step into the room and realized that GRUB was trapped in the box.

She stopped. Why was GRUB in the box? Should she let them go? As she took another step closer, the alien flashed red.

Emiko spun around as Max closed the door behind her. He grinned, yet his eyes were hard.

"I was wondering if you'd try to get out," he said.

"What's going on here?" Emiko pointed at GRUB. "Are the others on board?"

Max took a step towards her. "It's just you and me, sweetheart."

When Orin called her sweetheart, it was endearing. When Max said it, the word sounded dirty. Emiko backed away.

"I've been hoping you'd join me. You and me together—now that sounds like a great team."

"Join you?" Emiko struggled to keep her face neutral.

"I spent a decade serving Darla." He walked over to the floor-to-ceiling windows overlooking the ship's massive engines. "Hell, I'm the only one who stuck it out that long if you discount that tentacled monster."

"The ship's still running. Hwicce will make a good captain," she said, believing it even though he'd been so quick to suspect her.

"And that's the problem." Max pointed a finger at her. "Darla left the *Virdis* to him rather than me."

"Hwicce is Darla's family."

"He's just some dipshit who never even set foot on this ship." Max paced, becoming more agitated as he went.

Emiko licked her lips as she tried to subtly study the tank containing GRUB. Only a clasp held the lid closed. She took a tiny step closer—if she could open the lid, GRUB could come to her aid. The two of them could overpower Max.

"That bounty hunter was easy to find." Max turned towards her and smirked. "He paid handsomely too. All he wanted were a few updates on where we were heading. He's only an hour behind us now."

"But they destroyed the tracking device," Emiko said. "That you hid in my room."

"Sorry, sweetheart, that was a decoy. I needed someone who isn't me to take a fall."

Emiko shivered as she realized how thoroughly she'd been used.

"I saw you were the outsider. I suspected they'd be quick to turn on you."

"But...." Emiko's words trailed off. He was right. Even B had been quick to turn on her. Still, she wanted to warn the others that the bounty hunter was still on their tails. Even now, she still foolishly cared about them.

Max came over and stopped right in front of her. "The ship will be mine," he said. He reached a hand forward and traced a finger down her cheek. "It's not too late; you could still come with me."

"I...." Emiko wanted to back away from his touch, but he was between her and the tank. "I... would need time to think about it."

"You're going to have to decide now. The bounty hunter is willing to pay for you too—it seems even you have a price on your head. But I'm sure I can negotiate for your freedom."

Emiko swallowed.

"I've given him the codes to everyone's comms devices. Finding them will be easy for him."

Then she met his gaze. "Go to hell," she said as she shoved him backwards.

His surprise at her attack gave her enough time to reach the tank and unclip the lid. With a flash of purple and yellow, GRUB launched themself from the tank and leapt onto Max's head. The tank toppled onto its side, and the water sloshed out across the deck.

Max screamed and flailed at GRUB with his hands, but GRUB held on. Emiko sprinted to the supply cabinet and grabbed a handful of tie wraps and a large wrench.

GRUB emitted a series of sharp clicks as Max threw them off. "You're better off pretending to be a damn computer," he said, picking up a pry bar.

Flushing orange, GRUB lunged forward and wrapped their tentacles around Max's leg.

Max swung the pry bar, hitting GRUB's body. The alien lost their grip and tumbled across the floor.

"No wonder your species is nearly extinct." Max raised the pry bar and advanced on GRUB. "The bounty hunter will give me more than enough credits to get a proper AI."

GRUB let out a rapid series of soft clicks as their colour drained, leaving only grey skin.

Emiko looked at the tank on its side, then to Max. She grit her teeth and lunged towards him, wrench raised. She contacted his right forearm, and Max dropped the pry bar. Then Emiko swung and contacted the side of his left knee. Max screamed as he fell to the ground, clutching his leg.

"Help me," Emiko said as she started pushing Max towards the now empty tank.

Green dots swirled across their body as GRUB skittered forward and helped push. Max only feebly tried to resist. As soon as they had him in the tank, GRUB reached up with a single tentacle and pulled the door closed. They latched it shut.

Breathing heavily, Emiko stood and put her hands on her hips. "We did it."

GRUB flashed a pale green, then orange. The adult alien wasn't nearly as cute as Click, but they were far from monstrous.

"Now, how do I connect you back up with the ship?"

GRUB flashed cyan and lilac and made a popping sound. They reached up, unlocked the workshop door, and went out into the hallway. Emiko followed a few paces behind.

GRUB returned to the ship's garden and climbed up a trellis on the back wall. They disappeared into a panel at the top.

"Thank you." GRUB's voice now came from the ship's speaker. "I didn't expect Max would turn on the ship."

Emiko watched as GRUB swam down into the column, clearly more comfortable in water than air. She scratched the back of her neck. "The bounty hunter," she said.

"Yes, we need to warn the others." GRUB's tentacles splayed out as they communicated. "They took comms devices. However, the cloud layer will distort our signal."

She glanced over to the pink sheet rope she'd used to escape her room. Hwicce and B had accused her of doing something she'd never do. Yet, she couldn't bring herself to abandon them. Emiko swallowed. They might not evade the bounty hunter a second time—especially if they didn't know he was coming.

"I could go after them," Emiko said.

GRUB flashed vermillion. "Even after they turned on you?"

Emiko took a deep breath. She didn't owe them; she could just leave—find another ship and be gone before they got back. But she knew she couldn't live with herself if she did that.

"I still care."

GRUB flushed pink. "Then let's work together and come up with a plan."

Chapter Forty

As Veena leaned against the side of the pillar, she fiddled with her scarf, counting the hexagons in its honeycomb pattern. Her feet ached in her new fancy shoes, making her want to take them off and throw them over the nearest edge, letting them vanish forever into the Shimmer.

A gust of wind swept over her, pushing the whips of her hair that had escaped her ponytail into her mouth. As she wiped the hair away, she let her gaze resettle on their quarry.

Pam Long's guest had left an hour ago. Now the old woman sat alone, sipping tea and staring up at the clouds above. Still holding on to her messenger bag with one hand, Veena scratched her head. Even though Hwicce seemed to think otherwise, Mrs. Long didn't seem dangerous at all, and they'd seen no hint of any security detail. How could she possibly head a crime organization? It couldn't be true.

Veena glanced at Orin. "This is a waste of time. I'm thinking we should just get something to eat ourselves."

"We could join Mrs. Long," Orin suggested.

"Why would we do that?"

"We have proof of her involvement in the destruction of the *Garden Princess*. Maybe she'd trade info."

"Right, we have proof." Veena let out a slow exhale as she ran a hand over her head. The destruction of the *Garden Princess* to kill a single man had been the work of a stone-cold criminal —and that criminal was Mrs. Long. "Joining her is a bold plan."

"Maybe bold is what we need." Orin looked her in the eye. "I don't want to end up following her all day and finding out nothing. I haven't seen any hint of her security. Confronting her out in public would be safe."

"I don't want Hwicce and Baker to botch questioning her like they did with Boris."

Orin smiled. "Fair enough. Plus, I don't think I'd be able to break them out of prison here."

Veena glanced at the stone edifices on the buildings— nothing they'd seen so far seemed to be a prison. They had their jail hidden away somewhere—and the Islands' leaders probably had spared no expense in making sure it was secure. Having Hwicce thrown inside one of their cells would only delay getting Molly back and lead to more complications.

"We need to take matters into our own hands and ask Mrs. Long some questions," she said, running her hands down her pants and pulling herself up tall.

"I've got your back." Orin glanced to where Mrs. Long sat.

"No, I think only one of us should go—and it should be me. I need to confront that woman... convince her to help me get Mol back."

Orin frowned. "I don't want you going in there alone."

"It's a public restaurant patio sitting on a busy street—she's not going to do anything. Besides, if things go wrong, I need you to tell Hwicce what's happened and then pretend to be my lawyer like you did for Baker."

"You're assuming you'll be dealing with legitimate authorities."

Veena slowly inhaled as she stared at Mrs. Long—the

woman appeared harmless. Then she scanned the surroundings, looking for anyone that might be part of a security detail, and found no one. "I'm willing to make that assumption."

"Be careful. I don't want to explain to your husband what happened to you." Orin stepped out of her way.

"It's just talking."

Faking more confidence than she felt, Veena strode over to the nearly empty café and headed towards Mrs. Long's table.

"I'm sorry I'm late." A newcomer pushed past Veena and slid into the empty seat at Mrs. Long's table.

Forcing her face to remain neutral even though her heart was pounding, Veena continued past them without making eye contact. Another empty table was just beyond them, so Veena claimed it by taking a seat with her back to her targets.

She glanced over to the pillar where Orin waited. He was still there, leaning against the stonework in an exaggerated casual pose. The two of them were defiantly not cut out to be spies. She sighed and ordered a cup of tea from the server drone.

"I trust you have secured us access," Mrs. Long said.

Veena sat close enough to hear every word. As the server drone delivered her tea, she did her best to not look towards the other table. She took a sip from the fine china teacup and burned her tongue on the scalding liquid. In an awkward motion, she set the teacup down, spilling more of the tea over her hand.

"My contact will let my team in through the east door an hour before the auction," the other woman behind Veena said.

"And how many are on your team?"

"Just myself, Bob Singh, and Carie Drake. Both of them have done jobs for you in the past."

"You're very free with names. Does that mean your inside contact also knows who you are?" Mrs. Long's tone hinted at disapproval.

"Of course not. He just knows 'pink unicorn' is the password. Whoever says that to him at the side door will be let inside."

Mrs. Long snorted. "You sound like an amateur."

"Mrs. Long, I can guarantee—" The woman stopped talking abruptly as though Mrs. Long had gestured for her to shut up.

"I can't afford to lose that artifact." Mrs. Long's voice had taken on a more sinister tone. "Swa and her minions want it. Therefore, I want it in my hands first."

"Of course. Can you tell me what it is?"

"Some alien thing," Mrs. Long said. "If you're going to make it in this business, you need to stop asking so many questions of your clients. Now, is your team assembled?"

"Yes, they are on standby."

"And your exit plan?" Mrs. Long asked. "I will not be linked to you or your team if things go sour."

"We are professionals."

Mrs. Long snorted again, then stood. "Good, now go earn your pay." She strode away as if she didn't have a care in the world.

Mrs. Long's contact left shortly after, disappearing into a crowd that passed by. Orin came and joined Veena at her table.

"Did you get anything?" he asked.

"Mrs. Long hired her visitor to steal something from the auction house," she said, finally sopping up the spilled tea with a cloth napkin.

"That's something."

Veena glanced down at herself. Damp spots speckled the front of her jacket, several shades darker than the rest of the fabric. She sighed. "Crap. I've spilled tea all down my front."

Orin handed her the napkin from his side of the table. "Just dab at it. It'll be fine. Now back to Mrs. Long's acquaintance…."

"Right." Veena set the napkins down. "They have a way into the auction house and 'pink unicorn' is their password."

"Well, that's more successful than I expected."

Veena frowned. "I missed my chance to ask Mrs. Long for the location of Dr. Greer's lab." She twisted around and tried to see where the old woman had gone. "And now we've lost her."

"But you know she wants that artifact. We can negotiate with her once we have it."

"It sounded like Mrs. Long's contact was going to get the artifact before the auction. If we're going to beat them to it, we probably should head that way now." Veena resumed dabbing the damp spots on her jacket with the napkin.

"I'll message Hwicce." Orin pulled out his scroll and opened it. He frowned. "There's no net connection."

Veena checked her comms device. "I've got nothing either. They warned us about atmospheric interference."

"True." As Orin met her gaze, his brow wrinkled.

Veena stood and adjusted her scarf. Her pulse raced as she realized the window to get that artifact was now. Was going in without Hwicce and Baker really a good idea? She bit her lip. If Mrs. Long's people stole the artifact, it would be near impossible for them to get. They couldn't wait.

"Let's you and I do it. We know where to go, and we know the code. It sounded all arranged."

Orin nodded. "By the time we have the artifact in our hands, comms will probably work again, and we can tell the others."

"The sooner we have it, the sooner we can head out. I'm sure we can get Mol's location from either Mrs. Long or General Swa with the right leverage." Veena did her best to sound confident.

"Then we need to head towards the Island of Silver. I believe it's this way." He pointed down the street outside the teahouse.

Veena ran her hands down her pants. "Let's go then." The two of them started walking.

"I wonder how Baker is doing with her brother," Orin said as they headed down the street.

Chapter Forty-One

Hwicce followed Joseph and Baker out a back door to the bank. He felt the comms device in his pocket and told himself he'd message Veena once they got to the restaurant. The three of them now followed a narrow path between the back of the buildings and the edge of the island. Although a railing stood between them and empty air, it seemed so inadequate, especially now that the wind had picked up.

Hwicce put his hands on the top rail and studied the view. He didn't normally have a fear of heights, but with the wind and only a few rails to stop a fall, his gut churned.

Joseph stopped beside him. "It's spectacular."

"What if someone just falls off the edge?"

Joseph shrugged. "It's fine. One of the sentinel bots will grab them. The bots have a 99.8% capture rate."

"Sucks if you're one of the 0.2%," Baker said in a flat tone.

"Then don't fall over." Joseph frowned at his sister and resumed walking.

Hwicce fell into step beside him as Baker trailed behind.

"It's not just the Shimmer down there," Joseph continued. "Below are different layers. Rumour has it, more islands float down there along with possible alien life and even the wreckage of one of the lost generation ships."

They came around the edge of the building and proceeded down an alley. Once they reached the main square again, Joseph led them to a small, circular building that looked more like an iced cake than a structure for humans. Inside, pastel-painted vines added to the cake vibe. At the centre was a circular elevator big enough to hold a dozen people—currently, the doors were closed.

"And there's never any rain here," he said, apparently content to be the only one talking.

As they waited for the elevator, Hwicce turned and stared back out the door. A man in head-to-toe black stood still as the flow of humanity passed him out in the square. The man appeared to be watching them. A shiver rose up Hwicce's spine.

"That man," he said under his breath as a ping announced the elevator's arrival.

"What was that?" Joseph leaned towards him.

Hwicce shook his head. "Nothing. It's nothing."

Baker snorted. "I think a little rain would do this place some good and wash away the bullshit." Without waiting, she strode into the elevator car.

Joseph cocked his head. Hwicce shrugged and followed Baker.

A few moments later, the elevator doors whooshed open into a different world. The neon lights highlighted an impossible space. A strong sense of vertigo washed over Hwicce as he tried to take in everything at once. Baker and Joseph strode forward as though they were in just another ordinary room.

Just outside the elevator, a Mobius-strip-like staircase outlined in glowing blue rose towards the ceiling what seemed like two stories up. But the ceiling which really a ceiling. Instead, people walked on it as though it was the ground.

"If you ask me, this place is a waste of gravity plating." Baker's tone dripped with disdain.

"Oh, Fanny," Joseph said in a tone that suggested they'd had this conversation before. "This place is an engineering marvel."

Baker snorted in reply.

Hwicce couldn't take his eyes off the people above. "I had no idea anywhere was like this." He swallowed and focused on the staircase ahead of him.

"The transition is seamless. Just keep walking up the stairs. They keep the gravity plating tuned to perfection." Joseph smiled and started up the stairs.

Expecting a lurch or a jolt, Hwicce ascended the stairs. To his surprise, walking up felt normal, then he was standing on the ceiling looking down at the elevator.

"See, no problem. Now the Basement is this way." Joseph set off around a glittering jewelry store and through a door.

As he followed, Hwicce glanced back over his shoulder, and his gut clenched. The man he'd seen above just got off the elevator.

"This way, Mr. Baker," a waiting ma"tre d' said as they crossed the restaurant's threshold.

"What's up, sir?" Baker asked as she leaned in close.

Ahead Joseph followed the ma"tre d' towards a table. All around them, moody tones from mauve to burgundy cloaked the restaurant, creating a well-crafted, high-end ambiance. A thick carpet covered the floor, trapping the sounds of the busy restaurant.

"I saw someone who seems dodgy," he said, not sure how to describe the man. He had no evidence the man was following them, just a gut feeling.

"Ms. Baker, why don't you have a seat?" The ma"tre d' pulled out a chair and gestured to Baker to sit.

"Uh, thanks," she said as she slumped down. The yellow of her suit picked up the flickering lights at the centre of their table.

"Oh!" Hwicce looked up. The Shimmer arced over the ceiling. Fast-moving swirls of gold and silver storms moved across their view. Of course, he was actually looking down. He swallowed and took a seat beside Baker.

"So you're crew on a water tanker now?" Joseph asked from across the table.

"Yeah," Baker said.

Joseph frowned. "Doing what? Security? Scrubbing the decks?"

"No, she's—"

Baker cut Hwicce off.

"I'm crew and that's that." Baker stared her brother down. Hwicce noticed that Baker's tempered her normal colourful language around her brother.

"You could do better than that. There's still a spot for you at the bank."

Baker scowled. "Where I'd do what? Security? Scrubbing the floors?"

"Oh, come on, Fanny. Are we really going to have this argument again?" Joseph pushed himself back in his chair.

"There's nothing for me here." Baker crossed her arms over her chest.

"Maybe if you stay in one place, you'd meet someone, build a life."

"I did meet someone. She's…." Baker's words trailed off as she bit her lip.

"Then why didn't you bring her with you? I'd love to meet the woman that leaves you lost for words." Joseph leaned in, his demeanour softer now.

Hwicce shifted in his seat, knowing he was a big part of the reason Baker and Emiko weren't together.

"I screwed it up," Baker admitted as she stared down at the table.

Joseph reached across the table and put a hand on Baker's. "I just want you to know there's a place here for you."

She nodded, but said nothing.

After a few awkward moments, Joseph shifted his attention

to Hwicce. "How about you? With the guild, the water delivery business must be reasonably stable."

"I'm hoping so once we make those repairs." Hwicce smiled as a waiter set down glasses of water for everyone.

"Well, I'm confident that ugly rabbit will fetch you a fortune." Joseph smiled as he leaned in to talk to the waiter.

Hwicce surveyed the restaurant, his eyes lingering on all the patrons. Everyone seemed engaged with their own company, eating, chatting, and glancing up at the Shimmer. Still, the knot in his gut kept him on high alert. He pulled out his comms device. Still no signal.

"I'm sure she's fine," Baker said.

"I just wish I could reach her. We never should have split up." Hwicce twisted to slip the comms device back into his pocket and spotted a familiar form at the bar. It was the man from before. As soon as they made eye contact, the man stood and walked out of a nearby exit.

"If you would excuse me for a moment." Hwicce got up and headed towards the door.

Outside the restaurant, he stopped to survey the passing people. The crowd had picked up now. He turned to the right and moved as fast as he could through the throng of people. The man was nowhere; it was almost as though he'd vanished.

Then Hwicce saw the emergency exit. He pushed through a group of teenagers teetering on tall shoes and through the door. As the door shut out the sounds of humanity behind him, Hwicce looked around.

Something pierced the back of his suit and pricked into the skin of his lower back. He froze.

"Hands up where I can see them."

Moving slowly, Hwicce raised his hands up over his head. He twisted just enough to see his assailant in his peripheral vision. It was the man he'd seen at the bar.

"Who are you?" Hwicce asked.

"Up against the wall," the man said.

With a shuffle, Hwicce moved towards the wall. The man kept the knifepoint pricking his skin.

"Who are you?" Hwicce asked a second time.

"I'm nobody. But you are worth a fair bounty. Your wife, however, is worth a fortune. Why isn't she with you?"

"I have a comms device in my right pocket. Let me get it out, and I'll call her," Hwicce said, keeping his tone level.

"You're worth the same dead or alive, so don't try anything funny." The man shifted to the right, moving the knife back to allow Hwicce space to reach into his pocket.

Twisting to the left, Hwicce rammed his elbow into the side of the man's jaw. He continued rotating until the man was between him and the wall.

Barely slowing, the man lunged forward with his blade aimed at Hwicce's gut.

Swiping down with an open fist, Hwicce grabbed onto the man's wrist, twisting it until the blade fell. The nanite blade vanished, and the handle bounced off the floor and skidded into the corner.

"Who in the hell are you?" Hwicce said through clenched teeth.

The man didn't answer. Instead, he dropped his right hip below Hwicce's. Using his leverage, the man threw Hwicce to the ground, dropping on top of him.

The impact forced all the air in Hwicce's lungs out, and he gasped for his next breath.

"I'm just doing my job," the man said.

Hwicce arched his back and grabbed the man's neck. He continued to force his way out from under the man and rotated him into a chokehold.

The emergency exit crashed open as three of the teenagers burst into the space. Two of them were supporting a third between them. They stopped and stared at the two men on the floor.

"I was sure this was the way to the washroom," the first one said as she brushed a lock of deep purple hair over her shoulder.

"Oooooo, I can't wait." A teen with green hair in the middle bent over and vomited. The remnants of her last meal splattered across the floor.

Hwicce grimaced at the stench.

The green-haired girl fell to the ground, her face pale. Her friends hovered around, as if uncertain what to do. Hwicce couldn't live with himself if he let the green-haired girl choke on her own vomit. He let the man go and shifted over to the green-haired girl.

"Will she be okay?" asked the purple-haired girl.

The man jumped up and ran down the hallway, his soft boots making no sound on the industrial flooring. Hwicce opened his mouth to call after him—the man wasn't going to stop because he demanded it. He sighed.

He found the pulse on the passed-out teen—it was racing but strong. With a single push, he rolled her into the recovery position before looking up at her friends. "You need to call for medical help."

"Even though I warned Janie about the greenie liqueur, she still drank too much," the teen with purple hair said.

Hwicce sighed as he saw the man turn a corner and vanish from view. Teenage drama had thwarted him.

The green-haired teen finally opened her eyes, her face now the same shade as her hair. "Drake kept filling…" A series of hiccups interrupted her words.

Hwicce stood and faced the purple-haired teen. "You'll need to get her to a med clinic. Can you do that?"

The girl with purple hair nodded and turned to her friend. "Come on, let's go."

"My mom's going to kill me," the green-haired teen said as her friends led her back through the emergency exit letting the door slam shut behind them.

Relieved a door now separated him from the drunk teens,

Hwicce looked down the hall. The man was long gone. There was no point chasing after him. A glint from the corner pulled his attention—the knife's handle. Being careful to avoid the vomit, he bent down and picked it up.

The handle seemed to be formed out of a single piece of nacre that shimmered blues and greens beneath a milky white surface. It was a beautiful weapon. As he wrapped his hand around the hilt, the blade re-formed, the silver nanites created an impossibly sharp edge.

"This might come in handy," he said as he released the hilt and watched the blade vanish. He slid the safety on and put the knife in his pocket.

Chapter Forty-Two

Veena and Orin wove through the increasing crowds as the wind picked up. The brightly coloured banners hanging above snapped in the wind. Ahead, they could see the dome of the auction house behind a series of two-story buildings on the next island.

As they crossed over the last bridge to the Island of Silver, a gust of wind ruffled their clothes, and Veena had to grab onto her scarf to keep it from blowing away.

"The auction starts in two hours," Orin said.

Veena stopped at the apex of the bridge and stared off into the distance. Just above the swirling storms of the Shimmer, she could make out the dark structure of a mining platform. "This is a city of bizarre contradictions."

"The original settlers here got lucky to find so much wealth right beneath their feet."

The two of them kept moving, following the main road between several buildings and into a massive public square, this one ringed with statues. At the far end stood the auction house. A giant, squat, silver dome rose up above a white building defined by pillars and geometric lines. It was as though the builders had stolen all their ideas from the Ancient Greek buildings found in children's vids.

People milled about the square, and the cafe next to the auction house was packed.

"Should we head right to the side door or wait for Mrs. Long's goons?" Veena asked.

"Since we know the password, it's probably best we go straight there."

Veena nodded as she stared at the auction house. "Let me try Hwicce again." She pulled out her comms device and found the system was still offline.

With a sigh, she put the comms device away. Not taking advantage of the information she'd overheard seemed unthinkable—yet she'd promised Hwicce she'd be careful.

Her eyes fixed on the mauve and yellow banners flapping above the auction house—there were thirteen of them, a prime number. She bit her lip. The alien artifact had to be the key she needed to decode all the texts she had—once she'd decoded that text, she could use it as leverage to get Molly back. Going in was the right thing to do. Besides, it was an auction house, not a secret military facility. How risky could it be?

"You're right; we should go straight there. Get it and get out." She turned to look at Orin, but he was gone.

As she rotated around, she spotted him kneeling at the base of an abstract bright yellow statue. She went over to him.

"Are you okay?" she asked.

Orin looked up at the statue. "I've never seen this one before."

Veena glanced at the brass plaque at the base of the statue. It said 'an apology to my husband in yellow' by Mary Atkin.

"Your wife was a sculptor?"

Orin didn't answer. Instead, he buried his face in his hands. "She did this for me."

Veena bent down and looked at the date. "This is a new statue, only put up a few weeks ago."

"It's an apology because I got mad that she painted our kitchen that yellow." Orin pointed to the statue. Its yellow was vivid, more lemony than a lemon. "I left the next day. The day after that, bombs levelled New Haven."

"I didn't realize…." Veena let her words trail off. There was so much she didn't know about her former boss.

"The last conversation we ever had was about that yellow." He gestured to the statue. "She must have painted one of her works in progress right after I left."

Veena took a step back and studied the sculpture. It stood tall, at least twice her height, with the shape of a pine tree. At the top, an arm-width branch twisted up, then back on its self.

"It's a beautiful piece," Veena said, unsure of how she could comfort Orin.

He stood and looked up. "It is."

"Didn't you say it was her dream to have a statue here?"

Orin nodded as he reached forward and put a hand on the yellow surface. "My biggest regret is not apologizing." He let his forehead dip down and touch the statue.

Veena bit her lip.

"It was just yellow, not worth the fight."

"I think she understood," Veena said as she put a hand on Orin's shoulder.

"Yeah, I think she did." He sighed.

"We need to get to that door," Veena said, feeling guilty for dragging Orin away.

For a moment, he said nothing and just stared at the statue. Then he nodded. "You're right. Mary would have wanted me to follow through on my commitment. And we need to get there before Mrs. Long's hired goons."

"Are you okay?" Veena asked.

He smiled. "I haven't been okay since the bombing on New Haven and news of Mary's death. But I'm sticking to my commitment to help you get Molly back. It's a tragedy I can reverse."

Veena nodded. "Without your help, I wouldn't have made it this far."

"Let's find those goons." Orin looked up at the statue again. "We need that artifact."

Chapter Forty-Three

Nigel let himself float behind Molly and Click as they crawled through the vent. It was barely big enough for a child, so it was a good thing he could manipulate his pixels as needed. Click glowed a faint green, giving the three of them just enough light to see by. Nigel reminded himself that he could just depixelate, but he felt he needed to remain present—he was the only adult in their group.

"Okay, we need to remain hidden," he said.

"Yeah, yeah." Molly didn't even look back as she spoke. A little further on, she stopped at one of the vents.

Nigel flattened himself and drifted close enough to see what she saw. Below, a paisley swirling pattern in blue and white reminded him of his time on the Garden Princess. Pushing the nostalgia away, he looked further into the room. The paisley fabric was a bedspread; other than the bed, the room contained the usual bedroom furniture.

"It looks like someone's quarters."

"It's pretty fancy," Molly said as Clicked clicked.

"We need to keep moving."

"Do ya think that's Greer's room? He likes fancy stuff."

Nigel's brows pulled together as he tried to determine the room's owner. "I don't know—but we need to continue our escape."

"I think it's Greer's. I bet he has more Space Chew stashed." Molly turned to look Nigel in the eye. "And, you know, we need supplies for our escape."

"I don't think your mother would approve of all the candy…." Nigel's words trailed off as Click removed the vent cover. In a flash of orange and pink, they dropped to the room below, taking Nigel's transmitter with them.

Before he could say another word, Nigel blinked out of existence, then rematerialized, standing beside the bed.

Molly came feet first out of the vent and landed on the bed. She giggled as she bounced. Beneath her, the bed's springs groaned.

"Don't do that." Nigel reached a hand out towards Molly. A crash sounded behind him, and he spun—Click was pulling drawers out of the dresser. Clothes and drawers now covered the floor. "Look, we aren't here to wreck the place."

Molly hopped off the bed and opened the closet. "Jackpot." She held up a case of Space Chews as though it were a trophy.

Nigel groaned. The situation was getting out of hand. "And we aren't thieves."

"We need supplies." Molly frowned. "I wish I had my backpack."

An alarm sounded, and the white lights changed to red.

Nigel put his hands against his cheeks. "Oh, no! They've discovered we've escaped." He glitched, reappearing, facing the door. Rotating, he turned back to his two charges. Both Molly and Click stood staring at him with wide eyes.

"What do we do?" Molly whispered, her voice almost masked by the alarm.

Click flashed aqua, then made a popping sound.

For a moment, Nigel regretted helping in their escape. If he'd done nothing, both Molly and Click would still be safe in their cells. He was a steward AI, not a guardian, certainly not an escape artist.

An image from his memory banks surfaced, reminding him he'd promised to help reunite Molly with her mother. He rubbed his hands together, barely registering how his fingers passed through each other. If they were smart, escape was still possible.

"We hide here," he said.

"Won't they search everywhere?" Molly turned and looked at the still open closet.

Nigel went over to the closet and studied the row of pressed suits. For each one, he compared the fabric with what he'd seen Dr. Greer wearing on the Garden Princess. He got two matches.

"This is most likely Dr. Greer's quarters; I suspect this will be the last place they think to look."

Molly hugged the box of Space Chews against herself.

A click, then a squelch came from an overhead speaker.

"Subject... Molly." It was Dr. Greer's voice. "I'm worried about you. Please let us know where you are. I promise I won't be mad."

Nigel bit his lip. He needed a plan. Blinking out of existence, he used his full, but still inadequate, computing power to analyze the situation. A moment later, he rematerialized.

"Click, can you get into the computer system?" Nigel asked, wondering why hadn't he thought of this before.

Click flashed hot pink before crawling up the wall to the room's access port. For a moment, nothing happened.

"Are you in?" Nigel asked as Molly moved to stand by his side.

Emitting a sharp click, Click flashed green.

"Good. Now, can you find us the least occupied path to the shuttle bay?"

With a series of low pops, Click transferred the station's map into Nigel's storage.

"Oh! They're putting drones into the ventilation system."

Both Nigel and Molly looked up at the gaping hole above them. "Click, can you close that? Then we'll all hang out in the closet until the drones have passed."

After crawling up the wall, and across the ceiling, Click closed the vent.

"If the drones are in the vents, can we just head out?" Molly pointed to the door.

"I'm certain we'd be caught," Nigel said as he kept a watch on the map Click had given him. A red dot showed him the location of each drone—one was heading their way. "Time to get in the closet."

Molly and Click quickly complied. And the three of them waited out of sight from the ceiling vent.

The intercom squelched as it came back on. "Molly, if you let me know where you are, I'll let you call your mom," Greer said.

"I want to talk to my mom." Molly looked Nigel in the eye.

"We can't right now."

Molly's lower lip began to quiver. "But she must be worried, and I miss her."

"I know, sweetheart," he said as he watched the red dots on his map move away from their location. He now saw a direct path from where they were to the shuttle bay. "How about we call her once we're on the shuttle?"

She nodded.

"Okay, I need you two to move that—" Nigel pointed to a chair in the room's corner "—onto the bed so Molly can climb back up into the vent." It was a good thing the ceiling was low.

Molly and Click dragged the chair up onto the bed, then Click climbed the wall again to open the vent. From the ceiling, Click reached down to help steady Molly. She stood on the chair, and it wobbled on the mattress below.

Nigel froze as he watched—there was nothing he could do to help.

The first thing Molly did was pass up her box of Space

Chew to Click. Then she grabbed onto the rim of the vent. Click emitted a soft series of clicks as they helped Molly pull herself up and into the vent. With relief, Nigel let himself blink out and reappear in the vent.

"This way," he said in a whisper.

It took an hour of crawling through the vents, regularly pausing to stay out of view of the drones, to reach a vent leading into a storeroom off the shuttle bay. After checking that the coast was clear, Click opened the vent and jumped down, forcing Nigel to reform down on the floor. A table sat under the vent, giving Molly somewhere closer to drop onto. Once the three of them were down, they huddled together at the door as Click opened it a crack.

A row of shuttles sat parked in the bay. The closest was cherry red—reachable without going too far into the bay. No one was in sight.

Click clicked and faded to the same grey tone as the floor.

"Good idea. Go check," Nigel said.

Barely visible against the floor, Click scooted over to the nearest station terminal. They connected to the computer interface. A few moments later they flashed pink and orange.

"Is it?" Nigel stared at the shuttle Click was pointing at. It was a sleek model, the kind VIPs took for their travel.

"What?" Molly looked up at him.

"That shuttle is fully fuelled with enough food for a trip to Rock 13-5A."

"But I don't want to go there." Molly pursed her lips.

"No one is going to question our progress if we follow a pre-planned route." Nigel fidgeted, unsure how to convince a child to follow his plan. "Once we are en route, we can try to contact your parents."

"But I don't like it." Molly crossed her arms over her chest and scowled.

Nigel pulled his eyebrows together and vowed to download a

parenting manual the next time someone connected him to the net. "It's the best option we have."

Click flashed violet and headed over to the ship.

"It's too red." Molly wrinkled her nose as if something smelled funny.

Nigel looked back at the cherry red shuttle. "You're right, it is too red."

Nigel began second-guessing himself as Click started the engines. Was taking the shuttle a good idea? His hands began to glitch as he rubbed them together. The responsibility of watching Veena's little girl was almost too much for him. He was a steward AI from an adult-only luxury ship—not a nanny.

But if Dr. Greer was contemplating invasive experimentation on Molly, he needed to get her away. It was the only way to keep her safe. Nigel swallowed as his hands continued to glitch. Veena might never forgive him if he let anything happen to Molly.

Click let out a series of clicks as Molly buckled herself into the co-pilot's seat.

"This is going to be fun." She clapped her hands together. "Just like volume 3."

Clicked flashed pink in agreement, and Nigel sighed. Click eased back the controls, and the shuttle lifted off the ground.

"Shuttle 456-H, you are not authorized for departure," someone said over the comms.

"Click, you need to give me access to the ship," Nigel said.

Click clicked, then used a free tentacle to release the band around their neck. They then connected it to the ship's systems. For a moment, Nigel felt like he existed in two places at once, then his code settled on being part of the ship. The shuttle wasn't supposed to depart for an hour. He activated the external comms. "This is Shuttle 456-H. Our timeline has been accelerated," Nigel said in Dr. Greer's voice.

"We have not received proper authorization," the person on the other side said.

"There was a glitch in the station system," Nigel said, still impersonating Dr. Greer. "We can't wait for the technicians to troubleshoot. Open the outside doors now."

"Roger," the voice said, clearly recognizing Dr. Greer's voice. "Opening doors now."

As the large bay doors at the end of the hangar opened, Click flew them into the airlock. The inside doors closed behind them, then the outside doors opened, exposing them to the high winds of their moon.

Click flew forward like a pro, angling up towards the sky and gas giant that dominated it. They were free. Nigel let himself relax, dematerializing all together.

"Where'd you go?" Molly asked as she looked around.

"I'm here." Nigel rematerialized between the pilot's and co-pilot's seats. Still part of the ship's systems, he ran through their supplies. He only relaxed when he realized there were over six months' worth of food onboard.

"Can we call my mom now?"

"Of course."

Chapter Forty-Four

While telling himself to keep it together, Orin followed Veena around the east side of the auction house. An alley barely wide enough for them to walk side-by-side led them away from the public square and the people milling about.

Mary's yellow statue remained blazed across his thoughts. She shouldn't have felt the need to apologize to him—he was the one who should have said sorry. He should have messaged her; he should have arranged for a bouquet of flowers to have been delivered to her. Yellow, of course.

"Here we are," whispered Veena at his side.

At the end of the alley, a paint-chipped door stood out against the white facade, as though the stately building didn't want to admit it had a need for anything utilitarian.

"This is definitely it." Taking a deep breath, Orin pictured how proud Mary would be that he was helping get the little girl back. Mary had wanted kids, but it just hadn't been possible for them.

"Are you up for this?" Veena asked as she rewound her hexagon-patterned scarf around her neck.

As Orin met her gaze, he told himself yet again to focus on

the task at hand. Mary would be proud of him. He swallowed. "Let's do it."

Without waiting, he knocked on the door. Almost immediately, a short and stout woman answered.

"Code." She stared at Orin through narrow eyes.

"Pink unicorn." Orin used his most confident voice.

She snorted. "You aren't what I expected. And you're early."

"Is that going to be a problem?" Orin met her gaze.

"No. Your credits bought you flexibility," she said as she stepped out of the doorway. "Come in."

Orin and Veena exchanged a glance before stepping inside. A claustrophobic hallway greeted them. Beige walls and a scuffed floor suggested this space was meant only for staff.

The woman headed off to the left at a shuffle. "Come on then. And don't forget to shut the door. The wind is picking up."

She led them down a set of stairs into the heart of the island beneath the auction house. They went down several stories until the corridor opened up into a large cavern. One end gaped open. Three small 'sailboats' were tied up at a dock.

As they passed the naked edge, Orin glanced over. A wave of vertigo left him gasping for breath. There was nothing below but the shimmering metal layer. He pictured falling through the atmosphere, with the pressure getting greater and greater, crushing him long before he hit the ground.

A tremor rose from his feet and spread across his body. His hands were shaking now. The Shimmer seemed so close, like he could almost lean out and dip his hand in it. His heart began to pound.

"Orin?" Veena's voice sounded like she was somewhere far away.

Orin swallowed. Falling would ease his guilt about his last words to his wife. One step and….

Veena touched his arm. "Orin?"

With her touch, his promise to help her returned. He looked

at her, locking with her dark brown eyes. "Yeah...." His voice trailed off as he steadied himself. "Yes, yes, I'm fine."

"Quit dilly dallying," their guide said as she opened a door at the other end of the space—well away from the edge.

Lengthening his stride, Orin went over to the door. "Is the artifact in here?"

"The master keeps all the best artifacts in here," she said, sliding the door fully open. Inside, overhead lights automatically blinked on, filling the room with clinical illumination. Walls of roughly hewn rock surrounded metal tables and shelves filled with a seemingly random assortment of items.

Orin stepped inside and came face-to-face with a hippopotamus. Its immense face and glassy eyes were right at his level. A field of whiskers poked out from its cheeks; behind, its body bulged as though ready to charge his way. Orin swallowed and reminded himself such animals didn't—couldn't—exist; it was just another statue. With a trembling hand, he reached out towards it.

"Don't touch that," the woman said in a sharp tone. "That piece of taxidermy is worth more than this island."

Orin nodded and took a step backward. "Where's the alien artifact?"

"Over here." The woman wound her way past the tables and shelves to the back corner, past all sorts of stuff ranging from smaller taxidermy to ancient electronics to ornate vases and even a rusty bicycle. She stopped just past an old Earth samurai sword. "I don't get what all the fuss is about. It doesn't look like much."

The woman pointed to a palm-sized object nestled on a puce-toned velvet cushion. It was the colour of tarnished brass; the truncated icosahedron didn't appear special. The woman hadn't followed them into the storeroom, and he couldn't see another exit.

Orin frowned. "It's just a metal soccer ball."

Veena picked it up and bit her lip. She ran a finger over one of the hexagon sides. "This isn't what I expected—but then I don't know what I expected."

"The knot in my gut tells me we need to get out of here." Orin glanced around.

With a nod, she opened her messenger bag and slid the object inside. "We can study it when we get back to the ship." She strapped the bag over her shoulder.

"There they are," the woman said from the door.

Orin spun to face her and froze. A tall man in dark clothing stood beside her, holding a stun gun.

Veena's eyes went wide. "Shit, it's the bounty hunter. He caught up to us."

"Veena Oswiu." The bounty hunter's voice boomed out. "Once again, you are worth significantly more than your companion. My client is insisting I bring you back alive."

"Do you work for Swa?" Veena stared straight into the bounty hunter's eyes.

"Come with me peacefully, and I will let him go." He waved his gun towards Orin.

Orin put a hand on Veena's arm and leaned into her ear. "I'm not letting him take you."

Veena sighed. "I don't see how we can escape." She put up her hands. "I surrender," she said while looking directly at the bounty hunter.

The bounty hunter snorted, then shot her with his stun gun. Veena collapsed like a rag doll. With a lunge, Orin caught her before she face-planted into the shelving. He eased her to the floor.

"Now just back away," the bounty hunter said, moving to have a clear view of Orin.

Doing his best to not look at the ancient sword, Orin slowly rose to his feet. He lifted both hands and took a step towards the bounty hunter.

"What will you do with her?" He took another slow step forward. The hilt of the sword was now within reach.

"Hand her over to my client," the bounty hunter said. "After that, it's none of my business."

Orin grabbed the sword hilt with both hands, and in a single motion, he sprang towards the bounty hunter. He lifted the blade over his head and brought it down on the bounty hunter's blaster-holding forearm. The blade stopped dead, and a shutter reverberated back through Orin's body. The sword bounced out of his hands and skittered across the floor.

The bounty hunter laughed. "I've underestimated your group one time too many. This time, I'm prepared for a fight."

Kinetic armour. Orin gasped as he worked his hands, trying to get feeling back into them.

"There's no point trying to resist me," the bounty hunter said. "I will claim my prize."

Slowly, Orin shifted his feet under himself. Then he threw himself into the bounty hunter's midsection. The bounty hunter's kinetic armour didn't stop the two of them from toppling into the hippopotamus.

The bounty hunter lost his hold on the stun gun, and it bounced away. Orin darted after the weapon. As he grabbed it, he twisted to face the bounty hunter.

The bounty hunter now held a pistol, the kind that would kill Orin with a single shot. The bounty hunter's expression was of amusement.

"I'll give you full points for bravery. Almost as brave as her soldier husband." The bounty hunter gestured to Veena. "But—"

Orin fired.

The bounty hunter dodged to the right; he was fast but not quite fast enough. The stun bolt grazed his right shoulder, and he dropped the blaster.

"Fucking hell." The bounty hunter shook his right arm as though the motion would bring feeling back. "Now you've gone too far—the deal to let you go is off."

Before Orin could move, the bounty hunter launched himself at where he lay on the floor.

His knee impacted Orin's gut, driving all the air out of him. Orin gasped, unable to do anything to defend himself. His mind raced. He couldn't just give up. With everything he had, Orin willed himself to take a deep breath.

Before Orin could twist out of the way, the bounty hunter stood and grabbed Orin's leg.

"I can't take both of you in," the bounty hunter said as he started dragging Orin across the floor and out of the storeroom.

Orin reached out, grasping for anything to slow the bounty hunter down. But there was nothing to grab.

"And, as I said before, she's worth a hell of a lot more than you."

Orin dug his fingers into the metal floor, ripping his fingernails. "No, no, no…." He tried twisting his foot as the wind from the opening swirled around him.

The bounty hunter kicked Orin in the gut, knocking the wind out of him a second time.

Gasping for air, Orin struggled to breathe. A sharp pain in his chest suggested broken ribs. Panic swelled inside him as he realized what the bounty hunter planned.

"I don't have time for this shit." The bounty hunter dragged Orin parallel to the opening.

Orin tried to speak, tried to say anything to stop the bounty hunter. But no words would come.

"I hate to see good money wasted. But you've proven to be too much trouble." The bounty hunter put his right foot on Orin's shoulder and shoved him over the edge.

Orin couldn't even manage a scream as he fell.

Chapter Forty-Five

"Anything?" Hwicce asked as Baker fiddled with her comms device.

She shook her head. "The fucking storm is still messing with us."

The knot in Hwicce's gut twisted as he stared down into the auction house.

Joseph's balcony was the height of luxury. Maroon velvet covered the chairs, which were actually comfortable. The brocade pattern on the walls seamlessly melded into the curtain covering the door. Already, a server drone had brought them drinks.

Below, the main floor of the auction house seemed more like an old-fashion theatre than anything else. Lavish botanical prints separated by gilded panels carved to look like vines decorated the walls and ceiling.

"I'm sure Veena and Orin are smart enough to stay clear of the bounty hunter you encountered and Mrs. Long," Baker said as she tapped her comms device against the railing.

"I hope so."

Overdressed people started to fill the main floor below.

Human waiters with trays filled with Champaign flutes circled through the crowds. But Veena wasn't there. She hadn't been outside the front doors either. He swallowed.

Beside him, Baker unwound her datapad on her lap and scowled at it. "Fucking interference. The weather office says an electrical storm in a layer above is causing it."

"Great." Hwicce closed his eyes for a moment. The velvet of his chair felt smooth against his palms. Veena was smart. She would be okay.

"Check out those numb nuts," Baker said.

Hwicce opened his eyes and followed where she pointed. On the floor below were three people in the drabbest grey suits he'd ever seen.

"Didn't Veena say something about people in bloody grey suits?"

Hwicce pursed his lips as he watched the three fan out. "Yeah, people in grey suits took Molly. And that group is looking for someone."

Baker nodded. "They're probably looking for us."

Hwicce ran a hand through his hair. "I wonder if that bounty hunter tipped them off?"

"You think they're Swa's minions?" Baker put her electronics away.

"I think we have to assume that. But they want Veena, and since they are still looking, my guess is they don't have her." He tried to feel reassured by that. Nevertheless, the knot in his gut gnawed at him.

"It's only a matter of time until they start checking the balconies," Baker said.

"How long until the auction starts?" Hwicce glanced back to the single exit to their balcony.

Baker activated the auction house holographic program. "We've got ten minutes until things start." She started swiping through the inventory of items on offer. "It's quite a mish-mash of crap they're trying to make a fortune off of."

Hwicce glanced at the images. A full-sized hippopotamus, apparently authentic swords, and children's games stood out among other Old Earth goods. The stuff people had crammed on the generation ships was astounding. He scratched his head and returned his gaze to the auction house floor.

The three grey suits grouped together in discussion.

"Here it is." Baker brought up the alien artifact.

Hwicce glanced at the holographic image of what looked to him like a dirty soccer ball. A red banner appeared, claiming the item was no longer available.

"Shit. Let's hope your wife managed to somehow snatch it."

Hwicce let out a long exhale. "Crap, she wasn't supposed to—"

Baker cut him off. "We don't have time to lollygag around pondering things. We need to get the hell out of here right now."

The three people in grey suits below were now looking up at the balconies.

"Agreed."

Baker nodded, and the two of them stood just as a knock sounded at their balcony door. They glanced at each other, and Baker raised an eyebrow.

Hwicce looked over the railing. A grand piano was directly below. From there, it was a quick sprint to the door. He tilted his head over the railing, and Baker nodded.

Hwicce jumped, creating a cacophony as he landed on the piano. A leg gave way, and it dumped him onto the plush carpet. He rolled out of the way as Baker followed. She landed like a cat, then stood and dusted off her yellow suit.

The crowd parted as the two of them headed for the front doors. Hwicce hoped everyone would just assume they were some eccentric rich couple having a good time.

Someone behind yelled for them to stop. Instead, they sprinted. Hwicce followed Baker out of the auction house and towards the bridge leading off the island. A growing crowd milled about outside the auction house.

At the bridge on the other side of the square, Hwicce slowed to glance back. Two of the grey suits were chasing after them, causing a disturbance in the crowd as they went.

"Crap," he said, speeding up as he continued over the bridge.

Sirens sounded from somewhere up ahead. Baker dodged to the right and into a square ringed with more statues. She stopped behind one as yellow as her suit. Hwicce followed; it was a reasonable enough hiding spot for now.

"This is turning into a shit storm," Baker said, peeking around the abstract shape to watch the square.

The grey suits ran across the square and disappeared behind the next building.

"Are you sure they're after us?" Hwicce stretched to see where they went.

"Put your hands up," a synthetic voice said.

Hwicce put his hands up as he turned towards the voice. A police drone suspended by a balloon pointed a stun rifle at them.

"We've done nothing wrong, Officer," Hwicce said, hoping that was the right way to address the robot.

"You are charged with disturbing the peace," the drone said. "I will escort you to the station where another party is also waiting to speak with you."

"Right," Hwicce said. He stepped away from Baker as if to follow the drone's order. Baker took a step the other way.

As they separated, the drone couldn't keep its weapon on both of them at once. At first, it shifted in a jittery motion between them, then it focused on Baker as she continued stepping further away. The drone aimed its weapon directly at her centre of mass.

"Stop," it said. "I have called for reinforcements."

Hwicce dropped his arm and grabbed onto the hilt of the

nanite knife stashed in his pocket. Moving slowly to avoid catching the drone's attention, Hwicce pulled out the knife. He shifted so his body blocked the drone's view and flipped the knife's safety. The blade formed, glinting under the diffuse light.

He'd have one shot and couldn't afford to miss. The knot in his gut twisted as he threw the knife at the drone's balloon. The blade sunk into the fabric like it was nothing. With a hiss, the balloon vented its gas.

Still ordering them to surrender, the drone crashed to the ground. The deflated balloon covered the wreckage, preventing the robot from targeting them with its weapon.

"Let's get out of here before those reinforcements arrive," Hwicce called as he started sprinting away.

Baker quickly reached his side. "I know where we can go."

A few minutes later, they reached Baker's brother's bank and darted inside. Not even out of breath, Baker straightened her suit as she approached the front desk.

"Ms. Baker," the receptionist said with a smile. "You're back sooner than expected."

"I've decided to take my brother up on his offer of the use of one of his personal vehicles," Baker said.

"Good call," the receptionist said. He stood and gestured to a side staircase. "Two levels down, you'll find the garage."

Baker nodded, and the two of them headed down the stairs. The garage was as spacious and gleaming as the bank above. Best of all, no one was there.

Stopping to catch his breath, Hwicce pulled out his datapad. There was a message from GRUB. He opened and pursed his lips as he read it.

"Emiko never betrayed us," he said in a quiet voice as he hung his head.

"What?" Baker came over and read over his shoulder. "Oh… she'll never forgive me."

Hwicce let out a long exhale. "I think we both owe her an apology when we get back."

"Maybe we could stop somewhere…." Baker bit her lip and glanced back at the staircase. "I could get her a gift."

"If we have time. It looks like comms are back up," Hwicce said as he activated his comms device and tried to reach Veena. After several failed tries to connect with her, he tried Orin. He had no luck there either.

"Maybe that bloody storm's still causing interference." Baker put her hands on her hips.

"No, it's not the storm. I'm connecting to their devices, but no one's answering." He sent a message to GRUB asking them to track Veena's position.

A moment later, a map of the Seven Soaring Swans appeared on his datapad. He projected it into the space between himself and Baker. Veena wasn't on any of the islands. Hwicce swallowed as he zoomed out.

"There." Baker pointed to a mining rig to the west.

Hwicce zoomed in on her position and frowned.

"What's she doing out there?" Baker asked.

"Since she isn't answering my calls, I think we need to assume that bounty hunter found her," Hwicce said as a knot turned in his gut.

He turned and looked at the line of cherry red hovercraft against the wall. Each little car was suspended below a balloon twice its size. "We need to go after her."

Hwicce flew along the underside of the islands, being careful not to snag their balloon. The sleek craft couldn't go much faster than he could run, but it freed them from the maze of the islands above. Below, in the Shimmer, the reflective metal particles glinted in the sunlight.

"Do you have a direction?" he asked.

Baker scrunched up her face as she studied the map on her datapad. "Down three hundred metres and a kilometre west."

Hwicce angled the craft down. "How low can we go and still be able to breathe?"

In the distance, he could just make out the hulking shape of the extractor with its huge, statically charged nets extending below.

"This car has oxygen tanks," Baker said. "But I think the extractor's superstructure is as low as we should go without breathing devices."

"Let's put them on," Hwicce said.

Baker opened the glove compartment and pulled out two bundles. The first she unwound was a face mask with a tube connecting to a small oxygen bottle.

"Put the mask on and clip the tank to your belt," she said as she handed it to him.

Hwicce used one hand to pull it over his head. It was awkward, but he got it into place. By the time he stopped fiddling with it, Baker already had hers on.

"We should've stopped for some weapons," Baker said. "And I really miss my combat armour."

"You mean your yellow suit can't stop projectiles?" Hwicce said, forcing himself to smile.

She swatted him on the arm. "Dumbass."

Hwicce angled the car down, only levelling off once they'd reached the underside of the extractor. The glinting flakes of metal now fluttered around them like a colourful blizzard. It would be hard to see them from above. He slowed to the same speed as the extractor and stared up.

Below, the nets continued down as they dipped into the Shimmer, while above, the superstructure hung in the sky. It lacked any of the elegance of the buildings on the Seven

Soaring Swans, just utilitarian and minimalist. Catwalks extended out to the ends of the massive nets with a platform at the centre. No one was in view.

"What do you think is our best way in?" He turned his head to see Baker.

Baker squinted as she gazed up. "Can we come up under that catwalk?" She pointed to the one directly above.

Hwicce rose straight up, taking care to stay clear of the billowing fabric of the nets.

Chapter Forty-Six

"Mommy," Molly called from somewhere out of sight. Veena strained to see her little girl.

"Where are you, love bug?"

"You said you would always come for me."

A breath caught in Veena's throat. She'd made that promise, but every action she'd taken since Molly was kidnapped hadn't gotten her any closer. "Mol, I'm coming for you, but I don't know where you are."

"I'm in a lab. I'm afraid they're going to hurt us."

With a jolt, Veena woke. Every nerve in her body screamed at her. Fire seemed to rage across her skin. Then her body figured out she was okay, and the phantom pain subsided.

She tried to stretch, only to discover they bound her hands behind her back. She lay on her right side, her shoulder and hip digging into a cold, metal surface. The silk-like fabric of her scarf rested across her left cheek, the fabric moving with each breath she took.

Opening her eyes, she found herself in a control room of some sort. A floor-to-ceiling glass wall separated the room she was in from a larger space filled with machinery and conveyor belts. A door at the end of the clear wall connected the two spaces. Behind her, several workstations contained panels full of buttons and levers.

She had no idea where she was. Each breath she took came faster and faster as a dome of panic formed in her chest. Squeezing her eyes shut, she forced herself to take five deep breaths.

"It's old, I'll give it that," a familiar voice said from out of her view.

Veena flinched and flicked her eyes open. Shifting her leg and using it as leverage, she sat up and twisted towards the speaker. A shiver ran up her spine—she hadn't imagined it. The bounty hunter held her captive.

With his hands clasped behind his head, he sat slumped in the chair in front of a workstation. He rested his feet out in front of him, taking up way more space than he needed. It was as though he didn't have a care in the world—as though he was confident Veena was helpless.

Veena swallowed. She'd evaded him before; maybe she could evade him now.

"What's old?" She shifted so her shoulder rested against one of the workstations. She needed information, which meant she needed to play nice.

"This extractor." He stood and paced over to the floor-to-ceiling windows. "I suspect it may be the first one the original settlers built. That's almost two-hundred and fifty years of floating through this atmosphere, dipping its big gaping mouth into the layer below."

Veena drew her eyebrows together. She'd seen the mining platforms in the distance when their shuttle landed on Seven Soaring Swans. They'd seemed so far away, webs of dull coloured metal well out of reach. Her breathing sped up. Squeezing her eyes shut, she slowly counted back from ten.

"Why am I here?" she asked as she met the bounty hunter's gaze.

"The extractors are autonomous," he said, turning back towards her, his face unreadable. "Once every few months, a maintenance crew pops by to check on things and take the collected metal."

"So?"

He smiled, the expression not reaching his eyes. "Well, this is the perfect place to hand you off."

Veena swallowed and forced herself to take a deep breath. The extractor would be a tough place to escape from.

"Wait…." She swivelled her head. Only the two of them were there. Orin wasn't. "Did you keep your promise and let Orin go?"

"He refused to let you go without a fight. Quite the knight in shining armour."

A breath caught in Veena's throat as she leaned forward towards the bounty hunter. "Where is he?"

"I sent him over the edge. He'll fall until he reaches a layer with his density. Then, like this extractor, he'll circle the planet indefinitely."

Bile burned in the back of Veena's throat, and she thought she would vomit. Orin had died trying to save her. She squeezed her eyes shut as tears threatened to well up. Orin didn't deserve this.

"As for you…."

Veena opened her eyes and glared at her captor.

"What my client does with you is none of my business. Once the credits I'm owed are in my account, I'll hand you over, and I'll be on my way."

"You asshole." Veena spat as she spoke. "I'm going to make sure you pay for what you've done."

He shrugged. "I'm just doing my job; it wasn't personal until you threw me off a catwalk on Indigo Station."

Veena said nothing.

"The fall pulverized several vertebrae." He stood and stretched his hands over his head. "I can still feel those nanites working to fix things."

"You deserved it."

He scowled at her just as a loud thunk came from somewhere beyond the control room's walls.

"Hang tight. I'll check it out." He left through a door on the side wall.

As soon as she was alone, Veena pushed her shoulder joints to their limit as she scooted her bum over her hands. It was a stretch, but she passed her feet through the gap of her bound wrists. The metal of the cuffs cut into her wrists, but now her bound hands were at her front.

She studied the handcuffs. They were ordinary and would be easy to unlock, but she didn't have a key. Knowing she might not have much time, she awkwardly rose to her feet. She readjusted her scarf around her neck as she surveyed the room. No weapon-like tools lay about.

"I guess he isn't that kind of stupid," Veena muttered to herself as she started opening every drawer. Other than a few ration bars and a broken flashlight, the only thing she found was a small laser cutter—the kind one could open a package with. After checking it had enough charge to run, she pocketed it.

A moment later, the bounty hunter returned. He stopped in the doorway and stared at her, his eyes lingering on her hands, now at her front. For a moment, his nostrils flared, and he shook his head. "Don't fuck around with me. You're worth the same conscious or unconscious." He pointed his stun gun her way. "So get your ass back down on the floor."

Veena nodded as she noticed he now had her bag slung over his shoulder. Was the alien artifact still in it? She swallowed as she realized she'd need to retrieve the bag before she made an escape.

With a sigh, she returned to where she'd been sitting on the floor earlier. "I could use some water."

"And I could use a fancy hat, something splendid with extra feathers." He glanced down at his datapad and snorted. "Good. Comms are back up. My client will be here in about fifteen minutes."

Veena pursed her lips together and let her head tip back against the side of the workstation. She had to act now before Swa had her in their custody.

"They took my daughter."

"Don't care." He didn't even look up from his datapad. "Now keep quiet or...." He waved the stun gun her way.

Veena frowned. Appealing to his humanity had been a long shot. She didn't engage in any more conversation. Instead, she studied him. He was as big as Hwicce but leaner. He had said his back injury still pained him, but trying to overpower him was a bad idea—if he knew what he was doing, and considering his profession, he probably did, she wouldn't stand a chance. She needed another solution.

She stared out into the room full of automatic machinery on the other side of the window. Multiple catwalks led off between the equipment. There had to be hiding places—but she needed her bag, or their whole trip to New Venus would have been for nothing. The time to make a move was now before Swa's people came for her.

"Fucking hell." The bounty hunter frowned and shook his device.

She bit her lip as she watched him. The bounty hunter was as distracted as she could hope. In her peripheral vision, the door to the machinery room beckoned her. It stood two paces away, but she didn't know if it was locked or not. She took a deep breath. It was now or never.

Pushing off from the floor with her bound hands, she lurched to her feet and sprinted for the door. Luck was with her, and it slid open.

"Stop!" the bounty hunter's voice boomed out behind her.

Without even a glance his way, Veena sprinted down the

main catwalk. Her footfalls thumped against the metal grating and resonated throughout the space. Just as she turned behind an enormous machine, a blast from the stun gun narrowly missed her.

Running with her hands bound in front was awkward. With every turn she made, she risked losing her balance, but she didn't dare slow down.

At the far end of the machine room, she spotted another door. Unsure of how close the bounty hunter was behind her, she headed straight for it at her top speed.

In a single motion, she slid the door open and skidded to a stop. Empty sky extended out as far as she could see. Her chest heaved as she drew in ragged breaths, and her legs burned from the run.

A gust of wind buffeted her, almost pushing her back through the door. The hexagon-patterned scarf snapped around her face. Taking a single step forward, she pulled the door shut behind her.

"What now?" she said to herself while still panting.

Another gust of wind pushed a lock of hair over her eyes. With her bound hands, she pushed it behind her ear and approached the railing. A single metal bar was all that separated her from the same fate as Orin.

Her scarf came loose and floated away over the edge. The light fabric billowed as the wind buffeted it. Like a parachute, it floated down, drawing Veena's gaze with it.

The great nets filtering the metal-laced layer below gaped like the mouths of filter-feeding whales. Her heart continued to race as she considered options. No ladder led down from where she stood, but the catwalk extended to the right and left; she chose left.

Doing her best to ignore her mounting vertigo, she followed the catwalk around the edge and out of sight of the door. She stopped, surprised she'd gotten this far ahead of the bounty hunter.

"He must think I can't escape." She bit her lip—a remote mining platform might be the perfect place to hold someone. She scratched the side of her head and studied the building.

A few metres away, a ladder led up two stories to the roof of the machine room. Beside it, another ladder led down to the great nets below.

Without even a glance down, she took the ladder heading up, climbing as fast as her bound hands would allow. Counting each rung as she passed, she didn't even peek at her surroundings.

At the top, she lay on her belly on the flat roof and peered over the edge. Her stomach churned at the swirling interface of the Shimmer, but the bounty hunter sill wasn't in sight.

"He must be waiting for me somewhere." The relentless winds ripped away her words as fast as she said them. She didn't want to play such a high-stakes game of cat and mouse—hell, what she really wanted was to soak in a bubble bath back on *Virdis*.

Staying low, she leopard-crawled to the side where she'd exited the machine room. Peeking over the edge, all she could see was an empty catwalk with the Shimmer below. He wasn't there either. Continuing on, she periodically peered over the edge. Each time the catwalk below remained empty.

"Shit," Veena said as she glanced up at the sky above.

It glistened with its constant sunset hues. The islands of Seven Soaring Swans shone in the distance, the white surfaces of the buildings reflecting oranges and yellows. Hwicce was over there somewhere, probably wondering why she didn't meet him at the auction house.

"Get a grip," she told herself. Staying away from the edge, she stood and walked towards the front of the building. The roof dropped a story. She took another ladder down and stepped out onto the control room roof.

A landing pad connected to the front of the building. Currently, a single hover car occupied the space—presumably the hover car the bounty hunter used to bring her here. It looked like a rental, the kind anyone could fly.

Veena licked her lips; she could use the car to escape—but she needed the bag with the alien artifact in it first. Another ladder led down right beside the main doors.

She paused. The puny laser cutter was the only weapon she had. Nothing had changed—she wouldn't stand a chance against the bounty hunter. And he was waiting for her somewhere down below, like a cat waiting for its prey.

"Time's running out." With her heart racing again, she climbed down. Beside the foot of the ladder was a set of double doors.

Trying to look in all directions at once, she slid one door open and darted inside. With a cloud of dust that smelled like stale coffee, a lounge-like room greeted her. Two sofas sat perpendicular to each other, with a counter holding a coffee pot at the far end. Directly across from the entrance was a second set of doors with 'control room' stenciled on them. Beside those was another door labeled 'washroom.'

"Where are you?" she whispered. But the bounty hunter was nowhere to be seen.

She walked around the two sofas. They were mustard yellow and well worn, but their backs rose tall enough to hide behind. She would be out of view of both the front door and the door to the control room. But first, she needed a better weapon.

Her eyes focused on the coffee pot—more specifically on the metal carafe. Without looking at the pile of dirty mugs in the sink, she grabbed the carafe by the handle. It was heavy, but not too heavy.

Ignoring the dusty floor, she crouched down behind the sofa and waited. A strong sense of déjà vu washed over her. Her thoughts went back to the fancy stateroom she'd had on the *Garden Princess*, of how she'd confronted Dr. Greer there. She'd gotten away then, and she would get away now.

Chapter Forty-Seven

Veena didn't have to wait long. With a grinding metal sound, the door to the control room slid open. Forcing each breath to be slow and steady, she reminded herself she'd only have one chance, and she didn't want to squander it.

Heavy footfalls crossed the floor as she crouched lower and held her breath. After a pause, the sound moved past her sofa—meaning the bounty hunter's back should be facing her.

In a single motion, she lunged out and raised the carafe. Before the bounty hunter could turn, she slammed the carafe down on his head, resulting in a loud thunk.

He fell to his knees as Veena raised the carafe for a second blow. Then he spun and launched himself into her. He dropped a shoulder, focusing the force of his full weight into Veena's gut.

She toppled backwards, losing her grip on the carafe. It bounced across the floor as the bounty hunter landed on top of her, knocking the wind out of her.

He laughed. "I've got a pretty thick skull."

Veena coughed as she tried to breathe. The musky scent of his exertion wafted down as he studied her.

"I have to give one thing to you; you've put more effort into escape than any other bounty." He raised himself up just enough she could breathe.

She gasped, sucking in lung-fulls of air. "Please, just let me go."

"Hell no. I'm tempted to demand General Swa pay me extra for all the trouble you've caused."

Veena realized he had pinned her right hand against the pocket containing the pathetic laser cutter. Moving slowly, she started easing the cutter out of her pocket.

He snorted and rolled off her.

Free of his weight, she rolled to her side and forced herself to continue coughing. Now hidden from his view, she pulled out the cutter and activated it. She didn't know how much charge it had left. Keeping the cutter hidden behind her body, she pushed herself up to sitting.

The bounty hunter waved his stun gun in her face. "You going to cooperate now?"

She nodded.

"Good. You're the most frustrating academic mark I've dealt with." He leaned down, grabbed her upper right arm, and pulled her to her feet. "I'm definitely going to ask more for you."

A loud thunk vibrated through the structure. Keeping his hand on her arm, the bounty hunter pulled Veena over to the outside door. He opened it and pulled her through.

A large military shuttle now sat on the landing pad. Knowing once she was on that shuttle there would be no opportunity for escape, Veena glanced at the bounty hunter. He still had her bag slung over his shoulder. She shifted her gaze to his neck.

Veena swallowed, hating what she was about to do—then she remembered what he'd done to Orin.

Holding the cutter in both hands, she shoved the laser into the bounty hunter's neck. As soon as she pulled it out, blood started gushing out.

The bounty hunter made a choking sound and let go of her.

He put his hands to his neck. Veena grabbed her bag as more blood gushed out of him.

Without another word, she ran around the building. Her feet pounded on the catwalk, causing the metal structure to shake as she went. But she continued on all the way around to the far side of the building. At the top of the ladder going down, she stopped and looked back over her shoulder.

"Was that a fatal blow?" she muttered to herself, uncertain how she felt about that.

Through the bag, she could feel the alien artifact—at least she'd gotten it back.

With her hands shaking, she strapped the bag over her neck, letting it hang down her front. Handcuffs still held her wrists together, but there was nothing she could do about that.

She started down the ladder, counting each rung as she passed them. She was probably heading to a dead-end—or worst yet, a fall into the Shimmer.

Swallowing, she forced herself to focus on the rungs. At twenty-seven, her foot reached another catwalk. Taking the path that led under the structure above, she kept moving.

Shimmering dust swirled around her with each movement—like the glitter on Molly's pink backpack.

"Focus," she told herself. She could hear shouting coming from above—they were looking for her. She needed to find somewhere to hide.

A gust brought more dust, obscuring her view. Then a piece of fabric covered her face. Her heart felt like it was about to pound out of her chest—but no one pulled the fabric tight. She raised her hands and pulled it off her face.

She held her green hexagon scarf in her hands. Rotating around, she realized no one had followed her down—yet. She let out the breath she didn't realize she'd been holding.

"I still need to hide."

A gust of wind shoved her from behind as though urging her on. Pushing through a feeling of light-headedness, she continued down the catwalk. The glitter in the air was denser now, and she could barely make out the path ahead.

"Am I just going to a dead end?" she whispered to no one.

Mommy!

Veena stopped. Did she really hear Molly's voice, or was it just the wind? Squinting, she could see something—a figure, maybe. Her heart leapt into her throat.

"Molly!" she shouted, knowing it made no sense for Molly to be here.

She raced towards the shape, but thirteen paces on, she realized it was only the end of the catwalk—she'd chosen a dead-end after wall.

Placing both hands on the railing, she took a deep breath. Her light-headedness morphed into dizziness. Breathing in all the glittering metals couldn't be good for her, but she had no alternative.

A gust of wind cleared the glitter, and Veena could see the undersides of the islands of Seven Soaring Swans. The city seemed both close and impossibly far away. She'd failed; there was no escape. It was only a matter of time until Swa's people had her in their custody.

Chapter Forty-Eight

Hwicce slowed the car as they came up under the mining platform. The complicated web of metal supports, ladders, and catwalks created a three-dimensional maze, and he didn't want to snag the balloon that held them up.

"Over there," Baker shouted, pointing.

Hwicce looked that way. A lone figure in green stood at the end of the catwalk under the main platform. As a gust cleared the glittering particles out of the air, he could see it was Veena.

"I'm coming," he said as he angled the car in her direction.

Soon, he could see Veena's dark hair and the fact that her hands were bound. He sped up to reach the catwalk.

"Veena!" he shouted, his breathing apparatus muffling his words.

He couldn't tell if she heard him, but she looked his way, eyes wide and face spattered in blood.

"She won't be getting enough air." Baker leaned forward and rummaged in the glove compartment.

"Is there another oxygen bottle?" He spoke without taking his eyes off Veena. The metal structure was only a few car lengths away now.

"Found one." Baker put the oxygen bottle and mask on the floor and unbuckled.

Hwicce decelerated as he pulled the car up alongside the catwalk. A loud squeal sounded as the car rubbed along the catwalk—but he didn't dare leave a gap.

Baker stood and grabbed onto the railing. "Cross here," she said, but Veena was already moving their direction.

As Baker reached out to Veena, she climbed over the railing and stepped into the car.

Veena wrapped her bound hands over Hwicce's head and hugged him tightly. She was trembling. "I thought they had me for sure," she said, gasping for air between each word.

"Here." Baker strapped an oxygen mask over Veena's face.

Veena closed her eyes and took a deep breath.

"We got you." Hwicce wrapped his arms around her.

"Wait, where's Orin?" Baker twisted to see back along the catwalk.

"He… he… he fell." Veena bit her lip and met Hwicce's gaze. "He sacrificed himself for me."

"I'm sorry," he said, hugging her tight a second time.

"We should get the fucking hell out of here." Baker pointed to where two people were descending the ladder.

"Right. Swa's people are here. They parked their ship on the landing pad above." Veena shifted herself off Hwicce before looking around the car.

"It's a two-seater," Baker said.

"Whatever, as long as it gets us away from here." Veena settled herself onto Baker's lap. "At least I've got the artifact."

"This car isn't going to be able to outrun a military shuttle," Baker said as she glanced up.

"Yeah." Hwicce studied the surrounding structure. There was plenty of cover under the mining platform, but as soon as they left its shelter, they'd be exposed. He glanced at the car's display; they were ten metres above its maximum depth. He couldn't go down any further to hide.

Maybe Swa's people would be busy searching the platform for Veena. He swallowed, knowing it was a long shot. Any military shuttle could outrun them.

"We're going to have to run for it," he said, fixing his gaze on the distant floating islands. Even if they made it, the authorities would hunt for them there. But they had nowhere else to go.

With care, Hwicce navigated to the edge of the structure. The three of them looked up as though they expected a swarm of Swa's people to be looking down. Instead, they saw nothing.

"Hold on," Hwicce said.

Setting the throttle to maximum, he launched the car into a direct path for the nearest floating island. The engine whined but sped up. The wind buffeted them, forcing Hwicce to fight to maintain the course. Both Veena and Baker twisted to see the platform.

They got halfway.

"They've lifted off," Veena said.

"Fucking hell!" Baker said. "We've been spotted."

Hwicce didn't dare turn and look. Instead, he kept the car on its course. Maybe, just maybe, they'd make it.

Another military shuttle passed over the island, coming straight for them.

"Crap!" He swerved ninety degrees. There was no outrunning the shuttles and nowhere to go. He angled up with a faint hope of hiding in the cloud cover above.

For a few moments, no one said anything. The clouds above seemed to be getting closer. Hwicce eyed their depth gauge; they had a hundred metres until they reached the max height the car could navigate. He looked up at the clouds, trying to judge their height.

"They're gaining," Baker said, her tone flat.

With a sigh, Hwicce turned and looked. The two shuttles were flying in formation side-by-side less than two hundred metres behind them now. They were well within the shuttle's weapons range—likely only their desire to take Veena alive kept them from firing.

Gritting his teeth, Hwicce aimed upwards at a steeper angle.

One shuttle fired an energy weapon. The shimmering burst passed them on the right. He swallowed.

"We're not going to make it," Baker said, and Veena remained silent.

The clouds above grew darker as a rumble reverberated from them. Then a dark shape blocked out the sun above. The massive object sunk through the atmosphere just up ahead. Although flames came off the hull, it was clear what it was.

"It's a ship," Hwicce said as soon as he realized what he was looking at.

"It's the *Virdis*," Veena said.

"Well, fuck! I didn't realize it was atmosphere rated," Baker said.

"Of course it is. How else would we get water?" Hwicce craned his neck to watch the water tanker descend. At least with the fire, it was unlikely Swa's people would recognize it.

"Who's flying?" Veena said.

The *Virdis* continued down until it was flying right in front of them. The two shuttles backed off, maintaining a new position about five hundred metres behind.

The main cargo bay doors opened, an invitation the Hwicce didn't hesitate to accept. He flew right inside. Even before he had fully come to a stop on the deck, the colossal ship was already rising.

The two women were already out of the car as soon as it settled on the deck. He hopped out and embraced Veena. When he glanced down at her face, he frowned at the spatter of blood across one cheek.

"That's not yours, is it?" He wiped it away with his sleeve.

"No." She frowned. "I had to…." Her words trailed off.

"It's okay." He pulled her in tighter. "We're okay."

"Hey, lovebirds," Baker cut in. "We may not be out of the woods yet."

"Right." Hwicce released Veena.

"And you bloody well don't need those." Baker held up a bolt cutter.

Veena nodded and raised her bound hands. In a single motion, Baker cut the chain holding the cuffs together.

"I'll get the rest later. Right now, we got shit to do."

Taking Veena's hand, Hwicce raced up the stairs and down the long corridor to the bridge. When he burst through the door, he stopped dead.

"Orin!" Veena pulled away and raced down to the pilot's seat. "You're okay." She looked ready to throw her arms around the little man.

"Everyone buckle in," Orin said. "It's going to be rough leaving the planet, and the *Defiant* is in orbit."

Hwicce took the captain's chair. As he buckled himself in, he noticed Emiko sitting at the far console. She glanced his way, but her face remained blank. Without a word, she returned her attention to the displays.

"GRUB, are you there?" Hwicce asked as he confirmed both Veena and Baker were buckled in.

"Affirmative," GRUB replied. "The two shuttles are still following us."

"How much pressure can the hull handle?" Hwicce projected an image of New Venus into the air beside him.

"Roughly 90 bars," GRUB answered.

"And what do you think those shuttles can handle?" With a swipe, Hwicce cut across the projected planet to view the layer of atmosphere.

"Half that."

Hwicce let out a long exhale. The Shimmer below them was peppered with occasional floating islands—and they didn't have exact positions for them. Going down was a tremendous risk. "We dive."

"Diving," Orin said. A moment later, the ship's nose tilted downward.

They sunk below the floating island layer and into the Shimmer. Out the front windows, it was like they were flying into a glitter blizzard that got thicker and thicker as they descended.

"The outside atmosphere is now at fifteen bars. And our sensors are barely working." Orin levelled the ship off.

"It's all the metal in the Shimmer," Emiko said. "They won't be able to see us anymore either."

"GRUB, can you plot us a course to leave the atmosphere on a direct trajectory to the shipping lane headed to the gate?" Hwicce asked.

"Course is plotted," GRUB answered as they added the ship's path on the holographic globe.

Hwicce gripped the armrests on his chair. "Where's the *Defiant*?"

A miniature version of the military ship appeared. It was at the spaceport. Their course would avoid them.

A loud thunk reverberated through the ship.

"We've clipped a sunken island," GRUB said without emotion.

"Crap!" Hwicce shook his head. "Get us out of here, Orin, before we hit something else."

"Setting new course now."

The *Virdis* rose at a reasonable angle. The glitter storm outside thinned until they exited the layer. In the clear layer, a few islands were visible in the distance, but they didn't appear inhabited.

"Any news on the shuttles?" Hwicce turned to Emiko.

"Negative. I'm not picking up any other vessels."

"Keep rising," Hwicce said.

They passed into the cloud layer, the sunset hues filling the bridge. Orin kept them in the clouds until they reached their vector to the shipping lane. Only then did he lift the ship out of the atmosphere.

As the surrounding sky morphed into a field of stars, Hwicce held his breath. *Virdis* was no match for the *Defiant.* But the warship was nowhere to be seen. They'd made it.

Chapter Forty-Nine

After they'd traversed the first gate, Veena sat at the kitchen table and brought out the alien object. They'd made it. Even if the *Defiant* was following, they had enough of a head start to relax a bit. But GRUB seemed confident that the Water Guild's requirement of anonymity meant their ship hadn't been identified.

Hwicce came down from their quarters. His normally sandy blonde hair looked dark, meaning he'd just had a shower. Veena smiled, enjoying everything about him, from his bear-like posture down to the stubble of his current attempt at re-growing his beard. But just like when they first met, it was the blue of his eyes that drew her in.

"Hey, handsome," she said.

"Flirting like that could get you in trouble." He smiled as he went into the kitchen and filled two mugs with coffee.

"You mean I might wake up ten years from now and find you sleeping next to me?"

Hwicce sat down at the table. "It's a risk."

She reached out and took his hand. His palm was warm. "I can live with that level of risk."

"You were always the wild one."

Veena laughed out loud. They'd met in a library when she'd gone over to tell him and his friends to quiet down.

"Have you gotten anywhere with all this?" He waved to the pile of material before her.

"As a matter of fact, I have."

She turned the truncated isohedron over in her hand. Then she placed it on the base Theo65 gave her. Glowing orange patterns welled up in the shape, then a projection formed above the image.

"It's a star chart." Veena pointed to a glowing aqua ring. "Look, these shapes represent the gates."

Hwicce leaned in and scratched his chin. "There's more on there than our gate charts."

"Yeah, a hell of a lot more." Veena studied the image. There had to be dozens of unknown gates listed, creating more of a net than a figure-eight loop. This information was worth a fortune, but that didn't explain why Swa wanted it.

She took a sip of her coffee as Emiko stormed through the kitchen. Baker followed.

"Do you think they'll work it out?" Veena asked.

Hwicce frowned as his gaze followed the two women. Emiko went into her quarters and closed the door behind herself, leaving Baker outside.

"I hope so." He ran a hand through his hair. "I suspect Emiko won't be forgiving me anytime soon. Hell, I wouldn't be surprised if she gets off at the next port and never speaks with us again."

Baker banged on the door, but after a few moments and it not opening, she went into her own quarters, disappearing from view.

Veena returned her gaze back to the map. She pinpointed the Delta system gate and easily found two other off-loop gates. One of them would lead to where Molly was, but which one? And how did they access the new gates?

Orin came into the common room from the hall. "Wow," he said, walking over and taking a seat beside Veena. "That's quite the map." With his finger, he started tracing different paths through the gates.

Veena stared at Orin. "The bounty hunter said he threw you off the edge of the island."

Orin met her gaze and shrugged. "I tried to fight him off, but he was a tough bastard. And I lack fighting skills. He got the best of me and pushed me off the edge."

"How did you survive?" she asked.

"Turns out, people falling off the islands of Seven Soaring Swans is a known problem. They have a whole swarm of drones on standby to catch anyone who falls. One of them picked me up, and I headed straight back up to the ship." Orin smiled.

"We owe you," Hwicce said. "And GRUB and Emiko."

"I am disappointed by Max's betrayal," GRUB said in a flat tone.

Hwicce nodded. "We all are. I'd hoped...." His words trailed off. He'd hoped Max would give him a window into his late aunt's world. He'd certainly had hoped to keep Max on as chief engineer to honour Aunt Darla's decision to give him the job.

Orin leaned in closer to the gate map. "Does the projection give us any clues to translate the alien text?"

"Maybe." Veena returned her attention to the gate map. "I'll have to think—"

"There's a message you need to see," GRUB cut in. "It arrived encrypted and took a while for me to decode it."

"Can you show it here?" Hwicce asked.

"It is best you come to the bridge."

The three of them headed up to the bridge. Veena sank down into the seat next to the captain's chair as a flutter formed in her gut. Hwicce took the captain's chair, and Orin sat on the other side of him.

The windows facing outside darkened, and a new scene was projected. Molly's face appeared with a huge grin.

"We did it," she said as Click climbed up her arm and perched on her shoulder.

Veena clasped her hand to her mouth. Molly looked okay.

Nigel appeared behind her and said, "I think you need to explain."

Molly looked up at him, then back at the camera. "We escaped. Click, Nigel, and me. We were super smart and super sneaky. We've even stolen a shuttle." Her grin showed how proud she was of herself.

Nigel looked into the camera, his face glum. "It was the best choice out of a collection of terrible options." He pursed his lips. "This shuttle is a military transport, one that was fully kitted out with supplies for a long journey."

On Molly's shoulder, Click flashed yellow, then pink.

"Look, Mom. Click is real!" She pointed at the little octopus-like alien. "And waaaaay better than a stuffy!"

Nigel bent over next to Molly's empty shoulder. "You need to tell them where we're going."

"Right." She nodded, her tangled curls bouncing with the motion. "Mom, Dad, we're going to go home."

The message ended in static.

"GRUB, is there more?" Hwicce asked.

"Negative," GRUB answered.

"How long ago was the message recorded?" Veena asked.

"Nineteen hours ago," GRUB said. "The military equipment on that shuttle has masked their location."

"Crap." Veena grabbed onto her ponytail. "Where is Molly thinking home is now?"

Hwicce turned to her. "Do you think she'd head back to New Haven?"

"There's nothing left of our home there, and she knows it." Veena bit her lip. "Maybe they're going to Click's home."

"Would she go back to Rock 13-A5?" Orin asked.

"I suspect they'll be re-captured before they get too far," GRUB said. "The shuttle will have a tracking device on board."

"We need to track down Swa," Veena said. "She's the only one who can help us find Molly and Click."

Hwicce looked her in the eye. "Why would she help us?"

Veena ran a hand over the alien gate map and bit her lip. More alien knowledge sat on her kitchen table than she'd ever seen in one place. She glanced down at her datapad and the code she had stored.

"If I make sense of all this,"—she gestured to the codes and artifacts—"I can make a trade."

"May I suggest we keep all options on the table?" Orin said. "If Molly is indeed heading back to Rock 13-A5, my contacts will be able to help us."

Chapter Fifty

Swa sat behind her desk on the *Defiant*. That damn bounty hunter had failed to capture Dr. Oswiu, her team had failed to get that alien artifact, and now this. She clenched her teeth together and stared at the projected head hovering over her desk.

"Your Subject 34 escaped her cell and stole a shuttle." She sneered at Dr. Greer, noting that, for once, the celebrated doctor didn't look smug.

"The alien helped her," he said.

"The alien your research determined had the IQ of a watermelon." She pressed her lips together.

He let out an audible sigh. "I didn't suggest that. I simply had no proof they had an intellectual capacity anywhere near that of a human."

"But they somehow figured out how to make a gate system." Swa crossed her arms over her chest. "A feat our top engineers can't replicate."

"You know, the working theory was that the aliens had declined since their gate-building days." He frowned. "Some of my colleagues have even suggested their species devolved after some cataclysmic event."

"And yet one escaped from your facility like it was a public washroom," Swa said.

"I've already sent a party after the shuttle," Greer said, changing to the topic. "They'll capture it before they get out of the system."

"I want you to let them go," Swa said. "I'm going to use the girl as bait to capture her mother."

Greer frowned and shifted. "As much as a translation of the alien texts would accelerate my work, I don't think we should let an unsupervised child—."

Swa cut him off. "That is not for you to decide. Now did you obtain tissue samples from the girl before she escaped?"

"Yes. However, I need more to continue," Greer said. "I don't know how the Nader Alliance proceeded with this work so quickly unless, of course, they'd been defying the GenEn protocols for decades."

Swa studied Greer's face as she debated replacing him as the head of her research arm—but she knew she couldn't. Using the alien technology to replicate the super soldiers the Nader Alliance created would solidify her position and the need for her department. And, as distasteful as he was, Greer was integral to that.

"I want to move your department to Rock 13-A5," she said. "I need to keep a better eye on you."

Greer frowned. "There are too many eyes there."

"Prepare for the move. I expect your team to be installed there within the week." Swa clicked the comms link off. For a moment, she kept her eyes fixed on where Greer's head had been. If he wasn't brilliant, she would have replaced him months ago. The pompous ass needed to be taken down a notch.

Swa shifted her attention to Captain Von. "Have you located the shuttle the girl stole?"

"Yes, ma'am," Captain Von said with the proper level of respect. "It was preprogrammed for the trip to Rock 13-A5, and that has not been changed."

"Good. Leave it be," Swa said.

"Also, we have detected comms activity," Captain Von said.

"Oh?" Swa leaned forward and raised an eyebrow.

"A single, recorded message to her parents."

Swa smiled. "Perfect. Molly Oswiu has called her mom and dad." She stood and paced over to the vast windows filling one wall. "Tell your people to give the shuttle plenty of room on its way to Rock 13-A5. We'll pick it up once it enters the Alpha system."

"Yes, ma'am," Captain Von said.

"Dismissed," Swa said as she turned her back to the ship's captain.

Staring at the starfield beyond the window, Swa started working through all the puzzle pieces in play. Veena Oswiu had the alien codes and the alien artifact. Likely, she was already hard at work figuring out what they all meant. Greer was certain more knowledge of genetic engineering would be found in that work—a theory she suspected was true based on the earliest messages from the aliens.

She returned to her desk and opened the first of the messages. It had arrived on Earth 733 years ago, a decade before the first generation ships had started their voyage here.

It was an invitation, complete with suggestions on how humans could be genetically altered to tolerate long space voyages. Something had happened to the alien civilization between then and now, something cataclysmic that destroyed what they once were. But their advanced knowledge was still out there, and she would be the one to discover their secrets.

<<<<>>>>

Thanks for reading!

Thank you for reading *The Alien Algorithm*. I hope you enjoyed it!

Veena and Hwicce's quest to get Molly back continues in *Subject 34*.

To get news on new releases, free short stories and a peak into my world sign up for my mostly monthly newsletter here - http://jeannettebedard.com/

About the Author

By day I'm a scientist, by night I write science fiction. I have hard drives clogged with ideas and outlines—sometimes they dissolve into ones and zeros, but sometimes they coalesce to form an entire novel. My stories are filled with action and adventure where something always blows up, usually in the first fifty pages.

You can connect with me here: http://jeannettebedard.com/

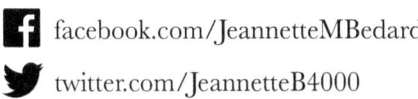

facebook.com/JeannetteMBedard

twitter.com/JeannetteB4000

Also by Jeannette Bedard

ENCODED ORBITS

Fractured Orbits

The Alien Algorithm

Subject 34

THE SETTLER CHRONICLES

Day 115 on an Alien World

Far Side of the Moon

Abandoned Ships, Hijacked Minds

The Alien Artifact

Acknowledgments

In no particular order I'd like to thank: Christine, Alana, and Amy for being kind enough to provide feedback on early drafts.

To Jeff Elkins and Tom Holbrook—their feedback made this book so much better.

To Gavin for giving me time to write and enduring hearing me talk about it.

www.ingramcontent.com/pod-product-compliance
Lightning Source LLC
Chambersburg PA
CBHW051329020726
47501CB00007B/1998